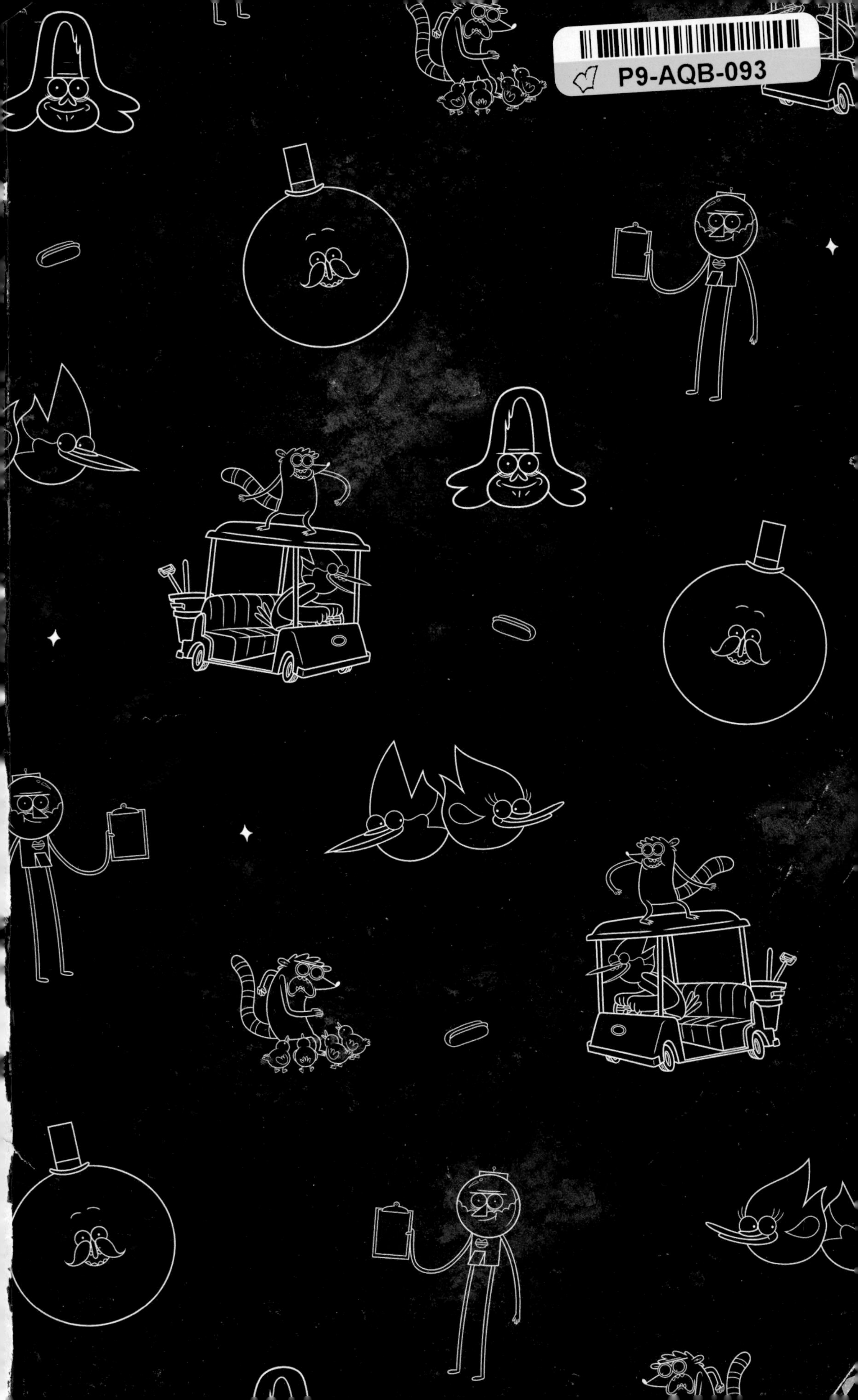

ROSS RICHIE CEO & Founder • MATT GAGNON Editor-in-Chief • FILIP SABLIK President of Publishing & Marketing • STEPHEN CHRISTY President of Development • LANCE KREITER VP of Licensing & Merchandising • PHIL BARBARO VP of Finance • BRYCE CARLSON Managing Editor • MEL CAYLO Marketing Manager • SCOTT NEWMAN Production Design Manager • KATE HENNING Operations Manager • SIERRA HAHN Senior Editor • DAFNA PLEBAN Editor, Talent Development • SHANNON WATTERS Editor • ERIC HARBURN Editor • WHITNEY LEOPARD Associate Editor • JASMINE AMIRI Associate Editor • CHRIS ROSA Associate Editor • ALEX GALER Associate Editor • CAMERON CHITTOCK Associate Editor • MATTHEW LEVINE Assistant Editor • KELSEY DIETERICH Production Designer • JILLIAN CRAB Production Designer • MICHELLE ANKLEY Production Designer • GRACE PARK Production Design Assistant • AARON FERRARA Operations Coordinator • ELIZABETH LOUGHRIDGE Accounting Coordinator • STEPHANIE HOCUTT Social Media Coordinator • JOSÉ MEZA Sales Assistant • JAMES ARRIOLA Mailroom Assistant • HOLLY AITCHISON Operations Assistant • SAM KUSEK Direct Market Representative • AMBER PARKER Administrative Assistant

REGULAR SHOW Volume Eight, April 2017. Published by KaBOOM!, a division of Boom Entertainment, Inc. REGULAR SHOW, CARTOON NETWORK, the logos, and all related characters and elements are trademarks of and © Cartoon Network. (S17) Originally published in single magazine form as REGULAR SHOW No. 29-32. © Cartoon Network. (S16) All rights reserved. KaBOOM!™ and the KaBOOM! logo are trademarks of Boom Entertainment, Inc., registered in various countries and categories. All characters, events, and institutions depicted herein are fictional. Any similarity between any of the names, characters, persons, events, and/or institutions in this publication to actual names, characters, and persons, whether living or dead, events, and/or institutions is unintended and purely coincidental. KaBOOM! does not read or accept unsolicited submissions of ideas, stories, or artwork.

A catalog record of this book is available from OCLC and from the BOOM! Studios website, www.boom-studios.com, on the Librarians Page.

BOOM! Studios, 5670 Wilshire Boulevard, Suite 450, Los Angeles, CA 90036-5679. Printed in China. First Printing.

ISBN: 978-1-60886-960-2, eISBN: 978-1-61398-631-8

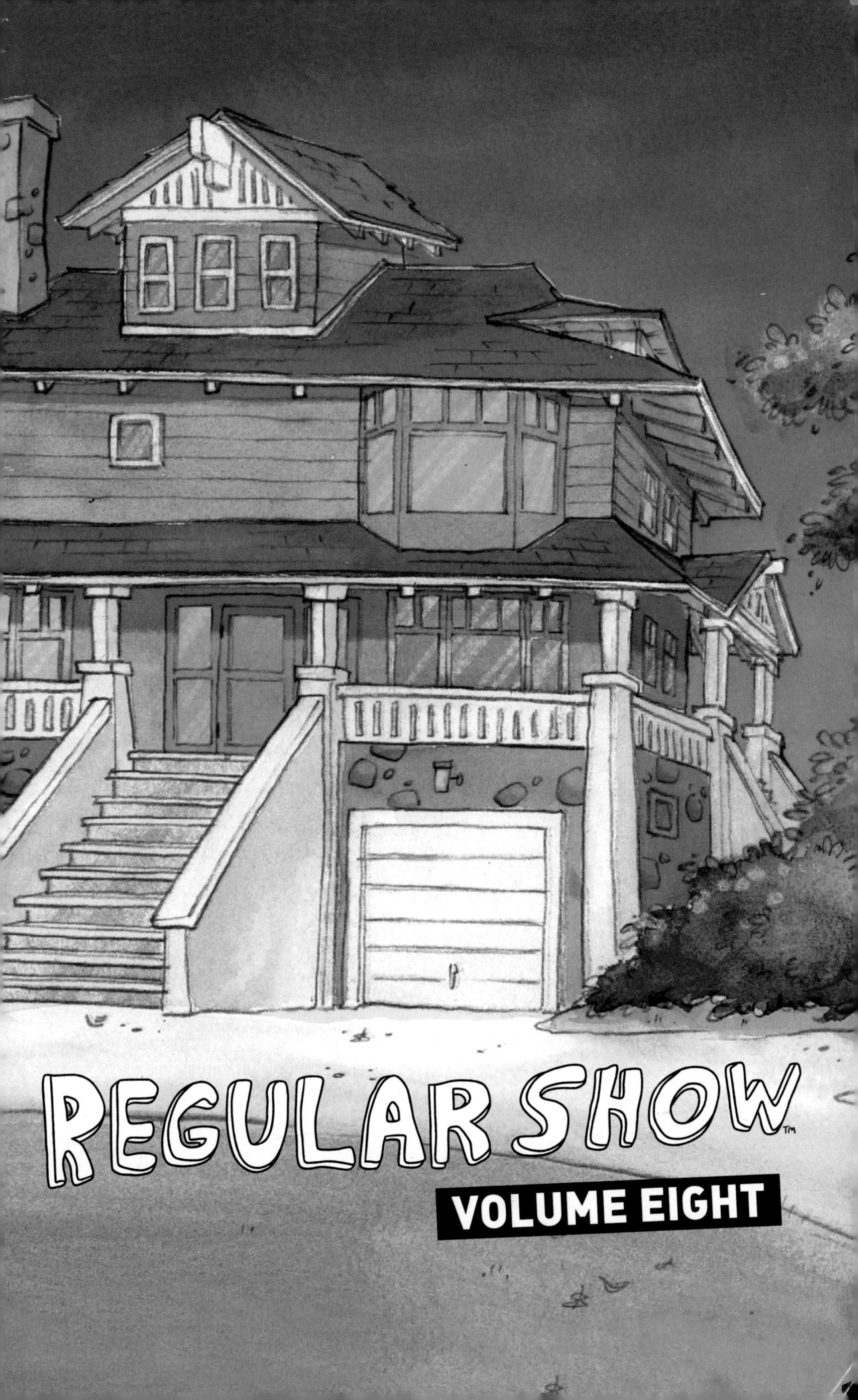
REGULAR SHOW™
VOLUME EIGHT

REGULAR

CREATED BY JG QUINTEL

SCRIPT BY MAD RUPERT

ART BY LAURA HOWELL

COLORS BY LISA MOORE

LETTERS BY STEVE WANDS

COVER BY
FELLIPE MARTINS

DESIGNER
MICHELLE ANKLEY

ASSISTANT EDITOR
MARY GUMPORT

ASSOCIATE EDITOR
CHRIS ROSA

EDITOR
SIERRA HAHN

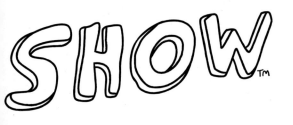

SHOW™

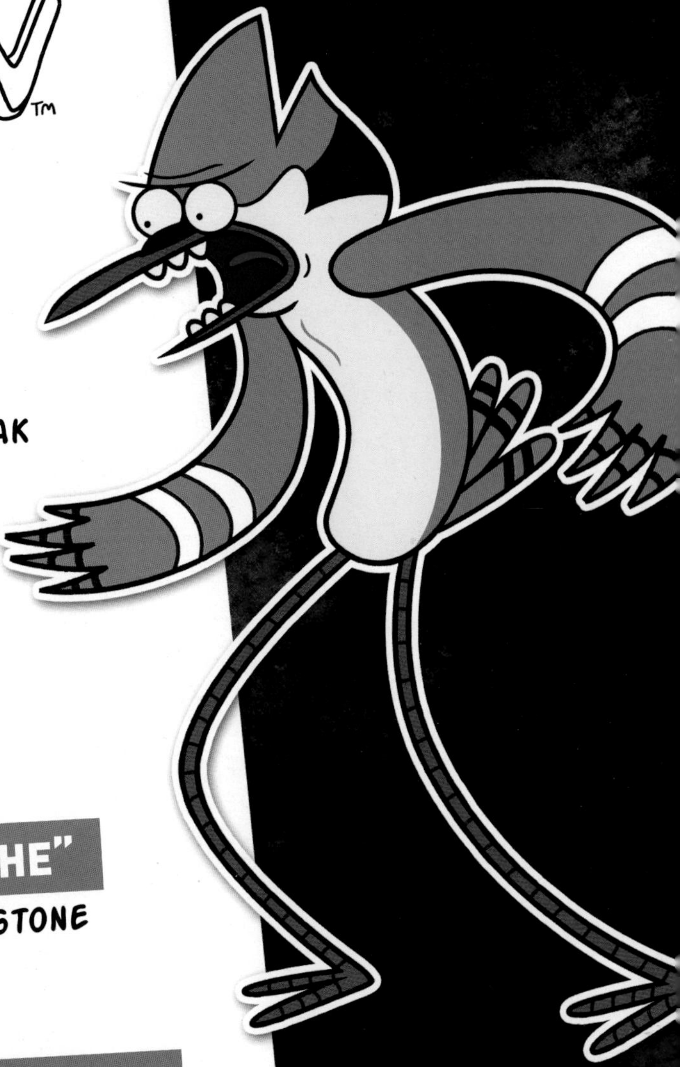

"DIS'N PIT"

SCRIPT BY **SHANNA MATUSZAK**
ART BY **WOOK JIN CLARK**

"TOUGH GUY"

SCRIPT BY **JON MORRIS**
ART BY **MATT SMIGIEL**

"CRAFT-TASTROPHE"

SCRIPT BY **ANDREW GREENSTONE**
ART BY **LIZ FLEMING**

"CUPPA FOR THE CREATURE"

SCRIPT BY **EDDIE WRIGHT**
ART BY **ADAM DEL RE**

"DANDY DRIVE-IN"

SCRIPT BY **EDDIE WRIGHT**
ART BY **CHRISTOPHER PETERSON**

WITH SPECIAL THANKS TO
MARISA MARIONAKIS, JANET NO, CURTIS LELASH, CONRAD MONTGOMERY, MEGHAN BRADLEY, KELLY CREWS, RYAN SLATER AND THE WONDERFUL FOLKS AT CARTOON NETWORK.

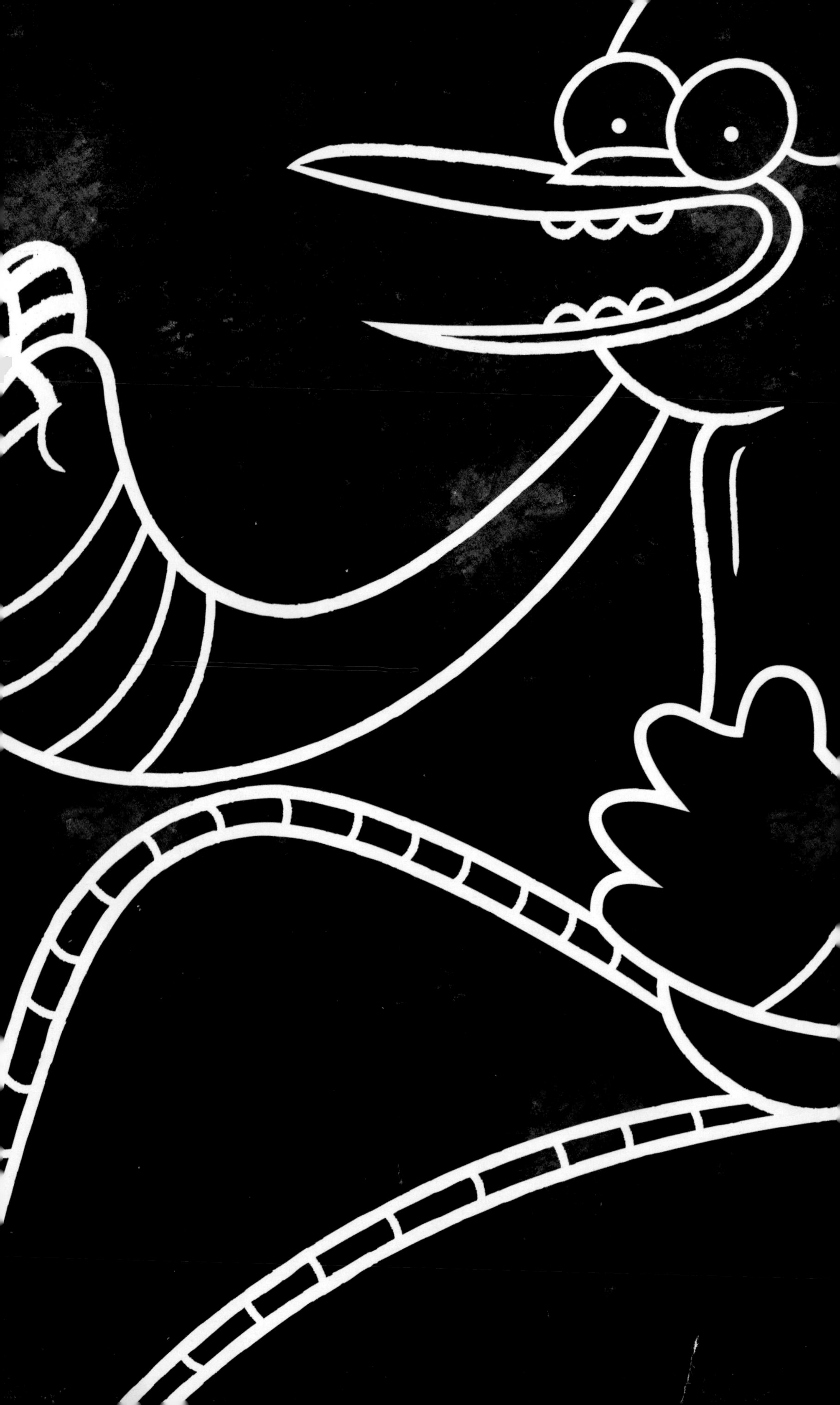

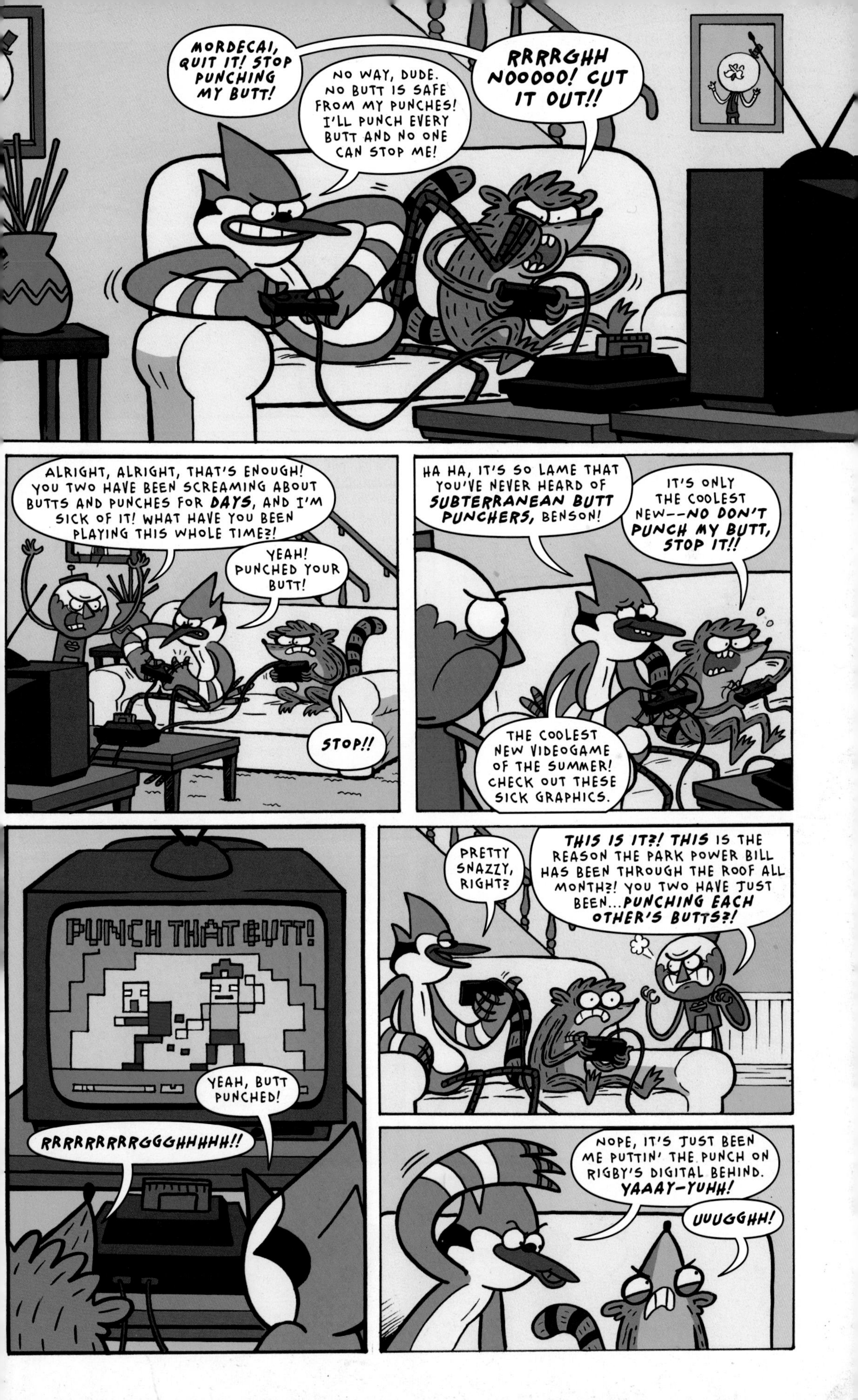

MORDECAI, QUIT IT! STOP PUNCHING MY BUTT!
NO WAY, DUDE. NO BUTT IS SAFE FROM MY PUNCHES! I'LL PUNCH EVERY BUTT AND NO ONE CAN STOP ME!
RRRRGHH NOOOOO! CUT IT OUT!!
ALRIGHT, ALRIGHT, THAT'S ENOUGH! YOU TWO HAVE BEEN SCREAMING ABOUT BUTTS AND PUNCHES FOR DAYS, AND I'M SICK OF IT! WHAT HAVE YOU BEEN PLAYING THIS WHOLE TIME?!
YEAH! PUNCHED YOUR BUTT!
STOP!!
HA HA, IT'S SO LAME THAT YOU'VE NEVER HEARD OF SUBTERRANEAN BUTT PUNCHERS, BENSON!
IT'S ONLY THE COOLEST NEW--NO DON'T PUNCH MY BUTT, STOP IT!!
THE COOLEST NEW VIDEOGAME OF THE SUMMER! CHECK OUT THESE SICK GRAPHICS.
PUNCH THAT BUTT!
YEAH, BUTT PUNCHED!
RRRRRRRRRGGGHHHHH!!
PRETTY SNAZZY, RIGHT?
THIS IS IT?! THIS IS THE REASON THE PARK POWER BILL HAS BEEN THROUGH THE ROOF ALL MONTH?! YOU TWO HAVE JUST BEEN...PUNCHING EACH OTHER'S BUTTS?!
NOPE, IT'S JUST BEEN ME PUTTIN' THE PUNCH ON RIGBY'S DIGITAL BEHIND. YAAAY-YUHH!
UUUGGHH!

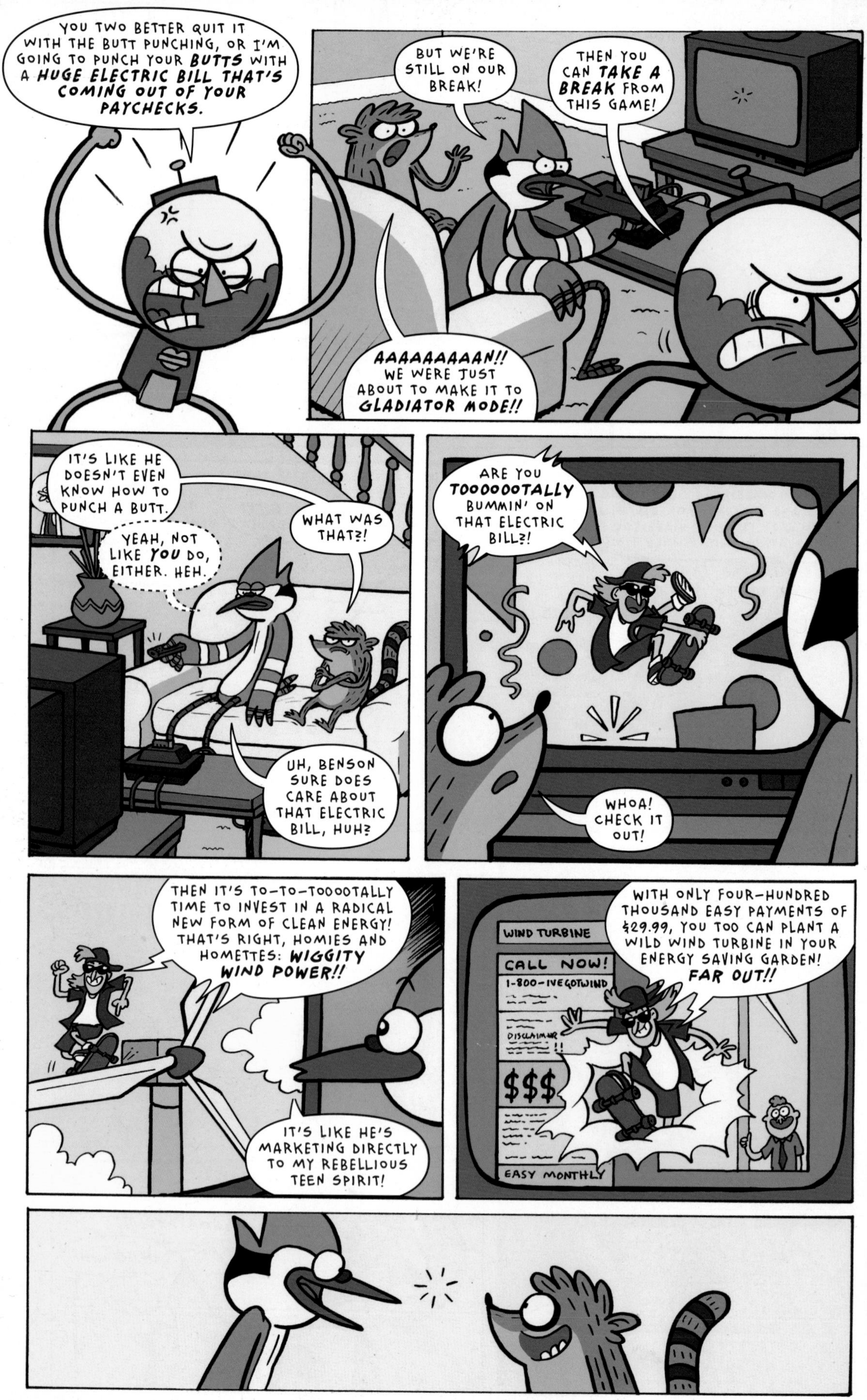
YOU TWO BETTER QUIT IT WITH THE BUTT PUNCHING, OR I'M GOING TO PUNCH YOUR BUTTS WITH A HUGE ELECTRIC BILL THAT'S COMING OUT OF YOUR PAYCHECKS.
BUT WE'RE STILL ON OUR BREAK!
THEN YOU CAN TAKE A BREAK FROM THIS GAME!
AAAAAAAAAN!! WE WERE JUST ABOUT TO MAKE IT TO GLADIATOR MODE!!
IT'S LIKE HE DOESN'T EVEN KNOW HOW TO PUNCH A BUTT.
WHAT WAS THAT?!
YEAH, NOT LIKE YOU DO, EITHER. HEH.
UH, BENSON SURE DOES CARE ABOUT THAT ELECTRIC BILL, HUH?
ARE YOU TOOOOOTALLY BUMMIN' ON THAT ELECTRIC BILL?!
WHOA! CHECK IT OUT!
THEN IT'S TO-TO-TOOOOTALLY TIME TO INVEST IN A RADICAL NEW FORM OF CLEAN ENERGY! THAT'S RIGHT, HOMIES AND HOMETTES: WIGGITY WIND POWER!!
IT'S LIKE HE'S MARKETING DIRECTLY TO MY REBELLIOUS TEEN SPIRIT!
WIND TURBINE
CALL NOW!
1-800-IVEGOTWIND
DISCLAIMER
$$$
EASY MONTHLY
WITH ONLY FOUR-HUNDRED THOUSAND EASY PAYMENTS OF $29.99, YOU TOO CAN PLANT A WILD WIND TURBINE IN YOUR ENERGY SAVING GARDEN! FAR OUT!!

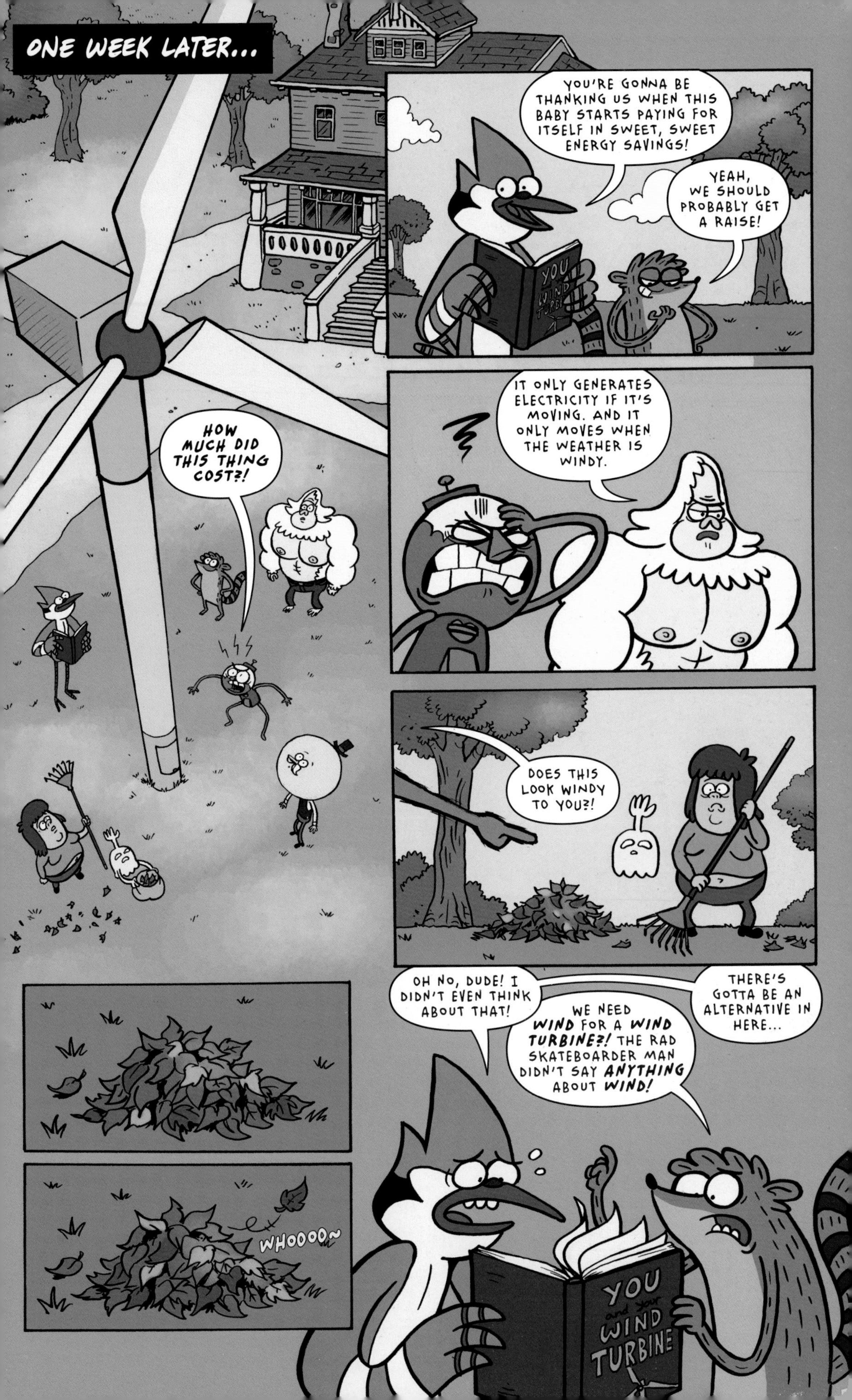

ONE WEEK LATER...
YOU'RE GONNA BE THANKING US WHEN THIS BABY STARTS PAYING FOR ITSELF IN SWEET, SWEET ENERGY SAVINGS!
YEAH, WE SHOULD PROBABLY GET A RAISE!
HOW MUCH DID THIS THING COST?!
IT ONLY GENERATES ELECTRICITY IF IT'S MOVING. AND IT ONLY MOVES WHEN THE WEATHER IS WINDY.
DOES THIS LOOK WINDY TO YOU?!
WHOOOO~
OH NO, DUDE! I DIDN'T EVEN THINK ABOUT THAT!
WE NEED WIND FOR A WIND TURBINE?! THE RAD SKATEBOARDER MAN DIDN'T SAY ANYTHING ABOUT WIND!
THERE'S GOTTA BE AN ALTERNATIVE IN HERE...
YOU and your WIND TURBINE

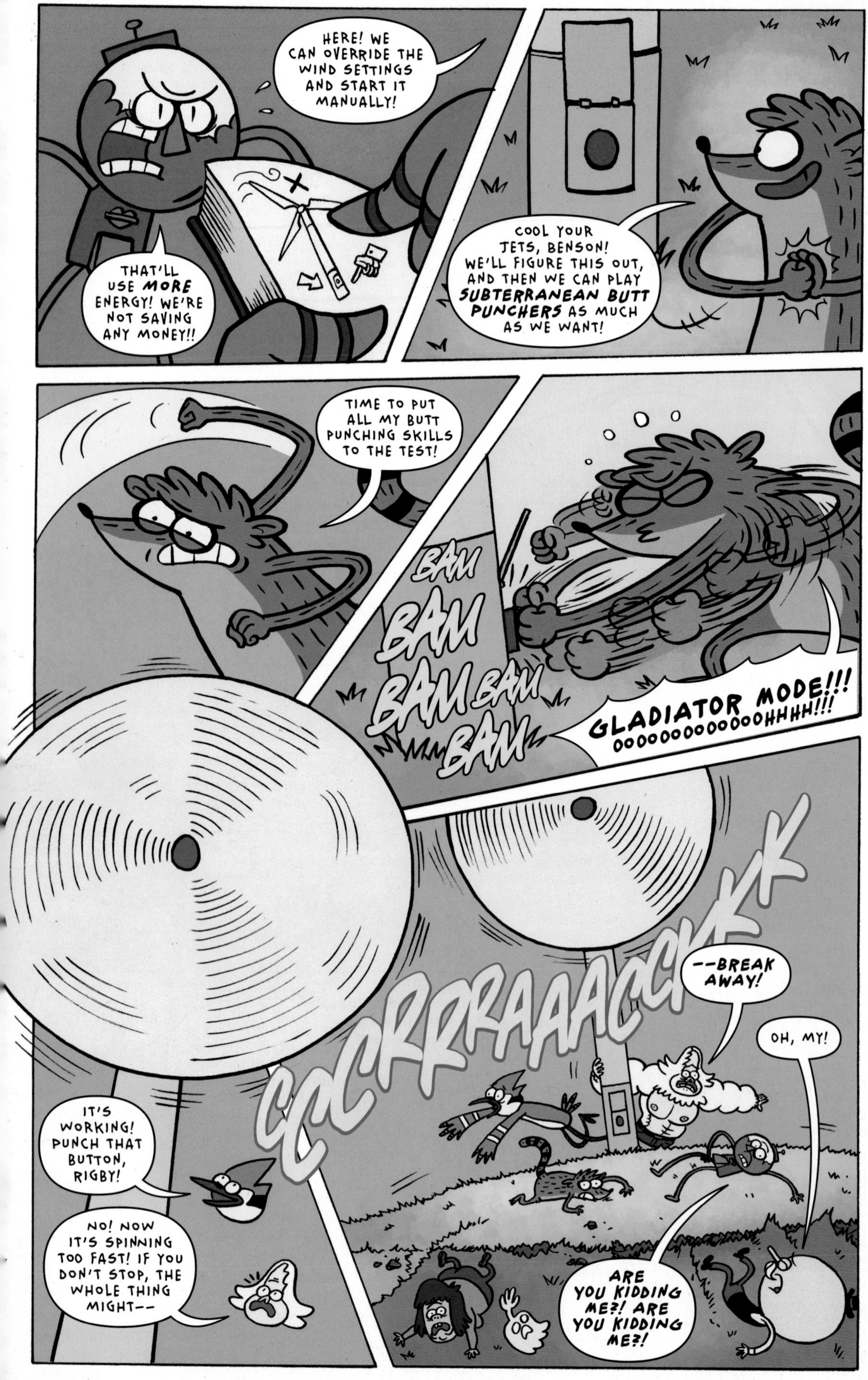
HERE! WE CAN OVERRIDE THE WIND SETTINGS AND START IT MANUALLY!
THAT'LL USE MORE ENERGY! WE'RE NOT SAVING ANY MONEY!!
COOL YOUR JETS, BENSON! WE'LL FIGURE THIS OUT, AND THEN WE CAN PLAY SUBTERRANEAN BUTT PUNCHERS AS MUCH AS WE WANT!
TIME TO PUT ALL MY BUTT PUNCHING SKILLS TO THE TEST!
BAM BAM BAM BAM BAM BAM
GLADIATOR MODE!!! OOOOOOOOOOOOHHHH!!!
IT'S WORKING! PUNCH THAT BUTTON, RIGBY!
NO! NOW IT'S SPINNING TOO FAST! IF YOU DON'T STOP, THE WHOLE THING MIGHT--
CCCRRRAAACCKKK
--BREAK AWAY!
OH, MY!
ARE YOU KIDDING ME?! ARE YOU KIDDING ME?!

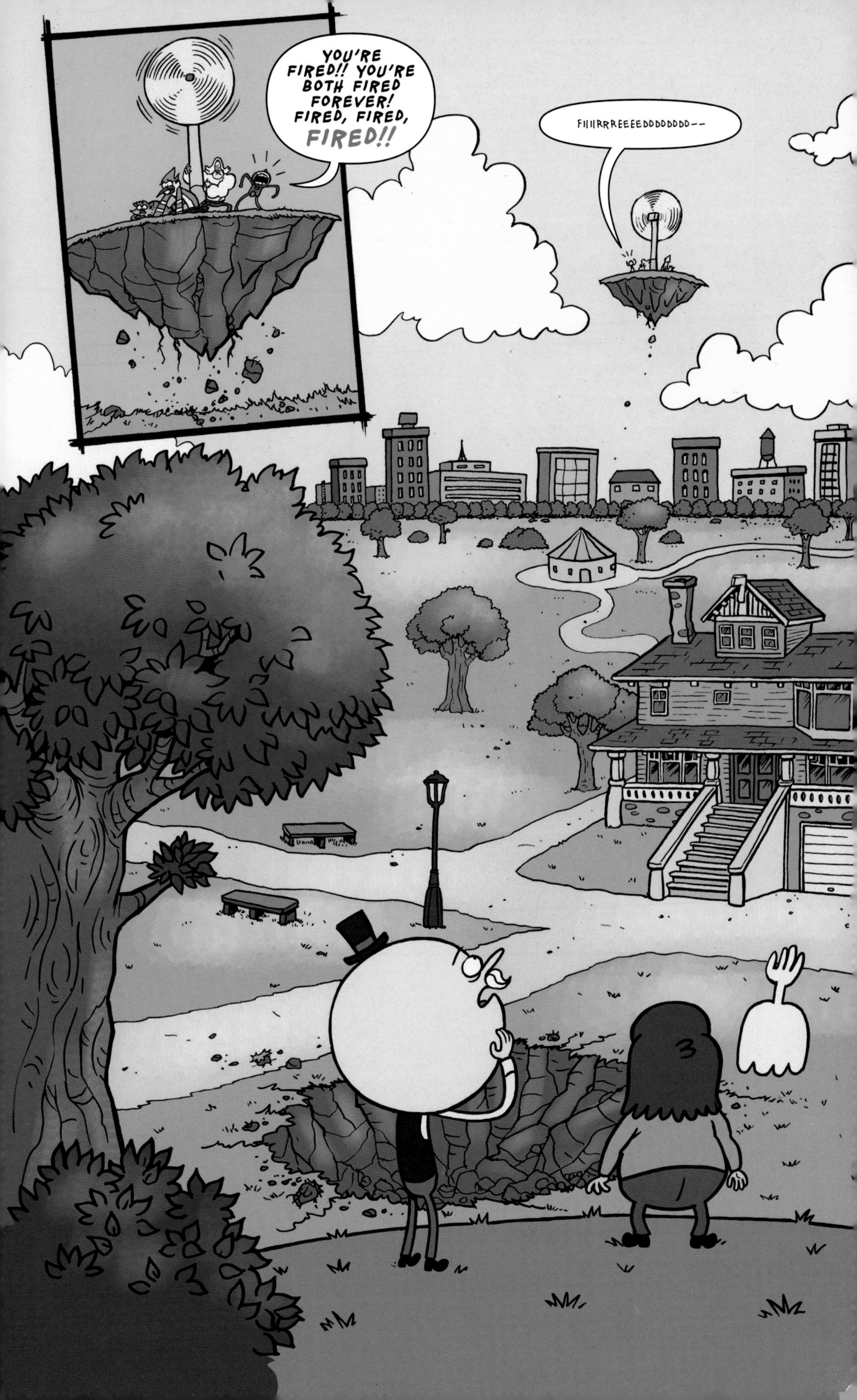

YOU'RE FIRED!! YOU'RE BOTH FIRED FOREVER! FIRED, FIRED, FIRED!!
FIIIIRRRREEEEEDDDDDDDD--

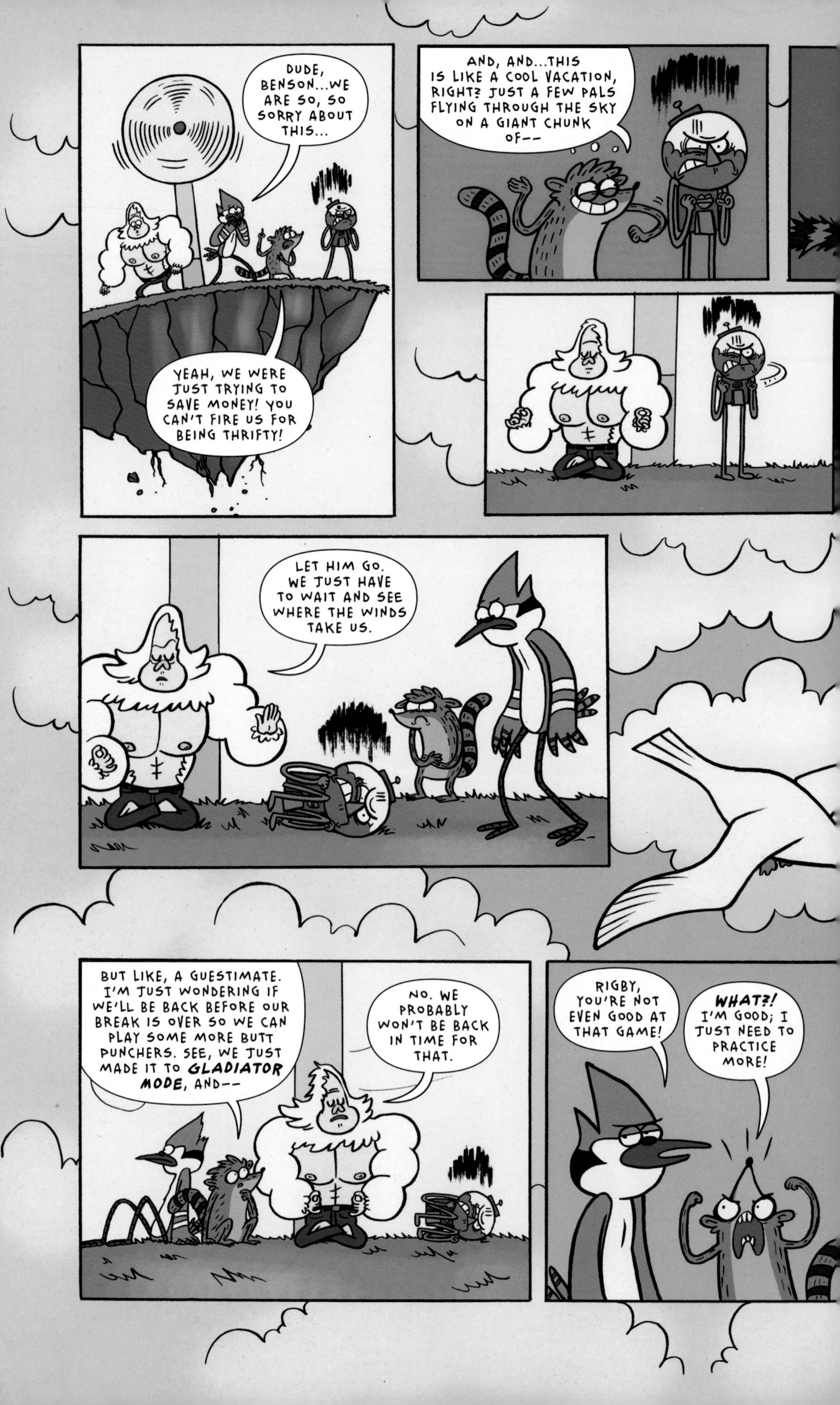
DUDE, BENSON...WE ARE SO, SO SORRY ABOUT THIS...
YEAH, WE WERE JUST TRYING TO SAVE MONEY! YOU CAN'T FIRE US FOR BEING THRIFTY!
AND, AND...THIS IS LIKE A COOL VACATION, RIGHT? JUST A FEW PALS FLYING THROUGH THE SKY ON A GIANT CHUNK OF--
LET HIM GO. WE JUST HAVE TO WAIT AND SEE WHERE THE WINDS TAKE US.
BUT LIKE, A GUESTIMATE. I'M JUST WONDERING IF WE'LL BE BACK BEFORE OUR BREAK IS OVER SO WE CAN PLAY SOME MORE BUTT PUNCHERS. SEE, WE JUST MADE IT TO GLADIATOR MODE, AND--
NO. WE PROBABLY WON'T BE BACK IN TIME FOR THAT.
RIGBY, YOU'RE NOT EVEN GOOD AT THAT GAME!
WHAT?! I'M GOOD; I JUST NEED TO PRACTICE MORE!

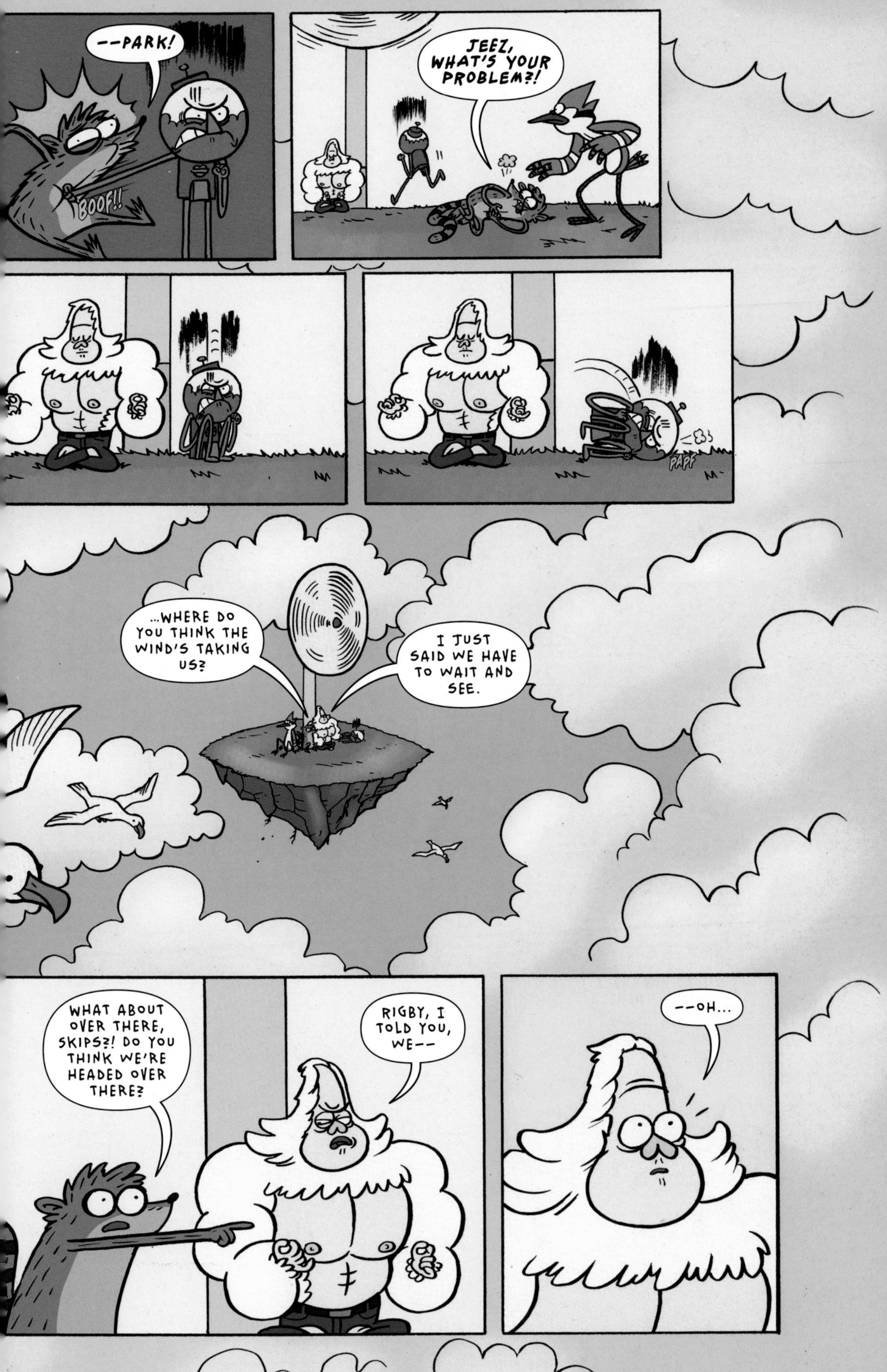
--PARK!
BOOF!!
JEEZ, WHAT'S YOUR PROBLEM?!
PAPF
...WHERE DO YOU THINK THE WIND'S TAKING US?
I JUST SAID WE HAVE TO WAIT AND SEE.
WHAT ABOUT OVER THERE, SKIPS?! DO YOU THINK WE'RE HEADED OVER THERE?
RIGBY, I TOLD YOU, WE--
--OH...

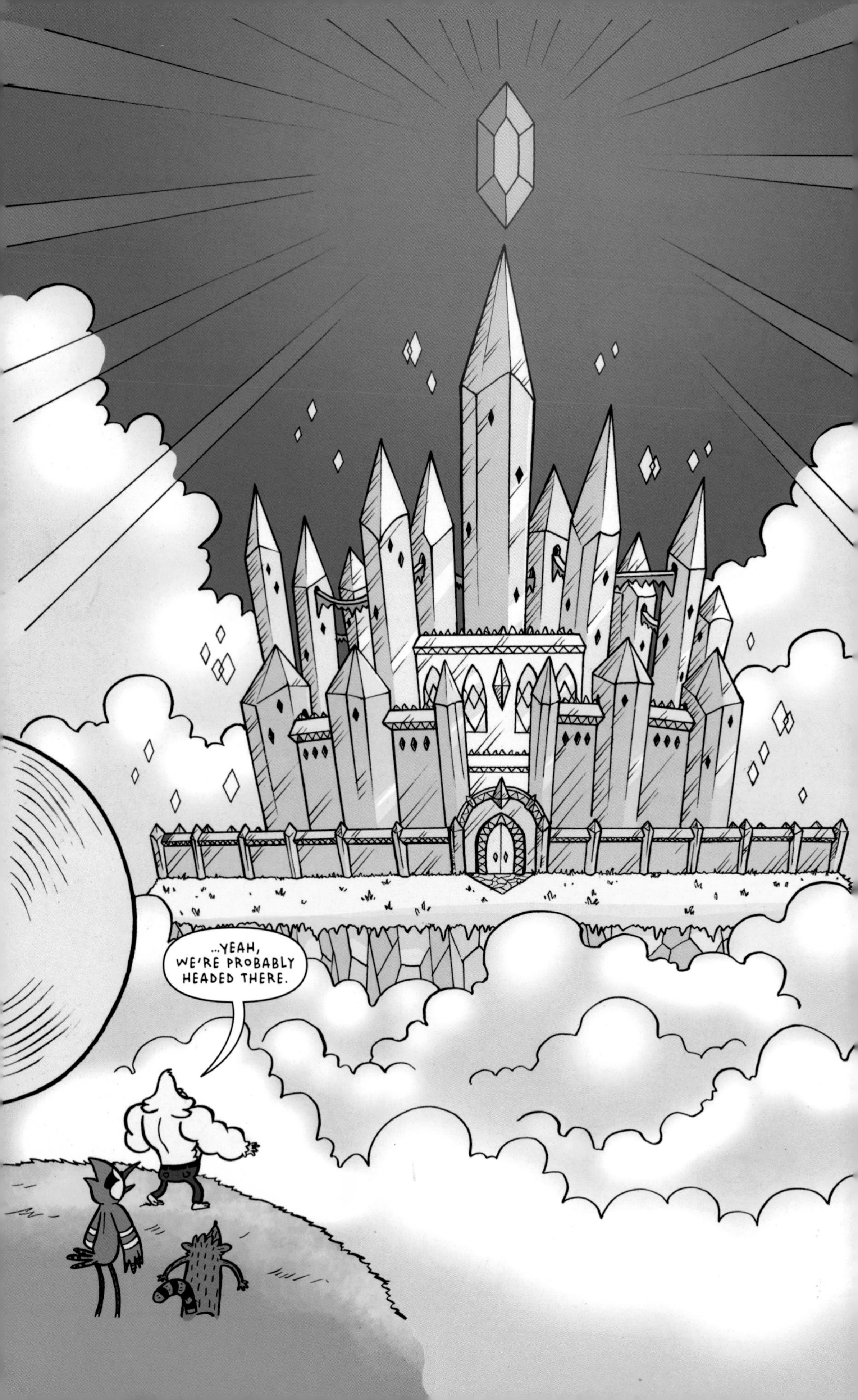
...YEAH, WE'RE PROBABLY HEADED THERE.

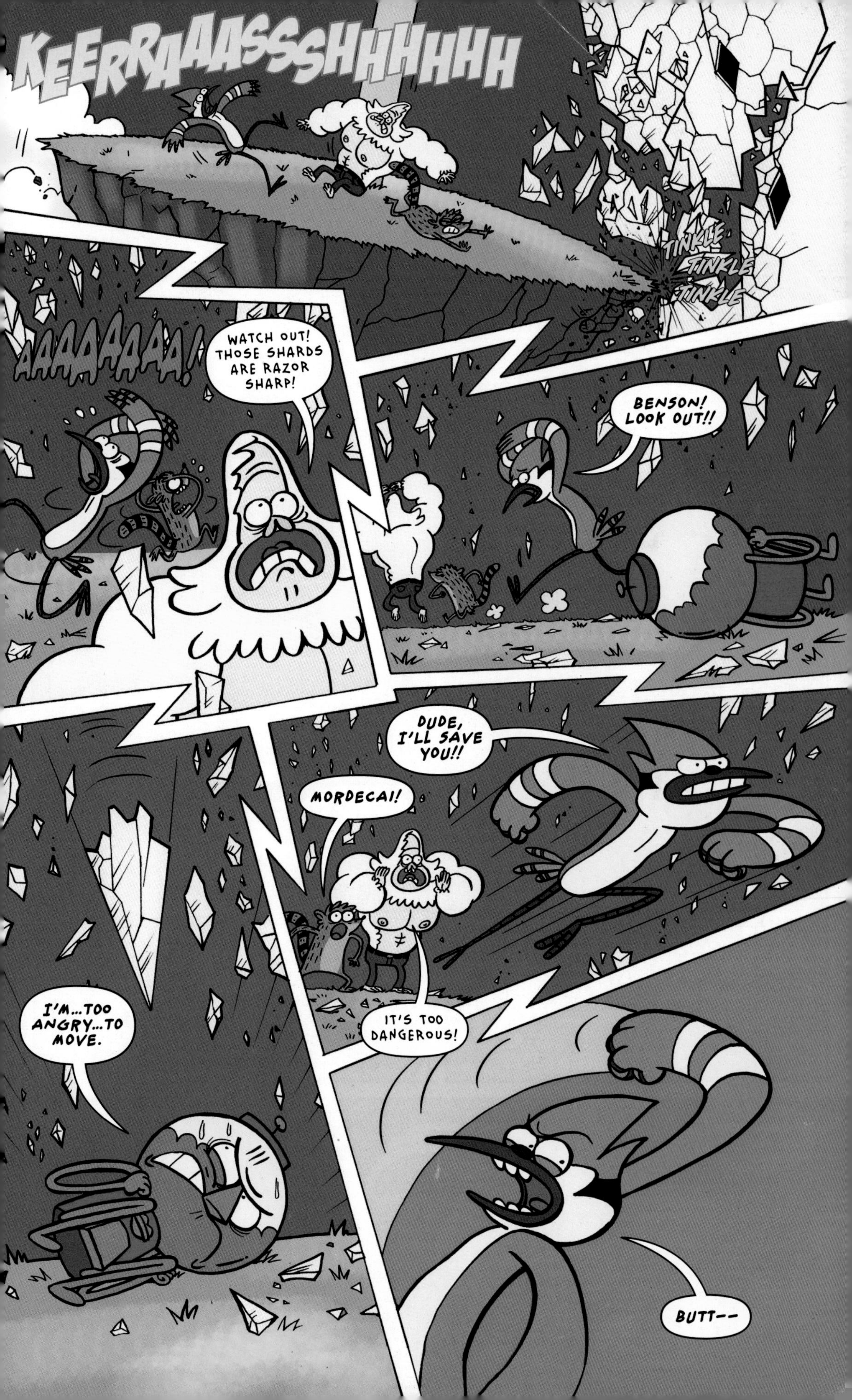
KEERRAAASSSHHHHHH
TINKLE
TINKLE
TINKLE
AAAAAAAA!
WATCH OUT! THOSE SHARDS ARE RAZOR SHARP!
BENSON! LOOK OUT!!
DUDE, I'LL SAVE YOU!!
MORDECAI!
IT'S TOO DANGEROUS!
I'M...TOO ANGRY...TO MOVE.
BUTT--

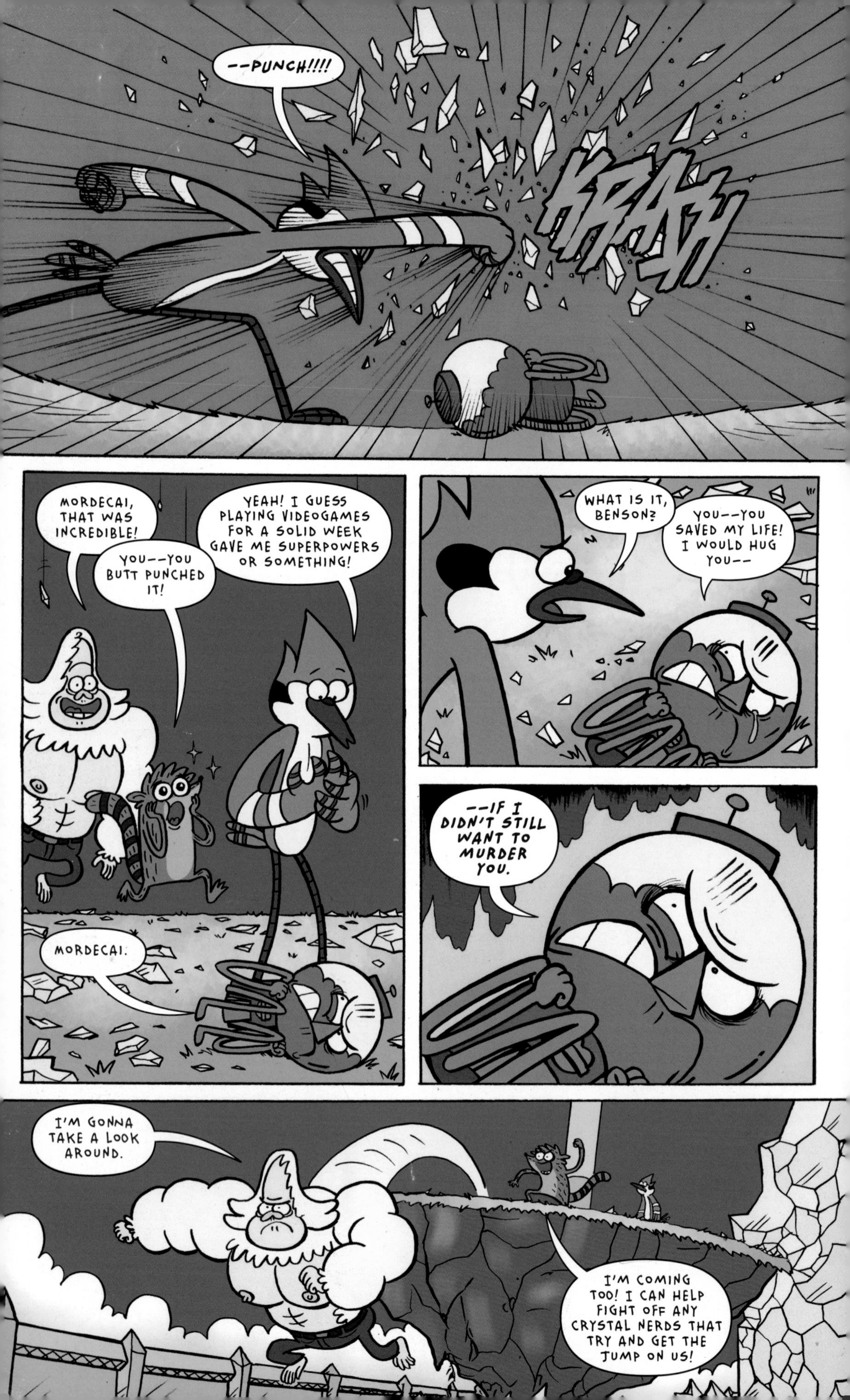
--PUNCH!!!!
KRASH
MORDECAI, THAT WAS INCREDIBLE!
YOU--YOU BUTT PUNCHED IT!
YEAH! I GUESS PLAYING VIDEOGAMES FOR A SOLID WEEK GAVE ME SUPERPOWERS OR SOMETHING!
MORDECAI.
WHAT IS IT, BENSON?
YOU--YOU SAVED MY LIFE! I WOULD HUG YOU--
--IF I DIDN'T STILL WANT TO MURDER YOU.
I'M GONNA TAKE A LOOK AROUND.
I'M COMING TOO! I CAN HELP FIGHT OFF ANY CRYSTAL NERDS THAT TRY AND GET THE JUMP ON US!

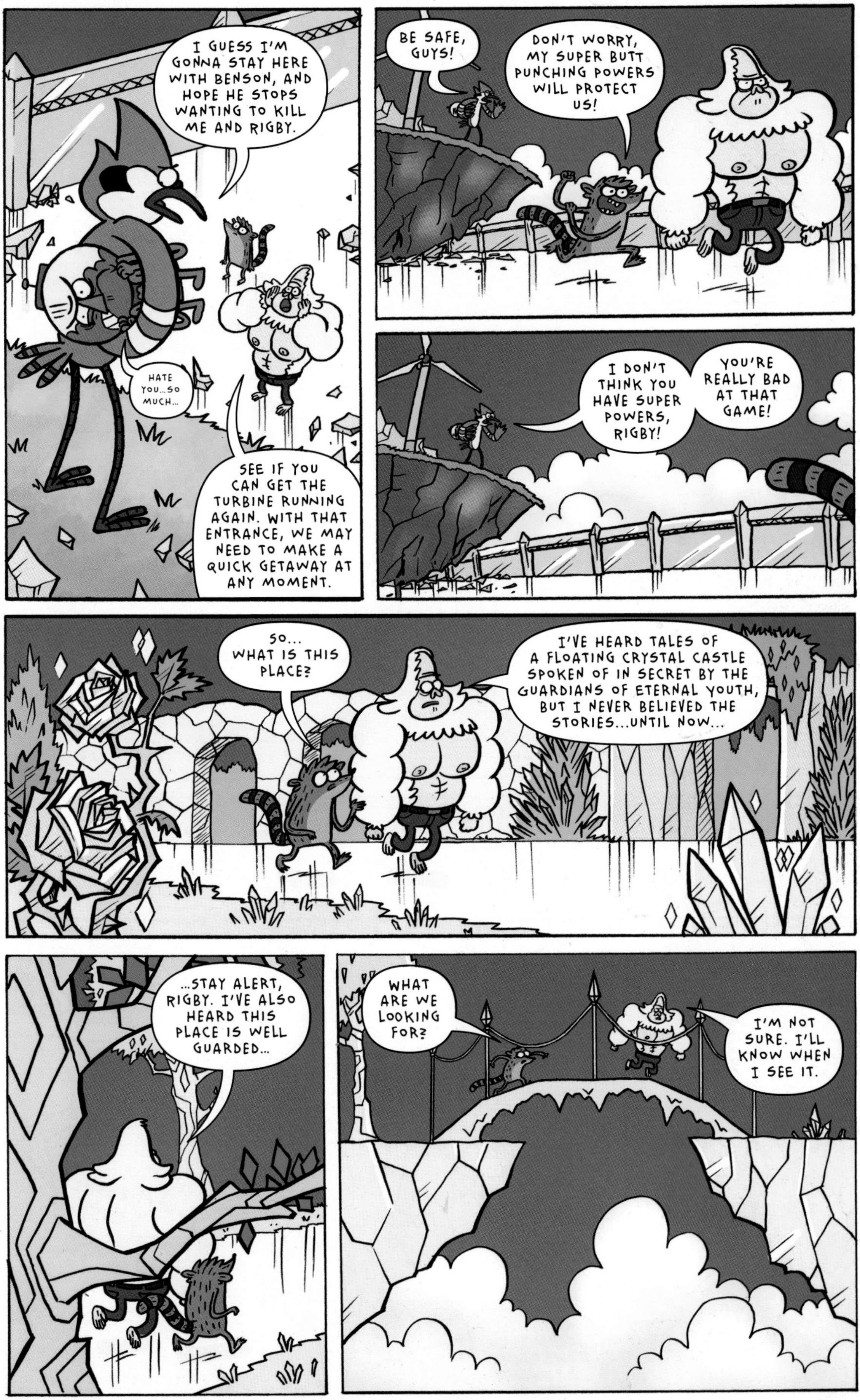
I GUESS I'M GONNA STAY HERE WITH BENSON, AND HOPE HE STOPS WANTING TO KILL ME AND RIGBY.
HATE YOU...SO MUCH...
SEE IF YOU CAN GET THE TURBINE RUNNING AGAIN. WITH THAT ENTRANCE, WE MAY NEED TO MAKE A QUICK GETAWAY AT ANY MOMENT.
BE SAFE, GUYS!
DON'T WORRY, MY SUPER BUTT PUNCHING POWERS WILL PROTECT US!
I DON'T THINK YOU HAVE SUPER POWERS, RIGBY!
YOU'RE REALLY BAD AT THAT GAME!
SO... WHAT IS THIS PLACE?
I'VE HEARD TALES OF A FLOATING CRYSTAL CASTLE SPOKEN OF IN SECRET BY THE GUARDIANS OF ETERNAL YOUTH, BUT I NEVER BELIEVED THE STORIES...UNTIL NOW...
...STAY ALERT, RIGBY. I'VE ALSO HEARD THIS PLACE IS WELL GUARDED...
WHAT ARE WE LOOKING FOR?
I'M NOT SURE. I'LL KNOW WHEN I SEE IT.

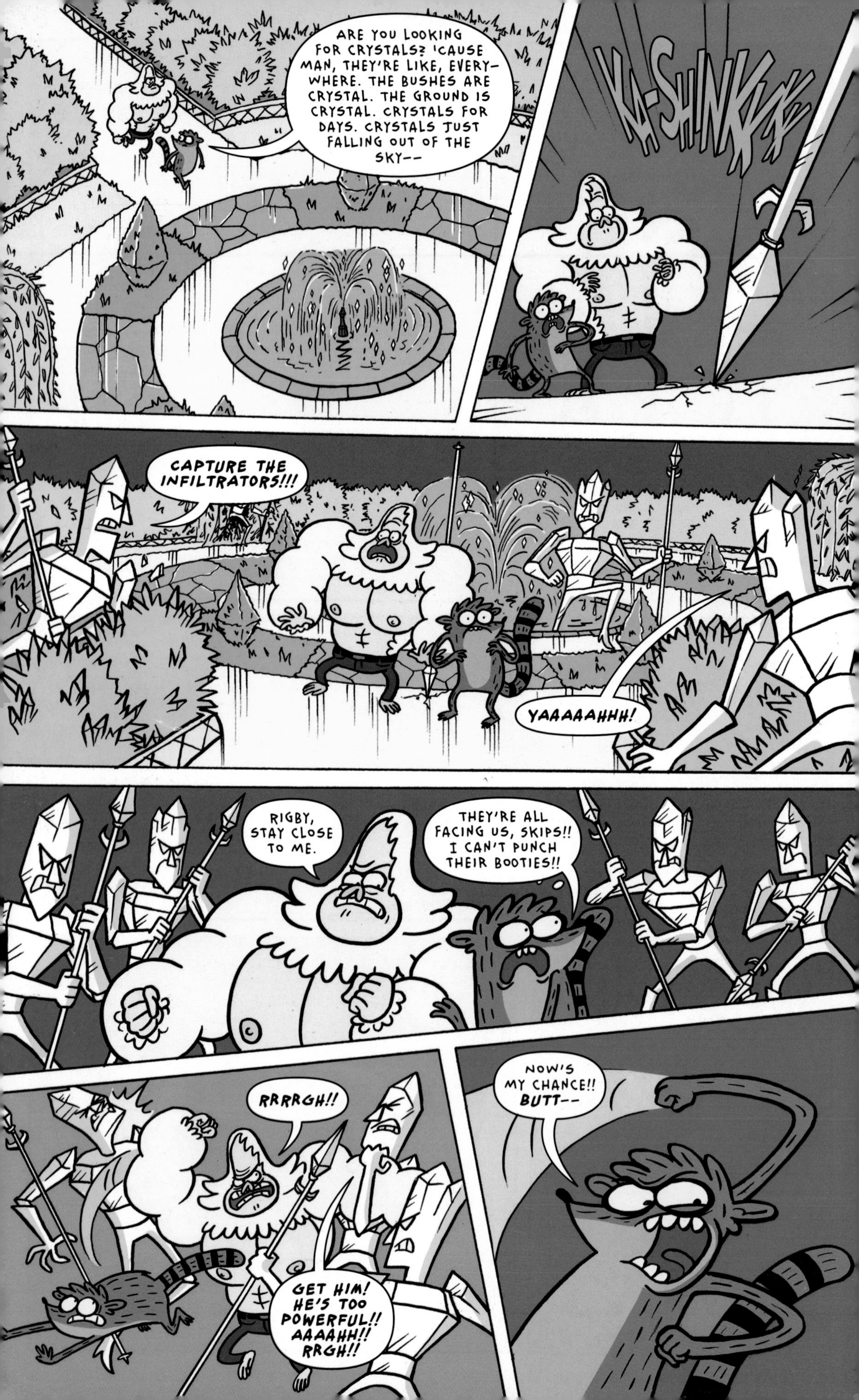
ARE YOU LOOKING FOR CRYSTALS? 'CAUSE MAN, THEY'RE LIKE, EVERYWHERE. THE BUSHES ARE CRYSTAL. THE GROUND IS CRYSTAL. CRYSTALS FOR DAYS. CRYSTALS JUST FALLING OUT OF THE SKY--
KA-SHINKKK
CAPTURE THE INFILTRATORS!!!
YAAAAAHHH!
RIGBY, STAY CLOSE TO ME.
THEY'RE ALL FACING US, SKIPS!! I CAN'T PUNCH THEIR BOOTIES!!
RRRRGH!!
GET HIM! HE'S TOO POWERFUL!! AAAAHH!! RRGH!!
NOW'S MY CHANCE!! BUTT--

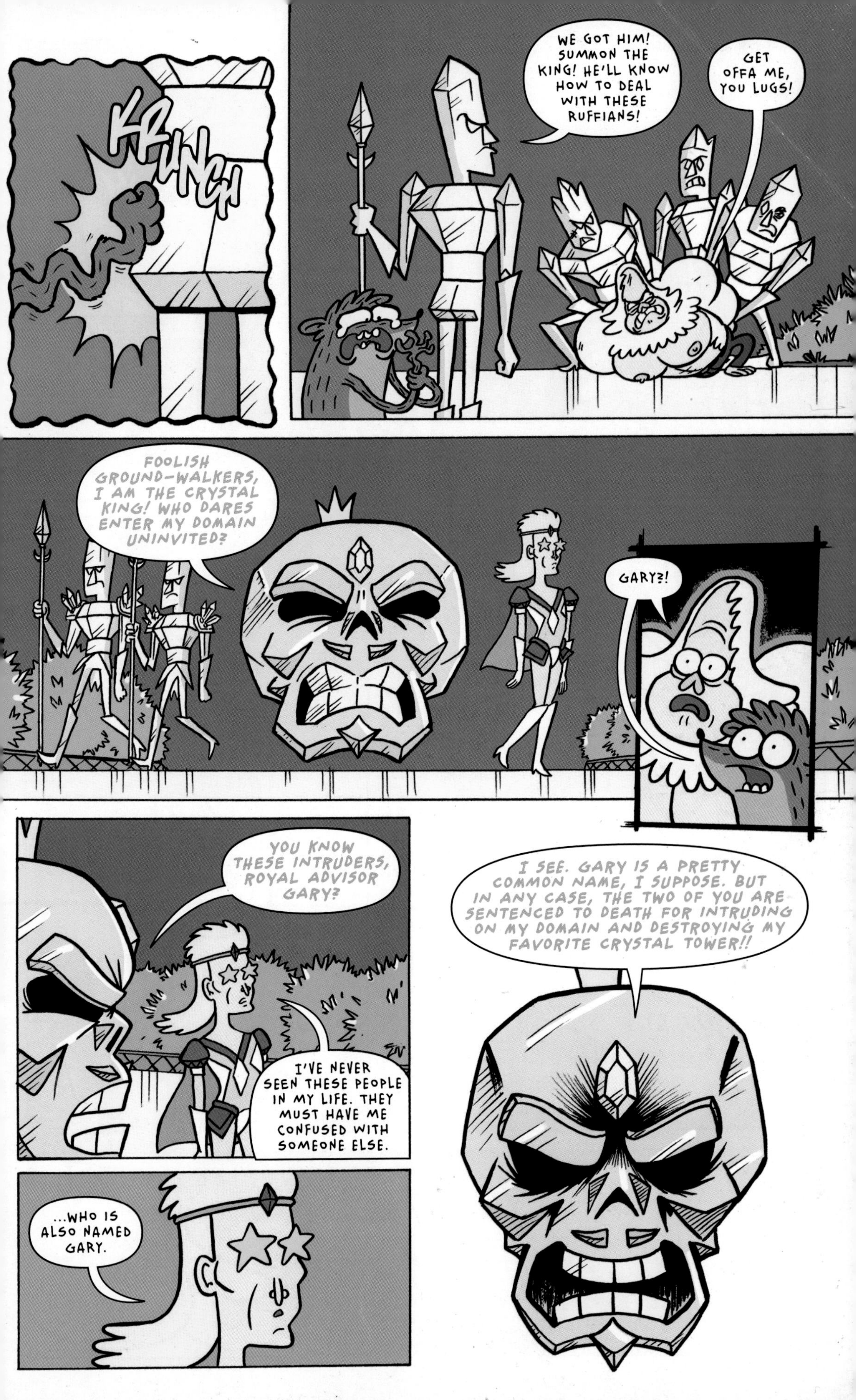
KRUNCH
WE GOT HIM! SUMMON THE KING! HE'LL KNOW HOW TO DEAL WITH THESE RUFFIANS!
GET OFFA ME, YOU LUGS!
FOOLISH GROUND-WALKERS, I AM THE CRYSTAL KING! WHO DARES ENTER MY DOMAIN UNINVITED?
GARY?!
YOU KNOW THESE INTRUDERS, ROYAL ADVISOR GARY?
I'VE NEVER SEEN THESE PEOPLE IN MY LIFE. THEY MUST HAVE ME CONFUSED WITH SOMEONE ELSE.
...WHO IS ALSO NAMED GARY.
I SEE. GARY IS A PRETTY COMMON NAME, I SUPPOSE. BUT IN ANY CASE, THE TWO OF YOU ARE SENTENCED TO DEATH FOR INTRUDING ON MY DOMAIN AND DESTROYING MY FAVORITE CRYSTAL TOWER!!

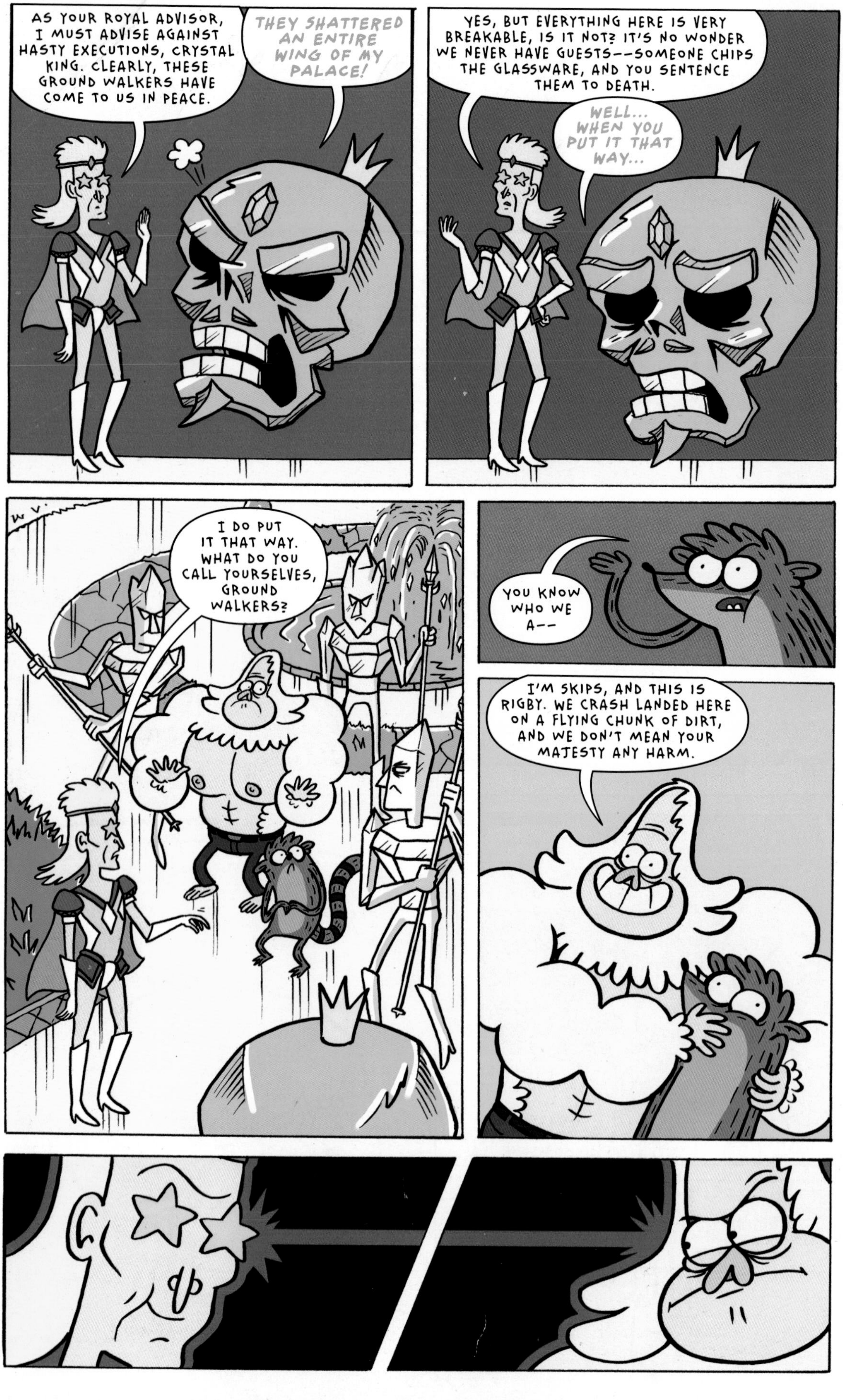
AS YOUR ROYAL ADVISOR, I MUST ADVISE AGAINST HASTY EXECUTIONS, CRYSTAL KING. CLEARLY, THESE GROUND WALKERS HAVE COME TO US IN PEACE.
THEY SHATTERED AN ENTIRE WING OF MY PALACE!
YES, BUT EVERYTHING HERE IS VERY BREAKABLE, IS IT NOT? IT'S NO WONDER WE NEVER HAVE GUESTS--SOMEONE CHIPS THE GLASSWARE, AND YOU SENTENCE THEM TO DEATH.
WELL... WHEN YOU PUT IT THAT WAY...
I DO PUT IT THAT WAY. WHAT DO YOU CALL YOURSELVES, GROUND WALKERS?
YOU KNOW WHO WE A--
I'M SKIPS, AND THIS IS RIGBY. WE CRASH LANDED HERE ON A FLYING CHUNK OF DIRT, AND WE DON'T MEAN YOUR MAJESTY ANY HARM.

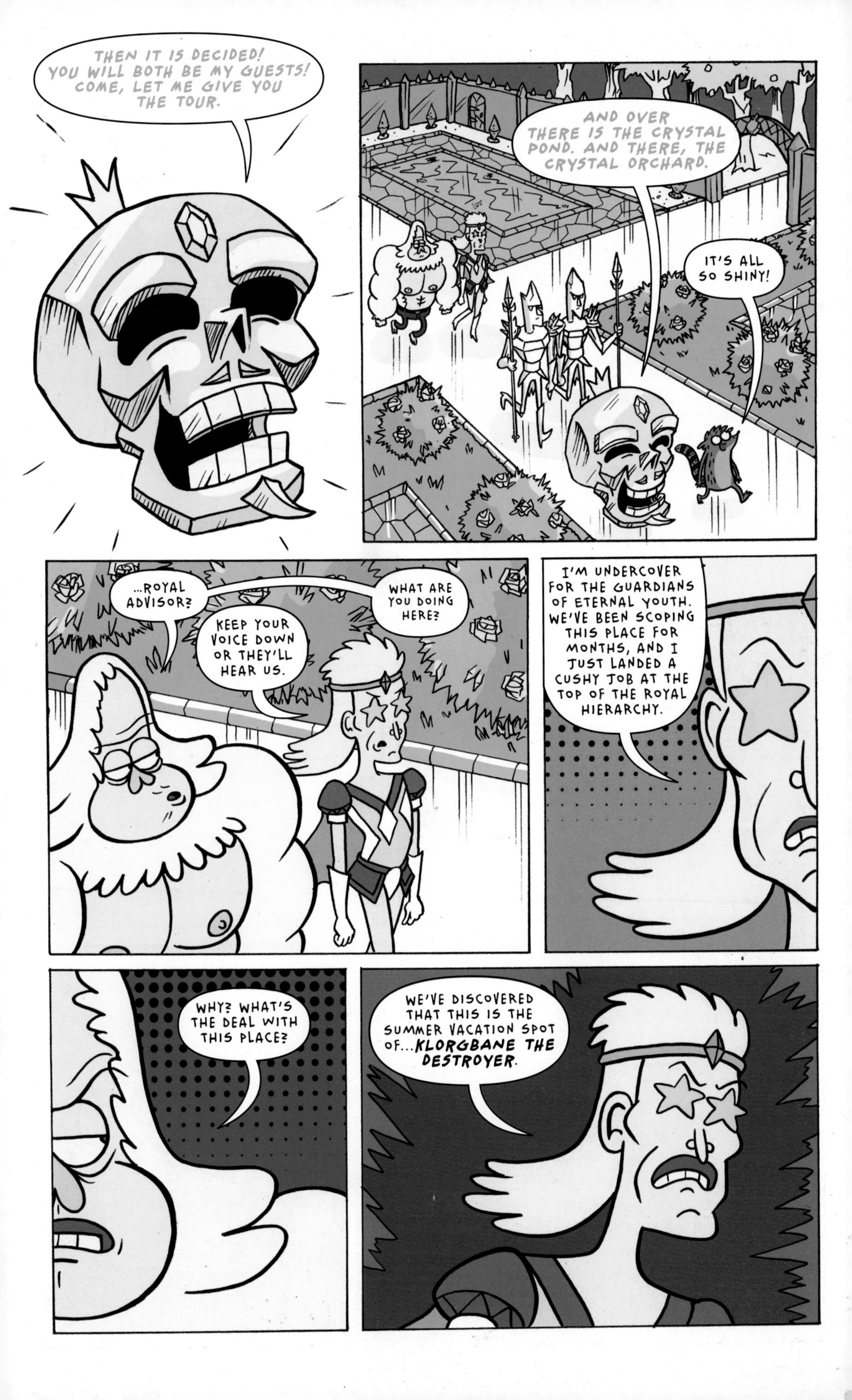
THEN IT IS DECIDED! YOU WILL BOTH BE MY GUESTS! COME, LET ME GIVE YOU THE TOUR.
AND OVER THERE IS THE CRYSTAL POND. AND THERE, THE CRYSTAL ORCHARD.
IT'S ALL SO SHINY!
...ROYAL ADVISOR?
WHAT ARE YOU DOING HERE?
KEEP YOUR VOICE DOWN OR THEY'LL HEAR US.
I'M UNDERCOVER FOR THE GUARDIANS OF ETERNAL YOUTH. WE'VE BEEN SCOPING THIS PLACE FOR MONTHS, AND I JUST LANDED A CUSHY JOB AT THE TOP OF THE ROYAL HIERARCHY.
WHY? WHAT'S THE DEAL WITH THIS PLACE?
WE'VE DISCOVERED THAT THIS IS THE SUMMER VACATION SPOT OF...**KLORGBANE THE DESTROYER**.

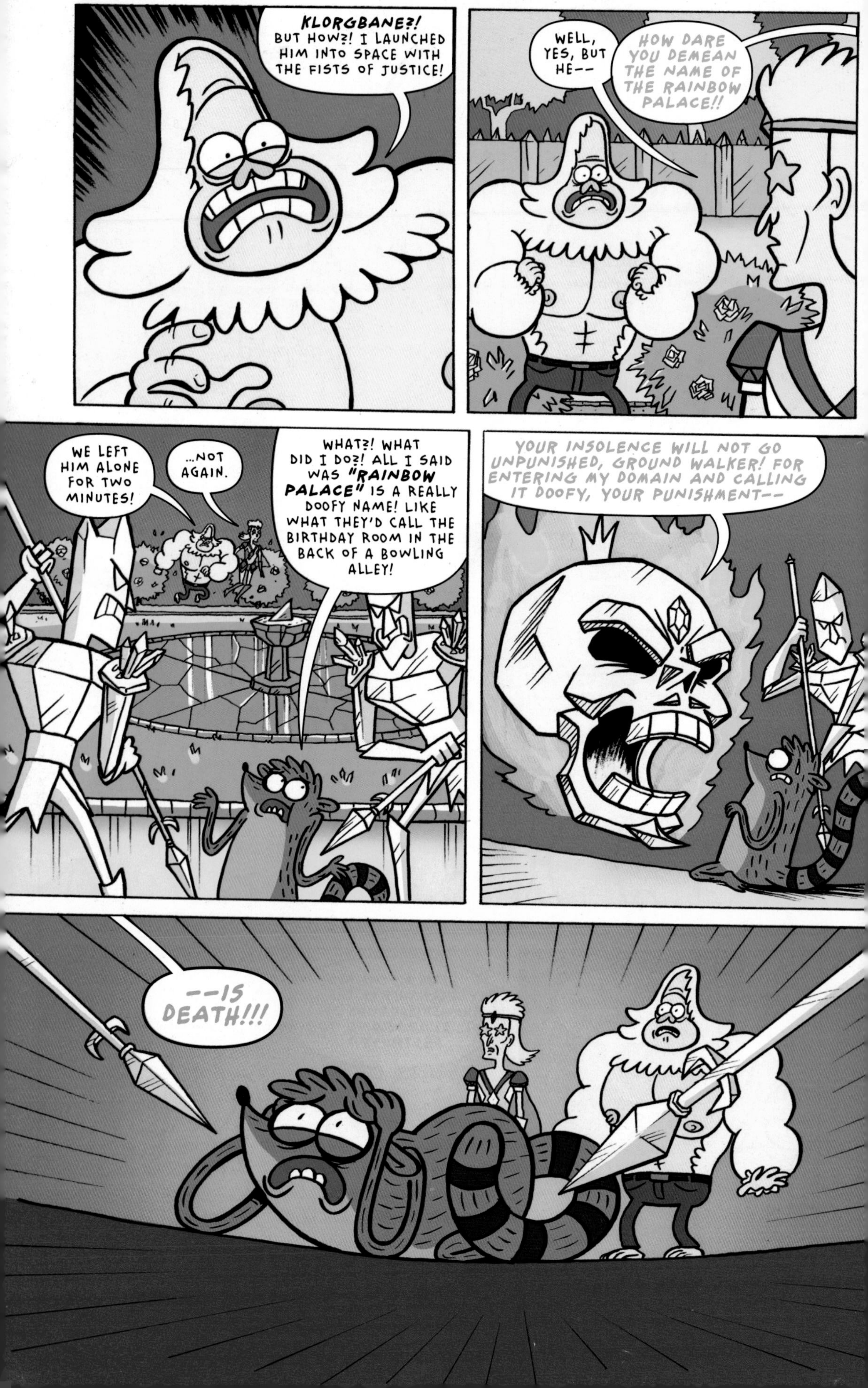
KLORGBANE?! BUT HOW?! I LAUNCHED HIM INTO SPACE WITH THE FISTS OF JUSTICE!
WELL, YES, BUT HE--
HOW DARE YOU DEMEAN THE NAME OF THE RAINBOW PALACE!!
WE LEFT HIM ALONE FOR TWO MINUTES!
...NOT AGAIN.
WHAT?! WHAT DID I DO?! ALL I SAID WAS "RAINBOW PALACE" IS A REALLY DOOFY NAME! LIKE WHAT THEY'D CALL THE BIRTHDAY ROOM IN THE BACK OF A BOWLING ALLEY!
YOUR INSOLENCE WILL NOT GO UNPUNISHED, GROUND WALKER! FOR ENTERING MY DOMAIN AND CALLING IT DOOFY, YOUR PUNISHMENT--
--IS DEATH!!!

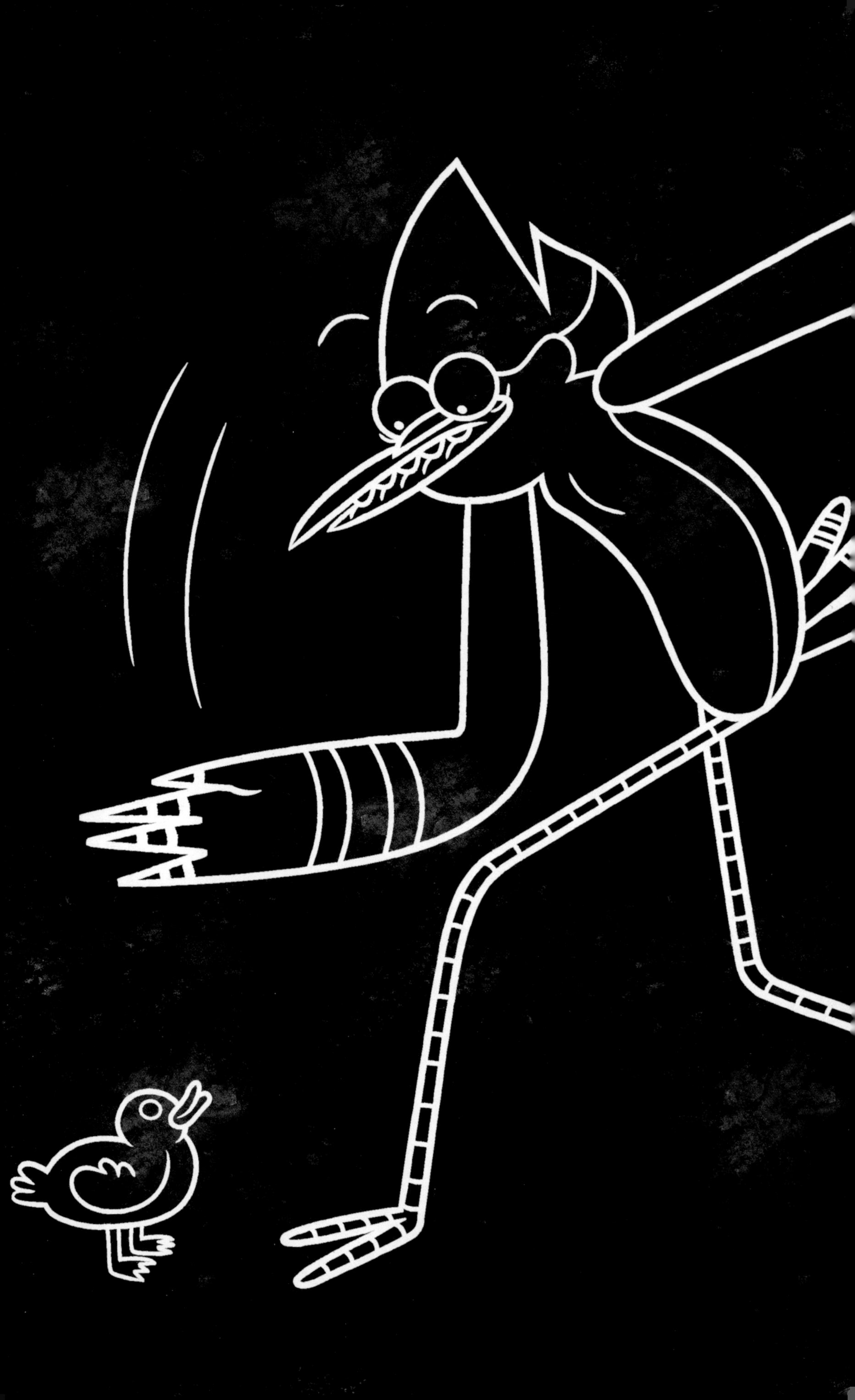

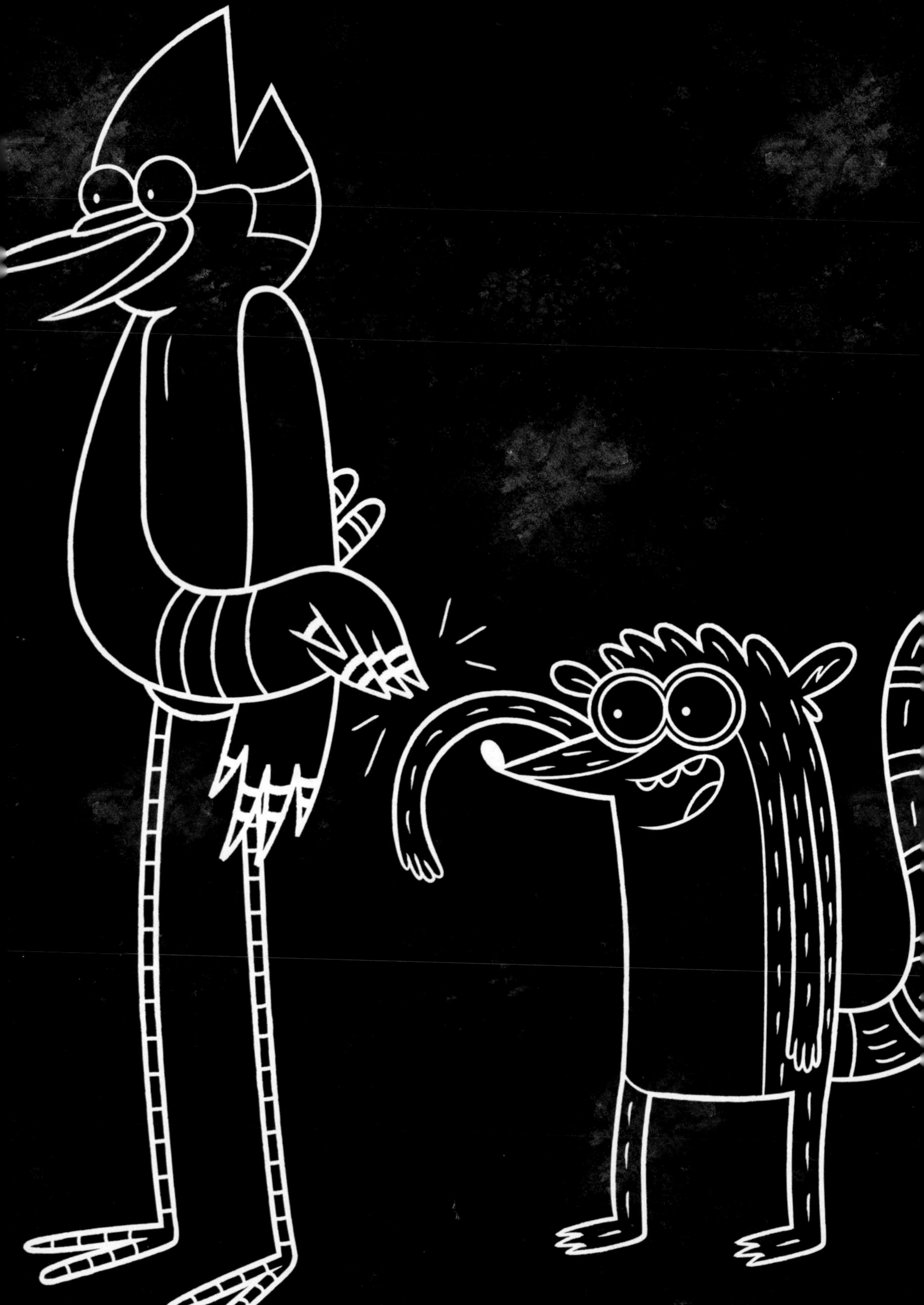

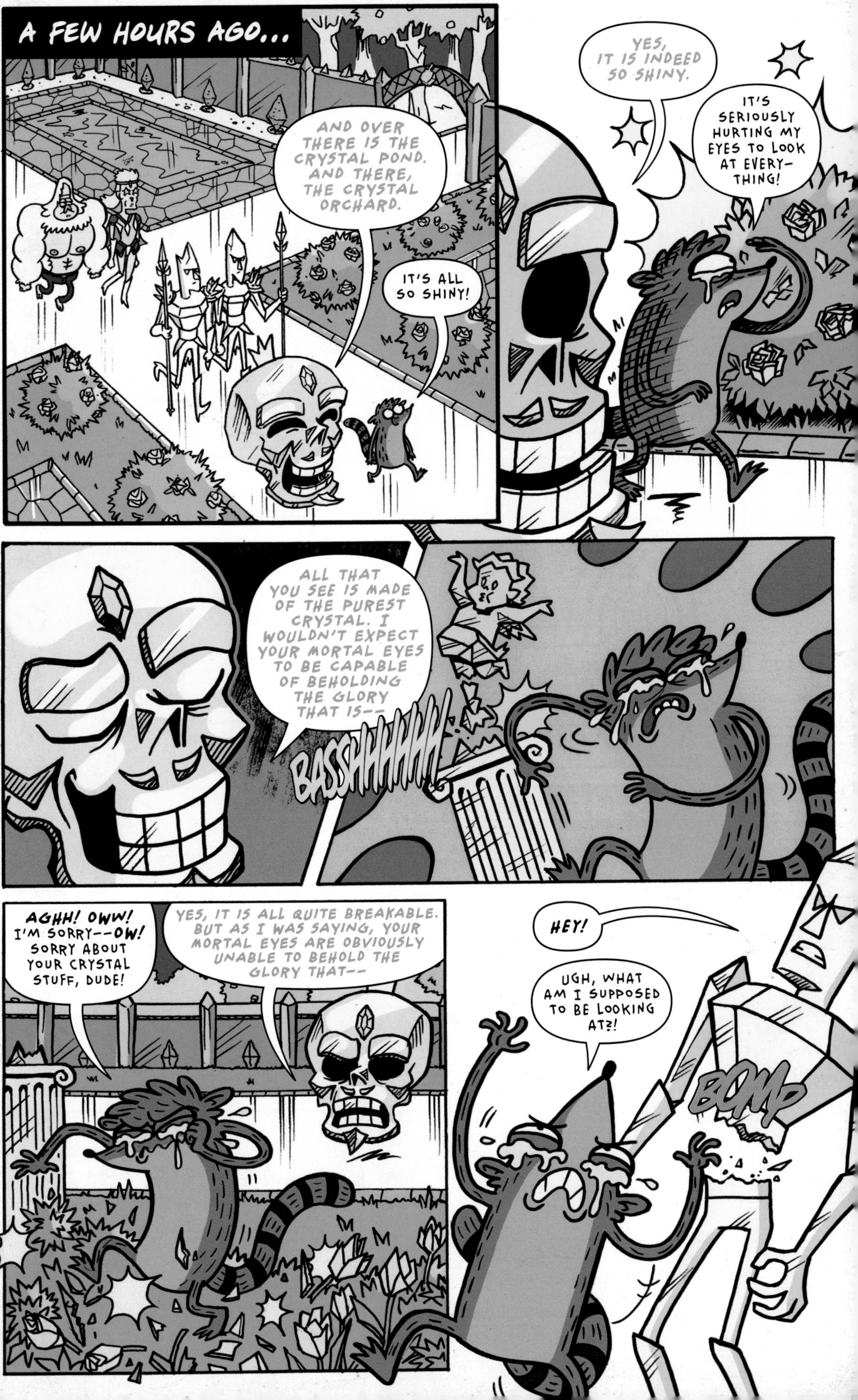

A FEW HOURS AGO...
AND OVER THERE IS THE CRYSTAL POND. AND THERE, THE CRYSTAL ORCHARD.
IT'S ALL SO SHINY!
YES, IT IS INDEED SO SHINY.
IT'S SERIOUSLY HURTING MY EYES TO LOOK AT EVERYTHING!
ALL THAT YOU SEE IS MADE OF THE PUREST CRYSTAL. I WOULDN'T EXPECT YOUR MORTAL EYES TO BE CAPABLE OF BEHOLDING THE GLORY THAT IS--
BASSHHHHHH!
AGHH! OWW! I'M SORRY--OW! SORRY ABOUT YOUR CRYSTAL STUFF, DUDE!
YES, IT IS ALL QUITE BREAKABLE. BUT AS I WAS SAYING, YOUR MORTAL EYES ARE OBVIOUSLY UNABLE TO BEHOLD THE GLORY THAT--
HEY!
UGH, WHAT AM I SUPPOSED TO BE LOOKING AT?!
BOMP

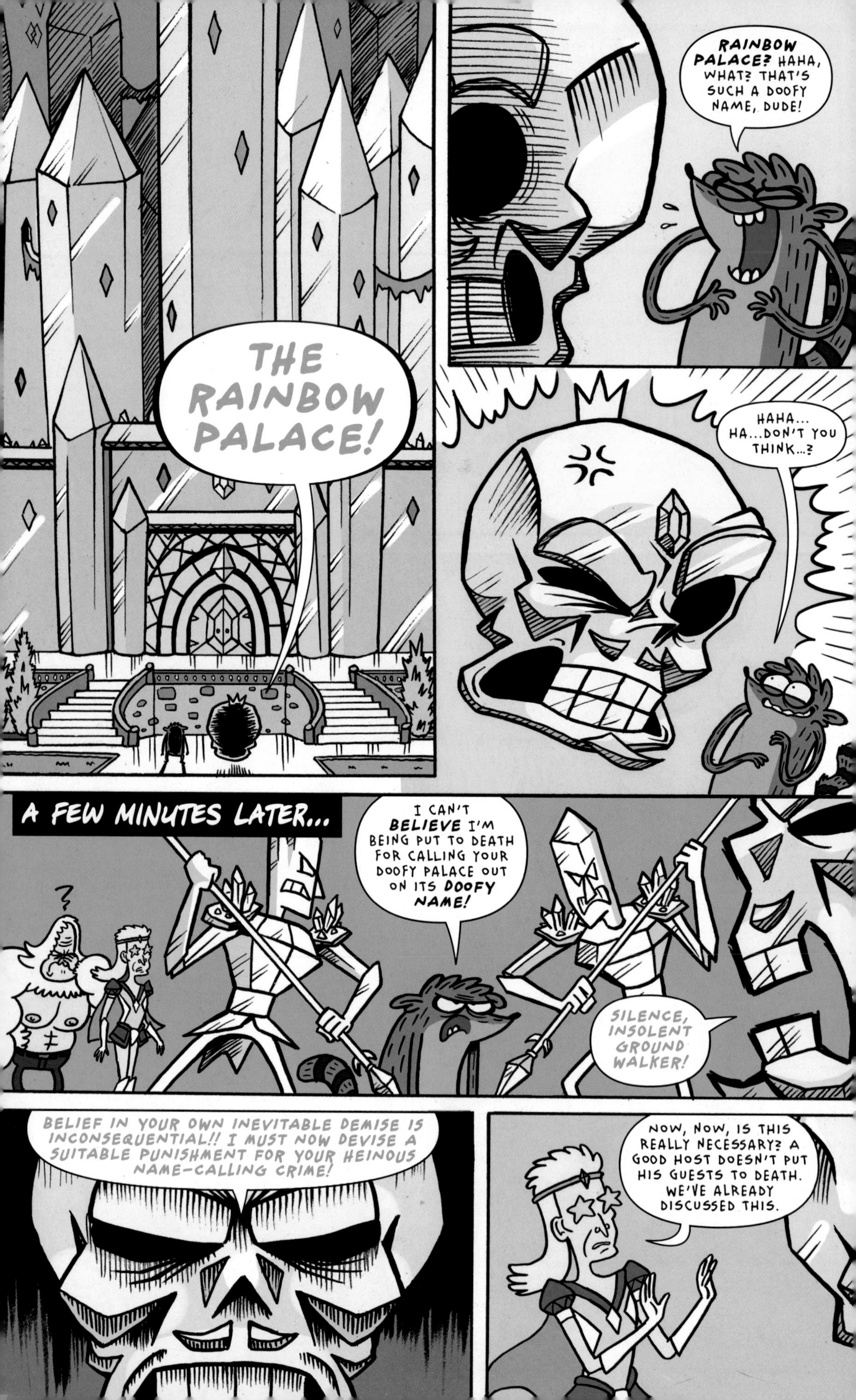
THE RAINBOW PALACE!
RAINBOW PALACE? HAHA, WHAT? THAT'S SUCH A DOOFY NAME, DUDE!
HAHA... HA...DON'T YOU THINK...?
A FEW MINUTES LATER...
I CAN'T BELIEVE I'M BEING PUT TO DEATH FOR CALLING YOUR DOOFY PALACE OUT ON ITS DOOFY NAME!
SILENCE, INSOLENT GROUND WALKER!
BELIEF IN YOUR OWN INEVITABLE DEMISE IS INCONSEQUENTIAL!! I MUST NOW DEVISE A SUITABLE PUNISHMENT FOR YOUR HEINOUS NAME-CALLING CRIME!
NOW, NOW, IS THIS REALLY NECESSARY? A GOOD HOST DOESN'T PUT HIS GUESTS TO DEATH. WE'VE ALREADY DISCUSSED THIS.

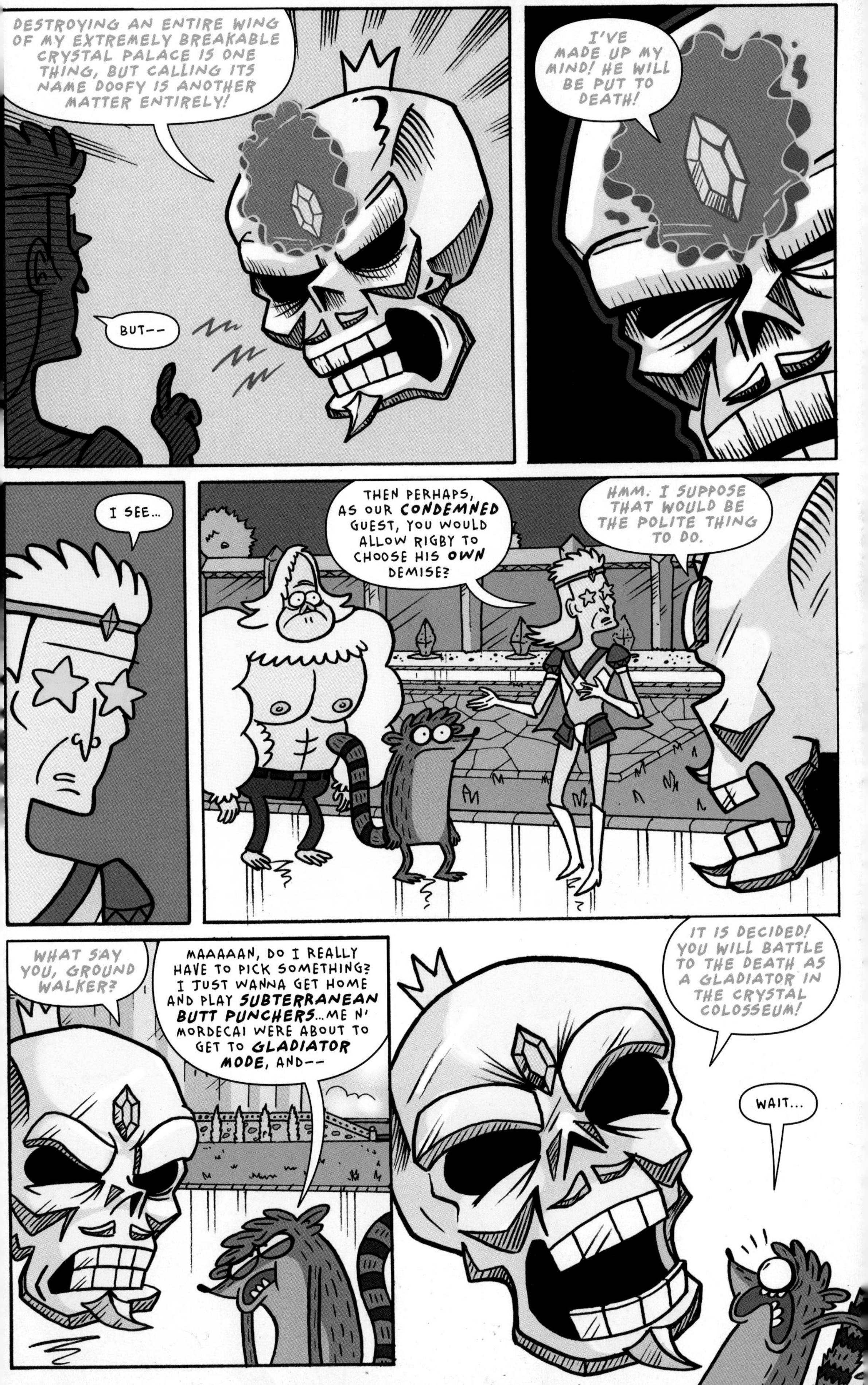
DESTROYING AN ENTIRE WING OF MY EXTREMELY BREAKABLE CRYSTAL PALACE IS ONE THING, BUT CALLING ITS NAME DOOFY IS ANOTHER MATTER ENTIRELY!
BUT--
I'VE MADE UP MY MIND! HE WILL BE PUT TO DEATH!
I SEE...
THEN PERHAPS, AS OUR CONDEMNED GUEST, YOU WOULD ALLOW RIGBY TO CHOOSE HIS OWN DEMISE?
HMM. I SUPPOSE THAT WOULD BE THE POLITE THING TO DO.
WHAT SAY YOU, GROUND WALKER?
MAAAAAN, DO I REALLY HAVE TO PICK SOMETHING? I JUST WANNA GET HOME AND PLAY SUBTERRANEAN BUTT PUNCHERS...ME N' MORDECAI WERE ABOUT TO GET TO GLADIATOR MODE, AND--
IT IS DECIDED! YOU WILL BATTLE TO THE DEATH AS A GLADIATOR IN THE CRYSTAL COLOSSEUM!
WAIT...

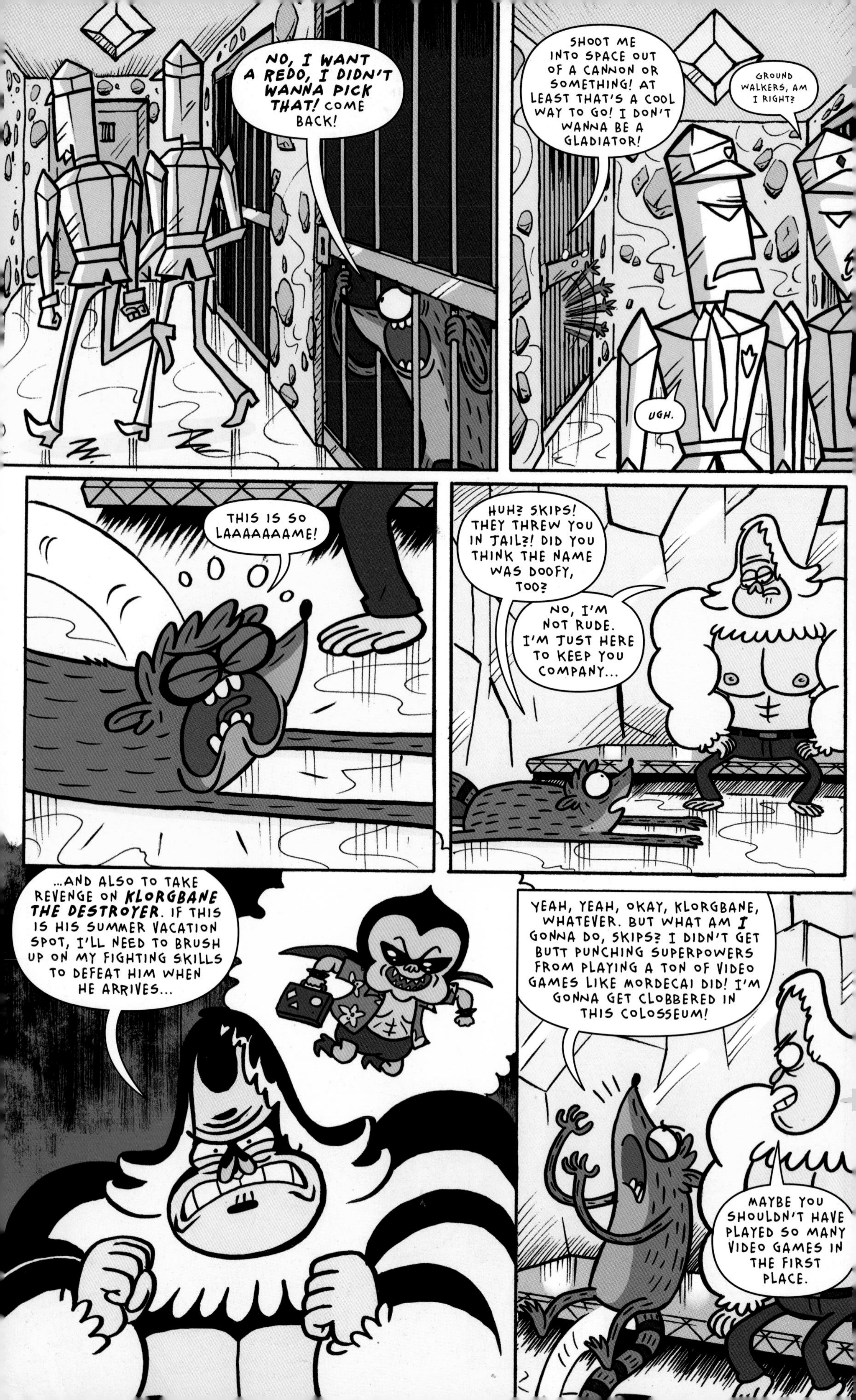
NO, I WANT A REDO, I DIDN'T WANNA PICK THAT! COME BACK!
SHOOT ME INTO SPACE OUT OF A CANNON OR SOMETHING! AT LEAST THAT'S A COOL WAY TO GO! I DON'T WANNA BE A GLADIATOR!
GROUND WALKERS, AM I RIGHT?
UGH.
THIS IS SO LAAAAAAAME!
HUH? SKIPS! THEY THREW YOU IN JAIL?! DID YOU THINK THE NAME WAS DOOFY, TOO?
NO, I'M NOT RUDE. I'M JUST HERE TO KEEP YOU COMPANY...
...AND ALSO TO TAKE REVENGE ON KLORGBANE THE DESTROYER. IF THIS IS HIS SUMMER VACATION SPOT, I'LL NEED TO BRUSH UP ON MY FIGHTING SKILLS TO DEFEAT HIM WHEN HE ARRIVES...
YEAH, YEAH, OKAY, KLORGBANE, WHATEVER. BUT WHAT AM I GONNA DO, SKIPS? I DIDN'T GET BUTT PUNCHING SUPERPOWERS FROM PLAYING A TON OF VIDEO GAMES LIKE MORDECAI DID! I'M GONNA GET CLOBBERED IN THIS COLOSSEUM!
MAYBE YOU SHOULDN'T HAVE PLAYED SO MANY VIDEO GAMES IN THE FIRST PLACE.

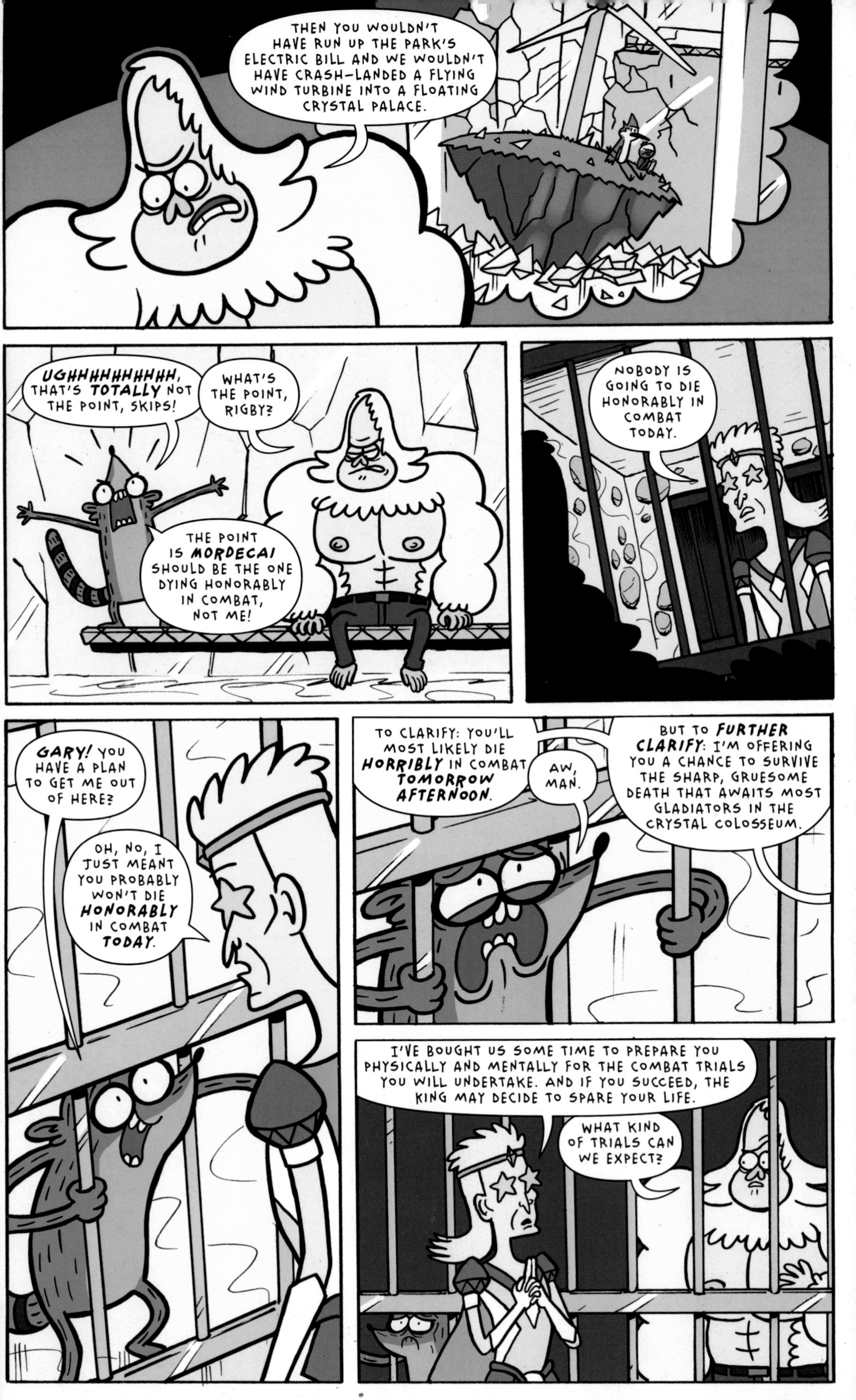
THEN YOU WOULDN'T HAVE RUN UP THE PARK'S ELECTRIC BILL AND WE WOULDN'T HAVE CRASH-LANDED A FLYING WIND TURBINE INTO A FLOATING CRYSTAL PALACE.
UGHHHHHHHHHH, THAT'S TOTALLY NOT THE POINT, SKIPS!
WHAT'S THE POINT, RIGBY?
THE POINT IS MORDECAI SHOULD BE THE ONE DYING HONORABLY IN COMBAT, NOT ME!
NOBODY IS GOING TO DIE HONORABLY IN COMBAT TODAY.
GARY! YOU HAVE A PLAN TO GET ME OUT OF HERE?
OH, NO, I JUST MEANT YOU PROBABLY WON'T DIE HONORABLY IN COMBAT TODAY.
TO CLARIFY: YOU'LL MOST LIKELY DIE HORRIBLY IN COMBAT TOMORROW AFTERNOON.
AW, MAN.
BUT TO FURTHER CLARIFY: I'M OFFERING YOU A CHANCE TO SURVIVE THE SHARP, GRUESOME DEATH THAT AWAITS MOST GLADIATORS IN THE CRYSTAL COLOSSEUM.
I'VE BOUGHT US SOME TIME TO PREPARE YOU PHYSICALLY AND MENTALLY FOR THE COMBAT TRIALS YOU WILL UNDERTAKE. AND IF YOU SUCCEED, THE KING MAY DECIDE TO SPARE YOUR LIFE.
WHAT KIND OF TRIALS CAN WE EXPECT?

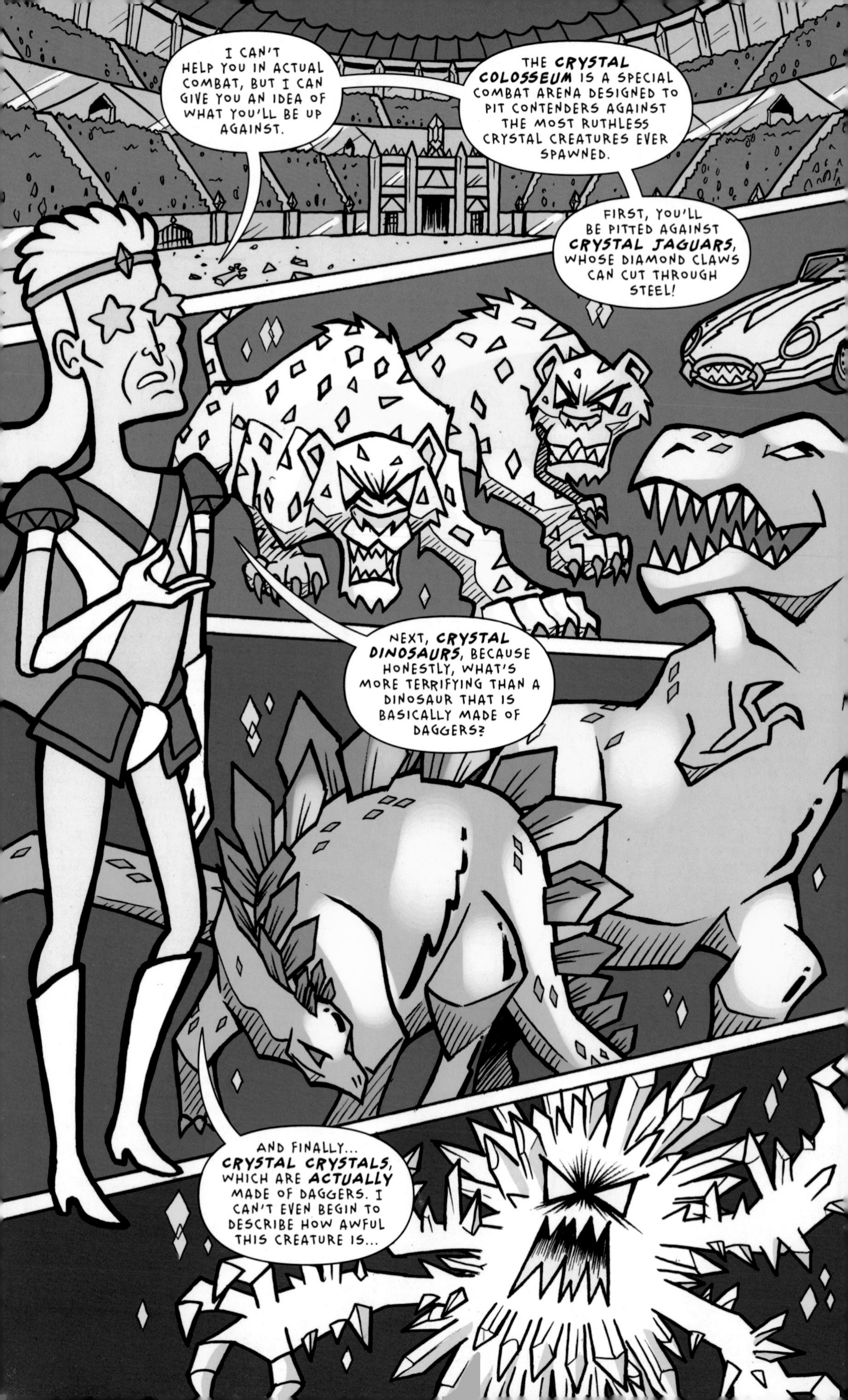
I CAN'T HELP YOU IN ACTUAL COMBAT, BUT I CAN GIVE YOU AN IDEA OF WHAT YOU'LL BE UP AGAINST.
THE CRYSTAL COLOSSEUM IS A SPECIAL COMBAT ARENA DESIGNED TO PIT CONTENDERS AGAINST THE MOST RUTHLESS CRYSTAL CREATURES EVER SPAWNED.
FIRST, YOU'LL BE PITTED AGAINST CRYSTAL JAGUARS, WHOSE DIAMOND CLAWS CAN CUT THROUGH STEEL!
NEXT, CRYSTAL DINOSAURS, BECAUSE HONESTLY, WHAT'S MORE TERRIFYING THAN A DINOSAUR THAT IS BASICALLY MADE OF DAGGERS?
AND FINALLY... CRYSTAL CRYSTALS, WHICH ARE ACTUALLY MADE OF DAGGERS. I CAN'T EVEN BEGIN TO DESCRIBE HOW AWFUL THIS CREATURE IS...

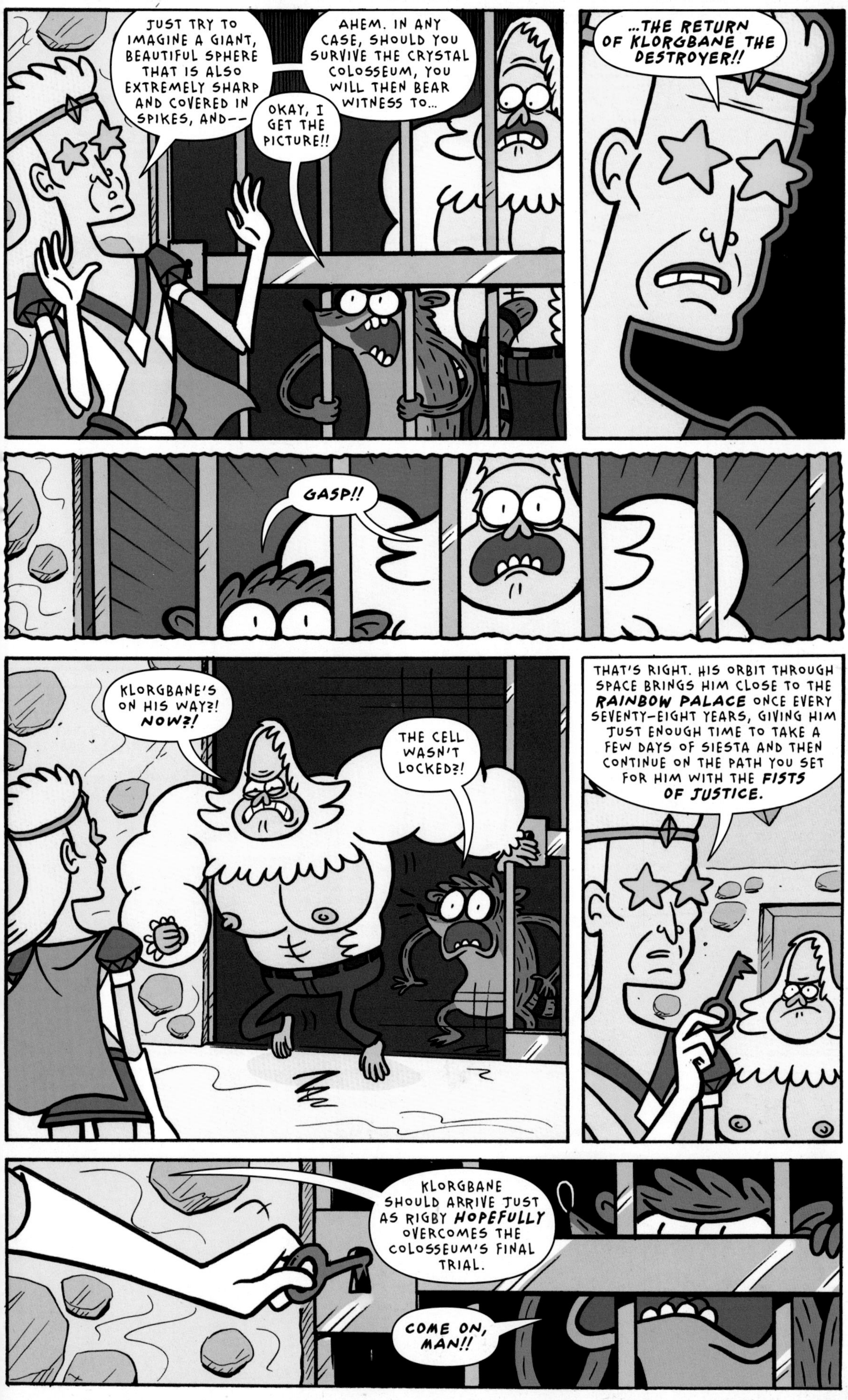
JUST TRY TO IMAGINE A GIANT, BEAUTIFUL SPHERE THAT IS ALSO EXTREMELY SHARP AND COVERED IN SPIKES, AND--
OKAY, I GET THE PICTURE!!
AHEM. IN ANY CASE, SHOULD YOU SURVIVE THE CRYSTAL COLOSSEUM, YOU WILL THEN BEAR WITNESS TO...
...THE RETURN OF KLORGBANE THE DESTROYER!!
GASP!!
KLORGBANE'S ON HIS WAY?! NOW?!
THE CELL WASN'T LOCKED?!
THAT'S RIGHT. HIS ORBIT THROUGH SPACE BRINGS HIM CLOSE TO THE RAINBOW PALACE ONCE EVERY SEVENTY-EIGHT YEARS, GIVING HIM JUST ENOUGH TIME TO TAKE A FEW DAYS OF SIESTA AND THEN CONTINUE ON THE PATH YOU SET FOR HIM WITH THE FISTS OF JUSTICE.
KLORGBANE SHOULD ARRIVE JUST AS RIGBY HOPEFULLY OVERCOMES THE COLOSSEUM'S FINAL TRIAL.
COME ON, MAN!!

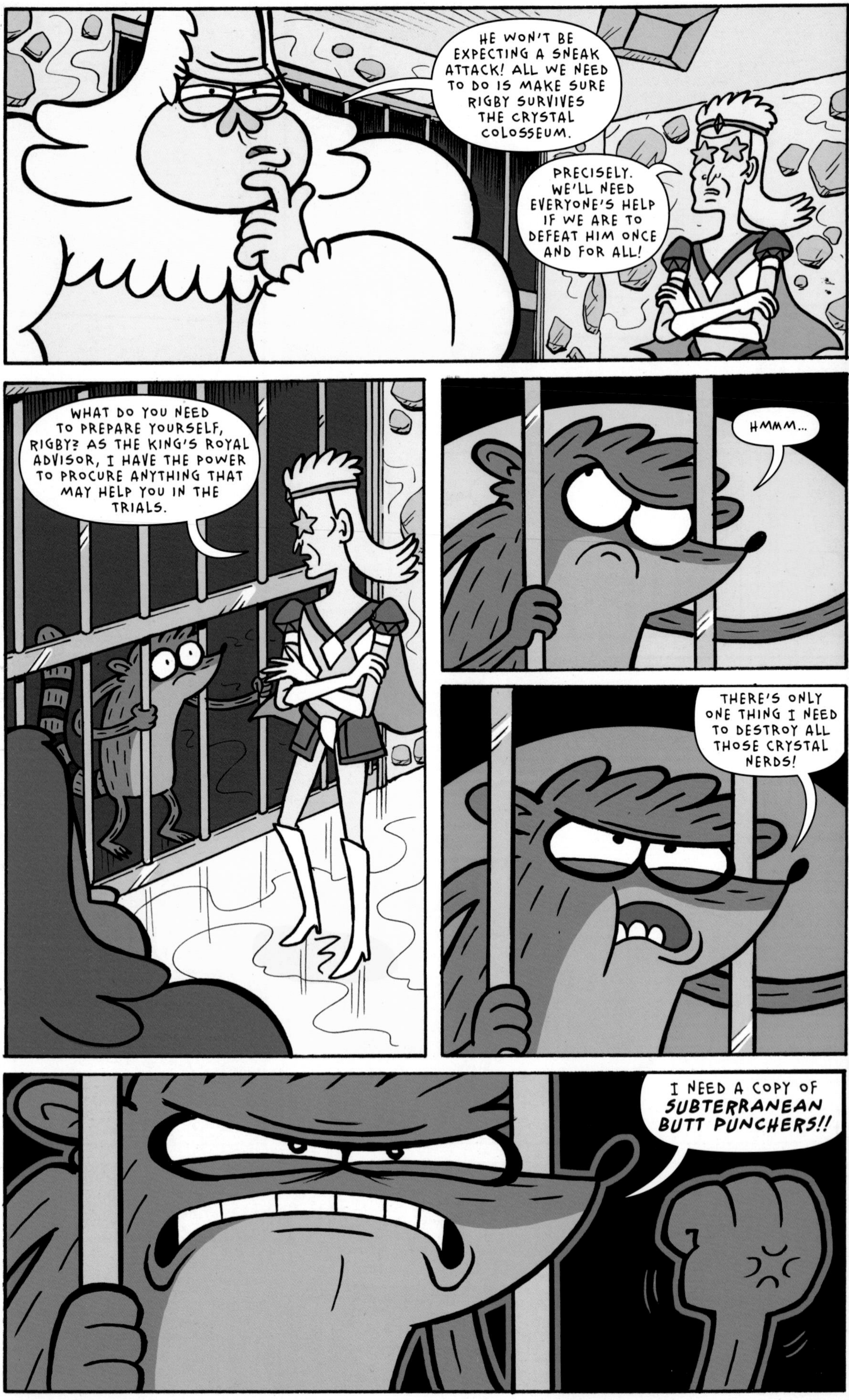
HE WON'T BE EXPECTING A SNEAK ATTACK! ALL WE NEED TO DO IS MAKE SURE RIGBY SURVIVES THE CRYSTAL COLOSSEUM.
PRECISELY. WE'LL NEED EVERYONE'S HELP IF WE ARE TO DEFEAT HIM ONCE AND FOR ALL!
WHAT DO YOU NEED TO PREPARE YOURSELF, RIGBY? AS THE KING'S ROYAL ADVISOR, I HAVE THE POWER TO PROCURE ANYTHING THAT MAY HELP YOU IN THE TRIALS.
HMMM...
THERE'S ONLY ONE THING I NEED TO DESTROY ALL THOSE CRYSTAL NERDS!
I NEED A COPY OF *SUBTERRANEAN BUTT PUNCHERS!!*

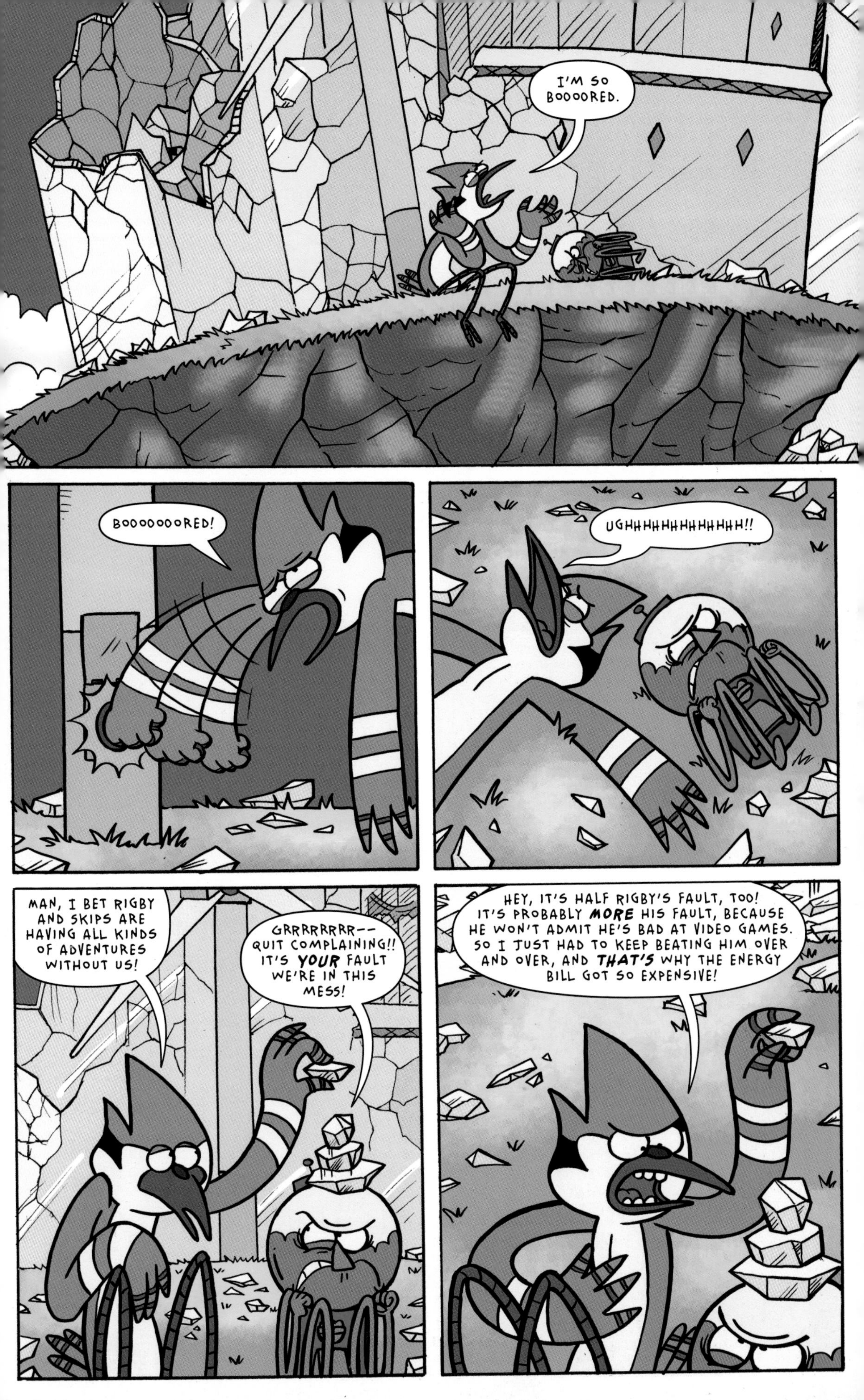
I'M SO BOOOORED.
BOOOOOOORED!
UGHHHHHHHHHHHH!!
MAN, I BET RIGBY AND SKIPS ARE HAVING ALL KINDS OF ADVENTURES WITHOUT US!
GRRRRRRRR-- QUIT COMPLAINING!! IT'S YOUR FAULT WE'RE IN THIS MESS!
HEY, IT'S HALF RIGBY'S FAULT, TOO! IT'S PROBABLY MORE HIS FAULT, BECAUSE HE WON'T ADMIT HE'S BAD AT VIDEO GAMES. SO I JUST HAD TO KEEP BEATING HIM OVER AND OVER, AND THAT'S WHY THE ENERGY BILL GOT SO EXPENSIVE!

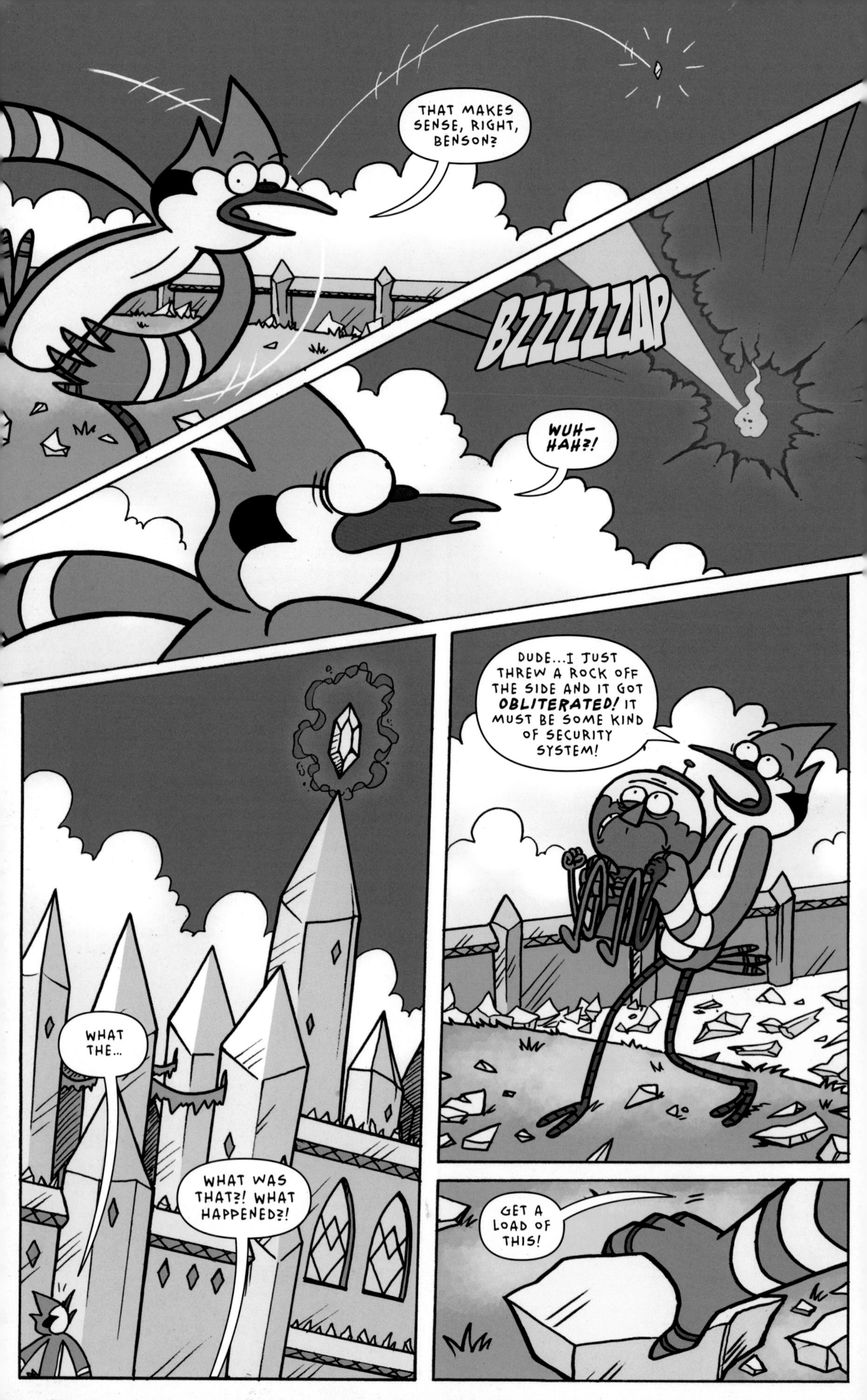
THAT MAKES SENSE, RIGHT, BENSON?
BZZZZZZAP
WUH-HAH?!
WHAT THE...
WHAT WAS THAT?! WHAT HAPPENED?!
DUDE...I JUST THREW A ROCK OFF THE SIDE AND IT GOT OBLITERATED! IT MUST BE SOME KIND OF SECURITY SYSTEM!
GET A LOAD OF THIS!

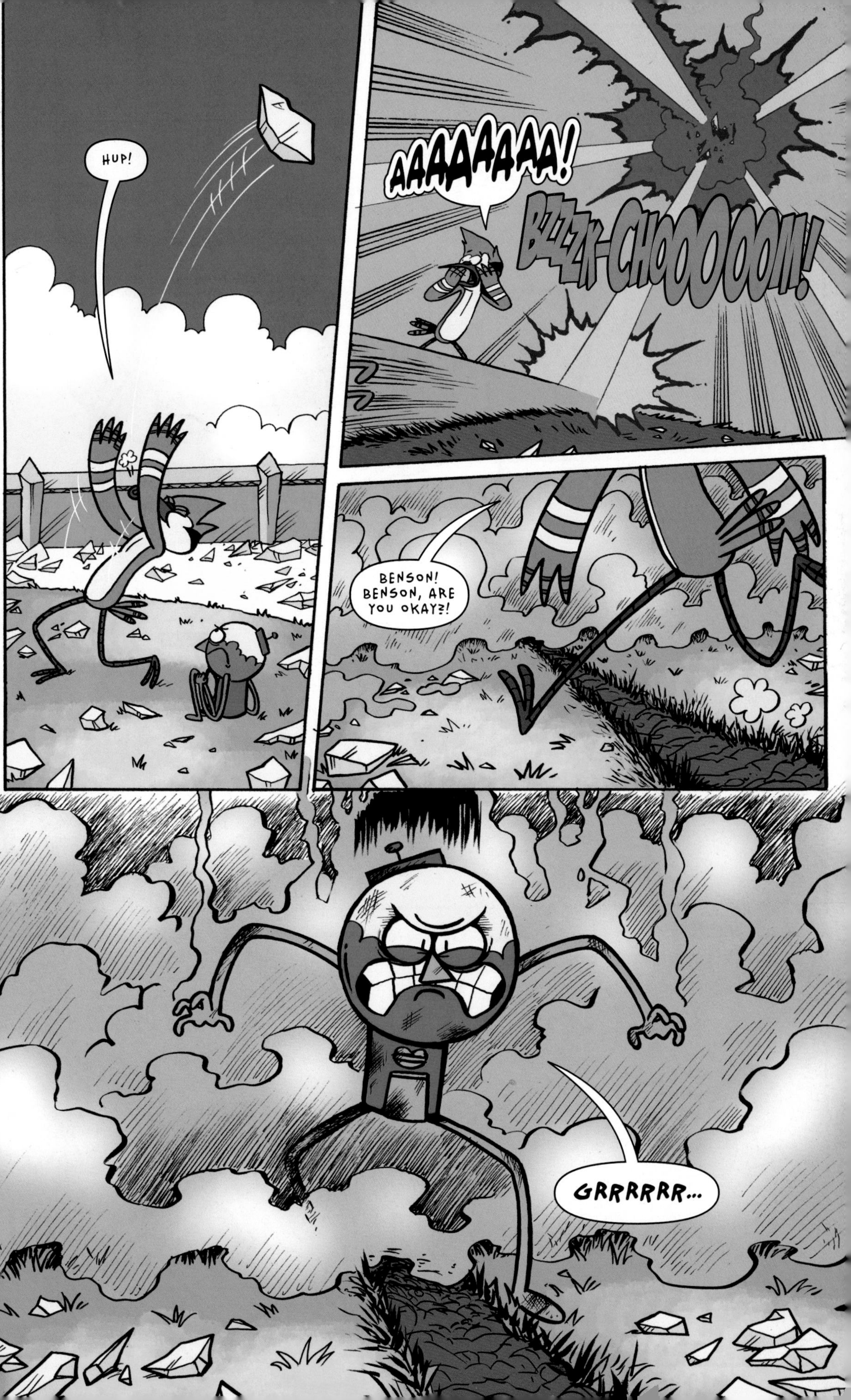
HUP!
AAAAAAAA!
BZZZK-CHOOOOOM!
BENSON! BENSON, ARE YOU OKAY?!
GRRRRRR...

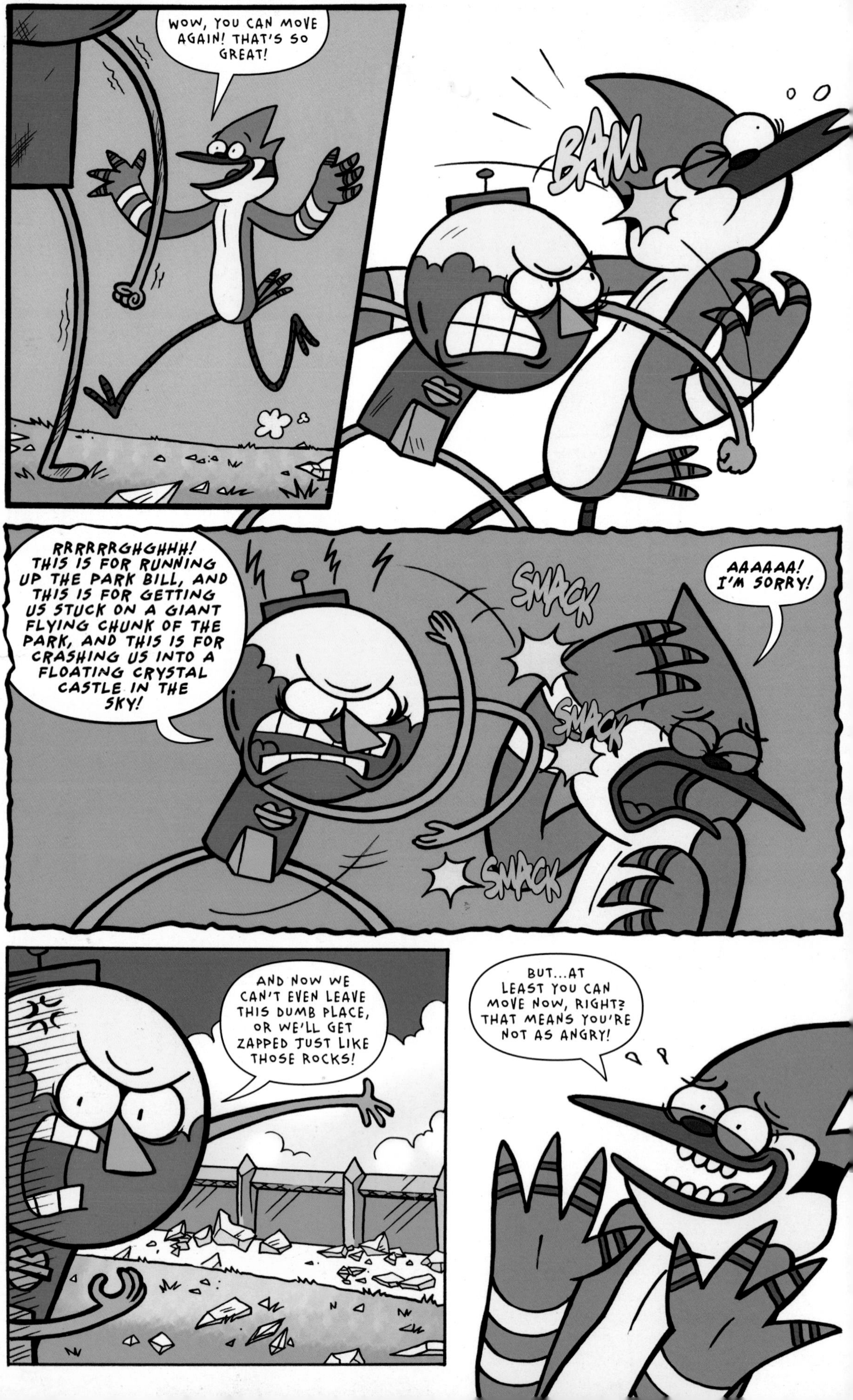
WOW, YOU CAN MOVE AGAIN! THAT'S SO GREAT!
BAM
RRRRRRGHGHHH! THIS IS FOR RUNNING UP THE PARK BILL, AND THIS IS FOR GETTING US STUCK ON A GIANT FLYING CHUNK OF THE PARK, AND THIS IS FOR CRASHING US INTO A FLOATING CRYSTAL CASTLE IN THE SKY!
SMACK
AAAAAA! I'M SORRY!
SMACK
SMACK
AND NOW WE CAN'T EVEN LEAVE THIS DUMB PLACE, OR WE'LL GET ZAPPED JUST LIKE THOSE ROCKS!
BUT...AT LEAST YOU CAN MOVE NOW, RIGHT? THAT MEANS YOU'RE NOT AS ANGRY!

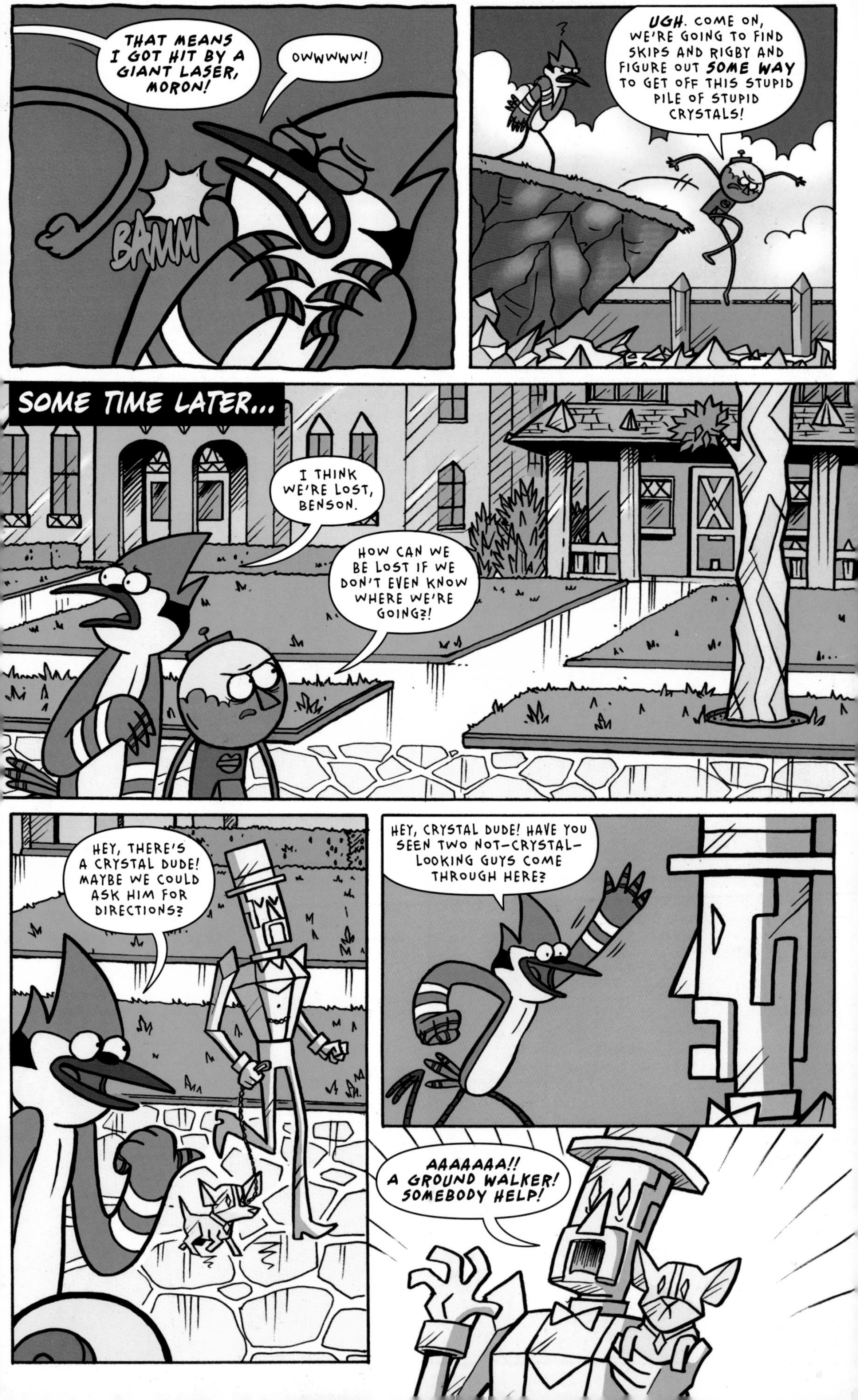

THAT MEANS I GOT HIT BY A GIANT LASER, MORON!
OWWWWW!
BAMM
UGH. COME ON, WE'RE GOING TO FIND SKIPS AND RIGBY AND FIGURE OUT SOME WAY TO GET OFF THIS STUPID PILE OF STUPID CRYSTALS!
SOME TIME LATER...
I THINK WE'RE LOST, BENSON.
HOW CAN WE BE LOST IF WE DON'T EVEN KNOW WHERE WE'RE GOING?!
HEY, THERE'S A CRYSTAL DUDE! MAYBE WE COULD ASK HIM FOR DIRECTIONS?
HEY, CRYSTAL DUDE! HAVE YOU SEEN TWO NOT-CRYSTAL-LOOKING GUYS COME THROUGH HERE?
AAAAAAA!! A GROUND WALKER! SOMEBODY HELP!

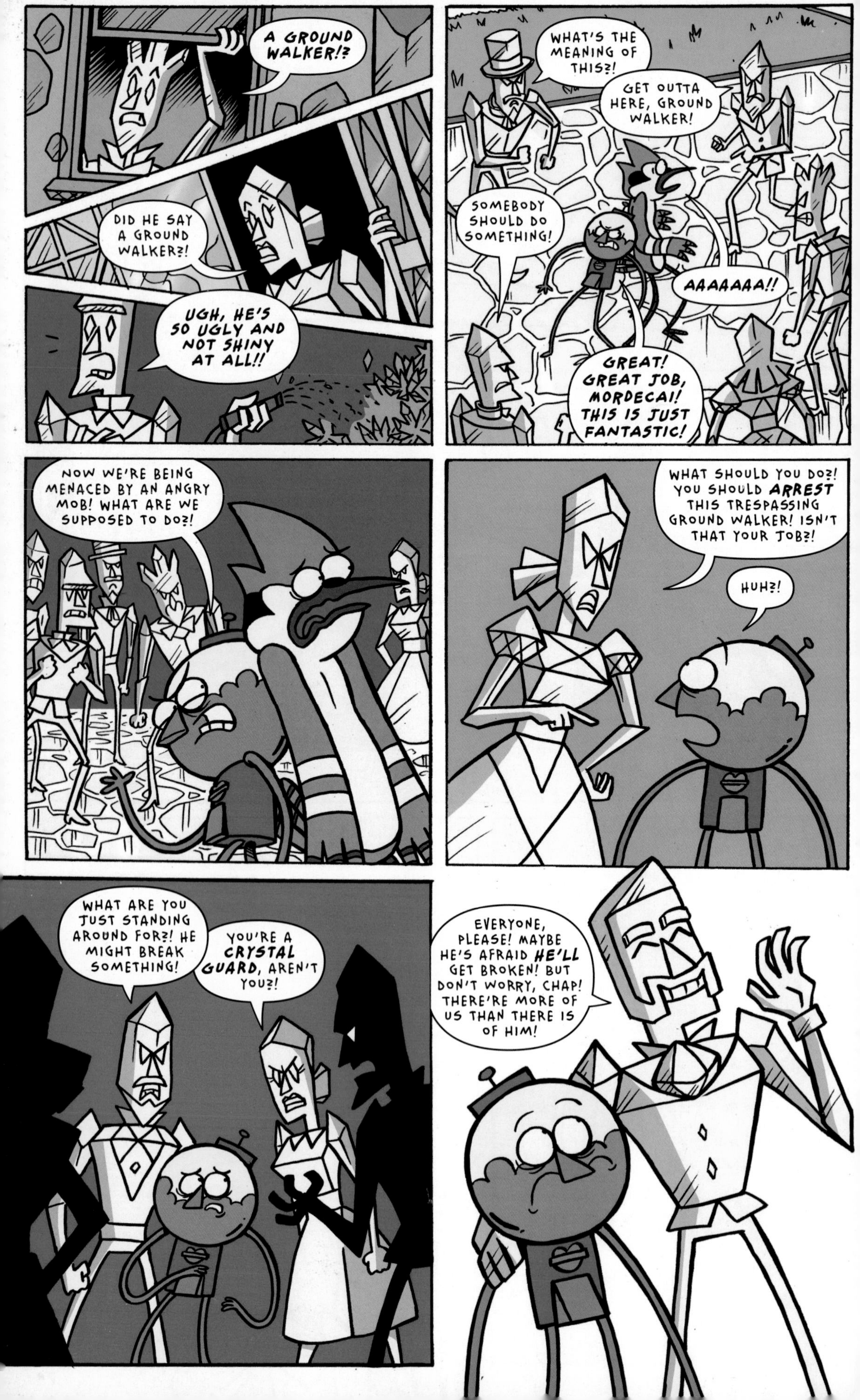
A GROUND WALKER!?
DID HE SAY A GROUND WALKER?!
UGH, HE'S SO UGLY AND NOT SHINY AT ALL!!
WHAT'S THE MEANING OF THIS?!
GET OUTTA HERE, GROUND WALKER!
SOMEBODY SHOULD DO SOMETHING!
AAAAAAA!!
GREAT! GREAT JOB, MORDECAI! THIS IS JUST FANTASTIC!
NOW WE'RE BEING MENACED BY AN ANGRY MOB! WHAT ARE WE SUPPOSED TO DO?!
WHAT SHOULD YOU DO?! YOU SHOULD ARREST THIS TRESPASSING GROUND WALKER! ISN'T THAT YOUR JOB?!
HUH?!
WHAT ARE YOU JUST STANDING AROUND FOR?! HE MIGHT BREAK SOMETHING!
YOU'RE A CRYSTAL GUARD, AREN'T YOU?!
EVERYONE, PLEASE! MAYBE HE'S AFRAID HE'LL GET BROKEN! BUT DON'T WORRY, CHAP! THERE'RE MORE OF US THAN THERE IS OF HIM!

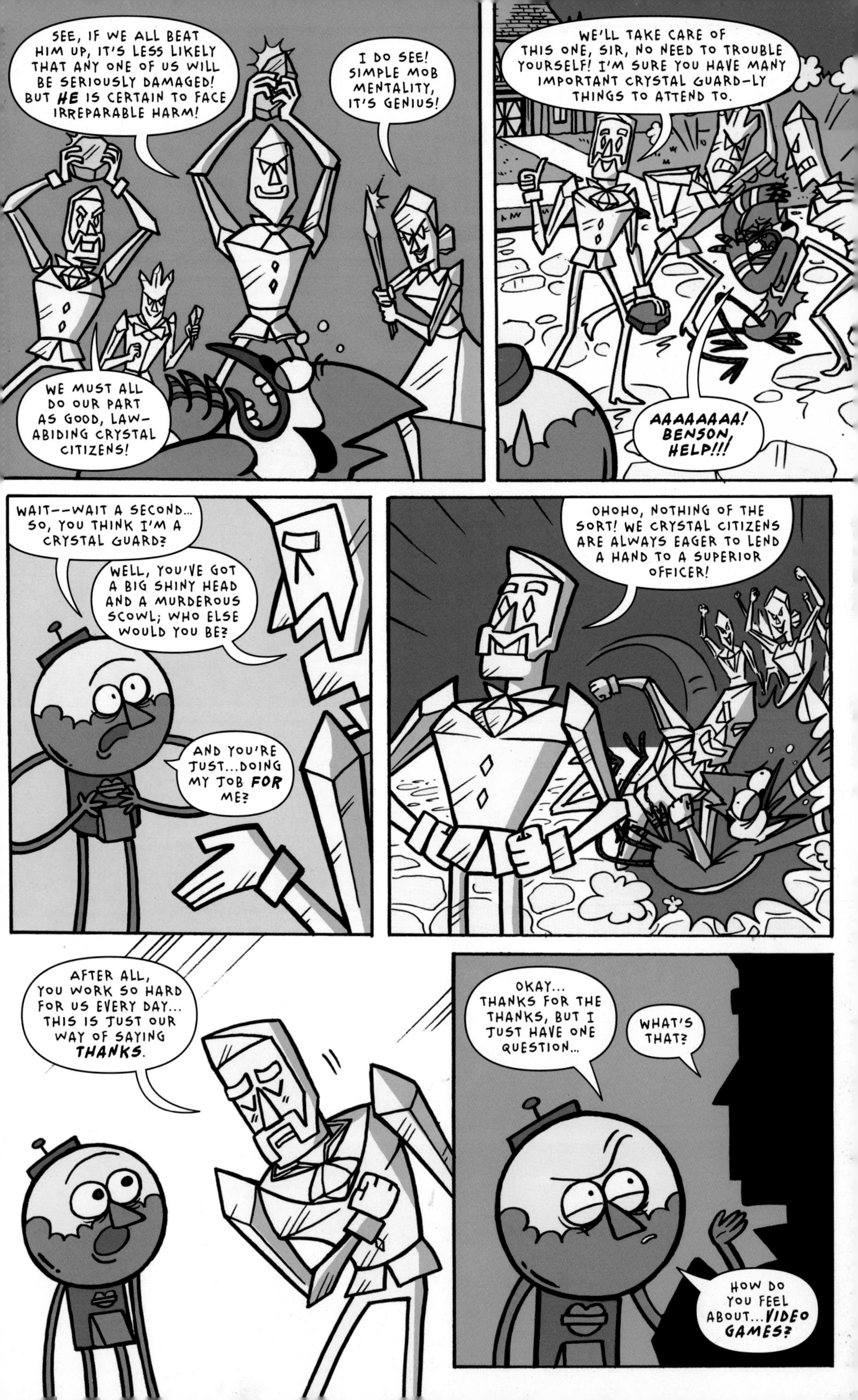
SEE, IF WE ALL BEAT HIM UP, IT'S LESS LIKELY THAT ANY ONE OF US WILL BE SERIOUSLY DAMAGED! BUT HE IS CERTAIN TO FACE IRREPARABLE HARM!
I DO SEE! SIMPLE MOB MENTALITY, IT'S GENIUS!
WE MUST ALL DO OUR PART AS GOOD, LAW-ABIDING CRYSTAL CITIZENS!
WE'LL TAKE CARE OF THIS ONE, SIR, NO NEED TO TROUBLE YOURSELF! I'M SURE YOU HAVE MANY IMPORTANT CRYSTAL GUARD-LY THINGS TO ATTEND TO.
AAAAAAAA! BENSON, HELP!!!
WAIT--WAIT A SECOND... SO, YOU THINK I'M A CRYSTAL GUARD?
WELL, YOU'VE GOT A BIG SHINY HEAD AND A MURDEROUS SCOWL; WHO ELSE WOULD YOU BE?
AND YOU'RE JUST...DOING MY JOB FOR ME?
OHOHO, NOTHING OF THE SORT! WE CRYSTAL CITIZENS ARE ALWAYS EAGER TO LEND A HAND TO A SUPERIOR OFFICER!
AFTER ALL, YOU WORK SO HARD FOR US EVERY DAY... THIS IS JUST OUR WAY OF SAYING THANKS.
OKAY... THANKS FOR THE THANKS, BUT I JUST HAVE ONE QUESTION...
WHAT'S THAT?
HOW DO YOU FEEL ABOUT...VIDEO GAMES?

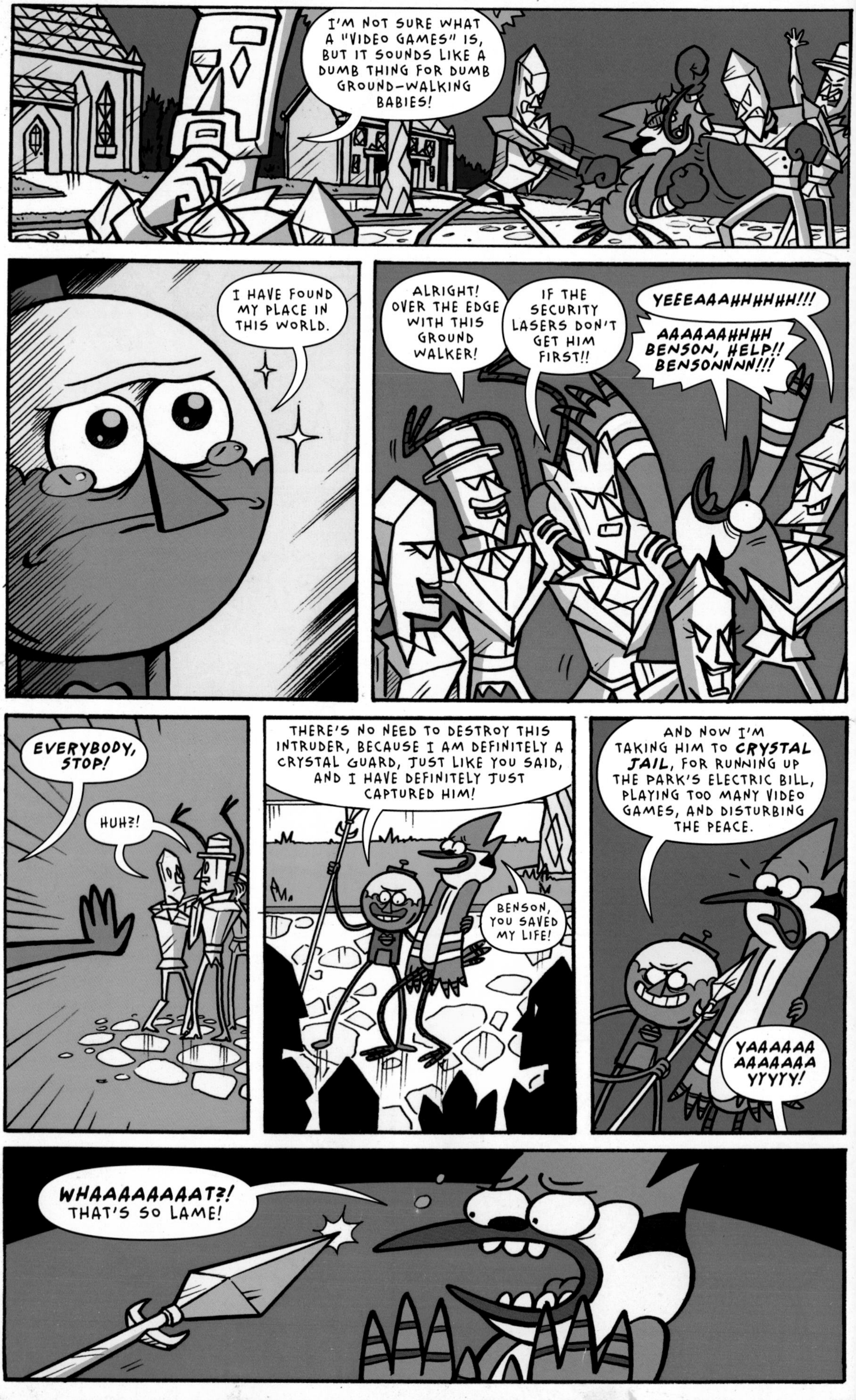
I'M NOT SURE WHAT A "VIDEO GAMES" IS, BUT IT SOUNDS LIKE A DUMB THING FOR DUMB GROUND-WALKING BABIES!
I HAVE FOUND MY PLACE IN THIS WORLD.
ALRIGHT! OVER THE EDGE WITH THIS GROUND WALKER!
IF THE SECURITY LASERS DON'T GET HIM FIRST!!
YEEEAAAHHHHHH!!!
AAAAAAHHHH BENSON, HELP!! BENSONNNN!!!
EVERYBODY, STOP!
HUH?!
THERE'S NO NEED TO DESTROY THIS INTRUDER, BECAUSE I AM DEFINITELY A CRYSTAL GUARD, JUST LIKE YOU SAID, AND I HAVE DEFINITELY JUST CAPTURED HIM!
BENSON, YOU SAVED MY LIFE!
AND NOW I'M TAKING HIM TO CRYSTAL JAIL, FOR RUNNING UP THE PARK'S ELECTRIC BILL, PLAYING TOO MANY VIDEO GAMES, AND DISTURBING THE PEACE.
YAAAAAA AAAAAAA YYYY!
WHAAAAAAAAT?! THAT'S SO LAME!

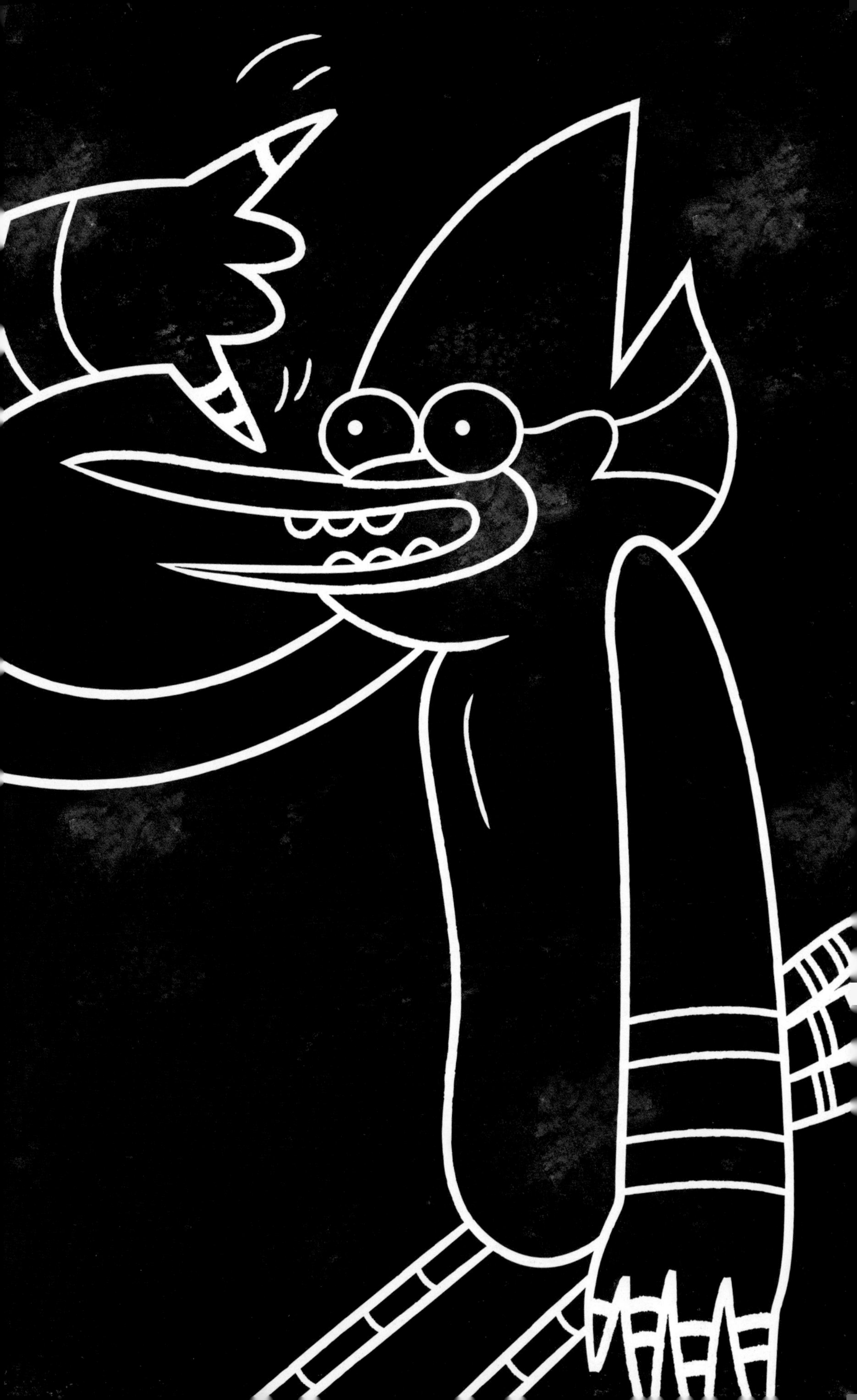

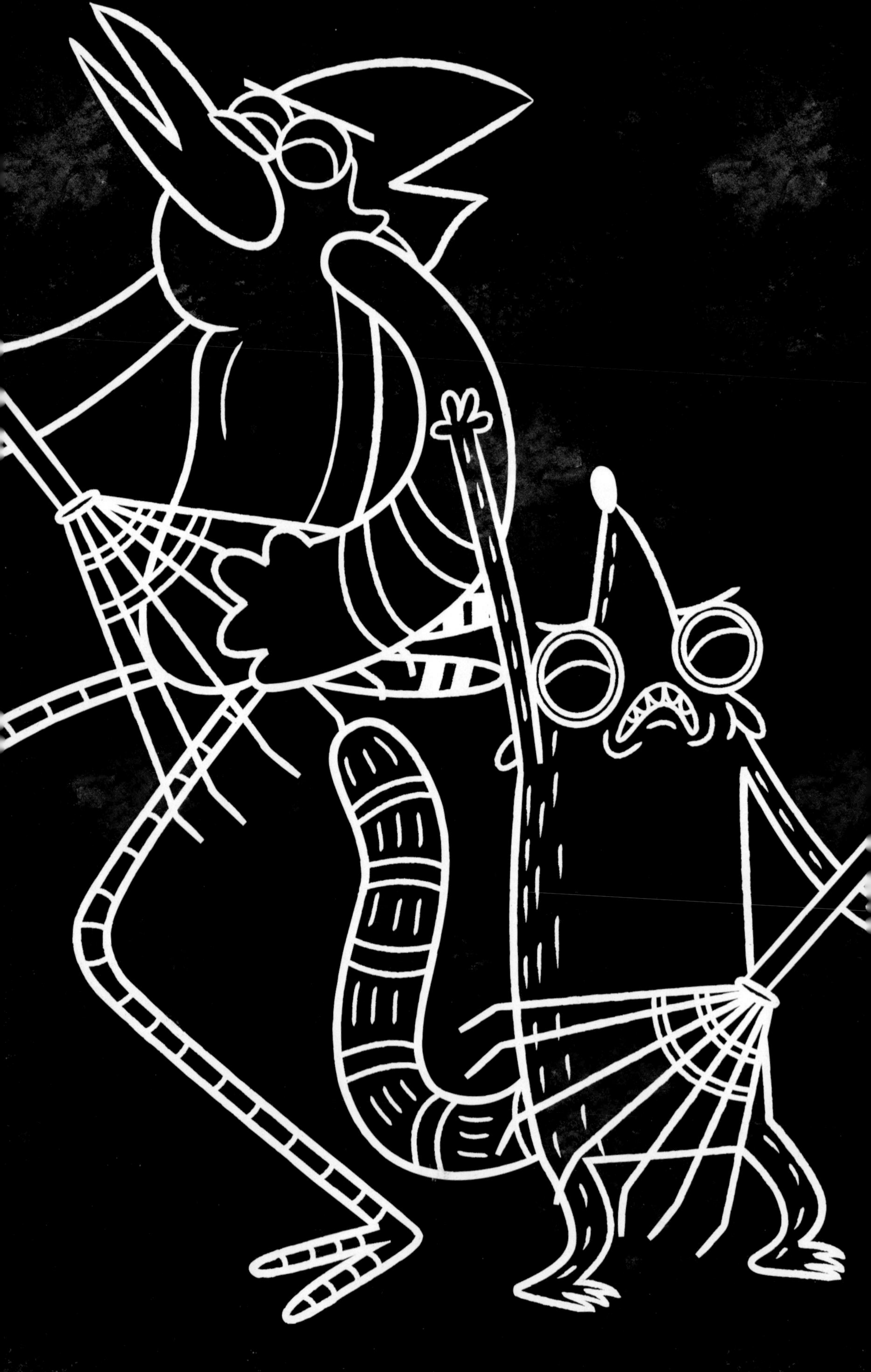

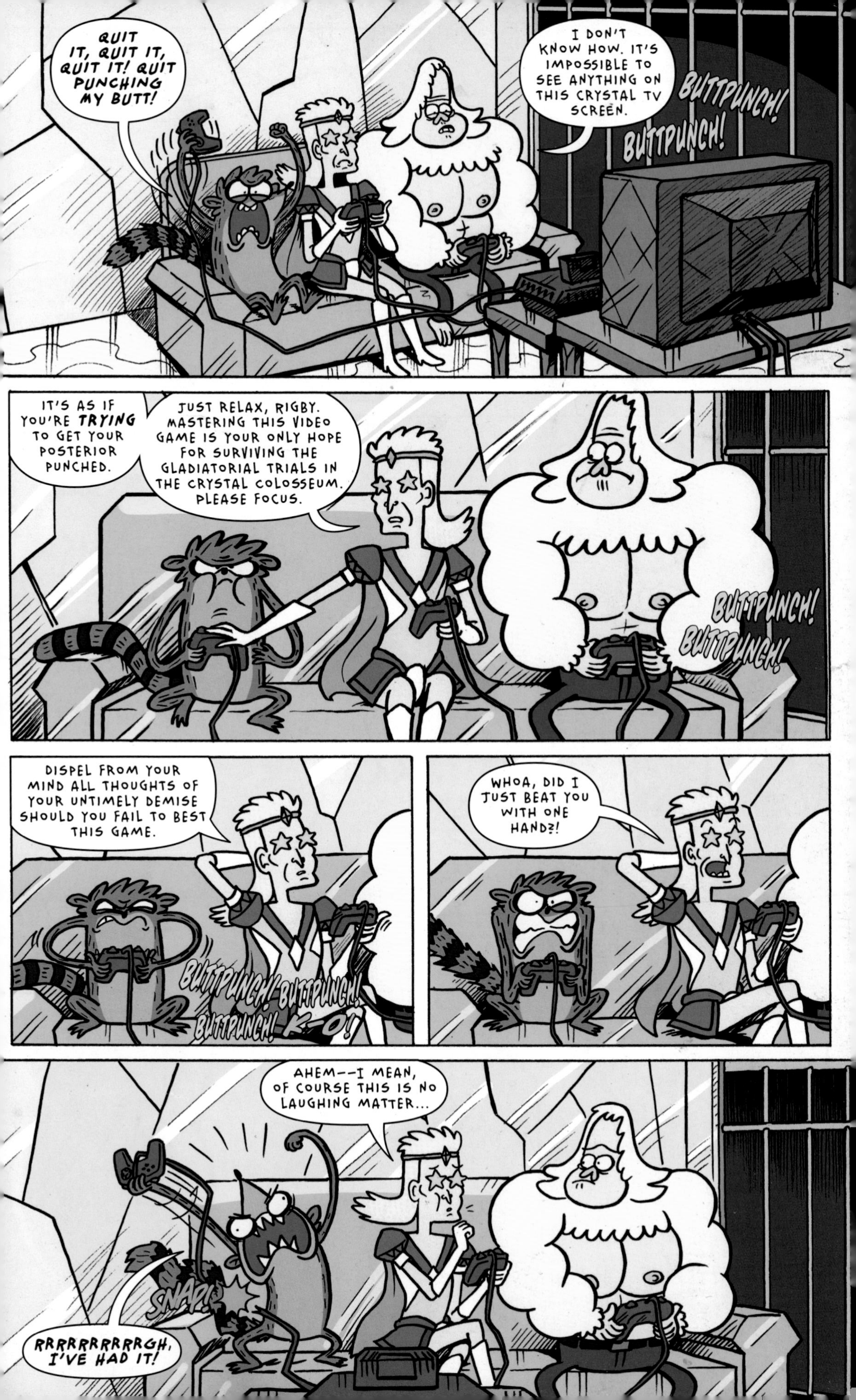
QUIT IT, QUIT IT, QUIT IT! QUIT PUNCHING MY BUTT!
I DON'T KNOW HOW. IT'S IMPOSSIBLE TO SEE ANYTHING ON THIS CRYSTAL TV SCREEN.
BUTTPUNCH!
BUTTPUNCH!
IT'S AS IF YOU'RE TRYING TO GET YOUR POSTERIOR PUNCHED.
JUST RELAX, RIGBY. MASTERING THIS VIDEO GAME IS YOUR ONLY HOPE FOR SURVIVING THE GLADIATORIAL TRIALS IN THE CRYSTAL COLOSSEUM. PLEASE FOCUS.
BUTTPUNCH!
BUTTPUNCH!
DISPEL FROM YOUR MIND ALL THOUGHTS OF YOUR UNTIMELY DEMISE SHOULD YOU FAIL TO BEST THIS GAME.
BUTTPUNCH! BUTTPUNCH!
BUTTPUNCH! K-O!
WHOA, DID I JUST BEAT YOU WITH ONE HAND?!
AHEM--I MEAN, OF COURSE THIS IS NO LAUGHING MATTER...
SNAP!
RRRRRRRRRRGH, I'VE HAD IT!

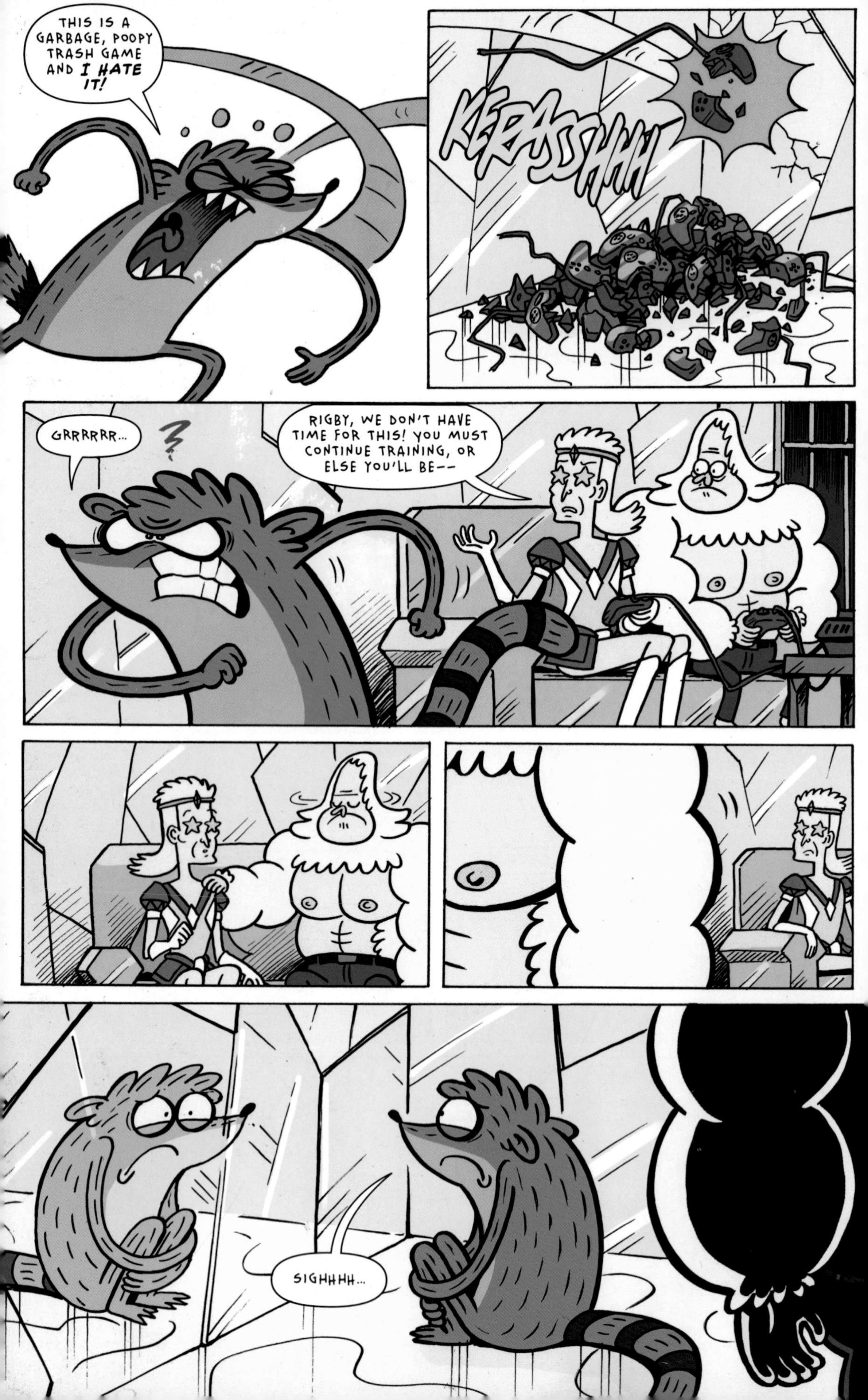
THIS IS A GARBAGE, POOPY TRASH GAME AND I HATE IT!
KERASSHHH
GRRRRRR...
RIGBY, WE DON'T HAVE TIME FOR THIS! YOU MUST CONTINUE TRAINING, OR ELSE YOU'LL BE--
SIGHHHH...

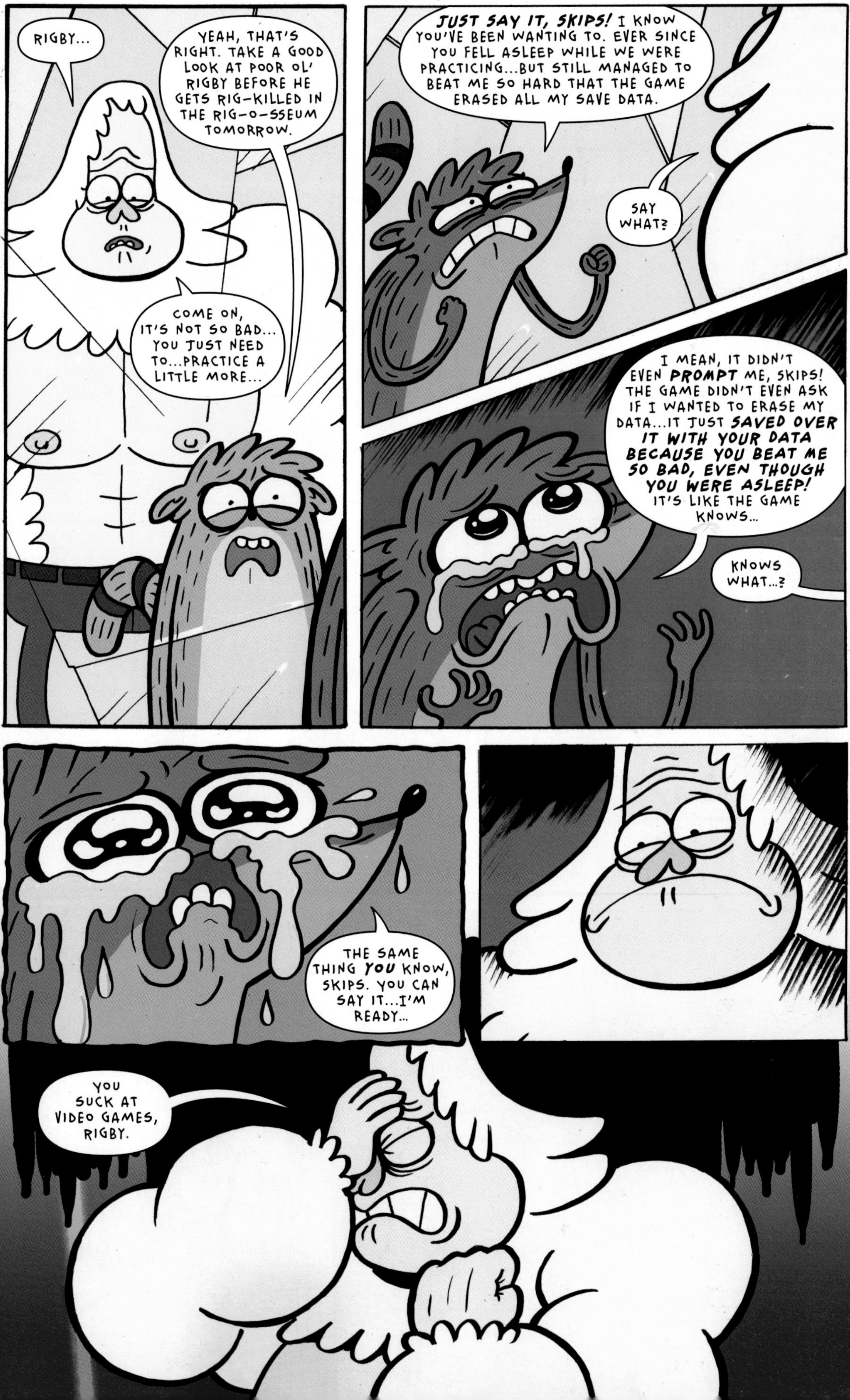
RIGBY...
YEAH, THAT'S RIGHT. TAKE A GOOD LOOK AT POOR OL' RIGBY BEFORE HE GETS RIG-KILLED IN THE RIG-O-SSEUM TOMORROW.
COME ON, IT'S NOT SO BAD... YOU JUST NEED TO...PRACTICE A LITTLE MORE...
JUST SAY IT, SKIPS! I KNOW YOU'VE BEEN WANTING TO. EVER SINCE YOU FELL ASLEEP WHILE WE WERE PRACTICING...BUT STILL MANAGED TO BEAT ME SO HARD THAT THE GAME ERASED ALL MY SAVE DATA.
SAY WHAT?
I MEAN, IT DIDN'T EVEN PROMPT ME, SKIPS! THE GAME DIDN'T EVEN ASK IF I WANTED TO ERASE MY DATA...IT JUST SAVED OVER IT WITH YOUR DATA BECAUSE YOU BEAT ME SO BAD, EVEN THOUGH YOU WERE ASLEEP! IT'S LIKE THE GAME KNOWS...
KNOWS WHAT...?
THE SAME THING YOU KNOW, SKIPS. YOU CAN SAY IT...I'M READY...
YOU SUCK AT VIDEO GAMES, RIGBY.

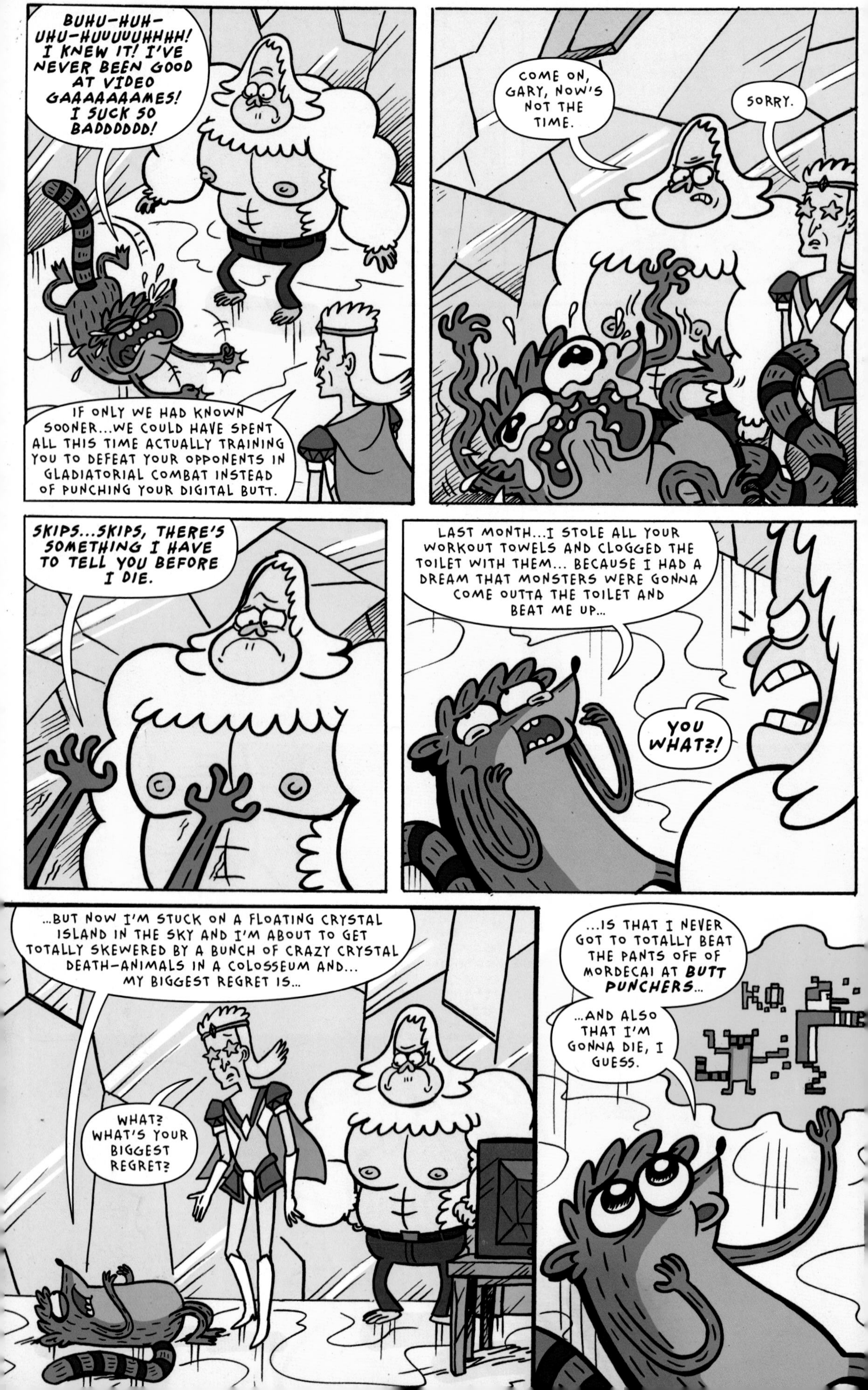
BUHU-HUH-UHU-HUUUUUHHHH! I KNEW IT! I'VE NEVER BEEN GOOD AT VIDEO GAAAAAAAMES! I SUCK SO BADDDDDD!
IF ONLY WE HAD KNOWN SOONER...WE COULD HAVE SPENT ALL THIS TIME ACTUALLY TRAINING YOU TO DEFEAT YOUR OPPONENTS IN GLADIATORIAL COMBAT INSTEAD OF PUNCHING YOUR DIGITAL BUTT.
COME ON, GARY, NOW'S NOT THE TIME.
SORRY.
SKIPS...SKIPS, THERE'S SOMETHING I HAVE TO TELL YOU BEFORE I DIE.
LAST MONTH...I STOLE ALL YOUR WORKOUT TOWELS AND CLOGGED THE TOILET WITH THEM... BECAUSE I HAD A DREAM THAT MONSTERS WERE GONNA COME OUTTA THE TOILET AND BEAT ME UP...
YOU WHAT?!
...BUT NOW I'M STUCK ON A FLOATING CRYSTAL ISLAND IN THE SKY AND I'M ABOUT TO GET TOTALLY SKEWERED BY A BUNCH OF CRAZY CRYSTAL DEATH-ANIMALS IN A COLOSSEUM AND... MY BIGGEST REGRET IS...
WHAT? WHAT'S YOUR BIGGEST REGRET?
...IS THAT I NEVER GOT TO TOTALLY BEAT THE PANTS OFF OF MORDECAI AT BUTT PUNCHERS...
K.O.
...AND ALSO THAT I'M GONNA DIE, I GUESS.

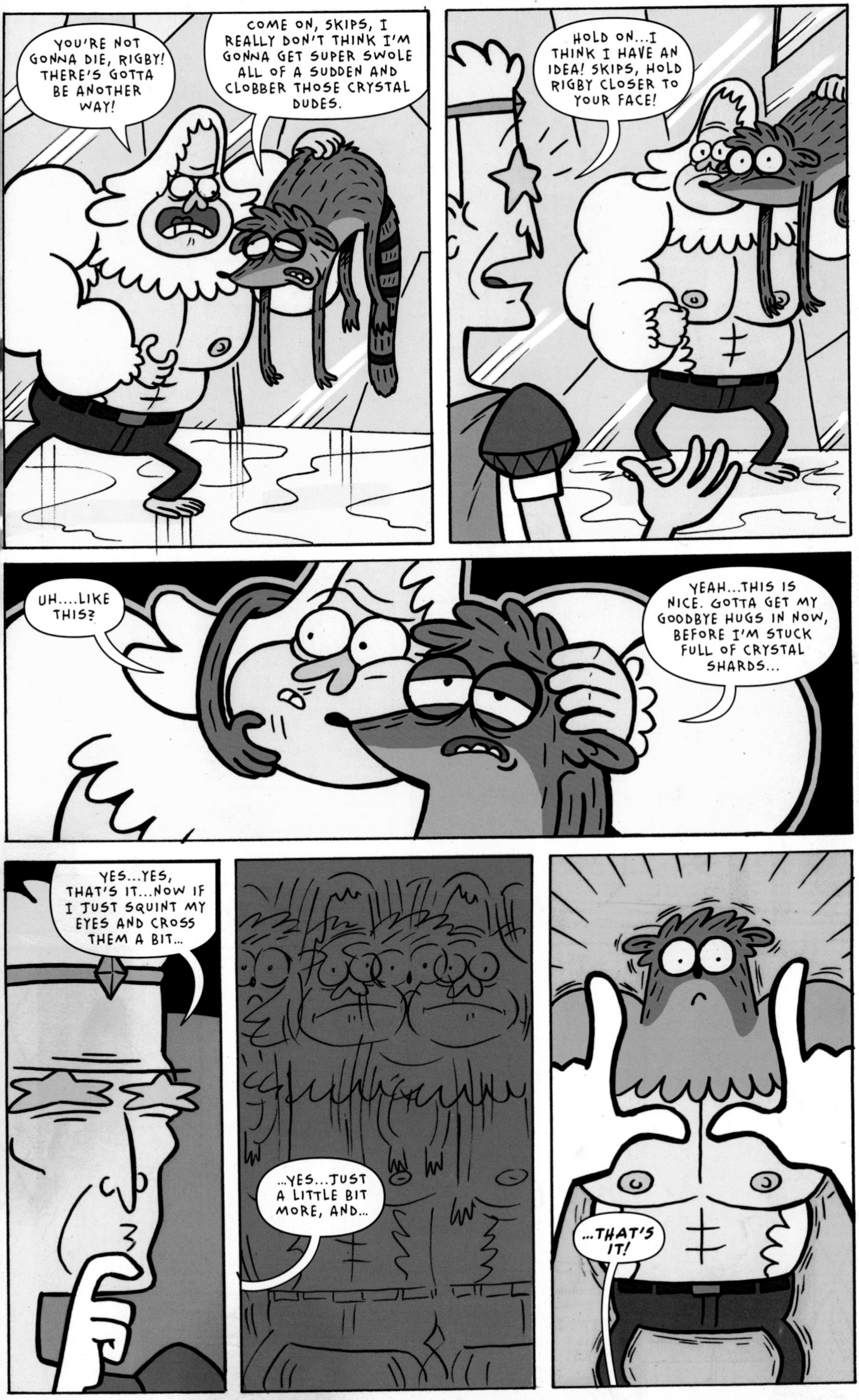
YOU'RE NOT GONNA DIE, RIGBY! THERE'S GOTTA BE ANOTHER WAY!
COME ON, SKIPS, I REALLY DON'T THINK I'M GONNA GET SUPER SWOLE ALL OF A SUDDEN AND CLOBBER THOSE CRYSTAL DUDES.
HOLD ON...I THINK I HAVE AN IDEA! SKIPS, HOLD RIGBY CLOSER TO YOUR FACE!
UH....LIKE THIS?
YEAH...THIS IS NICE. GOTTA GET MY GOODBYE HUGS IN NOW, BEFORE I'M STUCK FULL OF CRYSTAL SHARDS...
YES...YES, THAT'S IT...NOW IF I JUST SQUINT MY EYES AND CROSS THEM A BIT...
...YES...JUST A LITTLE BIT MORE, AND...
...THAT'S IT!

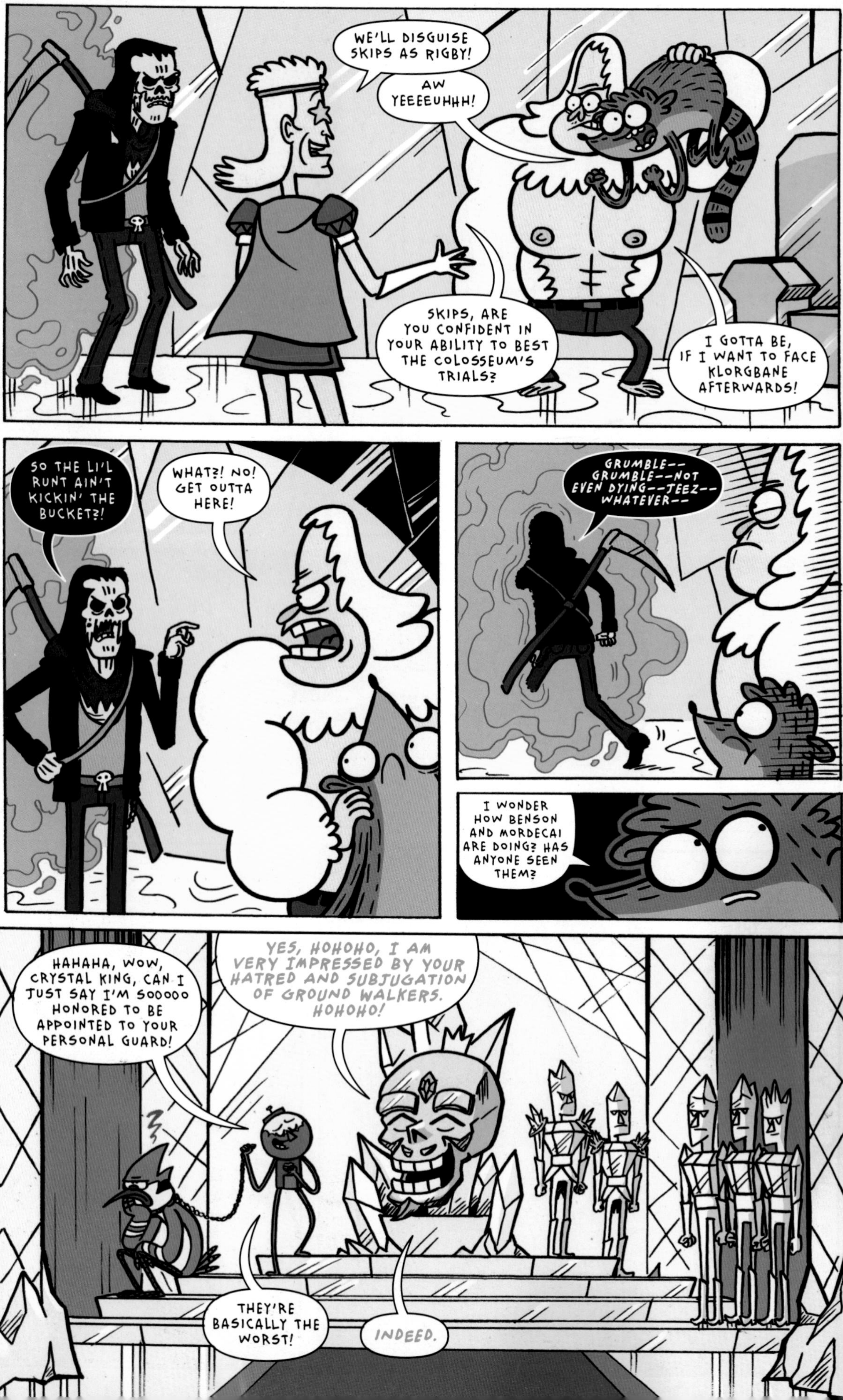
WE'LL DISGUISE SKIPS AS RIGBY!
AW YEEEEUHHH!
SKIPS, ARE YOU CONFIDENT IN YOUR ABILITY TO BEST THE COLOSSEUM'S TRIALS?
I GOTTA BE, IF I WANT TO FACE KLORGBANE AFTERWARDS!
SO THE LI'L RUNT AIN'T KICKIN' THE BUCKET?!
WHAT?! NO! GET OUTTA HERE!
GRUMBLE-- GRUMBLE--NOT EVEN DYING--JEEZ-- WHATEVER--
I WONDER HOW BENSON AND MORDECAI ARE DOING? HAS ANYONE SEEN THEM?
HAHAHA, WOW, CRYSTAL KING, CAN I JUST SAY I'M SOOOOO HONORED TO BE APPOINTED TO YOUR PERSONAL GUARD!
YES, HOHOHO, I AM VERY IMPRESSED BY YOUR HATRED AND SUBJUGATION OF GROUND WALKERS. HOHOHO!
THEY'RE BASICALLY THE WORST!
INDEED.

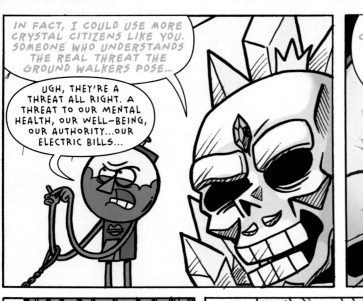

IN FACT, I COULD USE MORE CRYSTAL CITIZENS LIKE YOU. SOMEONE WHO UNDERSTANDS THE REAL THREAT THE GROUND WALKERS POSE...

UGH, THEY'RE A THREAT ALL RIGHT. A THREAT TO OUR MENTAL HEALTH, OUR WELL-BEING, OUR AUTHORITY...OUR ELECTRIC BILLS...

PRECISELY. YOU SAY OTHER CITIZENS HELPED YOU APPREHEND THIS BLUE GROUND WALKER, BUT THEY WOULD SIMPLY THROW HIM OFF THE ISLAND TO DISPOSE OF THE PROBLEM. I SEEK A MORE...PERMANENT SOLUTION.

UHHHH... YEAH...THEY'RE A REAL ISSUE...

WHOA, DUDE...

COME, THERE'S SOMETHING I MUST SHOW YOU.

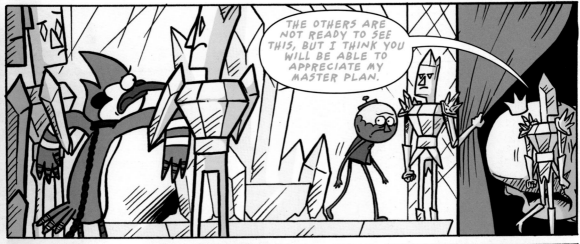

THE OTHERS ARE NOT READY TO SEE THIS, BUT I THINK YOU WILL BE ABLE TO APPRECIATE MY MASTER PLAN.

BEHOLD...

TOP SECRET
DO NOT LOOK AT THIS!! DIAMOND MASTER SUPERIORITY PLAN TO DESTROY THE ENTIRE SURFACE WORLD!
LOL
OMG
NOOO
UH, WOW... DID YOU DRAW THIS?
IT IS... DIFFICULT TO DRAW WITHOUT HANDS.
...YOU'RE PLANNING TO DESTROY THE WORLD? DON'T YOU THINK THAT'S A LITTLE OVERKILL?
WE HAVE BEEN EYEING THE SURFACE WITH SUSPICION FOR MANY YEARS, BUT NOW THAT THE GROUND WALKERS HAVE INFILTRATED MY DOMAIN, IT IS TIME TO SET THE PLAN INTO MOTION.
AND WHO'S "DIAMOND MASTER"?
I...AM DIAMOND MASTER.
"WE ARRIVED IN THIS PLACE MANY YEARS AGO, FROM THE FAR REACHES OF SPACE. THE PEOPLE ASSUMED WE WERE CRYSTAL, LIKE THEM..."
"BUT...AREN'T CRYSTALS AND DIAMONDS, LIKE...THE SAME THING?"
"NO, YOU FOOL! THEY'RE TOTALLY DIFFERENT, DIAMONDS ARE MUCH HARDER!!"
IF THEY KNEW MY TRUE NATURE, THE PEOPLE WOULD DEPOSE ME...BUT THIS IS A FRAIL, DELICATE PLACE...
CRASH
OH MY GOSH, DUDE, I'M SO SORRY! I JUST BUMPED YOU!
NAW, IT'S COOL, MAN. THIS HAPPENS ALL THE TIME.
SEE WHAT I MEAN?

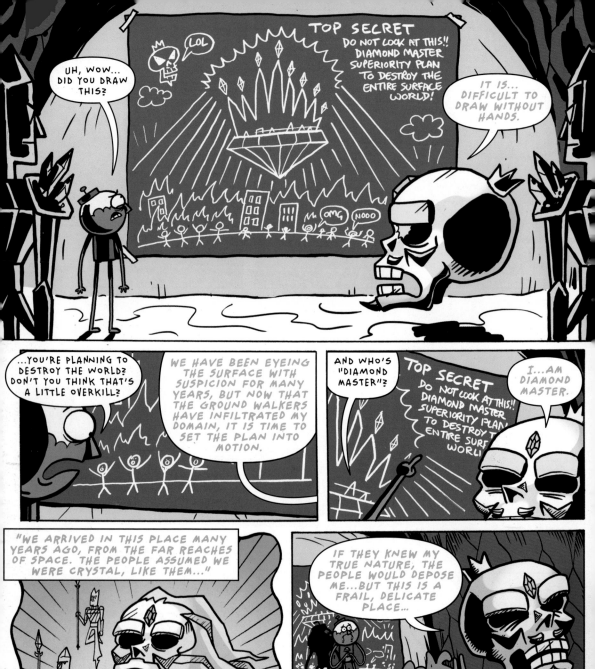

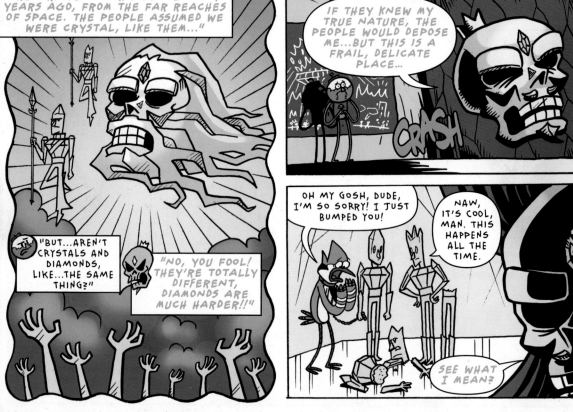

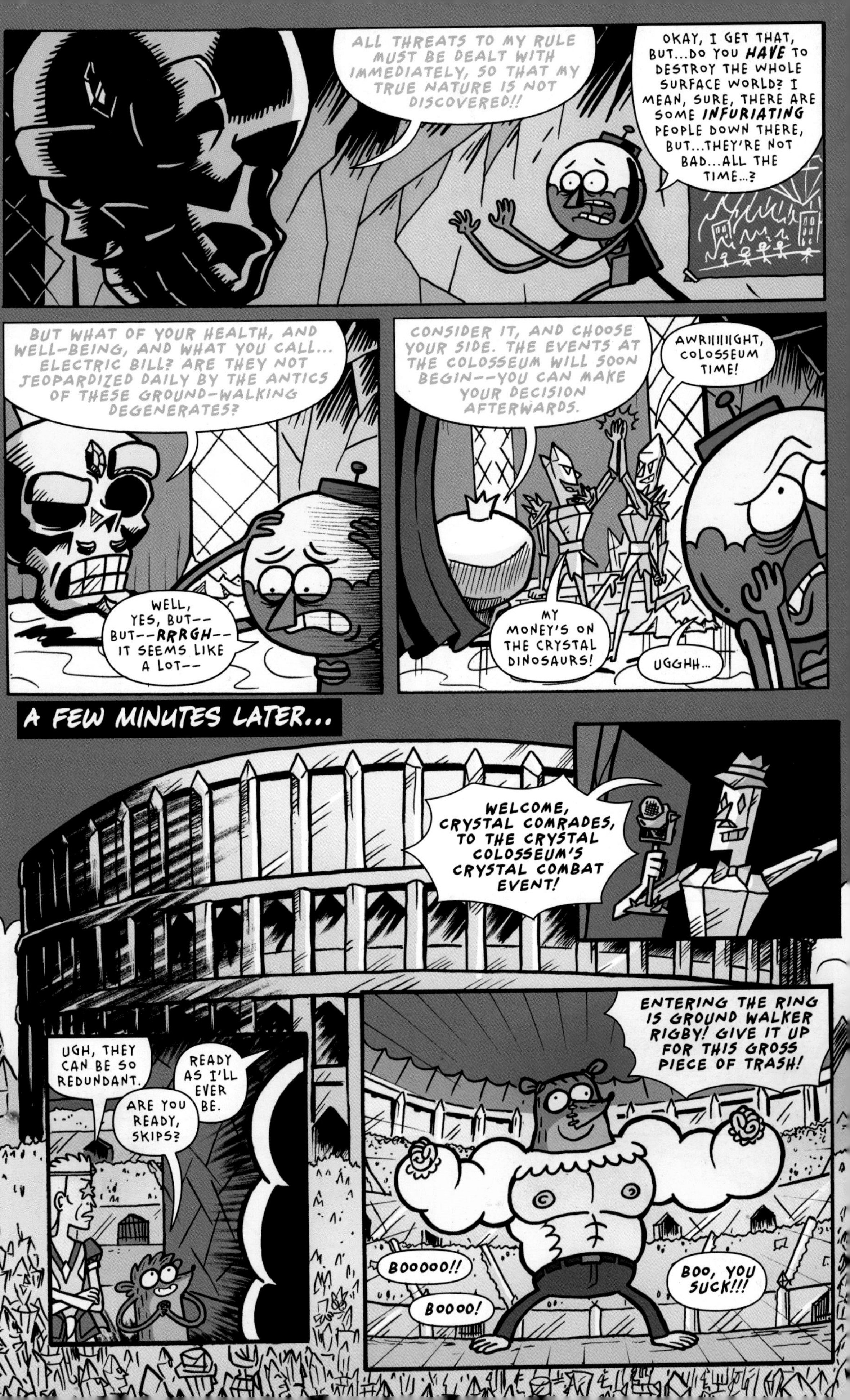

ALL THREATS TO MY RULE MUST BE DEALT WITH IMMEDIATELY, SO THAT MY TRUE NATURE IS NOT DISCOVERED!!
OKAY, I GET THAT, BUT...DO YOU HAVE TO DESTROY THE WHOLE SURFACE WORLD? I MEAN, SURE, THERE ARE SOME INFURIATING PEOPLE DOWN THERE, BUT...THEY'RE NOT BAD...ALL THE TIME...?
BUT WHAT OF YOUR HEALTH, AND WELL-BEING, AND WHAT YOU CALL... ELECTRIC BILL? ARE THEY NOT JEOPARDIZED DAILY BY THE ANTICS OF THESE GROUND-WALKING DEGENERATES?
WELL, YES, BUT-- BUT--RRRGH-- IT SEEMS LIKE A LOT--
CONSIDER IT, AND CHOOSE YOUR SIDE. THE EVENTS AT THE COLOSSEUM WILL SOON BEGIN--YOU CAN MAKE YOUR DECISION AFTERWARDS.
AWRIIIIIGHT, COLOSSEUM TIME!
MY MONEY'S ON THE CRYSTAL DINOSAURS!
UGGHH...
A FEW MINUTES LATER...
WELCOME, CRYSTAL COMRADES, TO THE CRYSTAL COLOSSEUM'S CRYSTAL COMBAT EVENT!
UGH, THEY CAN BE SO REDUNDANT.
ARE YOU READY, SKIPS?
READY AS I'LL EVER BE.
ENTERING THE RING IS GROUND WALKER RIGBY! GIVE IT UP FOR THIS GROSS PIECE OF TRASH!
BOOOOO!!
BOOOO!
BOO, YOU SUCK!!!

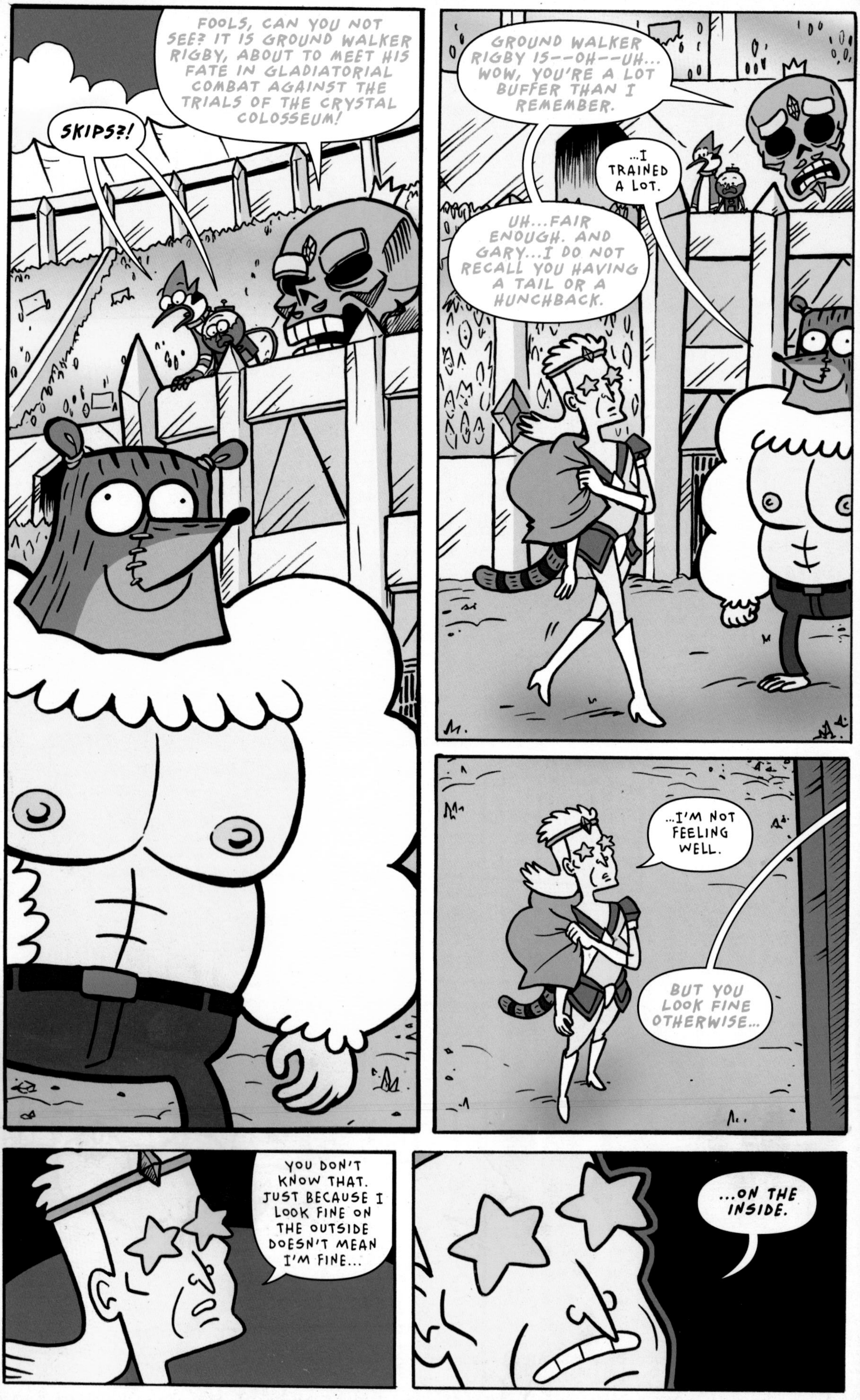
FOOLS, CAN YOU NOT SEE? IT IS GROUND WALKER RIGBY, ABOUT TO MEET HIS FATE IN GLADIATORIAL COMBAT AGAINST THE TRIALS OF THE CRYSTAL COLOSSEUM!
SKIPS?!
GROUND WALKER RIGBY IS--OH--UH... WOW, YOU'RE A LOT BUFFER THAN I REMEMBER.
...I TRAINED A LOT.
UH...FAIR ENOUGH. AND GARY...I DO NOT RECALL YOU HAVING A TAIL OR A HUNCHBACK.
...I'M NOT FEELING WELL.
BUT YOU LOOK FINE OTHERWISE...
YOU DON'T KNOW THAT. JUST BECAUSE I LOOK FINE ON THE OUTSIDE DOESN'T MEAN I'M FINE...
...ON THE INSIDE.

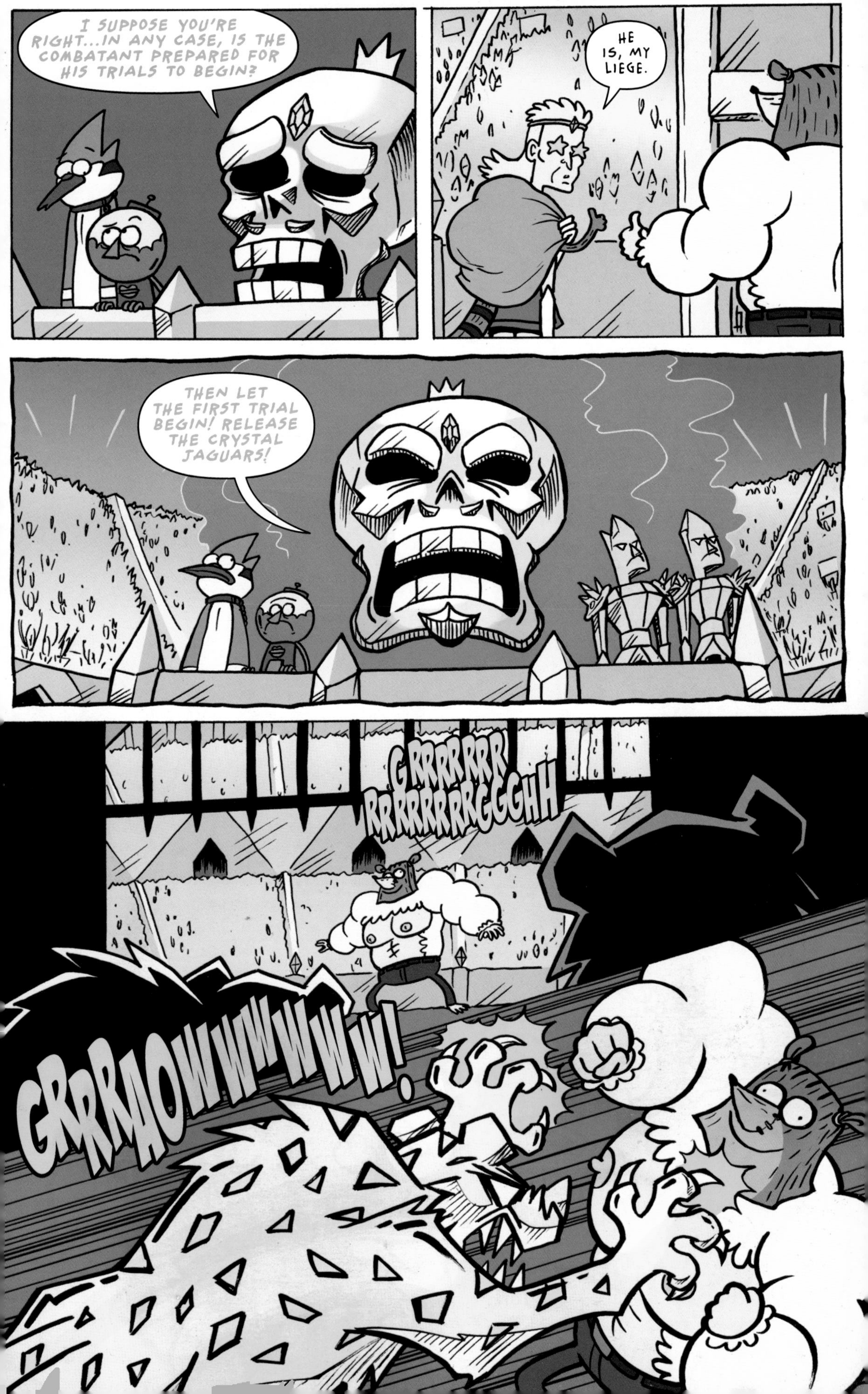
I SUPPOSE YOU'RE RIGHT...IN ANY CASE, IS THE COMBATANT PREPARED FOR HIS TRIALS TO BEGIN?
HE IS, MY LIEGE.
THEN LET THE FIRST TRIAL BEGIN! RELEASE THE CRYSTAL JAGUARS!
GRRRRRRR RRRRRRRGGGHH
GRRAOWWWWWW!

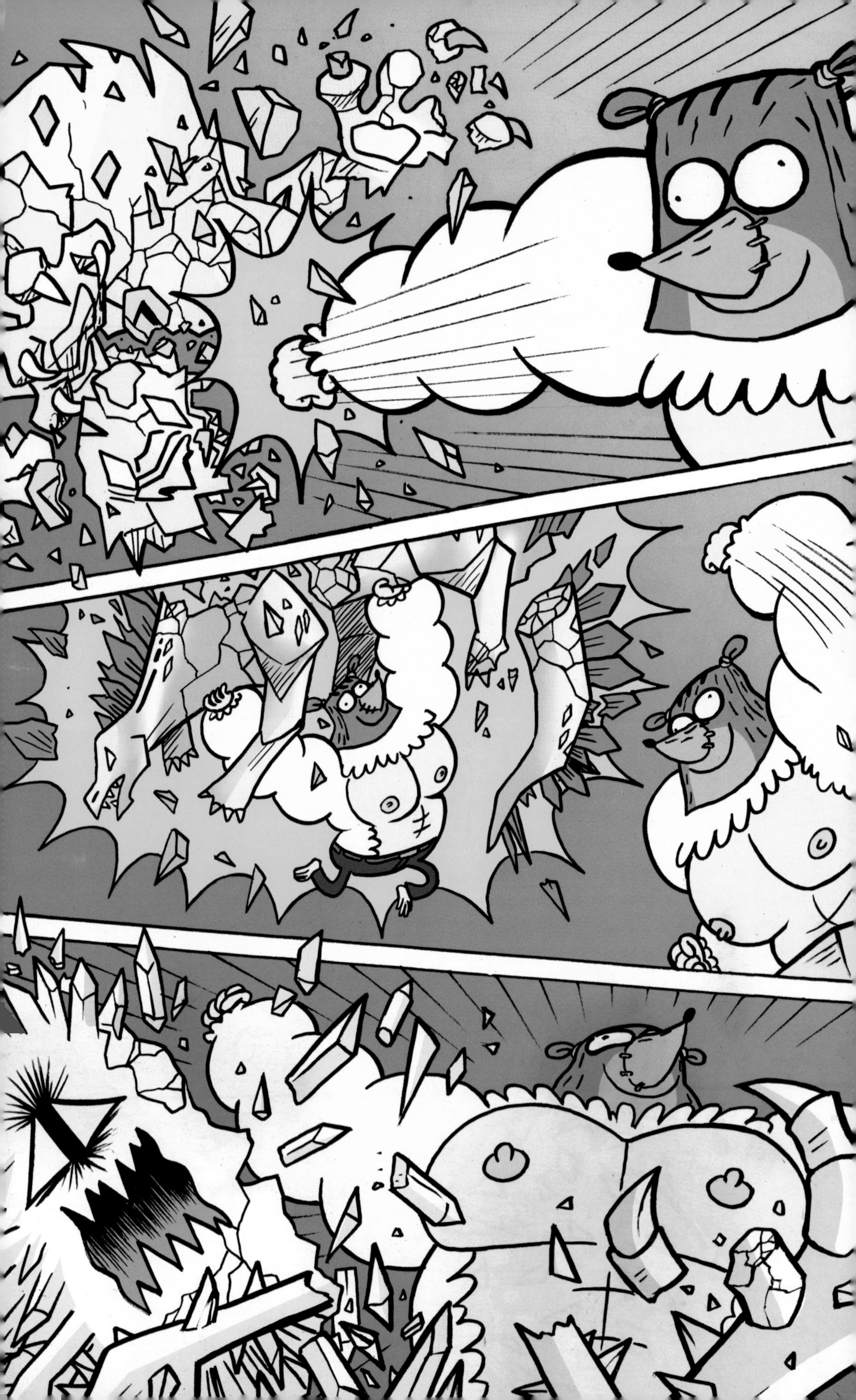

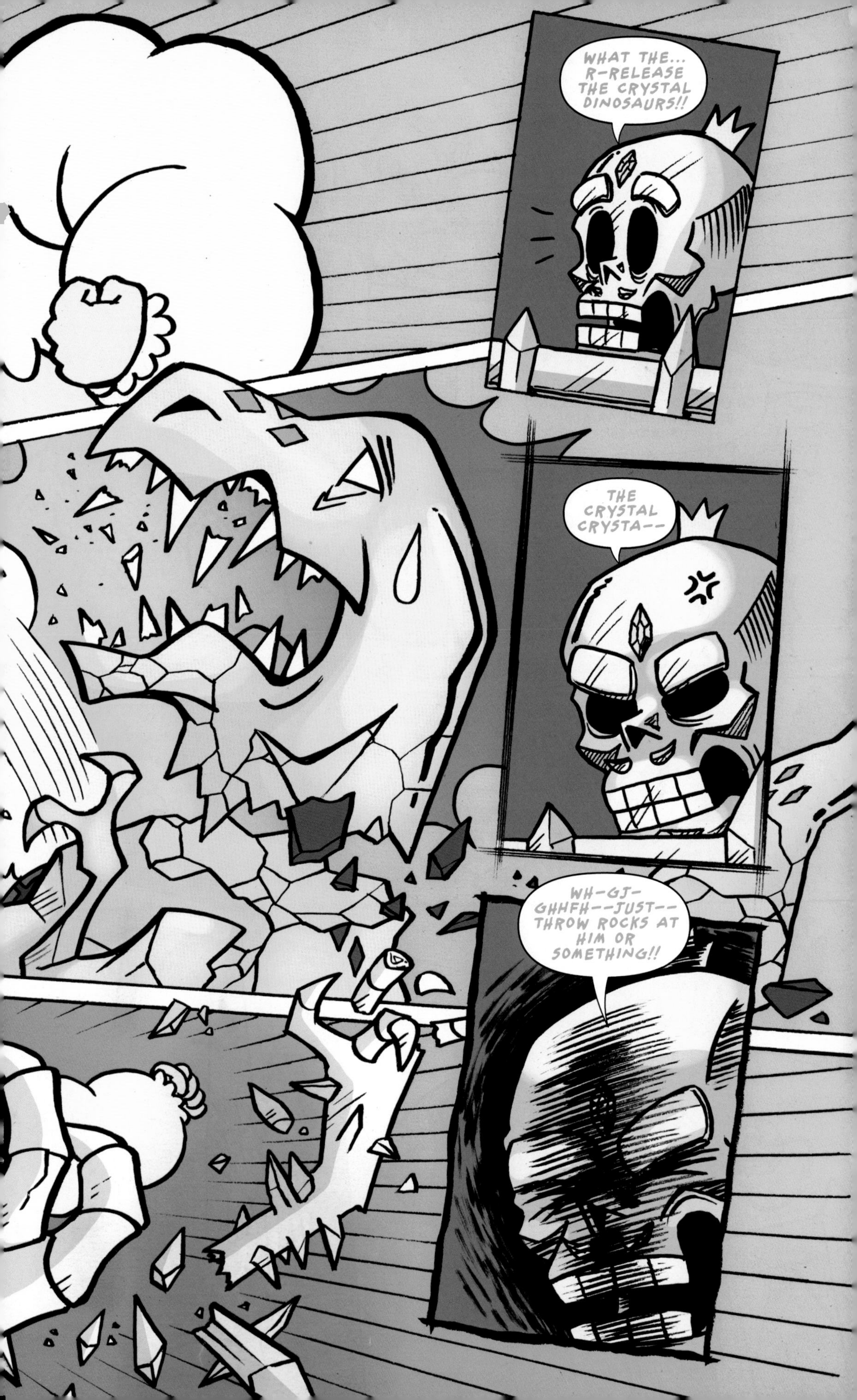
WHAT THE... R-RELEASE THE CRYSTAL DINOSAURS!!
THE CRYSTAL CRYSTA--
WH-GJ-GHHFH--JUST--THROW ROCKS AT HIM OR SOMETHING!!

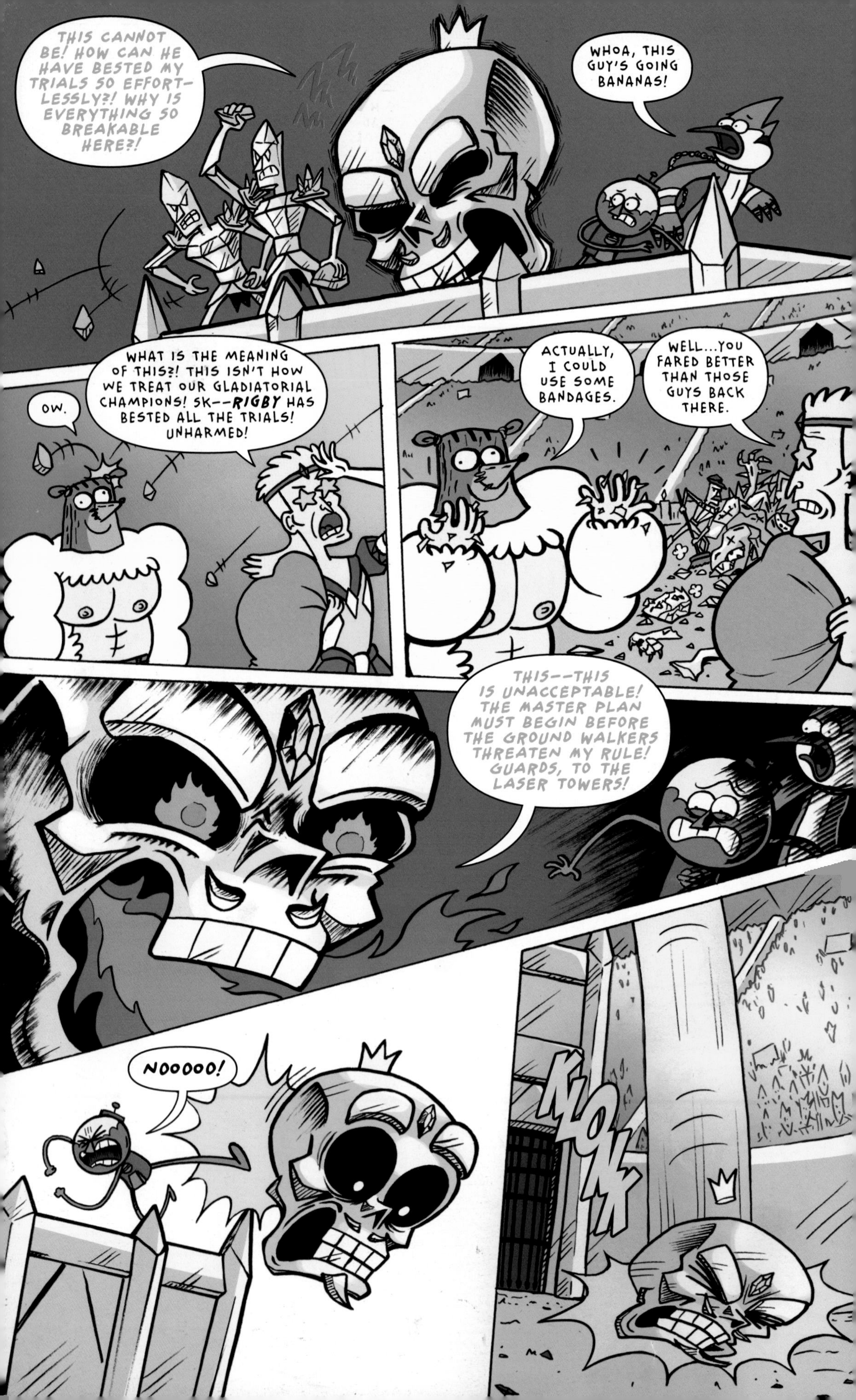
THIS CANNOT BE! HOW CAN HE HAVE BESTED MY TRIALS SO EFFORT-LESSLY?! WHY IS EVERYTHING SO BREAKABLE HERE?!
WHOA, THIS GUY'S GOING BANANAS!
OW.
WHAT IS THE MEANING OF THIS?! THIS ISN'T HOW WE TREAT OUR GLADIATORIAL CHAMPIONS! SK--RIGBY HAS BESTED ALL THE TRIALS! UNHARMED!
ACTUALLY, I COULD USE SOME BANDAGES.
WELL...YOU FARED BETTER THAN THOSE GUYS BACK THERE.
THIS--THIS IS UNACCEPTABLE! THE MASTER PLAN MUST BEGIN BEFORE THE GROUND WALKERS THREATEN MY RULE! GUARDS, TO THE LASER TOWERS!
NOOOOO!
KLONK

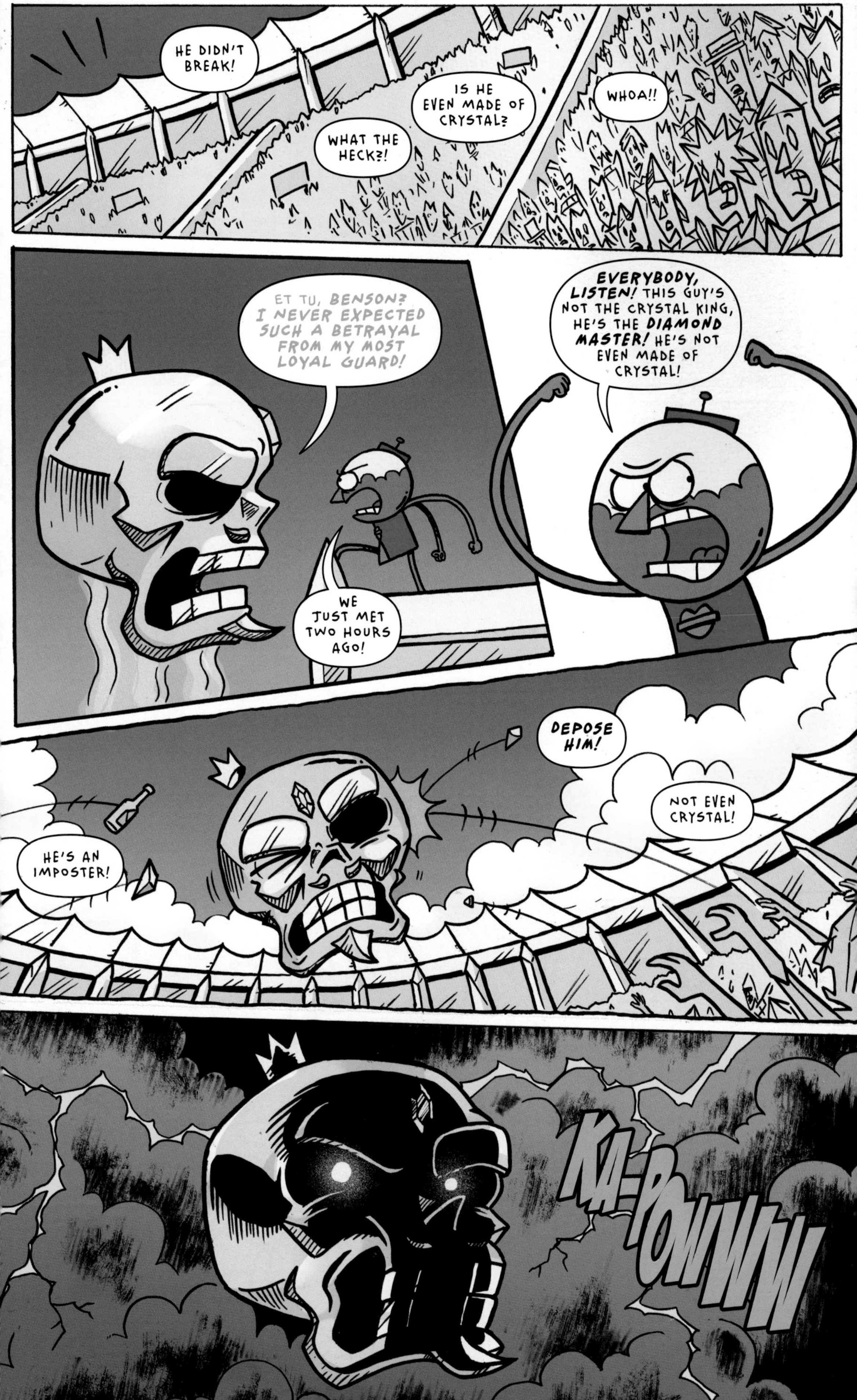
HE DIDN'T BREAK!
WHAT THE HECK?!
IS HE EVEN MADE OF CRYSTAL?
WHOA!!
ET TU, BENSON? I NEVER EXPECTED SUCH A BETRAYAL FROM MY MOST LOYAL GUARD!
WE JUST MET TWO HOURS AGO!
EVERYBODY, LISTEN! THIS GUY'S NOT THE CRYSTAL KING, HE'S THE DIAMOND MASTER! HE'S NOT EVEN MADE OF CRYSTAL!
HE'S AN IMPOSTER!
DEPOSE HIM!
NOT EVEN CRYSTAL!
KA-POWWW

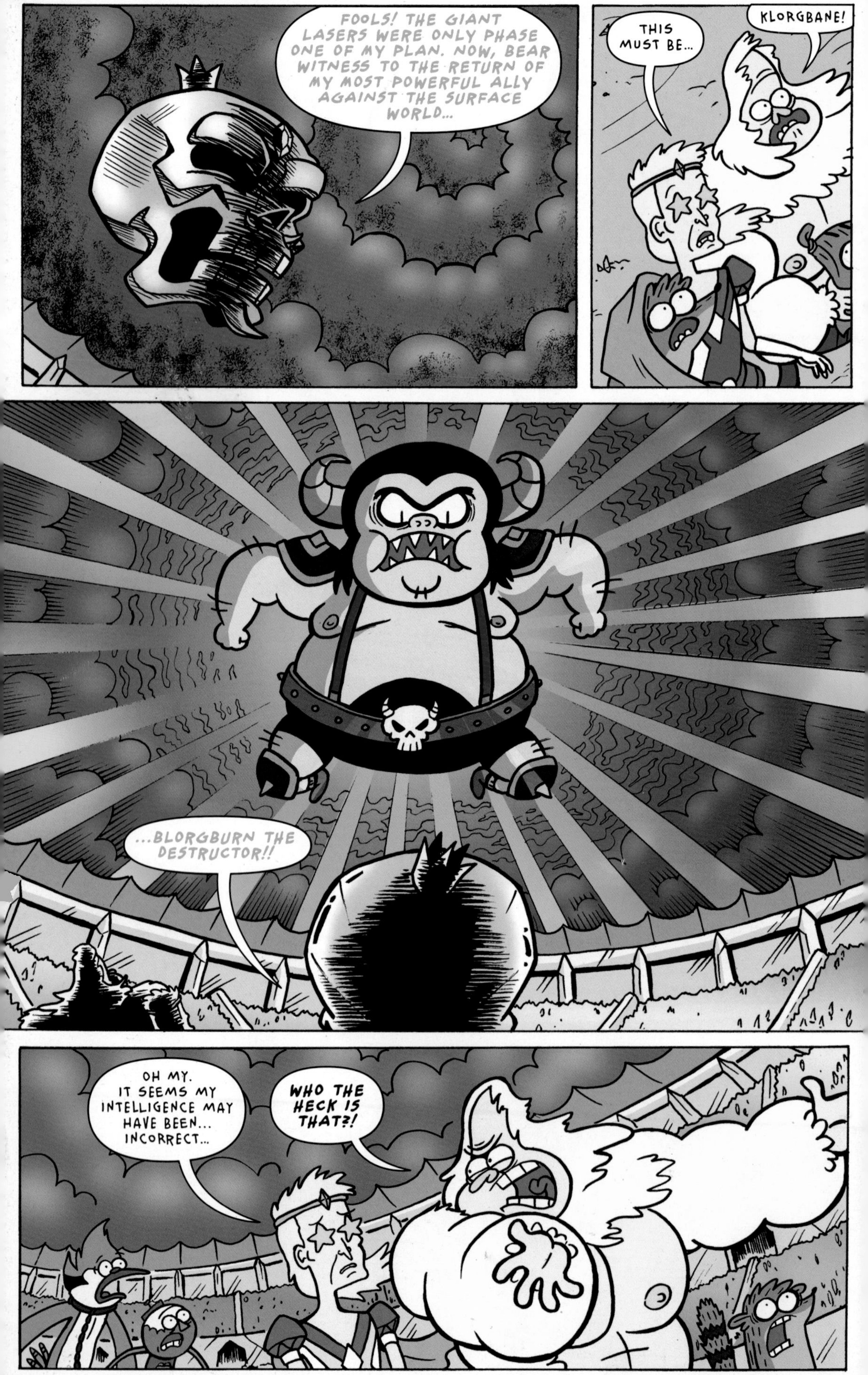
FOOLS! THE GIANT LASERS WERE ONLY PHASE ONE OF MY PLAN. NOW, BEAR WITNESS TO THE RETURN OF MY MOST POWERFUL ALLY AGAINST THE SURFACE WORLD...
THIS MUST BE...
KLORGBANE!
...BLORGBURN THE DESTRUCTOR!!
OH MY. IT SEEMS MY INTELLIGENCE MAY HAVE BEEN... INCORRECT...
WHO THE HECK IS THAT?!

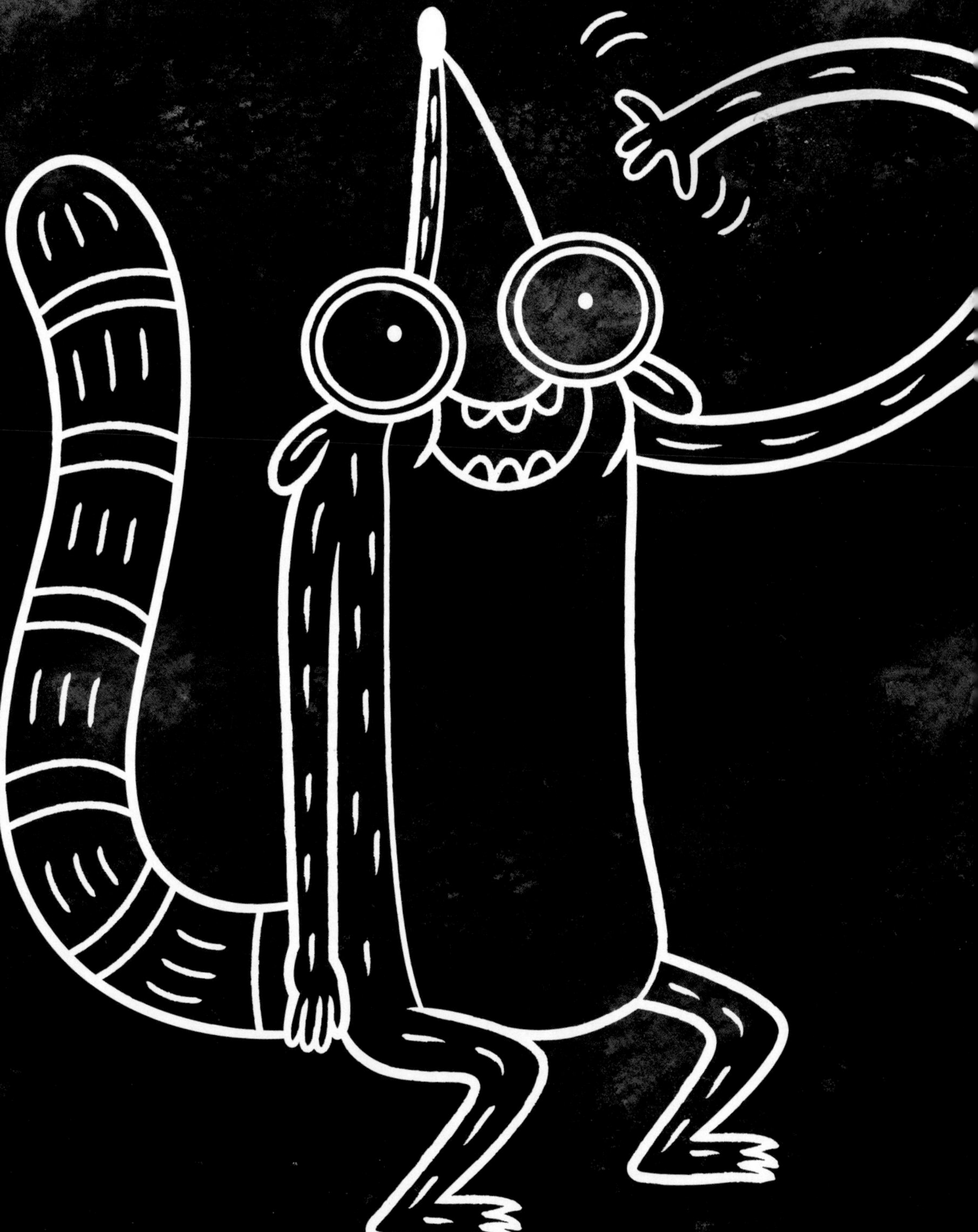

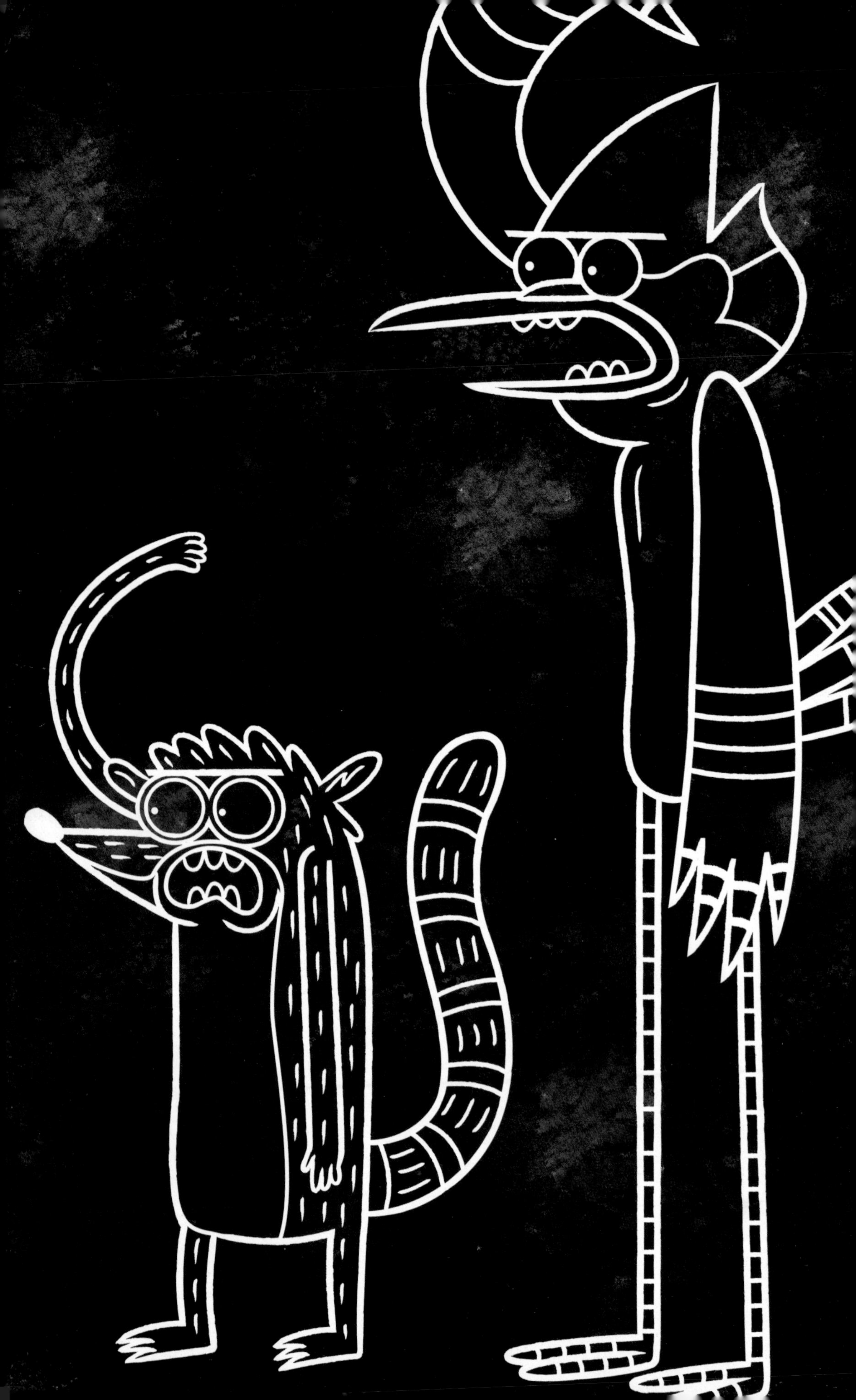

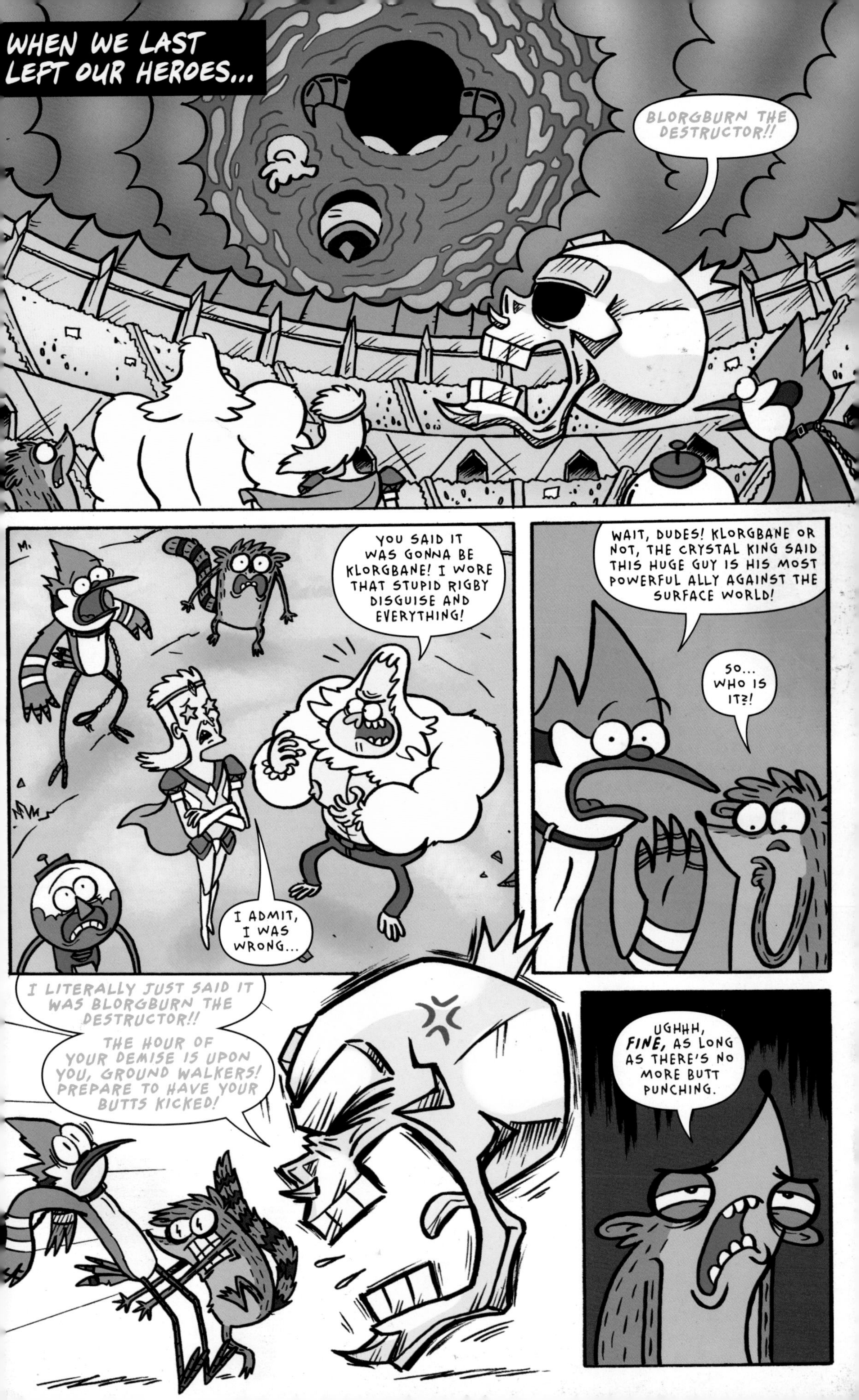
WHEN WE LAST LEFT OUR HEROES...
BLORGBURN THE DESTRUCTOR!!
YOU SAID IT WAS GONNA BE KLORGBANE! I WORE THAT STUPID RIGBY DISGUISE AND EVERYTHING!
I ADMIT, I WAS WRONG...
WAIT, DUDES! KLORGBANE OR NOT, THE CRYSTAL KING SAID THIS HUGE GUY IS HIS MOST POWERFUL ALLY AGAINST THE SURFACE WORLD!
SO... WHO IS IT?!
I LITERALLY JUST SAID IT WAS BLORGBURN THE DESTRUCTOR!!
THE HOUR OF YOUR DEMISE IS UPON YOU, GROUND WALKERS! PREPARE TO HAVE YOUR BUTTS KICKED!
UGHHH, FINE, AS LONG AS THERE'S NO MORE BUTT PUNCHING.

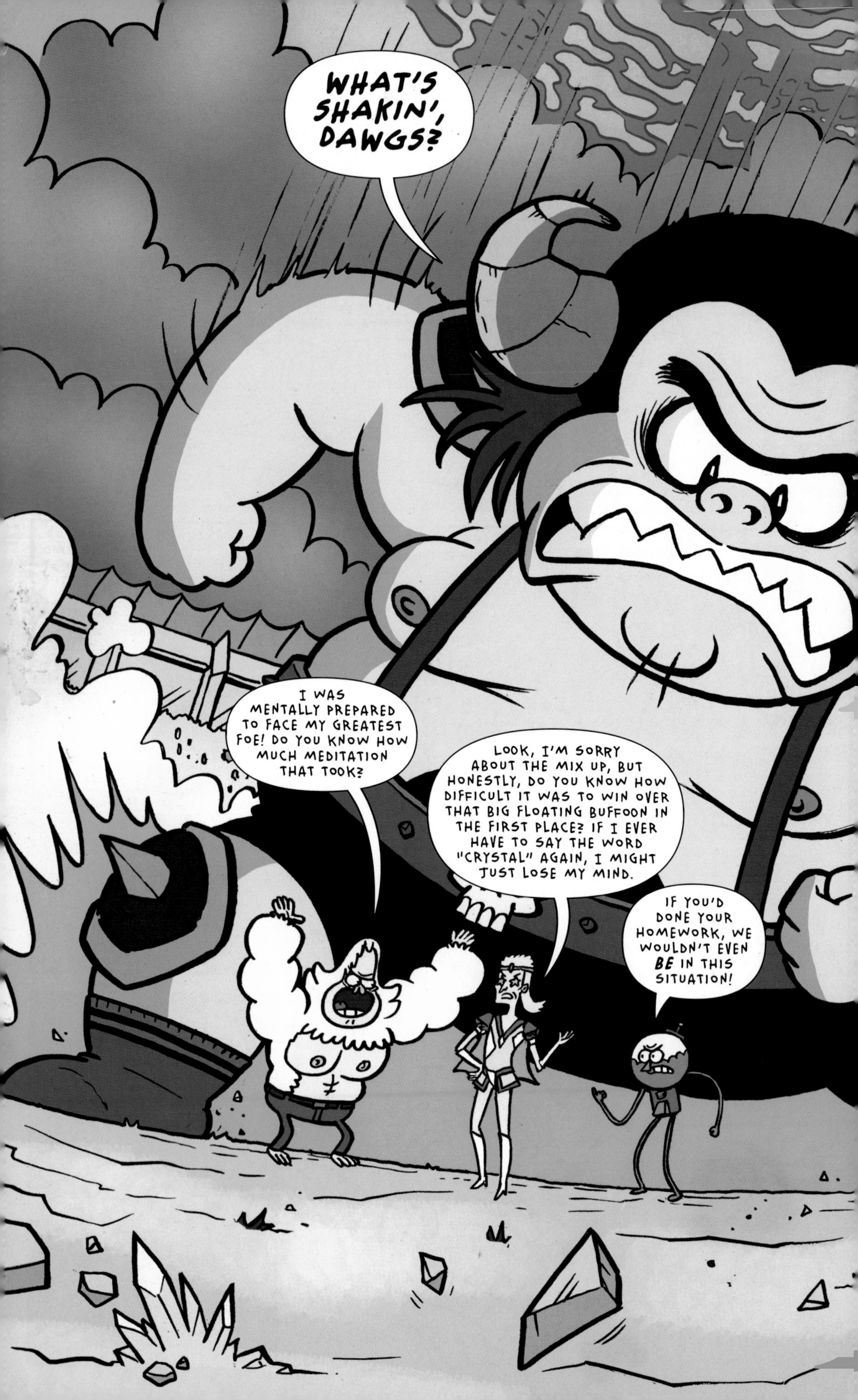
WHAT'S SHAKIN', DAWGS?
I WAS MENTALLY PREPARED TO FACE MY GREATEST FOE! DO YOU KNOW HOW MUCH MEDITATION THAT TOOK?
LOOK, I'M SORRY ABOUT THE MIX UP, BUT HONESTLY, DO YOU KNOW HOW DIFFICULT IT WAS TO WIN OVER THAT BIG FLOATING BUFFOON IN THE FIRST PLACE? IF I EVER HAVE TO SAY THE WORD "CRYSTAL" AGAIN, I MIGHT JUST LOSE MY MIND.
IF YOU'D DONE YOUR HOMEWORK, WE WOULDN'T EVEN BE IN THIS SITUATION!

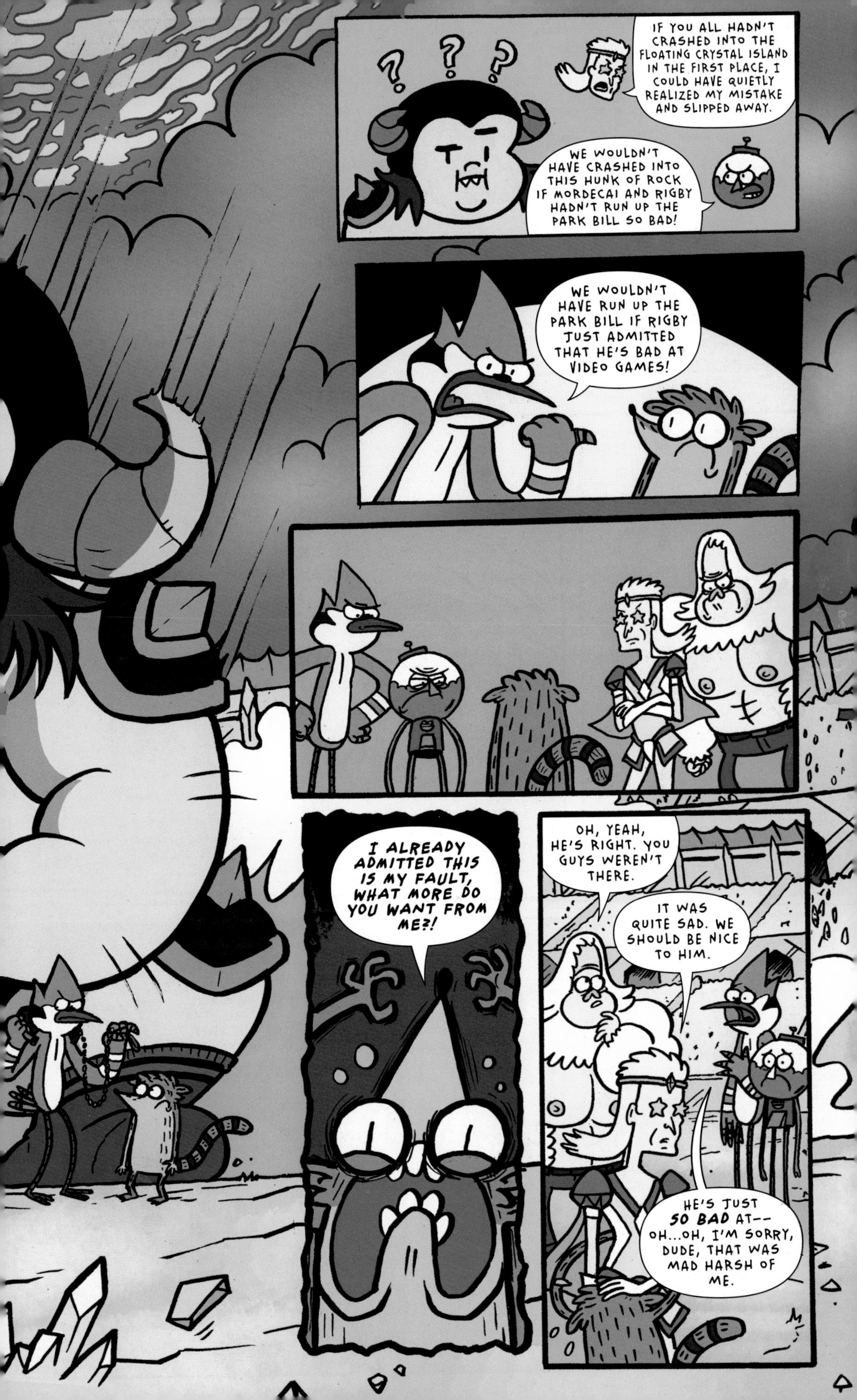
IF YOU ALL HADN'T CRASHED INTO THE FLOATING CRYSTAL ISLAND IN THE FIRST PLACE, I COULD HAVE QUIETLY REALIZED MY MISTAKE AND SLIPPED AWAY.
WE WOULDN'T HAVE CRASHED INTO THIS HUNK OF ROCK IF MORDECAI AND RIGBY HADN'T RUN UP THE PARK BILL SO BAD!
WE WOULDN'T HAVE RUN UP THE PARK BILL IF RIGBY JUST ADMITTED THAT HE'S BAD AT VIDEO GAMES!
I ALREADY ADMITTED THIS IS MY FAULT, WHAT MORE DO YOU WANT FROM ME?!
OH, YEAH, HE'S RIGHT. YOU GUYS WEREN'T THERE.
IT WAS QUITE SAD. WE SHOULD BE NICE TO HIM.
HE'S JUST SO BAD AT-- OH...OH, I'M SORRY, DUDE, THAT WAS MAD HARSH OF ME.

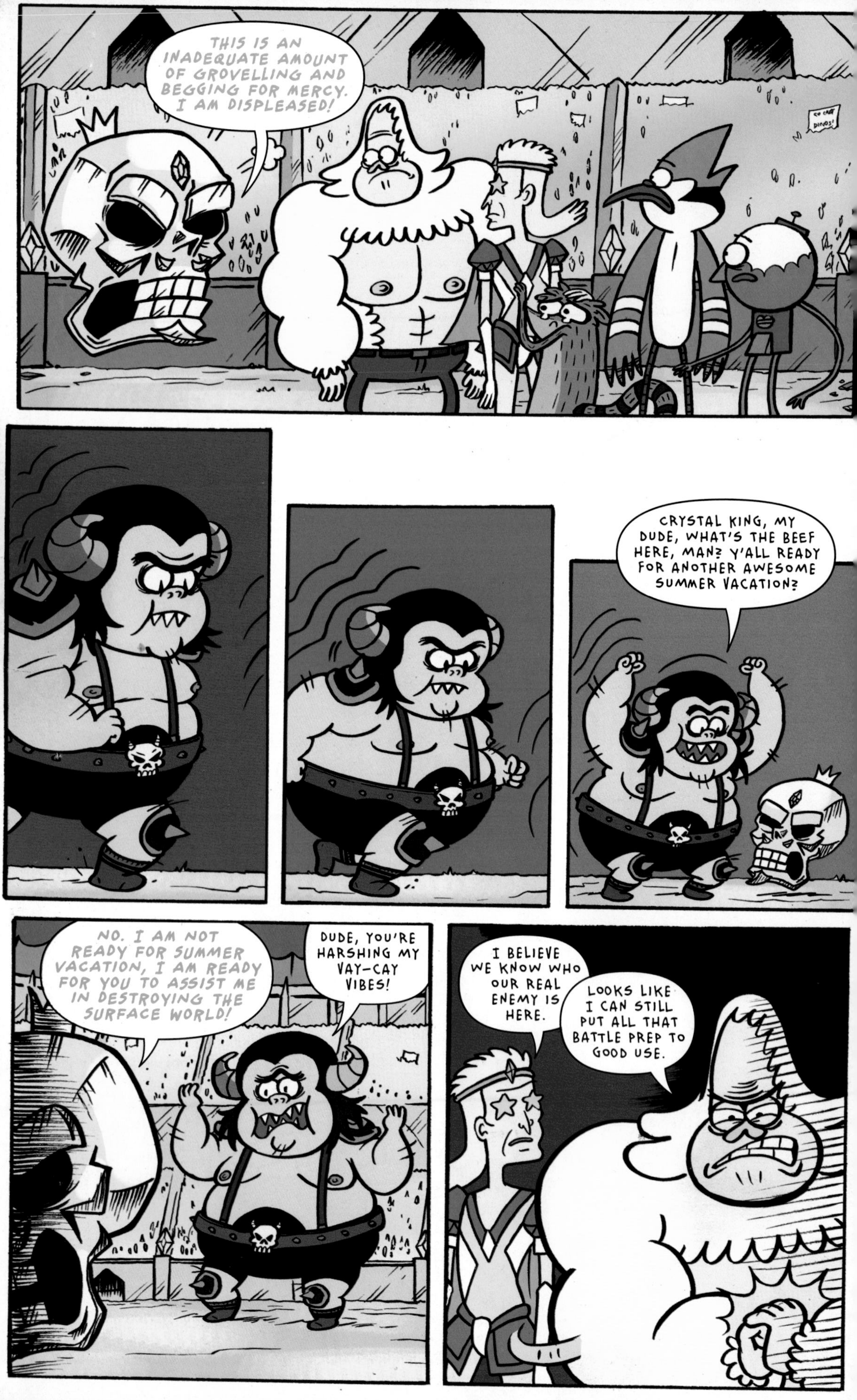
THIS IS AN INADEQUATE AMOUNT OF GROVELLING AND BEGGING FOR MERCY. I AM DISPLEASED!
CRYSTAL KING, MY DUDE, WHAT'S THE BEEF HERE, MAN? Y'ALL READY FOR ANOTHER AWESOME SUMMER VACATION?
NO. I AM NOT READY FOR SUMMER VACATION, I AM READY FOR YOU TO ASSIST ME IN DESTROYING THE SURFACE WORLD!
DUDE, YOU'RE HARSHING MY VAY-CAY VIBES!
I BELIEVE WE KNOW WHO OUR REAL ENEMY IS HERE.
LOOKS LIKE I CAN STILL PUT ALL THAT BATTLE PREP TO GOOD USE.

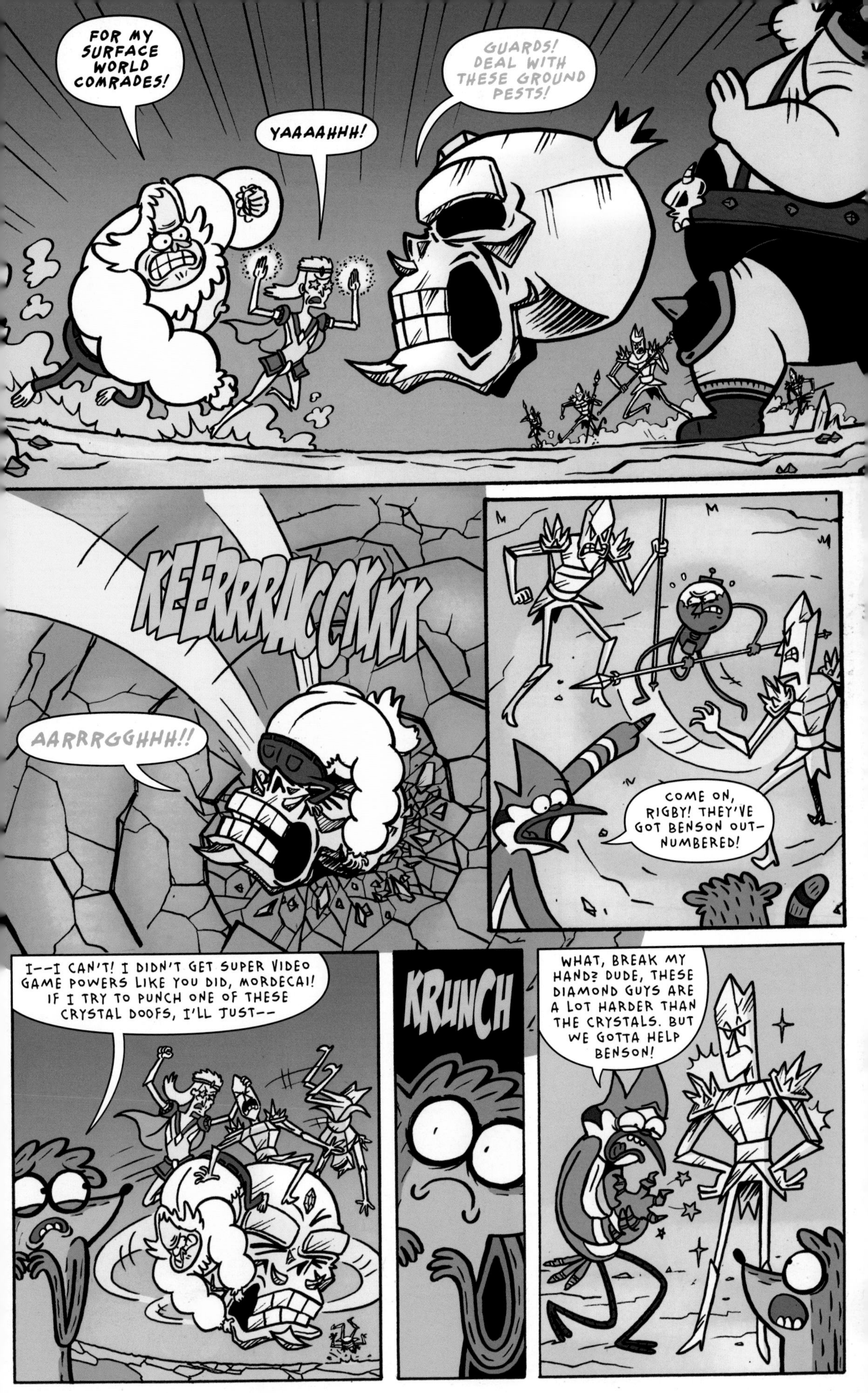
FOR MY SURFACE WORLD COMRADES!
YAAAAHHH!
GUARDS! DEAL WITH THESE GROUND PESTS!
KEERRRACCKKK
AARRRGGHHH!!
COME ON, RIGBY! THEY'VE GOT BENSON OUT-NUMBERED!
I--I CAN'T! I DIDN'T GET SUPER VIDEO GAME POWERS LIKE YOU DID, MORDECAI! IF I TRY TO PUNCH ONE OF THESE CRYSTAL DOOFS, I'LL JUST--
KRUNCH
WHAT, BREAK MY HAND? DUDE, THESE DIAMOND GUYS ARE A LOT HARDER THAN THE CRYSTALS. BUT WE GOTTA HELP BENSON!

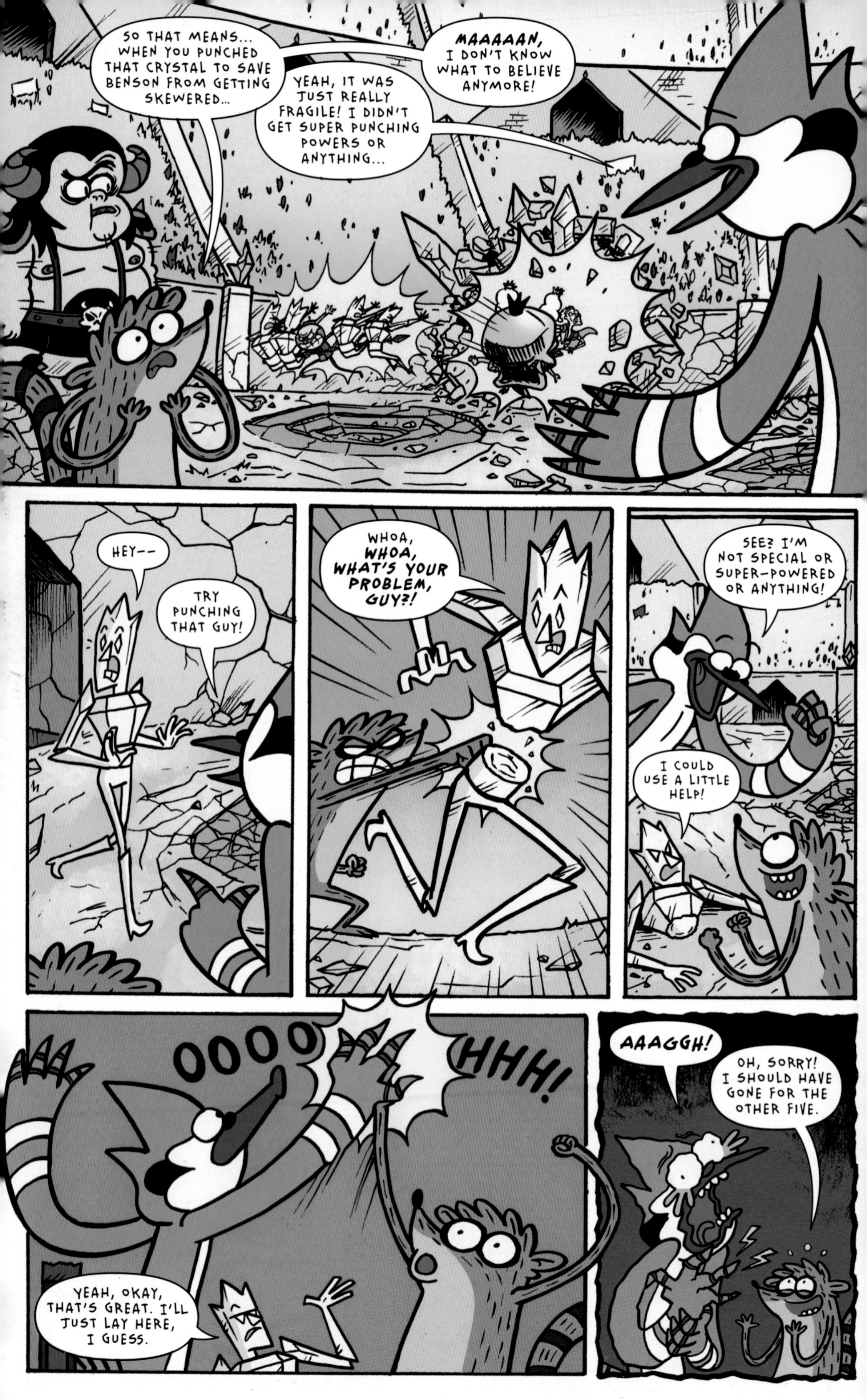
SO THAT MEANS... WHEN YOU PUNCHED THAT CRYSTAL TO SAVE BENSON FROM GETTING SKEWERED...
YEAH, IT WAS JUST REALLY FRAGILE! I DIDN'T GET SUPER PUNCHING POWERS OR ANYTHING...
MAAAAAN, I DON'T KNOW WHAT TO BELIEVE ANYMORE!
HEY--
TRY PUNCHING THAT GUY!
WHOA, WHOA, WHAT'S YOUR PROBLEM, GUY?!
SEE? I'M NOT SPECIAL OR SUPER-POWERED OR ANYTHING!
I COULD USE A LITTLE HELP!
OOOOHHH!
YEAH, OKAY, THAT'S GREAT. I'LL JUST LAY HERE, I GUESS.
AAAGGH!
OH, SORRY! I SHOULD HAVE GONE FOR THE OTHER FIVE.

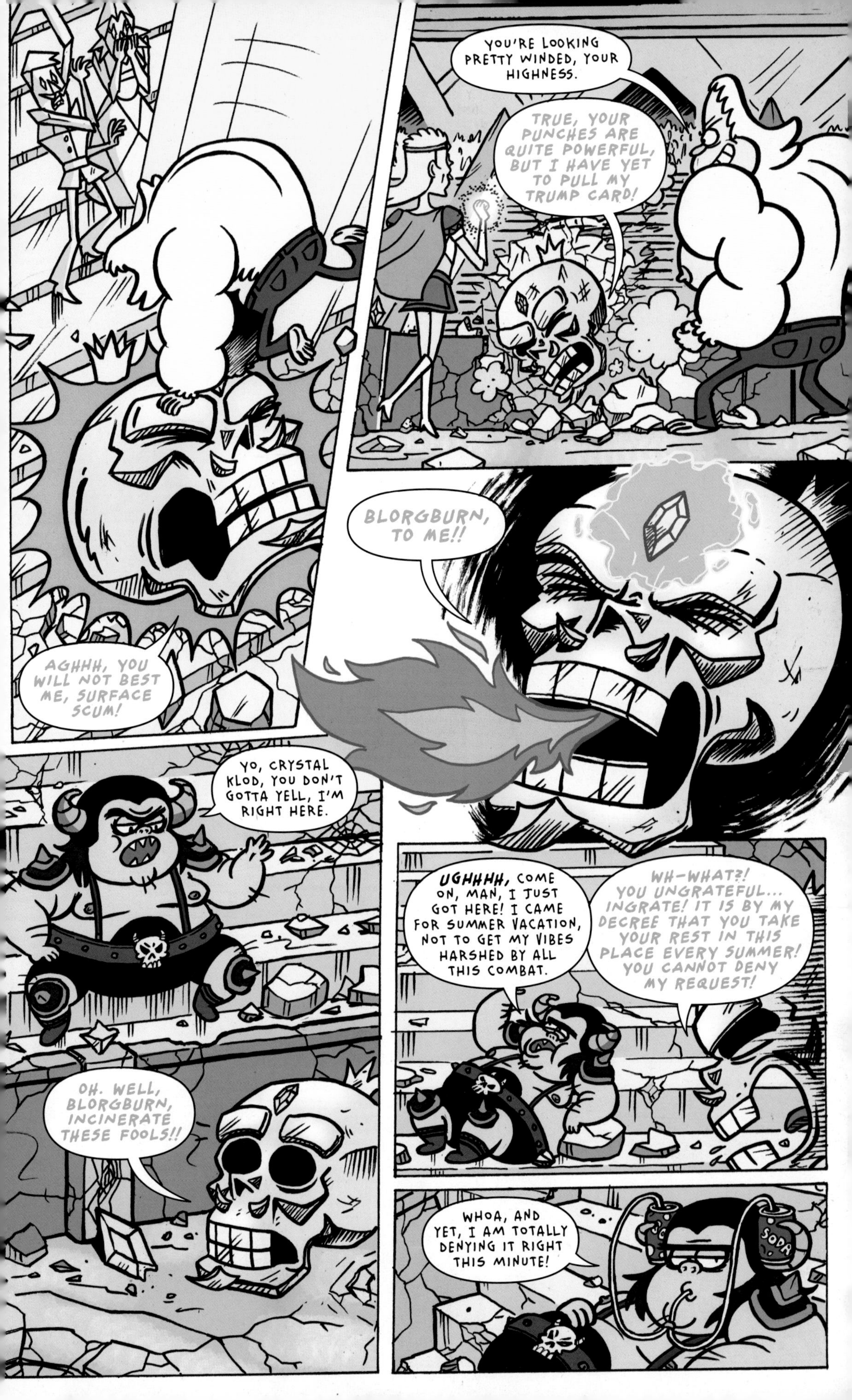

YOU'RE LOOKING PRETTY WINDED, YOUR HIGHNESS.
TRUE, YOUR PUNCHES ARE QUITE POWERFUL, BUT I HAVE YET TO PULL MY TRUMP CARD!
AGHHH, YOU WILL NOT BEST ME, SURFACE SCUM!
BLORGBURN, TO ME!!
YO, CRYSTAL KLOD, YOU DON'T GOTTA YELL, I'M RIGHT HERE.
OH. WELL, BLORGBURN, INCINERATE THESE FOOLS!!
UGHHHH, COME ON, MAN, I JUST GOT HERE! I CAME FOR SUMMER VACATION, NOT TO GET MY VIBES HARSHED BY ALL THIS COMBAT.
WH-WHAT?! YOU UNGRATEFUL... INGRATE! IT IS BY MY DECREE THAT YOU TAKE YOUR REST IN THIS PLACE EVERY SUMMER! YOU CANNOT DENY MY REQUEST!
WHOA, AND YET, I AM TOTALLY DENYING IT RIGHT THIS MINUTE!
SODA

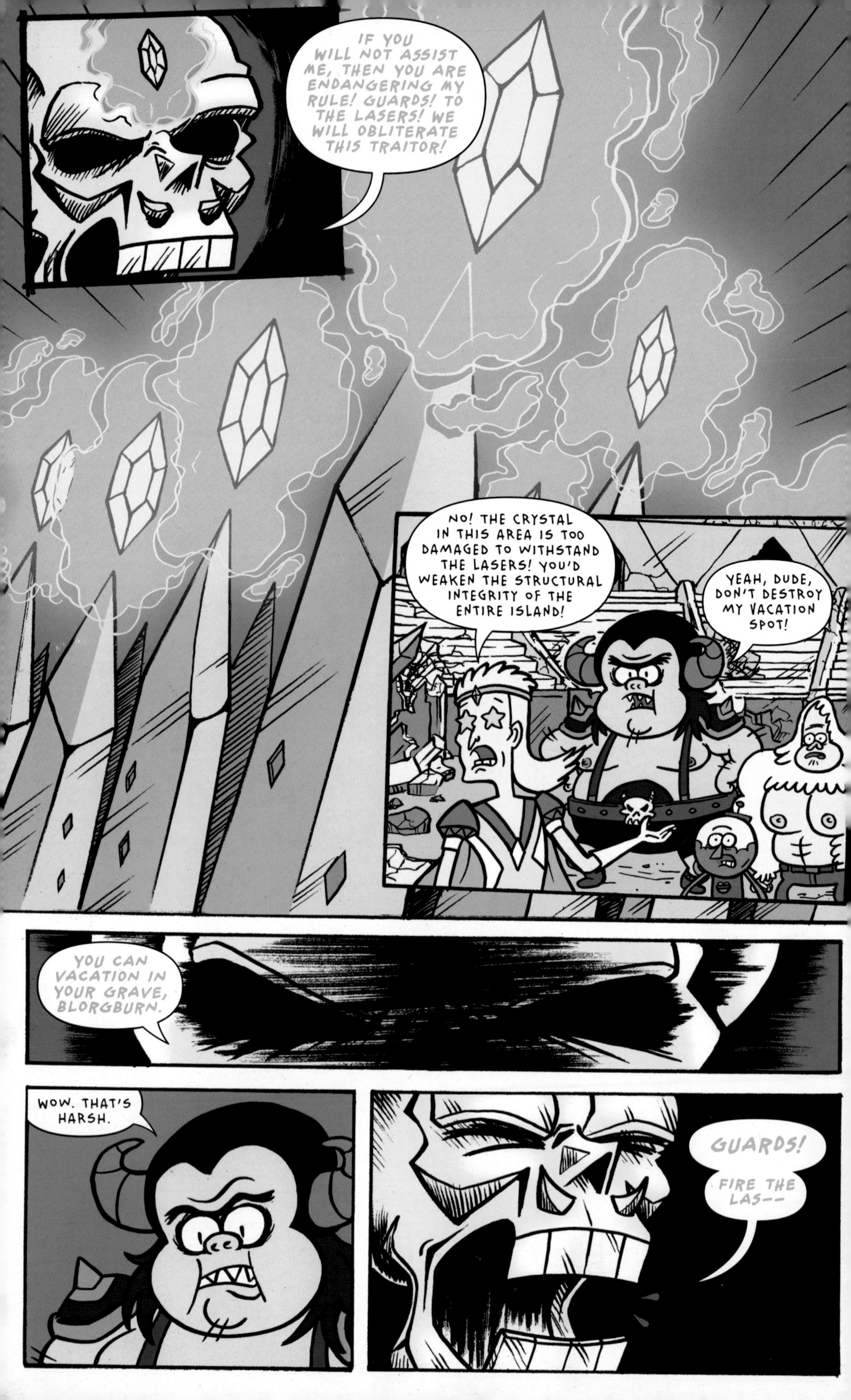
IF YOU WILL NOT ASSIST ME, THEN YOU ARE ENDANGERING MY RULE! GUARDS! TO THE LASERS! WE WILL OBLITERATE THIS TRAITOR!
NO! THE CRYSTAL IN THIS AREA IS TOO DAMAGED TO WITHSTAND THE LASERS! YOU'D WEAKEN THE STRUCTURAL INTEGRITY OF THE ENTIRE ISLAND!
YEAH, DUDE, DON'T DESTROY MY VACATION SPOT!
YOU CAN VACATION IN YOUR GRAVE, BLORGBURN.
WOW. THAT'S HARSH.
GUARDS!
FIRE THE LAS--

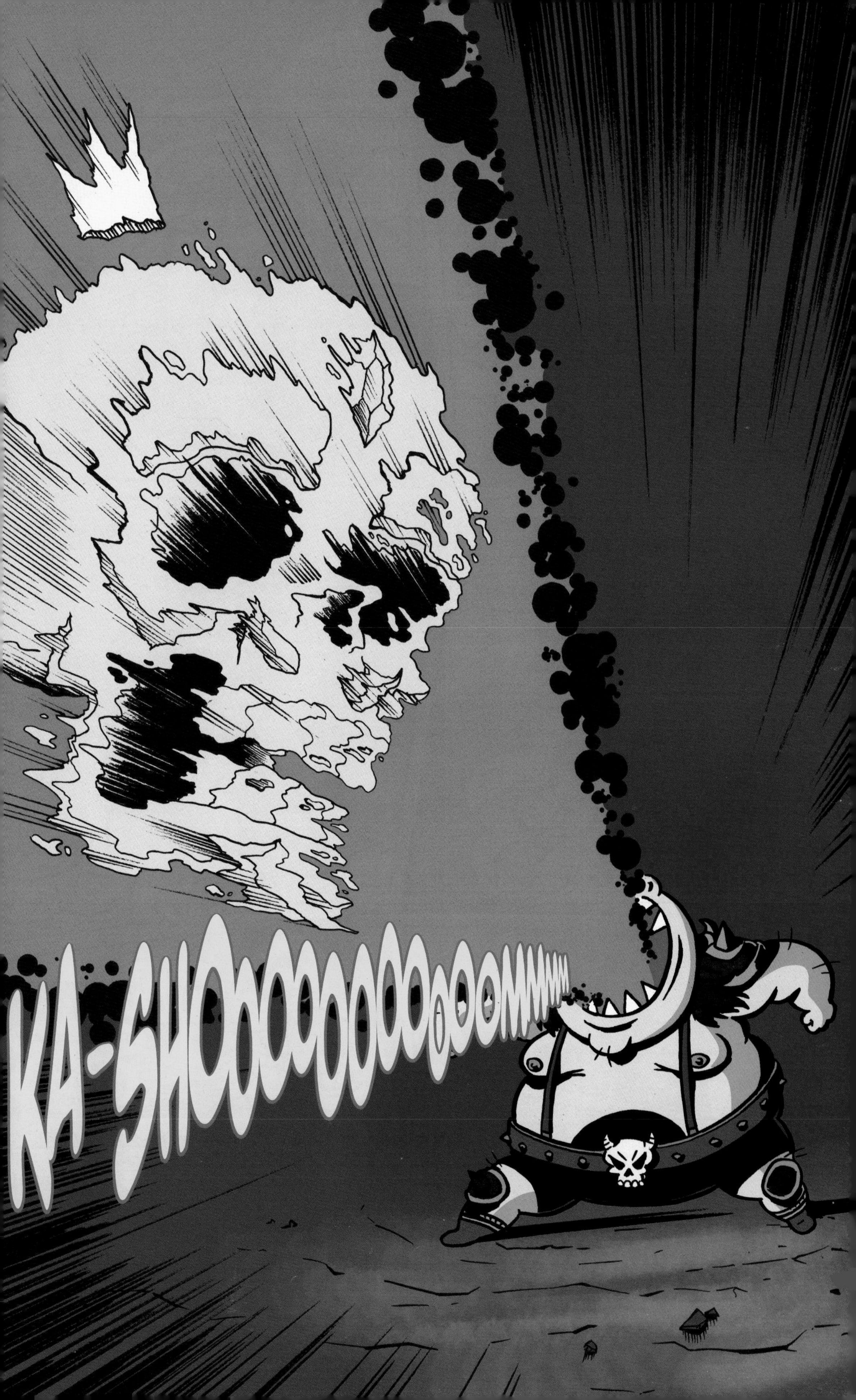
KA-SHOOOOOOOOOOMMMMM

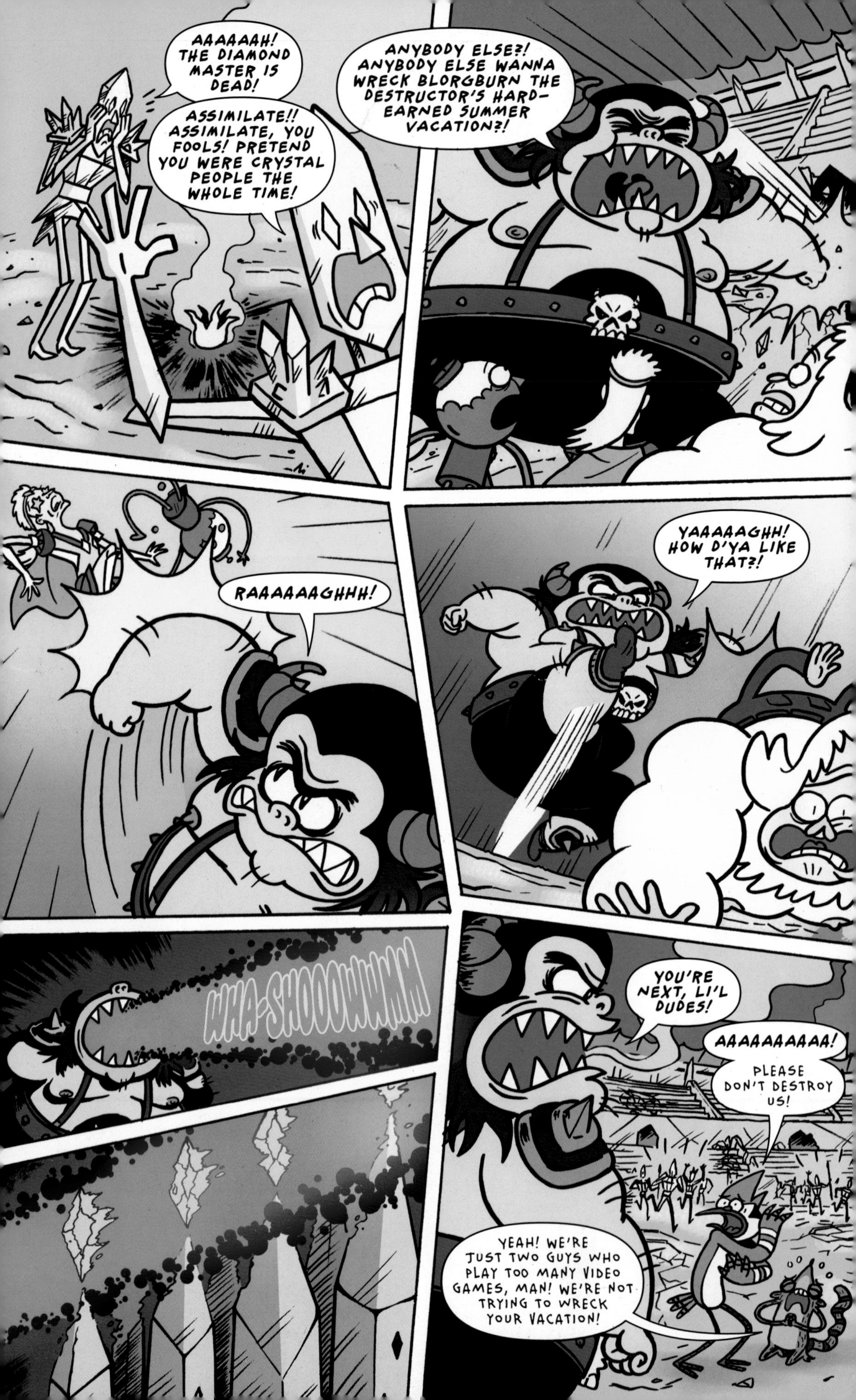
AAAAAAH! THE DIAMOND MASTER IS DEAD!
ASSIMILATE!! ASSIMILATE, YOU FOOLS! PRETEND YOU WERE CRYSTAL PEOPLE THE WHOLE TIME!
ANYBODY ELSE?! ANYBODY ELSE WANNA WRECK BLORGBURN THE DESTRUCTOR'S HARD-EARNED SUMMER VACATION?!
RAAAAAAGHHH!
YAAAAAGHH! HOW D'YA LIKE THAT?!
WHA-SHOOOWWMM
YOU'RE NEXT, LI'L DUDES!
AAAAAAAAAA!
PLEASE DON'T DESTROY US!
YEAH! WE'RE JUST TWO GUYS WHO PLAY TOO MANY VIDEO GAMES, MAN! WE'RE NOT TRYING TO WRECK YOUR VACATION!

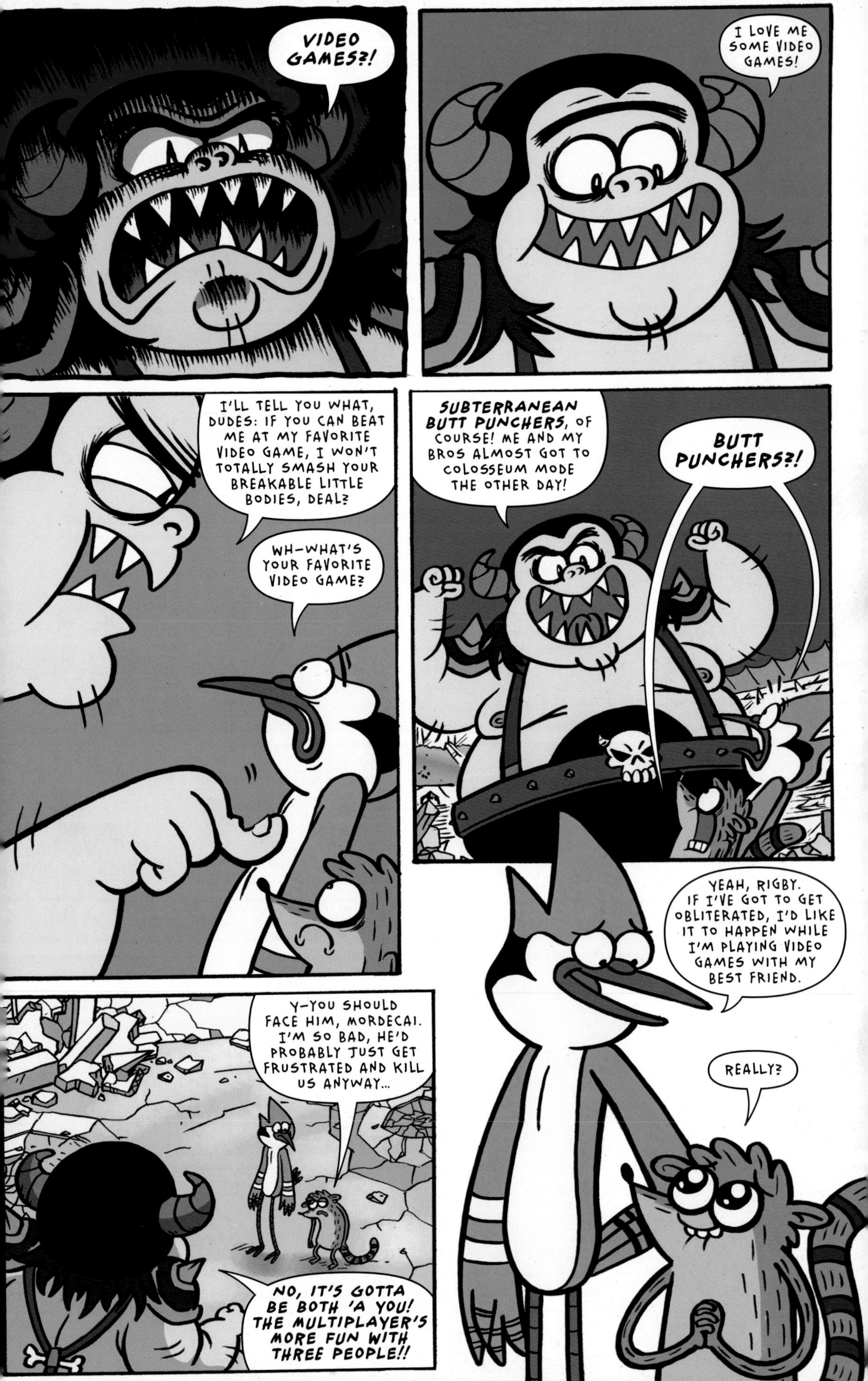
VIDEO GAMES?!
I LOVE ME SOME VIDEO GAMES!
I'LL TELL YOU WHAT, DUDES: IF YOU CAN BEAT ME AT MY FAVORITE VIDEO GAME, I WON'T TOTALLY SMASH YOUR BREAKABLE LITTLE BODIES, DEAL?
WH-WHAT'S YOUR FAVORITE VIDEO GAME?
SUBTERRANEAN BUTT PUNCHERS, OF COURSE! ME AND MY BROS ALMOST GOT TO COLOSSEUM MODE THE OTHER DAY!
BUTT PUNCHERS?!
Y-YOU SHOULD FACE HIM, MORDECAI. I'M SO BAD, HE'D PROBABLY JUST GET FRUSTRATED AND KILL US ANYWAY...
NO, IT'S GOTTA BE BOTH 'A YOU! THE MULTIPLAYER'S MORE FUN WITH THREE PEOPLE!!
YEAH, RIGBY. IF I'VE GOT TO GET OBLITERATED, I'D LIKE IT TO HAPPEN WHILE I'M PLAYING VIDEO GAMES WITH MY BEST FRIEND.
REALLY?

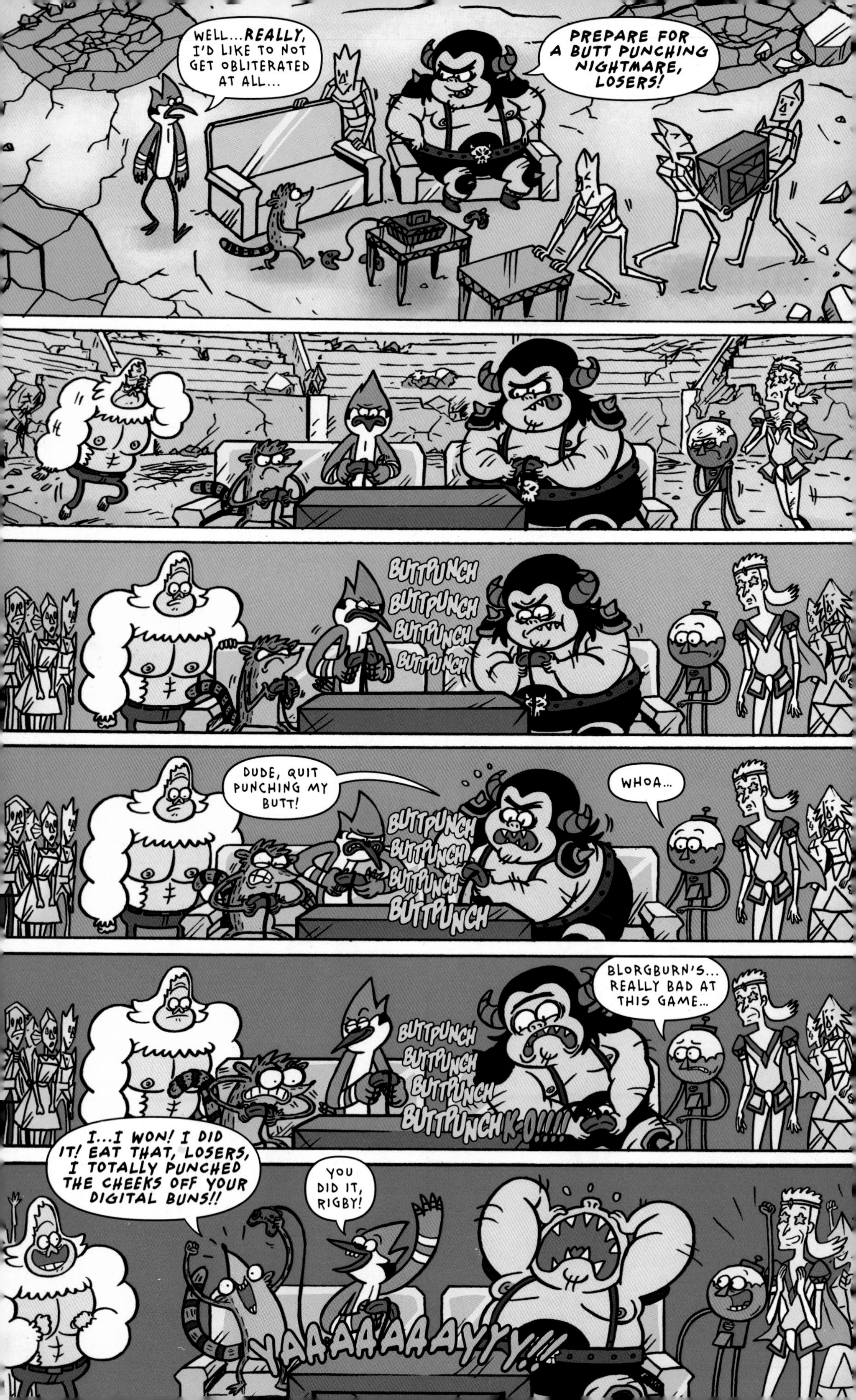
WELL... REALLY, I'D LIKE TO NOT GET OBLITERATED AT ALL...
PREPARE FOR A BUTT PUNCHING NIGHTMARE, LOSERS!
BUTTPUNCH
BUTTPUNCH
BUTTPUNCH
BUTTPUNCH
DUDE, QUIT PUNCHING MY BUTT!
BUTTPUNCH
BUTTPUNCH
BUTTPUNCH
BUTTPUNCH
WHOA...
BLORGBURN'S... REALLY BAD AT THIS GAME...
BUTTPUNCH
BUTTPUNCH
BUTTPUNCH
BUTTPUNCH K-O!!!!!
I...I WON! I DID IT! EAT THAT, LOSERS, I TOTALLY PUNCHED THE CHEEKS OFF YOUR DIGITAL BUNS!!
YOU DID IT, RIGBY!
YAAAAAAAAYYY!!

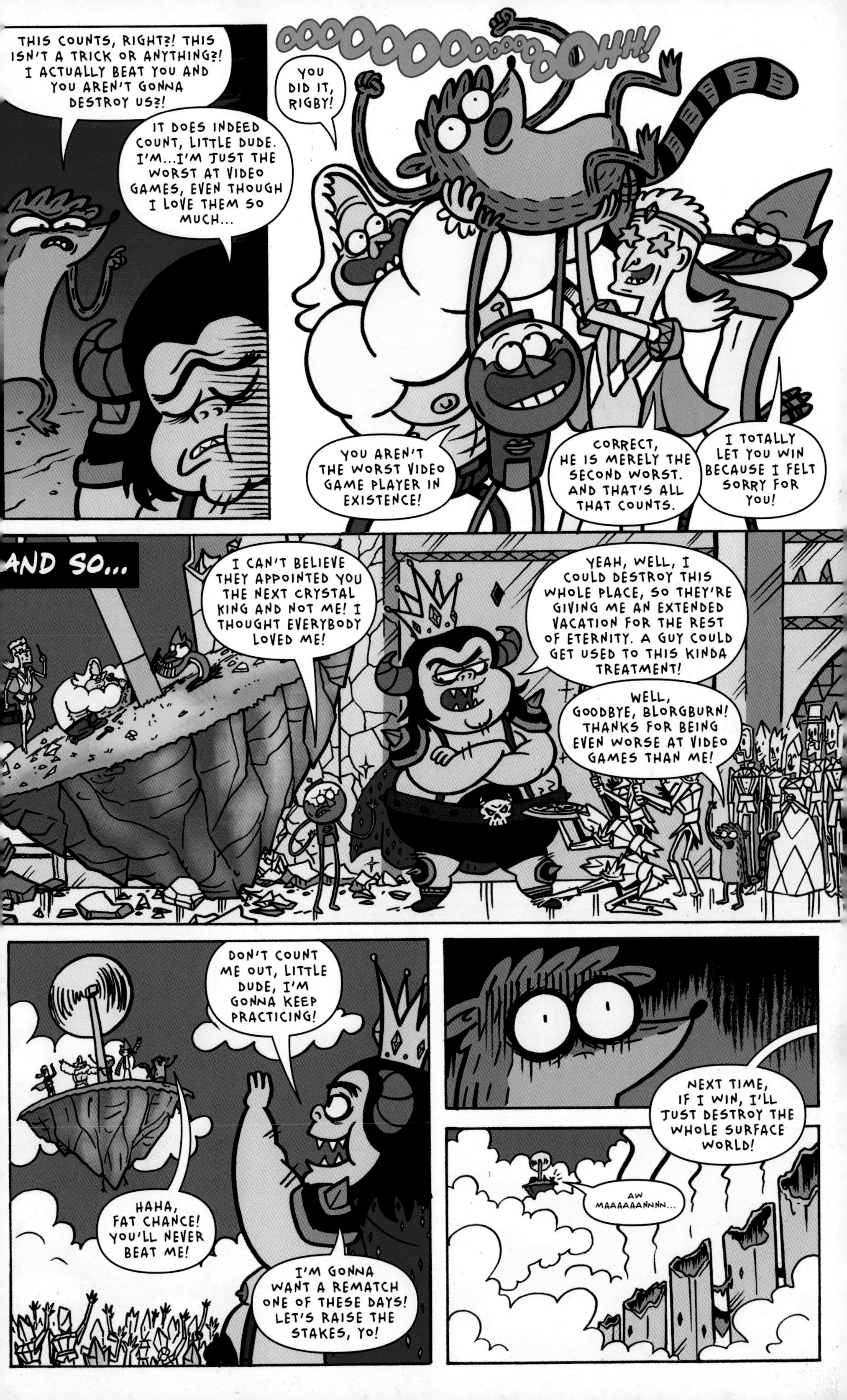
THIS COUNTS, RIGHT?! THIS ISN'T A TRICK OR ANYTHING?! I ACTUALLY BEAT YOU AND YOU AREN'T GONNA DESTROY US?!
IT DOES INDEED COUNT, LITTLE DUDE. I'M...I'M JUST THE WORST AT VIDEO GAMES, EVEN THOUGH I LOVE THEM SO MUCH...
OOOOOOOOOOooooooOOHHH!
YOU DID IT, RIGBY!
YOU AREN'T THE WORST VIDEO GAME PLAYER IN EXISTENCE!
CORRECT, HE IS MERELY THE SECOND WORST. AND THAT'S ALL THAT COUNTS.
I TOTALLY LET YOU WIN BECAUSE I FELT SORRY FOR YOU!
AND SO...
I CAN'T BELIEVE THEY APPOINTED YOU THE NEXT CRYSTAL KING AND NOT ME! I THOUGHT EVERYBODY LOVED ME!
YEAH, WELL, I COULD DESTROY THIS WHOLE PLACE, SO THEY'RE GIVING ME AN EXTENDED VACATION FOR THE REST OF ETERNITY. A GUY COULD GET USED TO THIS KINDA TREATMENT!
WELL, GOODBYE, BLORGBURN! THANKS FOR BEING EVEN WORSE AT VIDEO GAMES THAN ME!
DON'T COUNT ME OUT, LITTLE DUDE, I'M GONNA KEEP PRACTICING!
HAHA, FAT CHANCE! YOU'LL NEVER BEAT ME!
I'M GONNA WANT A REMATCH ONE OF THESE DAYS! LET'S RAISE THE STAKES, YO!
NEXT TIME, IF I WIN, I'LL JUST DESTROY THE WHOLE SURFACE WORLD!
AW MAAAAAAANNNN...

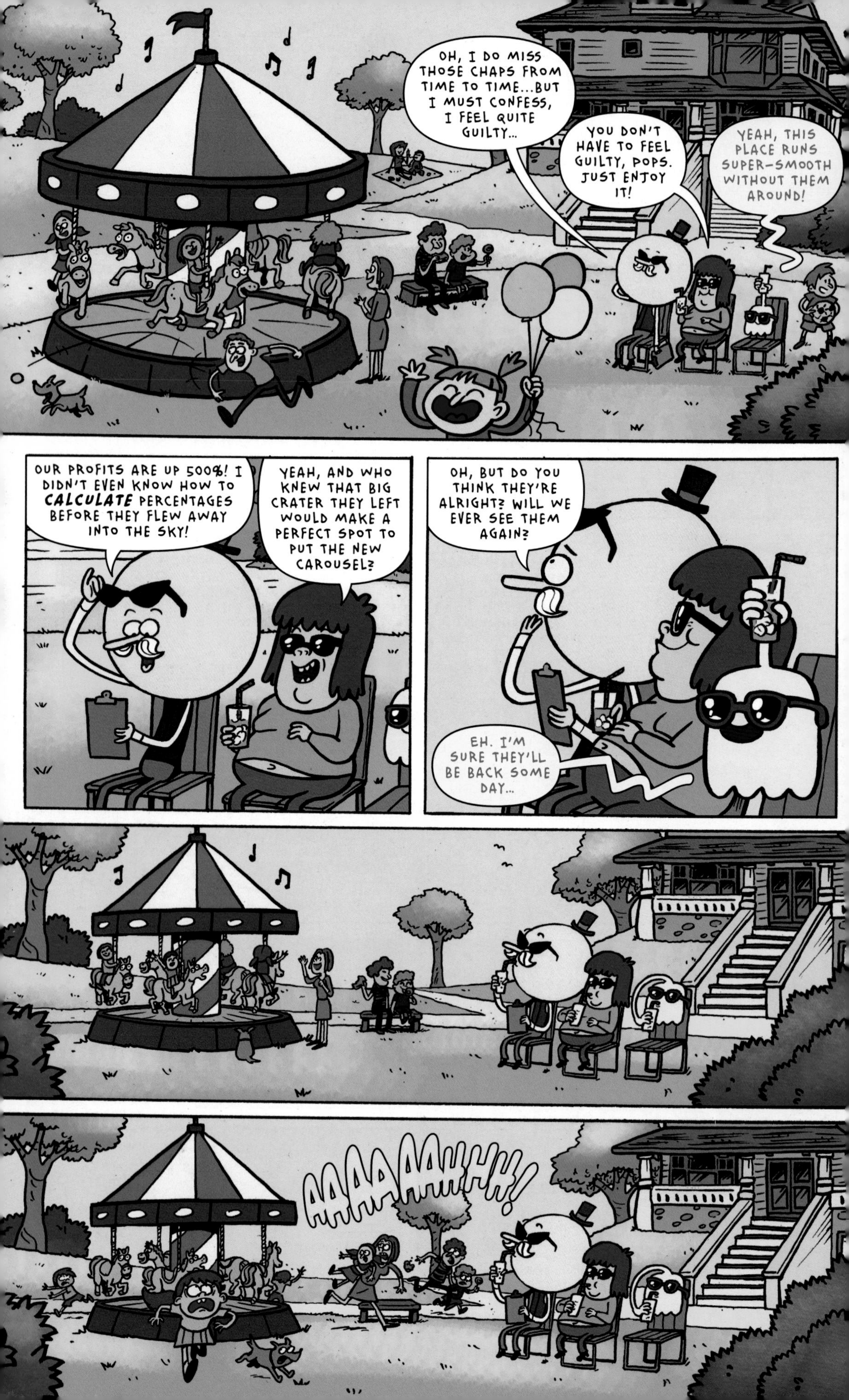

OH, I DO MISS THOSE CHAPS FROM TIME TO TIME...BUT I MUST CONFESS, I FEEL QUITE GUILTY...
YOU DON'T HAVE TO FEEL GUILTY, POPS. JUST ENJOY IT!
YEAH, THIS PLACE RUNS SUPER-SMOOTH WITHOUT THEM AROUND!
OUR PROFITS ARE UP 500%! I DIDN'T EVEN KNOW HOW TO CALCULATE PERCENTAGES BEFORE THEY FLEW AWAY INTO THE SKY!
YEAH, AND WHO KNEW THAT BIG CRATER THEY LEFT WOULD MAKE A PERFECT SPOT TO PUT THE NEW CAROUSEL?
OH, BUT DO YOU THINK THEY'RE ALRIGHT? WILL WE EVER SEE THEM AGAIN?
EH. I'M SURE THEY'LL BE BACK SOME DAY...
AAAAAAHHH!

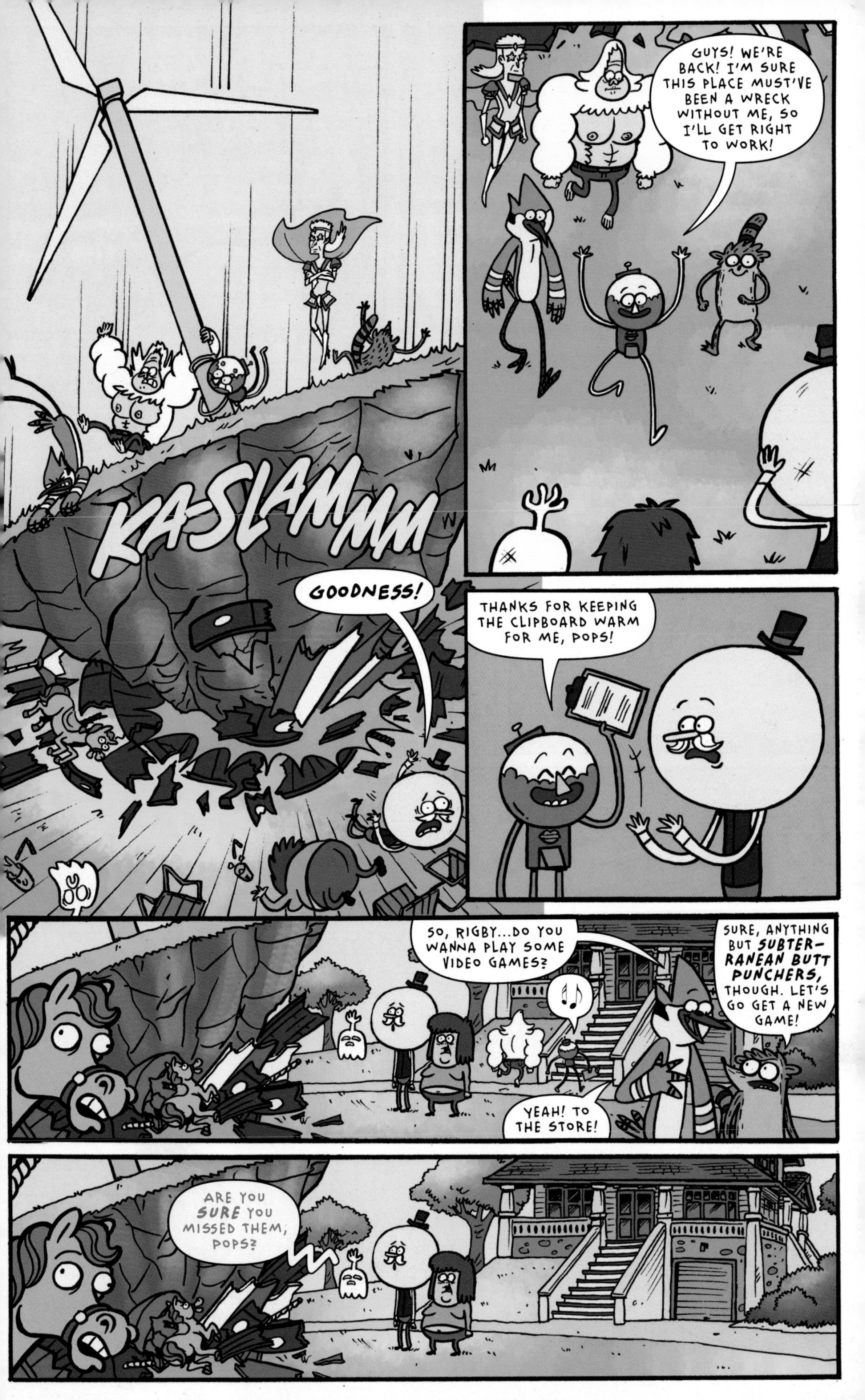
KA-SLAMMMM
GOODNESS!
GUYS! WE'RE BACK! I'M SURE THIS PLACE MUST'VE BEEN A WRECK WITHOUT ME, SO I'LL GET RIGHT TO WORK!
THANKS FOR KEEPING THE CLIPBOARD WARM FOR ME, POPS!
SO, RIGBY...DO YOU WANNA PLAY SOME VIDEO GAMES?
SURE, ANYTHING BUT SUBTER-RANEAN BUTT PUNCHERS, THOUGH. LET'S GO GET A NEW GAME!
YEAH! TO THE STORE!
ARE YOU SURE YOU MISSED THEM, POPS?

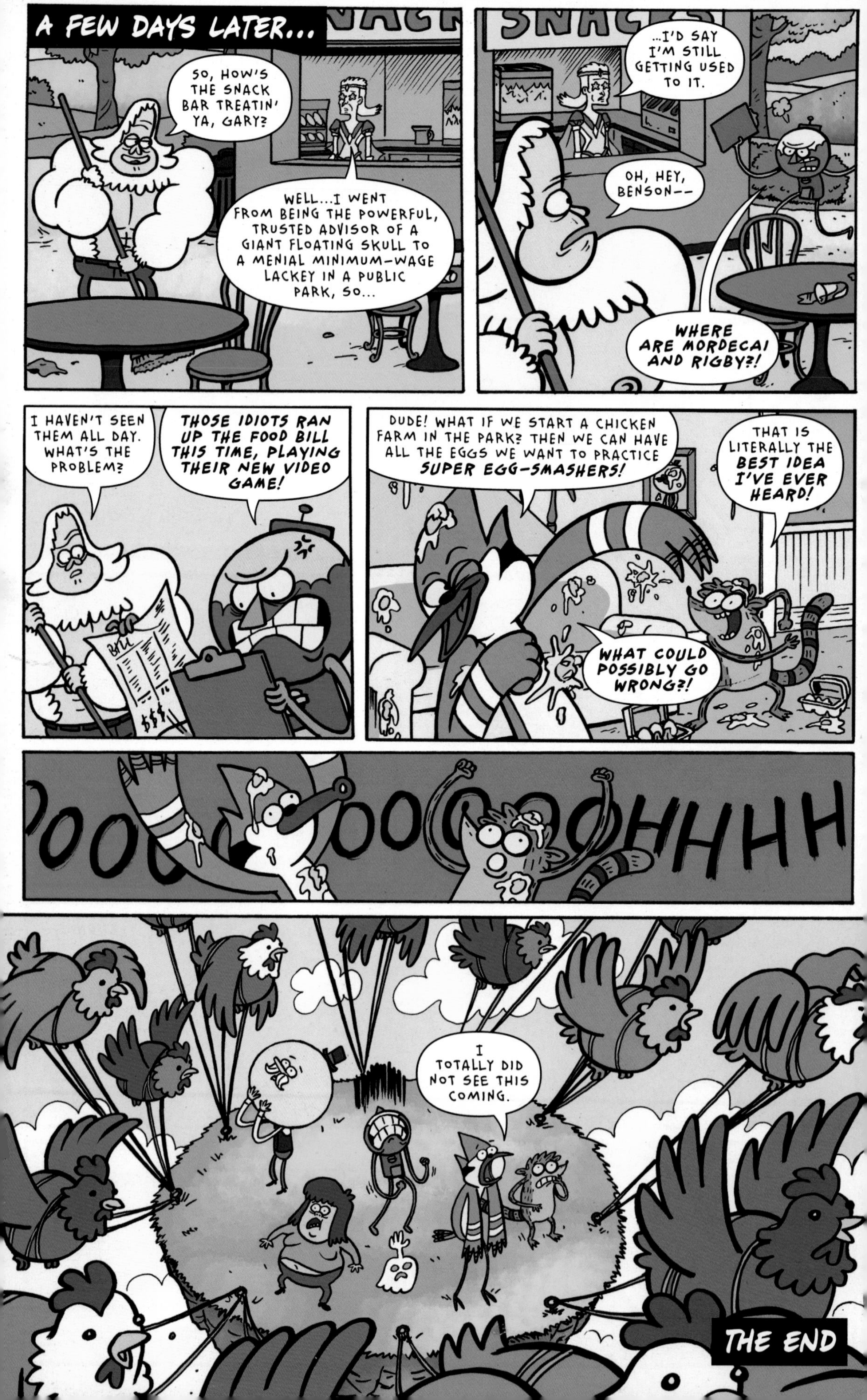
A FEW DAYS LATER...
SO, HOW'S THE SNACK BAR TREATIN' YA, GARY?
WELL...I WENT FROM BEING THE POWERFUL, TRUSTED ADVISOR OF A GIANT FLOATING SKULL TO A MENIAL MINIMUM-WAGE LACKEY IN A PUBLIC PARK, SO...
...I'D SAY I'M STILL GETTING USED TO IT.
OH, HEY, BENSON--
WHERE ARE MORDECAI AND RIGBY?!
I HAVEN'T SEEN THEM ALL DAY. WHAT'S THE PROBLEM?
THOSE IDIOTS RAN UP THE FOOD BILL THIS TIME, PLAYING THEIR NEW VIDEO GAME!
DUDE! WHAT IF WE START A CHICKEN FARM IN THE PARK? THEN WE CAN HAVE ALL THE EGGS WE WANT TO PRACTICE SUPER EGG-SMASHERS!
THAT IS LITERALLY THE BEST IDEA I'VE EVER HEARD!
WHAT COULD POSSIBLY GO WRONG?!
OOOOOOOOHHHH
I TOTALLY DID NOT SEE THIS COMING.
THE END

SHORT STORIES, BRO

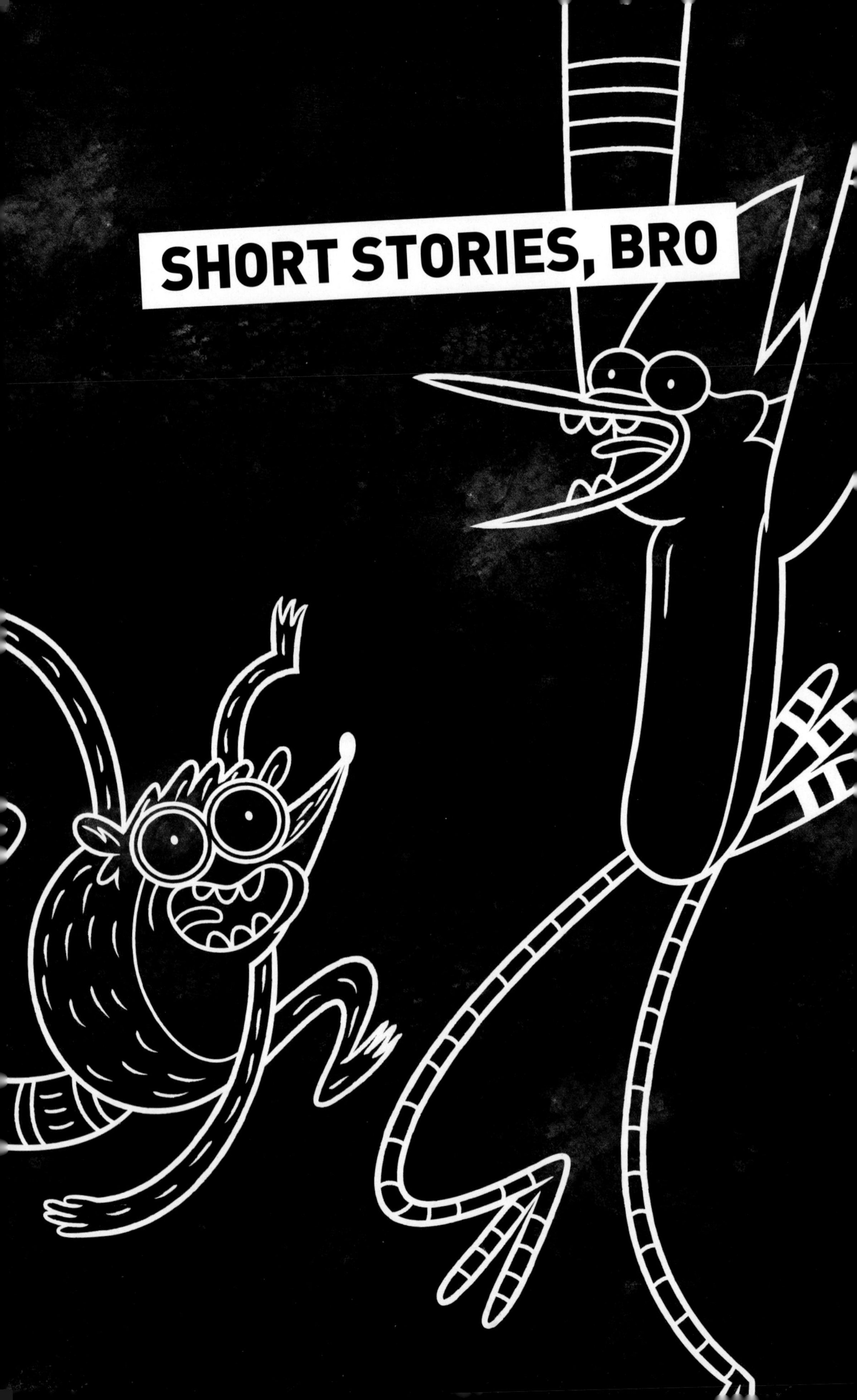

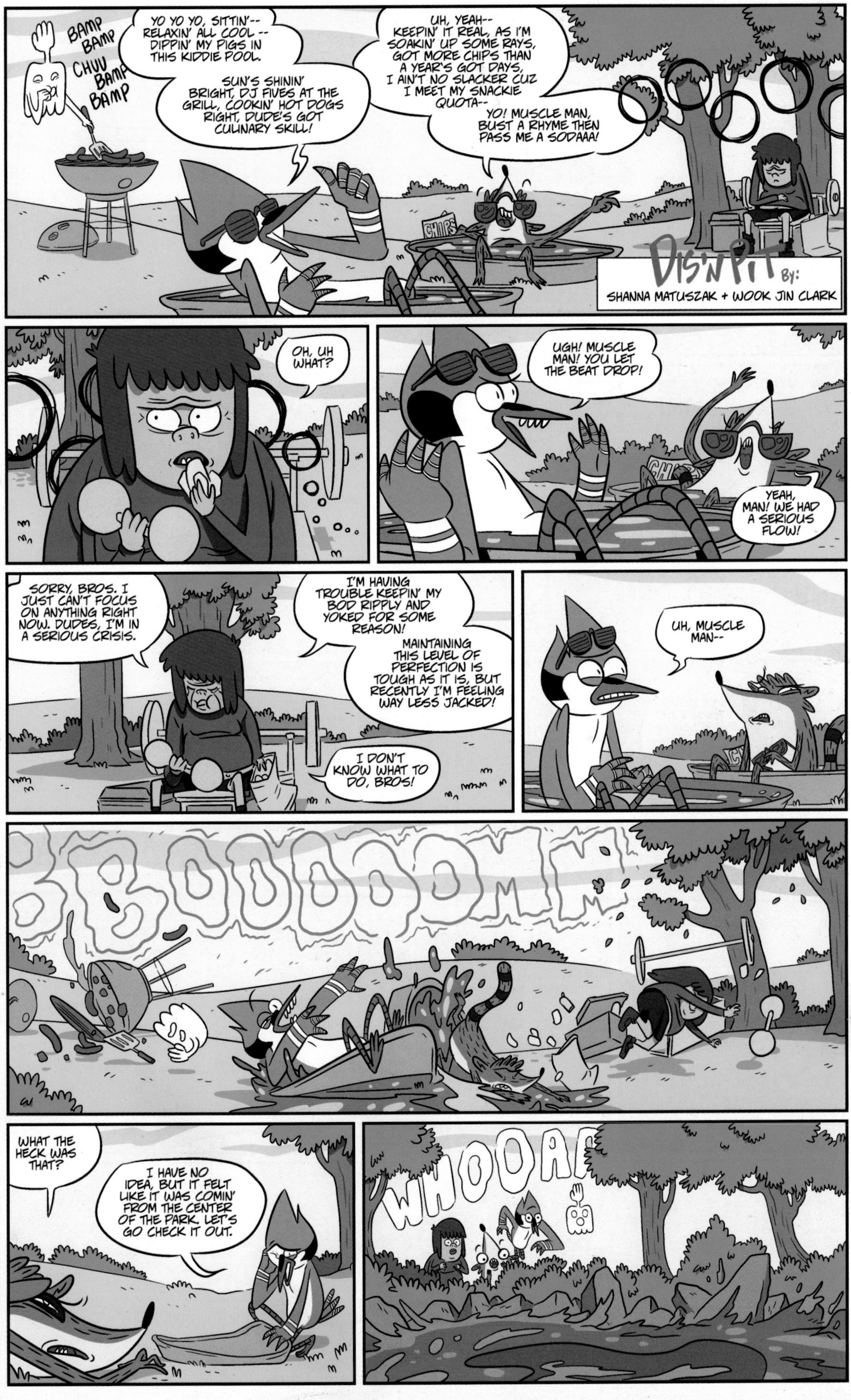
BAMP BAMP CHUU BAMP BAMP
YO YO YO, SITTIN'-- RELAXIN' ALL COOL -- DIPPIN' MY PIGS IN THIS KIDDIE POOL.
SUN'S SHININ' BRIGHT, DJ FIVES AT THE GRILL, COOKIN' HOT DOGS RIGHT, DUDE'S GOT CULINARY SKILL!
UH, YEAH-- KEEPIN' IT REAL, AS I'M SOAKIN' UP SOME RAYS, GOT MORE CHIPS THAN A YEAR'S GOT DAYS, I AIN'T NO SLACKER CUZ I MEET MY SNACKIE QUOTA--
YO! MUSCLE MAN, BUST A RHYME THEN PASS ME A SODAAA!
CHIPS
DIS'N PIT By:
SHANNA MATUSZAK + WOOK JIN CLARK
OH, UH WHAT?
UGH! MUSCLE MAN! YOU LET THE BEAT DROP!
YEAH, MAN! WE HAD A SERIOUS FLOW!
SORRY, BROS. I JUST CAN'T FOCUS ON ANYTHING RIGHT NOW. DUDES, I'M IN A SERIOUS CRISIS.
I'M HAVING TROUBLE KEEPIN' MY BOD RIPPLY AND YOKED FOR SOME REASON!
MAINTAINING THIS LEVEL OF PERFECTION IS TOUGH AS IT IS, BUT RECENTLY I'M FEELING WAY LESS JACKED!
I DON'T KNOW WHAT TO DO, BROS!
UH, MUSCLE MAN--
BOOOOOM
WHAT THE HECK WAS THAT?
I HAVE NO IDEA, BUT IT FELT LIKE IT WAS COMIN' FROM THE CENTER OF THE PARK. LET'S GO CHECK IT OUT.
WHOOA

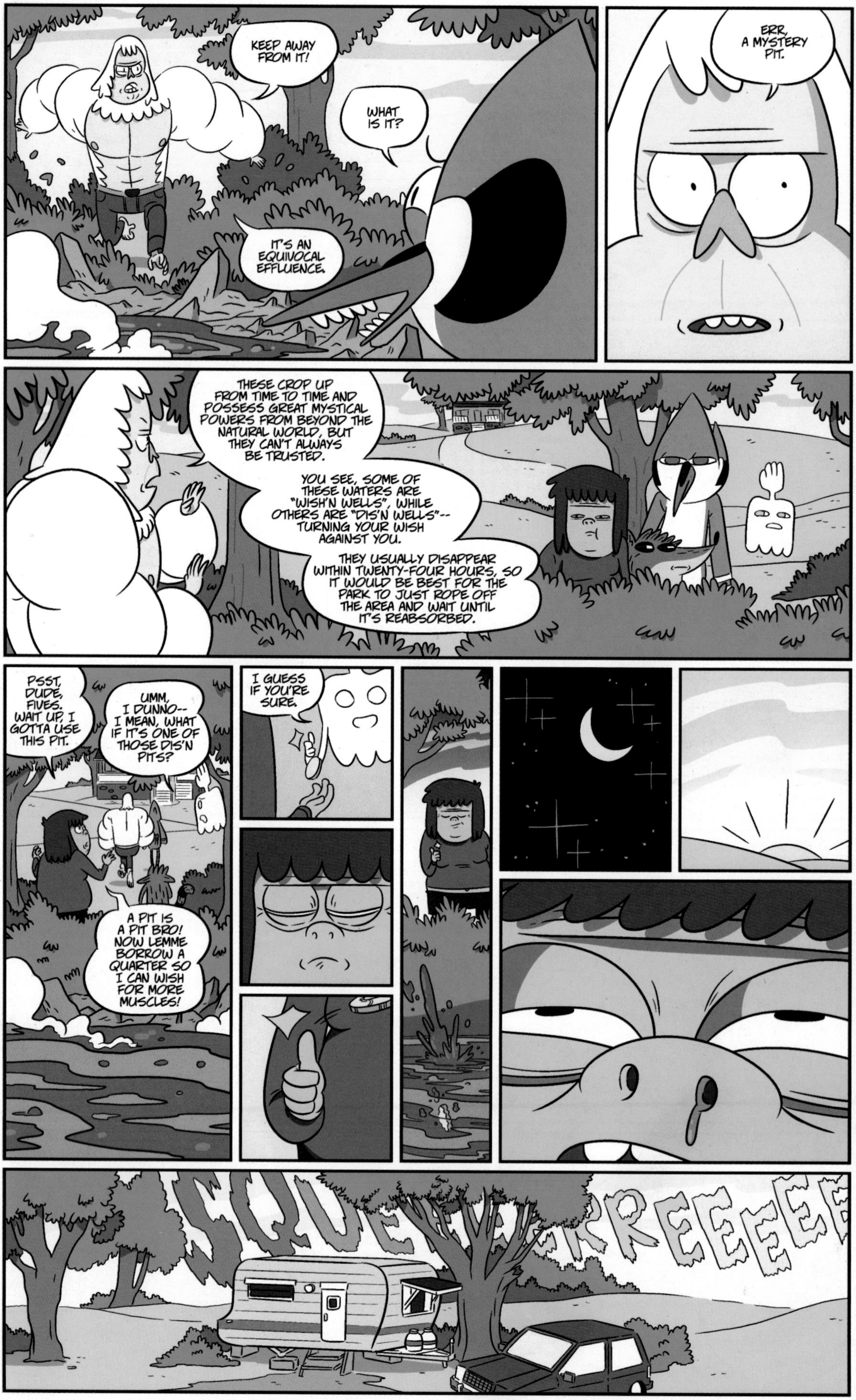
KEEP AWAY FROM IT!
WHAT IS IT?
IT'S AN EQUIVOCAL EFFLUENCE.
ERR, A MYSTERY PIT.
THESE CROP UP FROM TIME TO TIME AND POSSESS GREAT MYSTICAL POWERS FROM BEYOND THE NATURAL WORLD, BUT THEY CAN'T ALWAYS BE TRUSTED.
YOU SEE, SOME OF THESE WATERS ARE "WISH'N WELLS", WHILE OTHERS ARE "DIS'N WELLS"-- TURNING YOUR WISH AGAINST YOU.
THEY USUALLY DISAPPEAR WITHIN TWENTY-FOUR HOURS, SO IT WOULD BE BEST FOR THE PARK TO JUST ROPE OFF THE AREA AND WAIT UNTIL IT'S REABSORBED.
PSST, DUDE, FIVES. WAIT UP, I GOTTA USE THIS PIT.
UMM, I DUNNO-- I MEAN, WHAT IF IT'S ONE OF THOSE DIS'N PITS?
A PIT IS A PIT BRO! NOW LEMME BORROW A QUARTER SO I CAN WISH FOR MORE MUSCLES!
I GUESS IF YOU'RE SURE.
SQUEEEARRREEEEEE

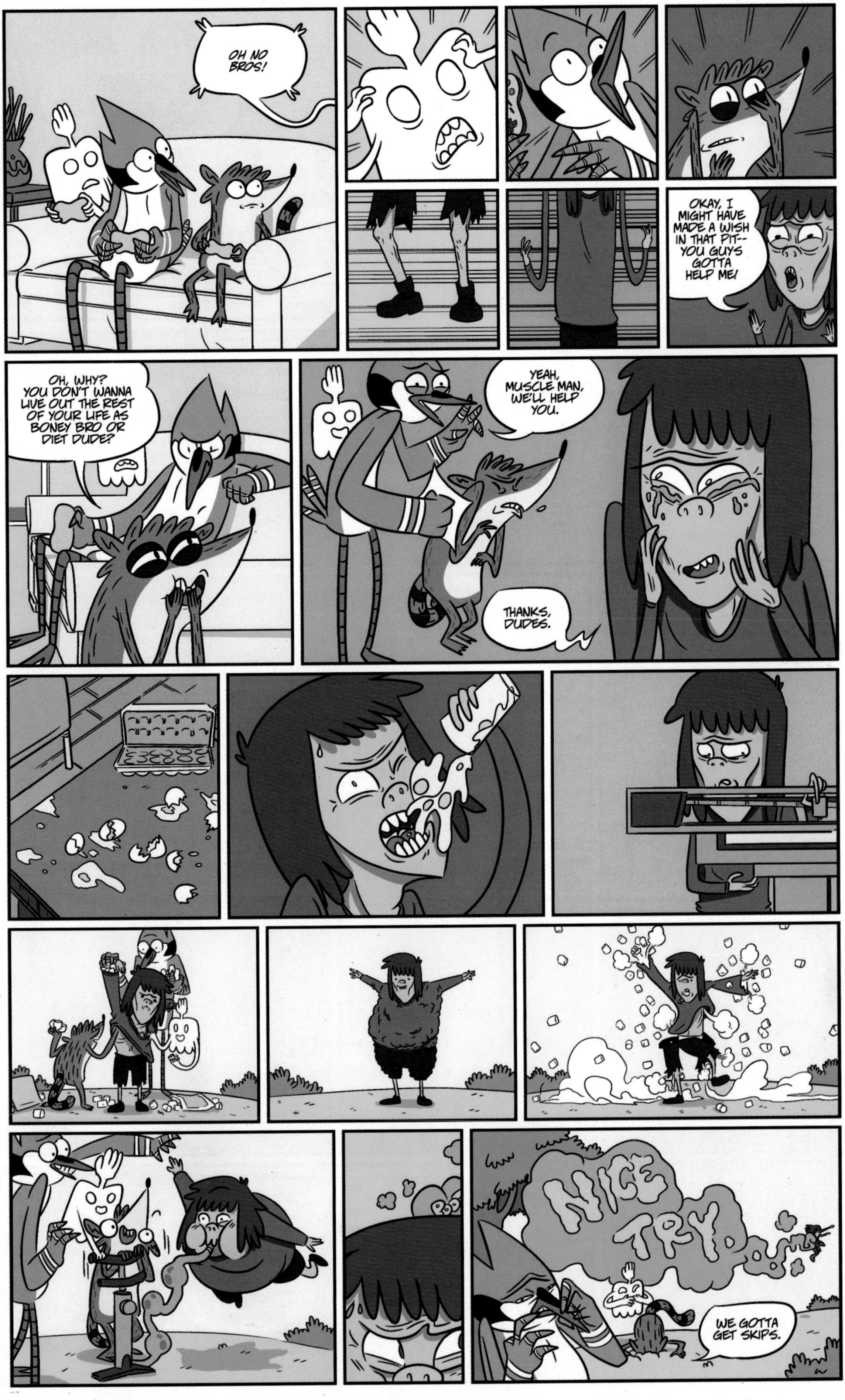
OH NO BROS!
OKAY, I MIGHT HAVE MADE A WISH IN THAT PIT-- YOU GUYS GOTTA HELP ME!
OH, WHY? YOU DON'T WANNA LIVE OUT THE REST OF YOUR LIFE AS BONEY BRO OR DIET DUDE?
YEAH, MUSCLE MAN, WE'LL HELP YOU.
THANKS, DUDES.
NICE TRY.
WE GOTTA GET SKIPS.

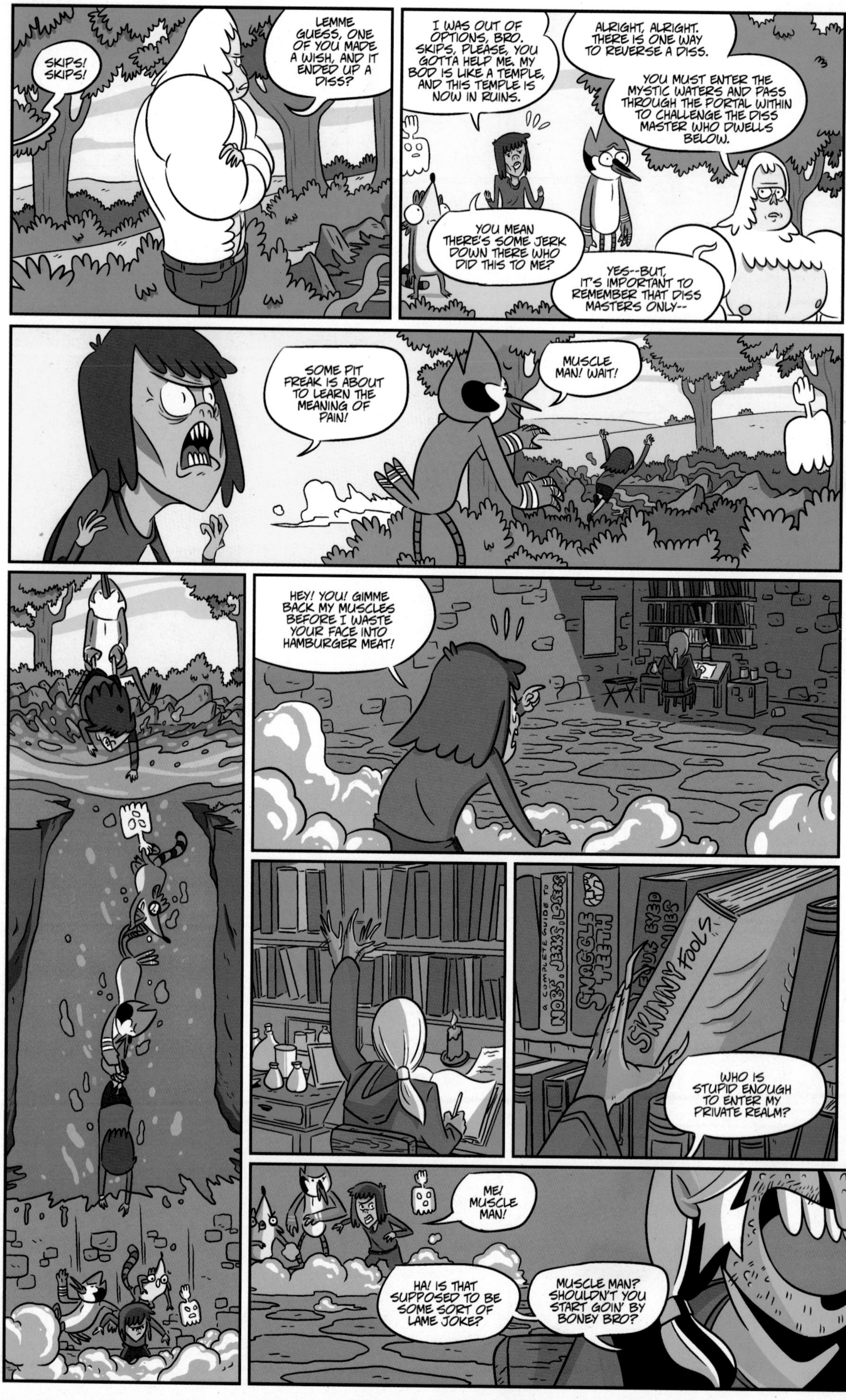
SKIPS! SKIPS!
LEMME GUESS, ONE OF YOU MADE A WISH, AND IT ENDED UP A DISS?
I WAS OUT OF OPTIONS, BRO. SKIPS, PLEASE, YOU GOTTA HELP ME. MY BOD IS LIKE A TEMPLE, AND THIS TEMPLE IS NOW IN RUINS.
ALRIGHT, ALRIGHT. THERE IS ONE WAY TO REVERSE A DISS.
YOU MUST ENTER THE MYSTIC WATERS AND PASS THROUGH THE PORTAL WITHIN TO CHALLENGE THE DISS MASTER WHO DWELLS BELOW.
YOU MEAN THERE'S SOME JERK DOWN THERE WHO DID THIS TO ME?
YES--BUT, IT'S IMPORTANT TO REMEMBER THAT DISS MASTERS ONLY--
SOME PIT FREAK IS ABOUT TO LEARN THE MEANING OF PAIN!
MUSCLE MAN! WAIT!
HEY! YOU! GIMME BACK MY MUSCLES BEFORE I WASTE YOUR FACE INTO HAMBURGER MEAT!
A COMPLETE GUIDE TO NOBS, JERKS, LOSERS
SNAGGLE TEETH
SKINNY FOOLS
WHO IS STUPID ENOUGH TO ENTER MY PRIVATE REALM?
ME! MUSCLE MAN!
HA! IS THAT SUPPOSED TO BE SOME SORT OF LAME JOKE?
MUSCLE MAN? SHOULDN'T YOU START GOIN' BY BONEY BRO?

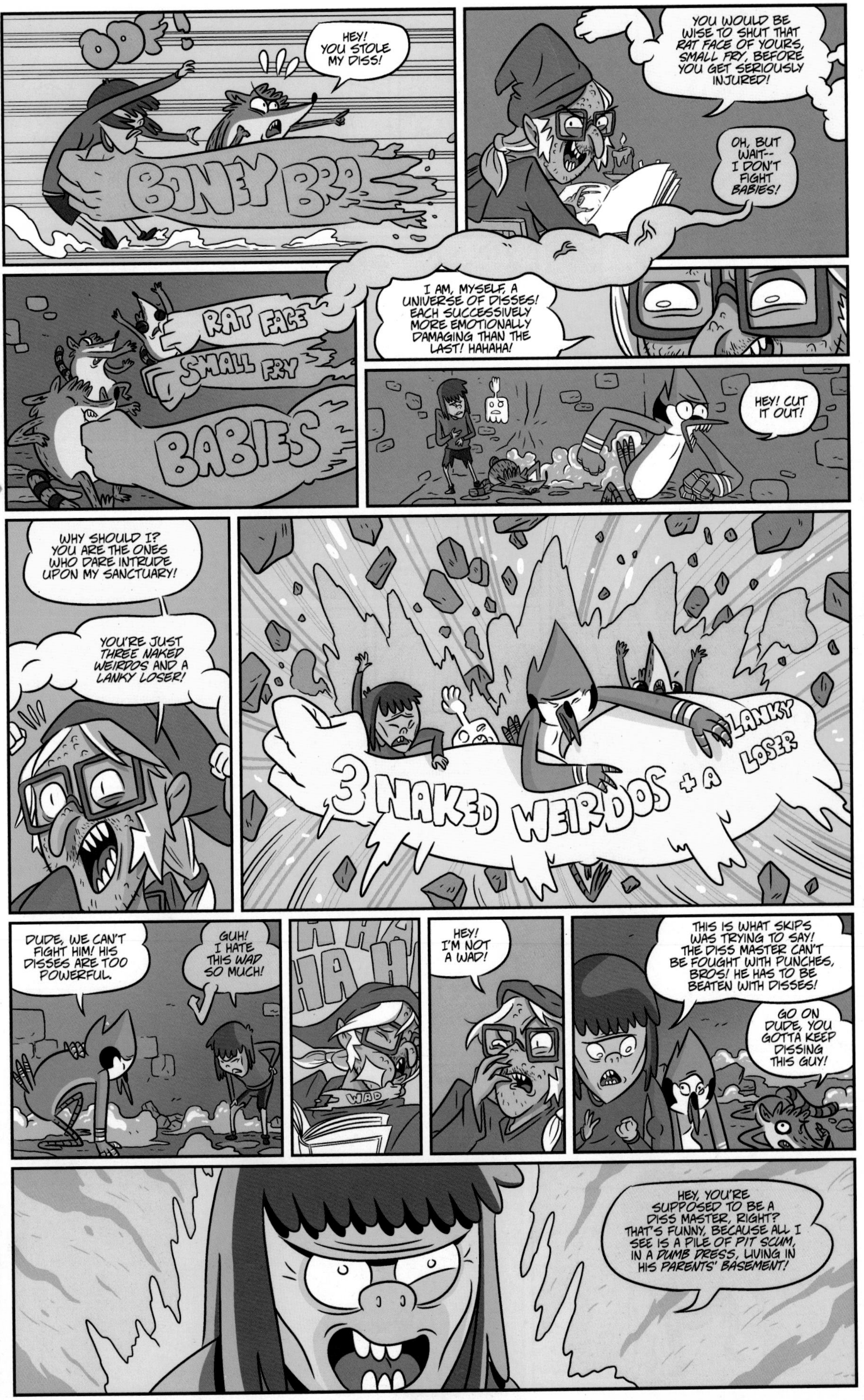
OOF!
HEY! YOU STOLE MY DISS!
BONEY BRO
YOU WOULD BE WISE TO SHUT THAT RAT FACE OF YOURS, SMALL FRY, BEFORE YOU GET SERIOUSLY INJURED!
OH, BUT WAIT-- I DON'T FIGHT BABIES!
RAT FACE
SMALL FRY
BABIES
I AM, MYSELF, A UNIVERSE OF DISSES! EACH SUCCESSIVELY MORE EMOTIONALLY DAMAGING THAN THE LAST! HAHAHA!
HEY! CUT IT OUT!
WHY SHOULD I? YOU ARE THE ONES WHO DARE INTRUDE UPON MY SANCTUARY!
YOU'RE JUST THREE NAKED WEIRDOS AND A LANKY LOSER!
3 NAKED WEIRDOS + A LANKY LOSER
DUDE, WE CAN'T FIGHT HIM! HIS DISSES ARE TOO POWERFUL.
GUH! I HATE THIS WAD SO MUCH!
HA HA HA H
WAD
HEY! I'M NOT A WAD!
THIS IS WHAT SKIPS WAS TRYING TO SAY! THE DISS MASTER CAN'T BE FOUGHT WITH PUNCHES, BROS! HE HAS TO BE BEATEN WITH DISSES!
GO ON DUDE, YOU GOTTA KEEP DISSING THIS GUY!
HEY, YOU'RE SUPPOSED TO BE A DISS MASTER, RIGHT? THAT'S FUNNY, BECAUSE ALL I SEE IS A PILE OF PIT SCUM, IN A DUMB DRESS, LIVING IN HIS PARENTS' BASEMENT!

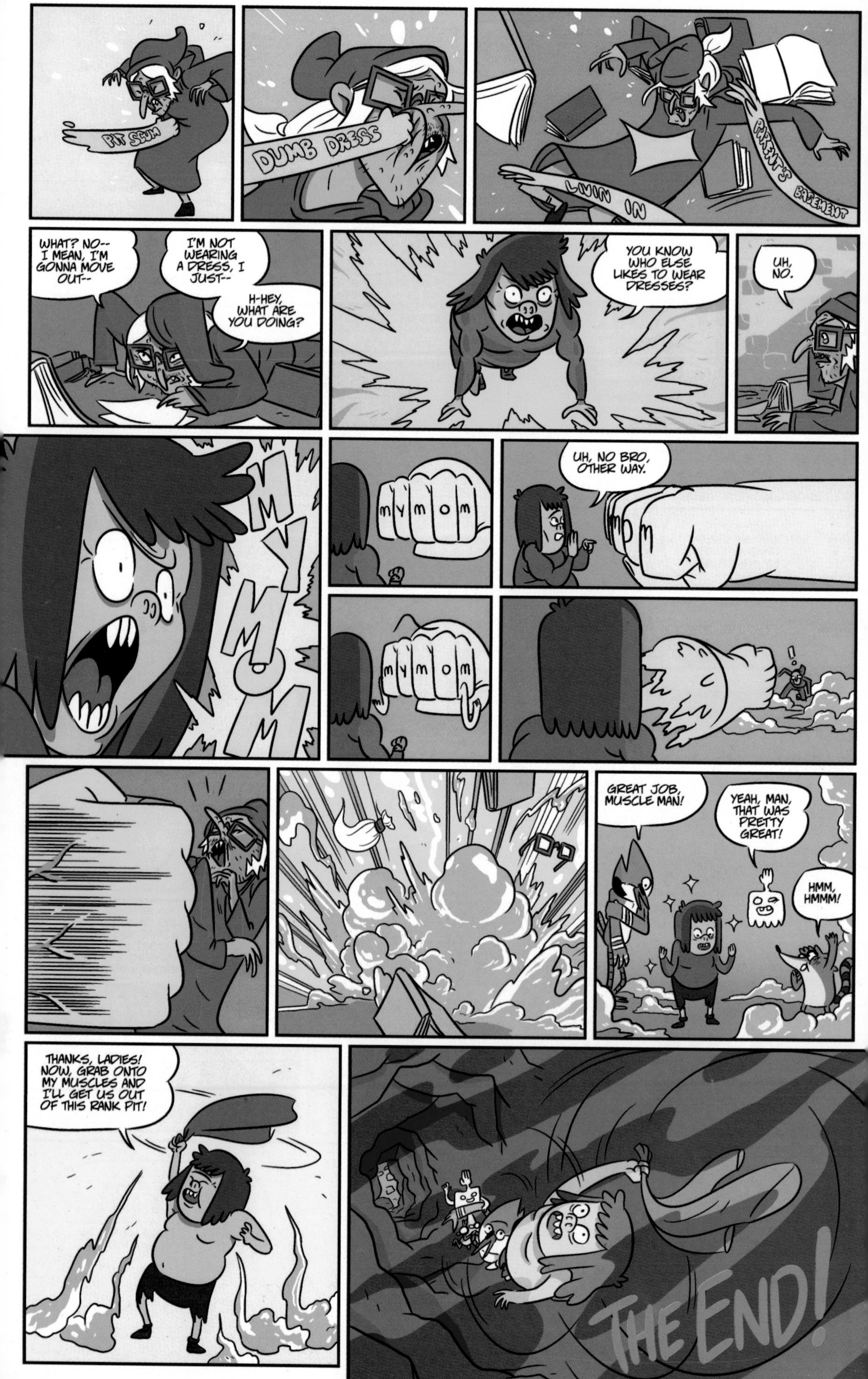

PIT SCUM
DUMB DRESS
LIVIN IN
PARENT'S BASEMENT
WHAT? NO-- I MEAN, I'M GONNA MOVE OUT--
I'M NOT WEARING A DRESS, I JUST--
H-HEY, WHAT ARE YOU DOING?
YOU KNOW WHO ELSE LIKES TO WEAR DRESSES?
UH, NO.
MY MOM
mymom
UH, NO BRO, OTHER WAY.
mymom
!
GREAT JOB, MUSCLE MAN!
YEAH, MAN, THAT WAS PRETTY GREAT!
HMM, HMMM!
THANKS, LADIES! NOW, GRAB ONTO MY MUSCLES AND I'LL GET US OUT OF THIS RANK PIT!
THE END!

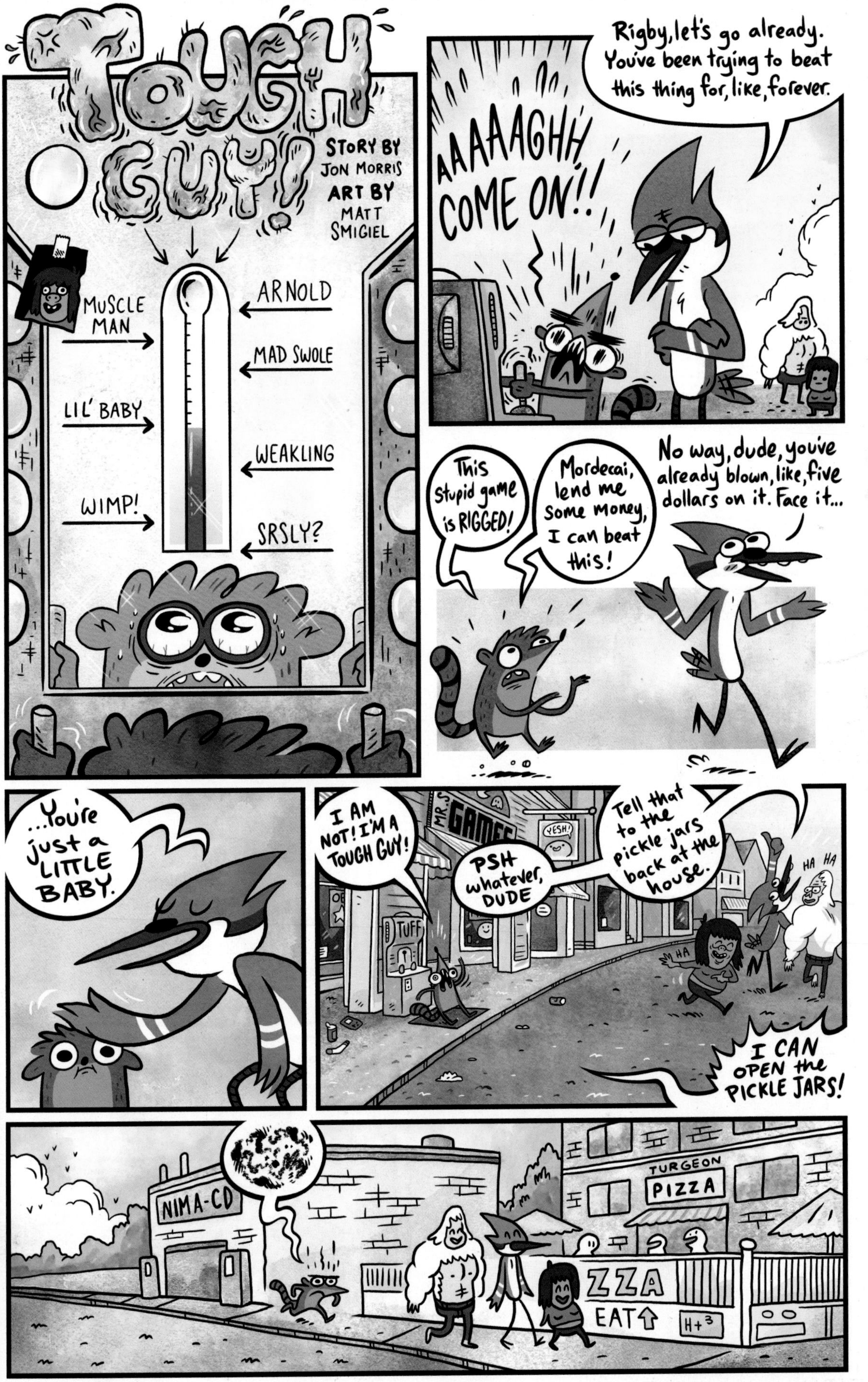

TOUGH GUY!
STORY BY JON MORRIS
ART BY MATT SMIGIEL
MUSCLE MAN
ARNOLD
MAD SWOLE
LIL' BABY
WEAKLING
WIMP!
SRSLY?
Rigby, let's go already. You've been trying to beat this thing for, like, forever.
AAAAAGHH, COME ON!!
This stupid game is RIGGED!
Mordecai, lend me some money, I can beat this!
No way, dude, you've already blown, like, five dollars on it. Face it...
...You're just a LITTLE BABY.
I AM NOT! I'M A TOUGH GUY!
PSH whatever, DUDE
Tell that to the pickle jars back at the house.
MR. S GAMES
YESH!
TUFF
HA HA
HA
I CAN OPEN the PICKLE JARS!
NIMA-CD
TURGEON PIZZA
ZZA
EAT

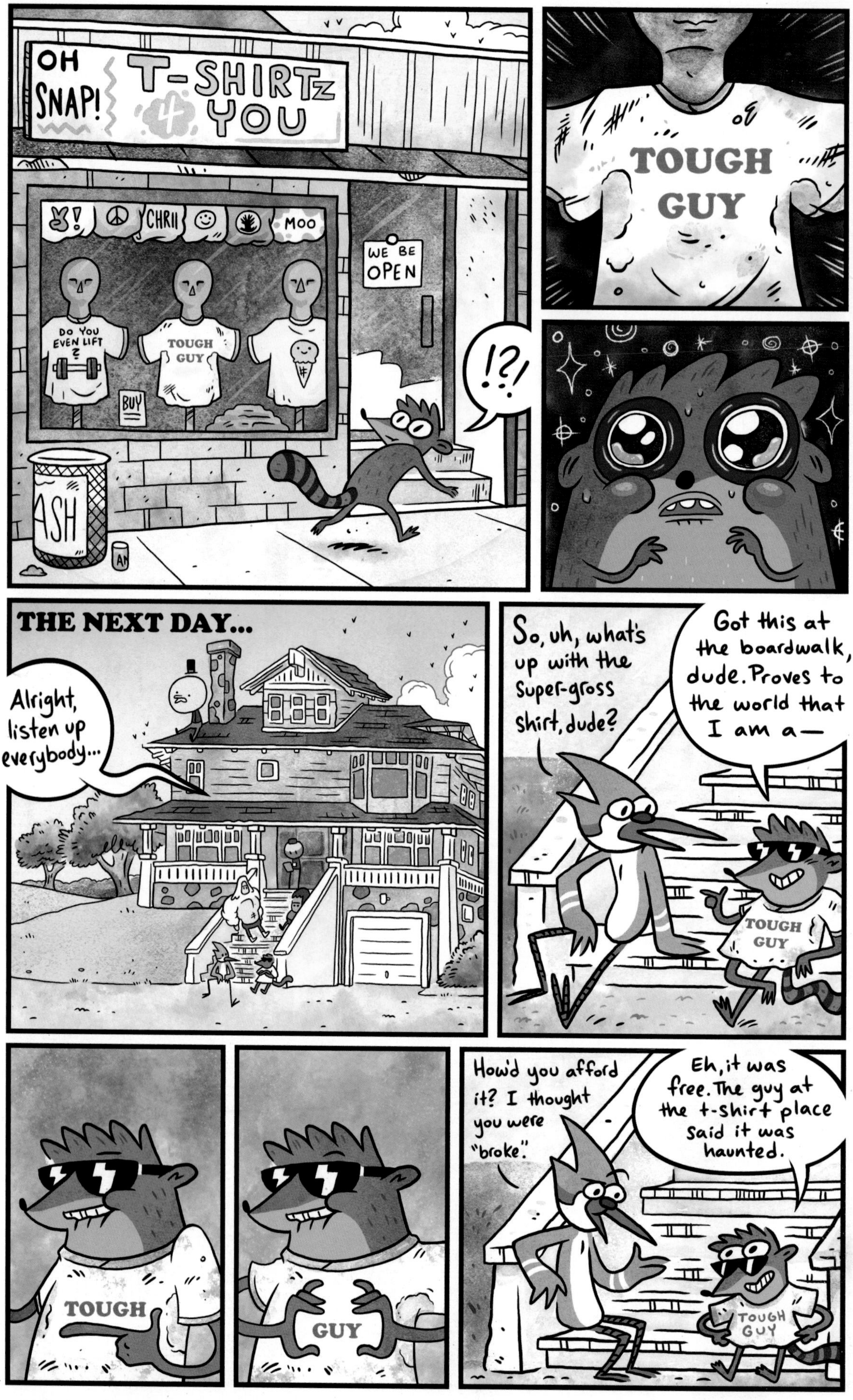
OH SNAP! T-SHIRTz 4 YOU
CHRII
MOO
WE BE OPEN
DO YOU EVEN LIFT ?
TOUGH GUY
BUY
ASH
!?!
TOUGH GUY
THE NEXT DAY...
Alright, listen up everybody...
So, uh, what's up with the super-gross shirt, dude?
Got this at the boardwalk, dude. Proves to the world that I am a—
TOUGH GUY
TOUGH
GUY
How'd you afford it? I thought you were "broke."
Eh, it was free. The guy at the t-shirt place said it was haunted.
TOUGH GUY

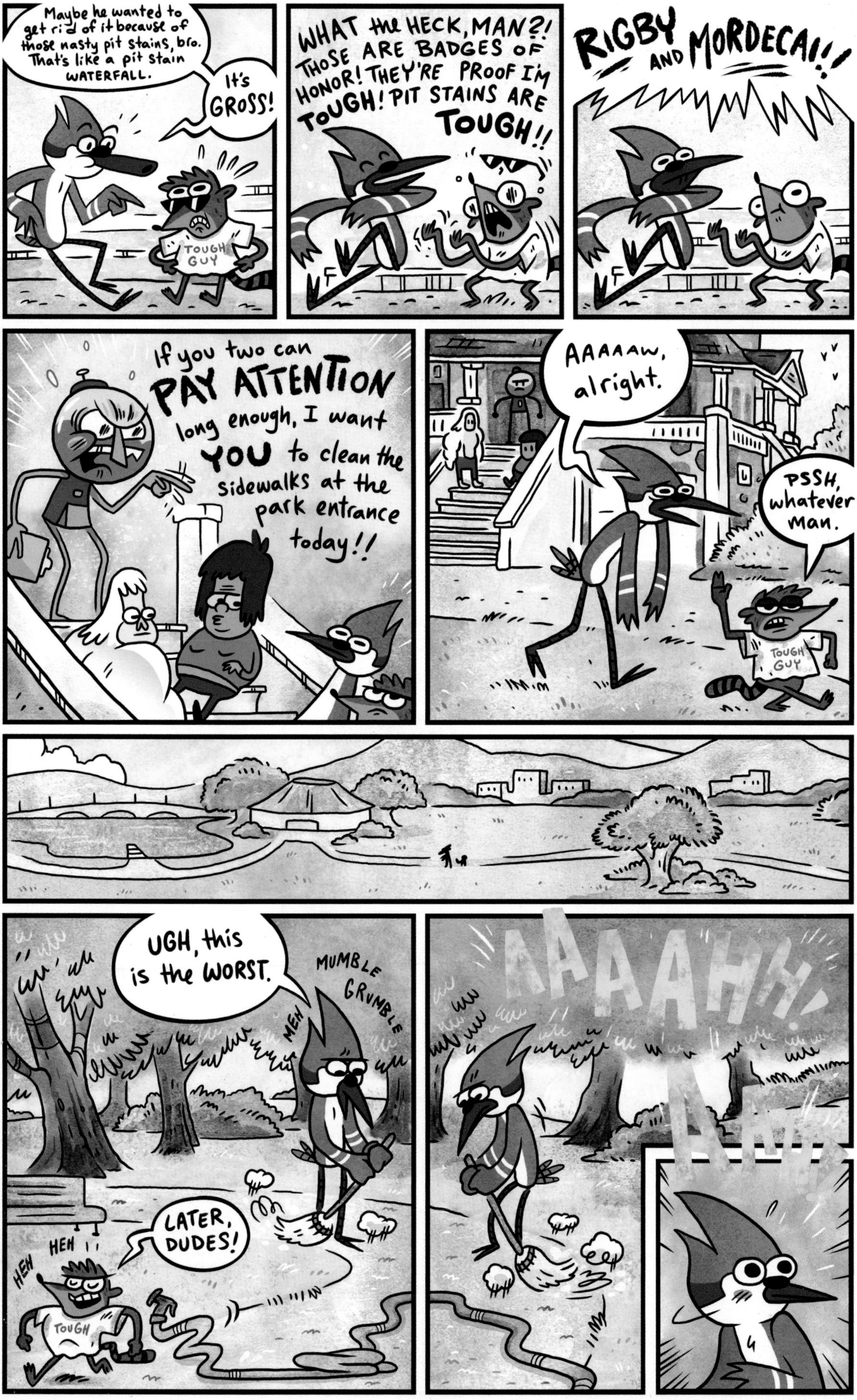
Maybe he wanted to get rid of it because of those nasty pit stains, bro. That's like a pit stain WATERFALL.
It's GROSS!
TOUGH GUY
WHAT the HECK, MAN?! THOSE ARE BADGES OF HONOR! THEY'RE PROOF I'M TOUGH! PIT STAINS ARE TOUGH!!
RIGBY AND MORDECAI!!
If you two can PAY ATTENTION long enough, I want YOU to clean the sidewalks at the park entrance today!!
AAAAAW, alright.
PSSH, whatever man.
TOUGH GUY
UGH, this is the WORST.
MUMBLE GRUMBLE
MEH
LATER, DUDES!
HEH HEH
TOUGH
AAAAHH! AAAH

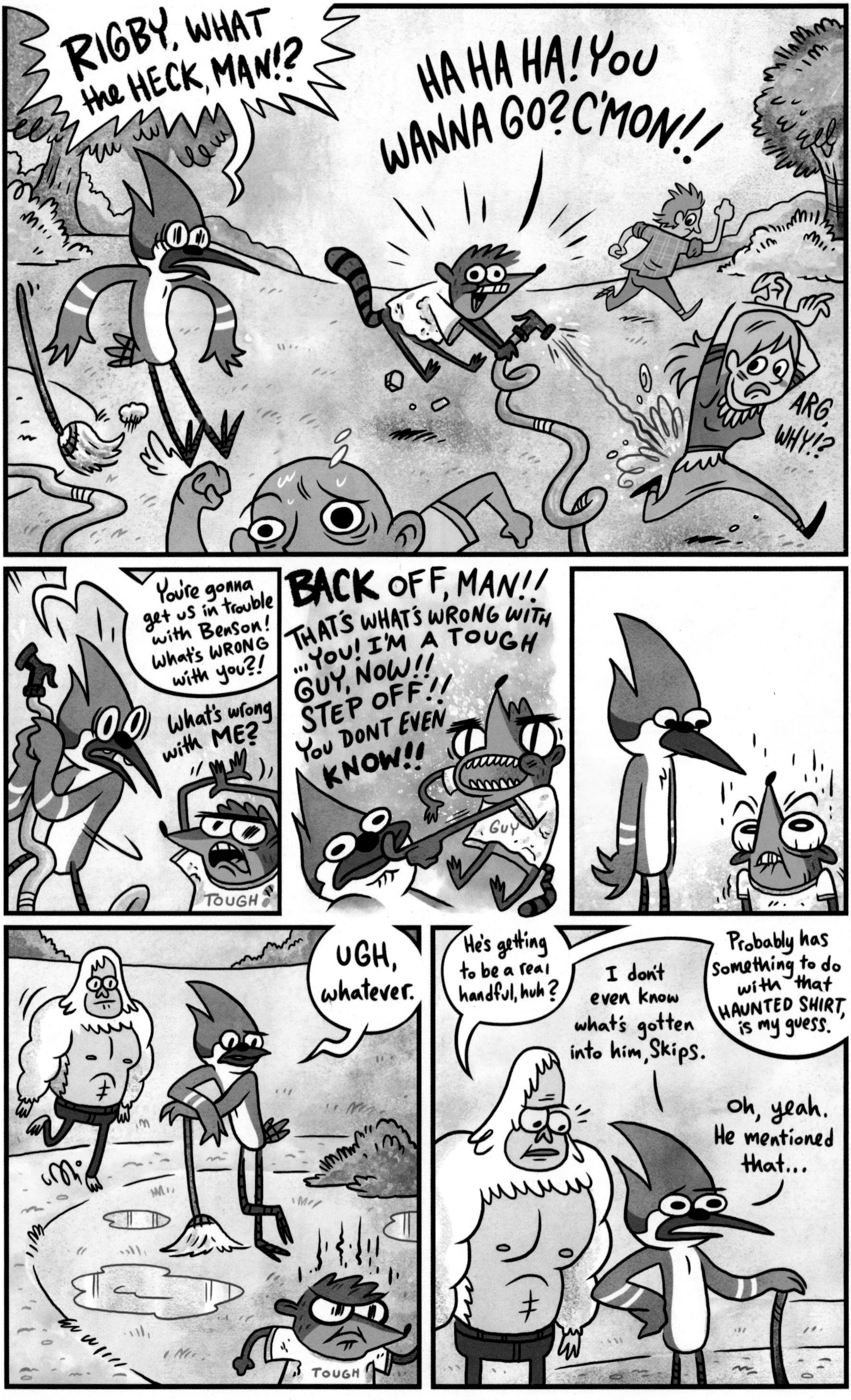
RIGBY, WHAT the HECK, MAN!?
HA HA HA! YOU WANNA GO? C'MON!!
ARG, WHY!?
You're gonna get us in trouble with Benson! What's WRONG with you?!
What's wrong with ME?
TOUGH
BACK OFF, MAN!!
THAT'S WHAT'S WRONG WITH ...YOU! I'M A TOUGH GUY, NOW!! STEP OFF!! You DONT EVEN KNOW!!
GUY
UGH, whatever.
TOUGH
He's getting to be a real handful, huh?
I don't even know what's gotten into him, Skips.
Probably has something to do with that HAUNTED SHIRT, is my guess.
Oh, yeah. He mentioned that...

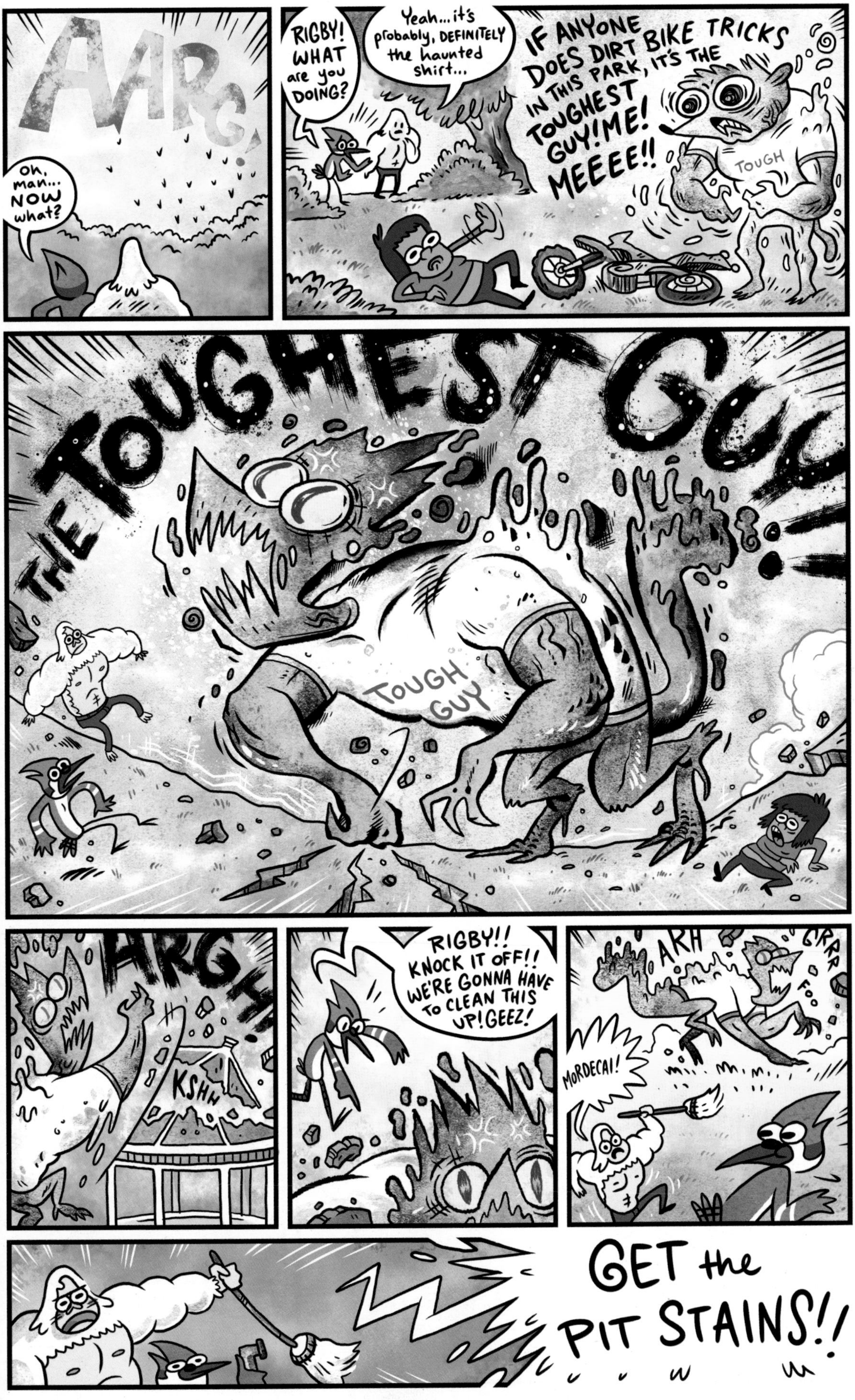
AARG
Oh, man... NOW what?
RIGBY! WHAT are you DOING?
Yeah... it's probably, DEFINITELY the haunted shirt...
IF ANYONE DOES DIRT BIKE TRICKS IN THIS PARK, IT'S THE TOUGHEST GUY! ME! MEEEE!!
TOUGH
THE TOUGHEST GUY
TOUGH GUY
ARGH
KSHH
RIGBY!! KNOCK IT OFF!! WE'RE GONNA HAVE TO CLEAN THIS UP! GEEZ!
ARH
GRRR
FOO
MORDECAI!
GET the PIT STAINS!!

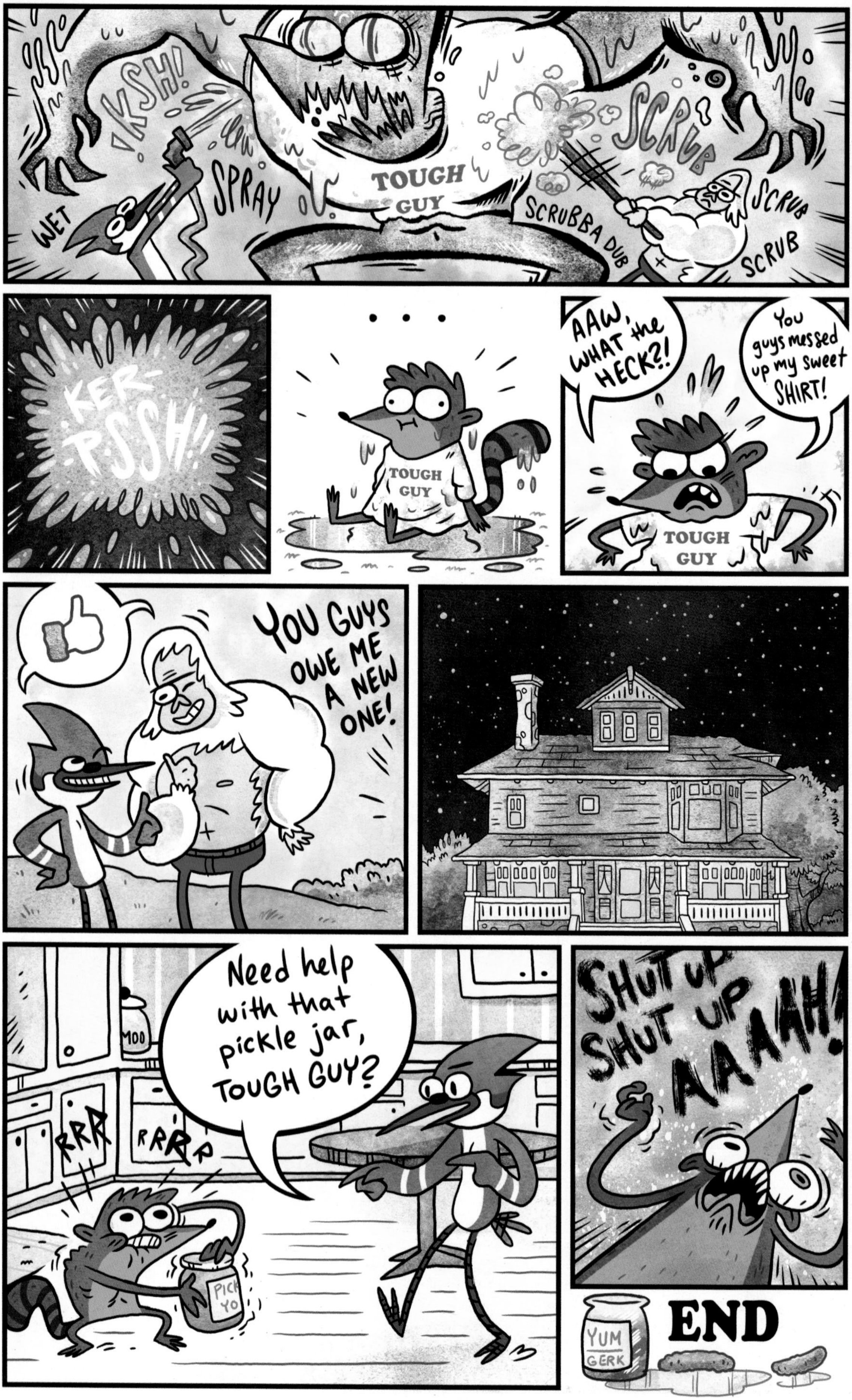
KSH!
WET
SPRAY
TOUGH GUY
SCRUB
SCRUBBA DUB
SCRUB
SCRUB
KER-PSSH!!
. . .
TOUGH GUY
AAW, WHAT the HECK?!
You guys messed up my sweet SHIRT!
TOUGH GUY
YOU GUYS OWE ME A NEW ONE!
MOO
RRR
RRRR
Need help with that pickle jar, TOUGH GUY?
PICK YO
SHUT UP SHUT UP AAAAH!
YUM GERK
END

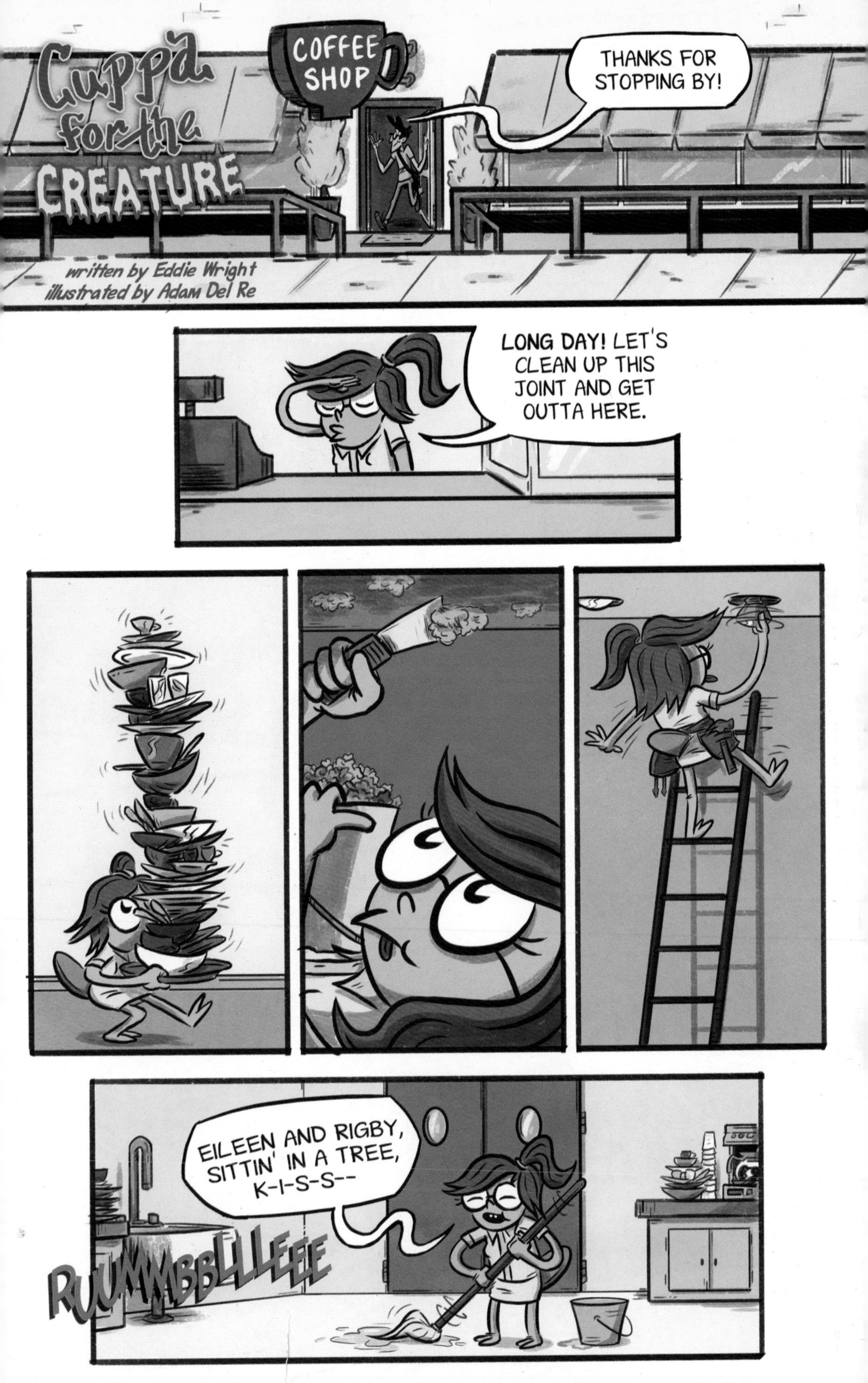
Cuppa for the CREATURE
COFFEE SHOP
THANKS FOR STOPPING BY!
written by Eddie Wright
illustrated by Adam Del Re
LONG DAY! LET'S CLEAN UP THIS JOINT AND GET OUTTA HERE.
EILEEN AND RIGBY, SITTIN' IN A TREE, K-I-S-S--
RUUMMBBLLLEEE

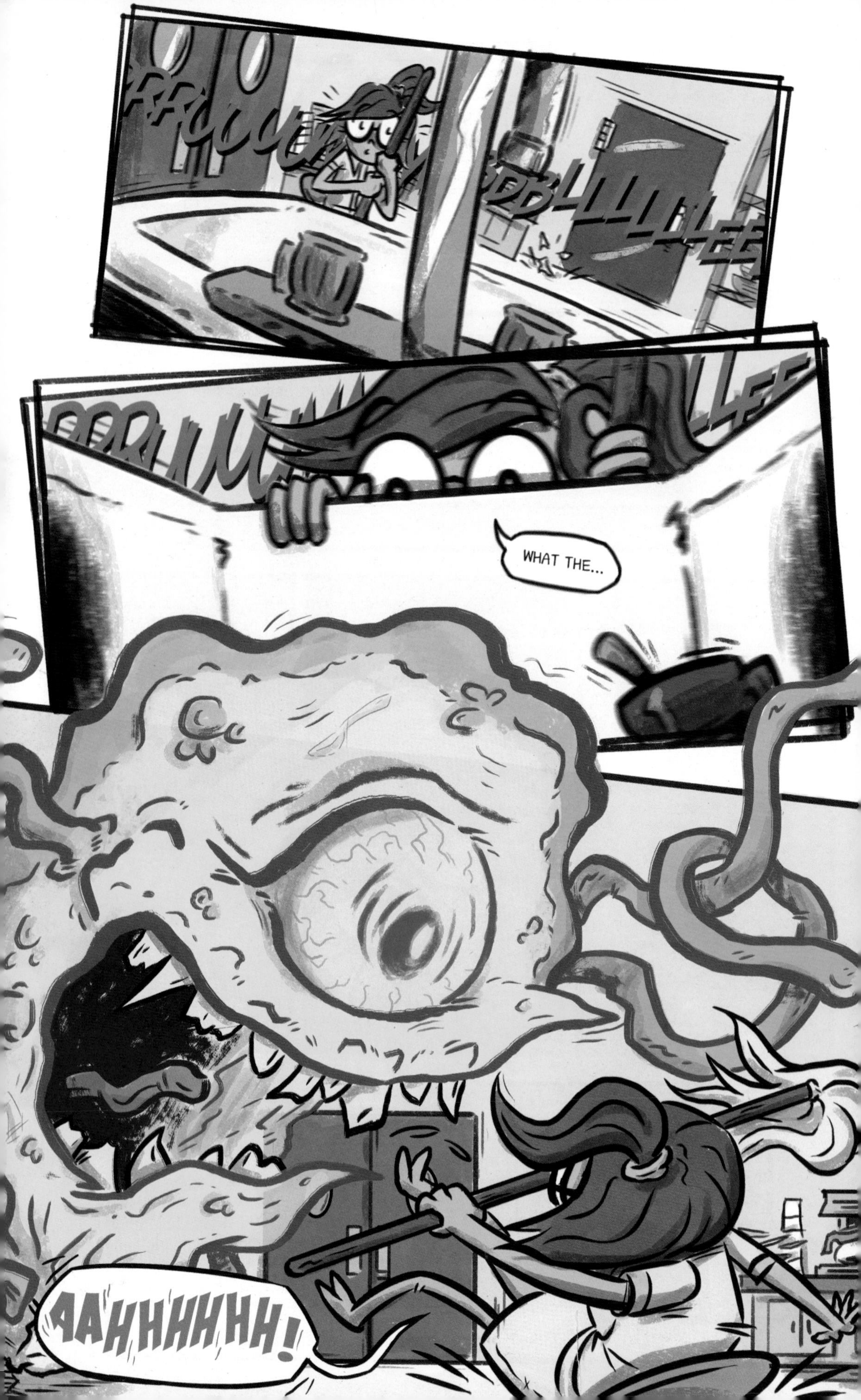
WHAT THE...
AAHHHHHH!

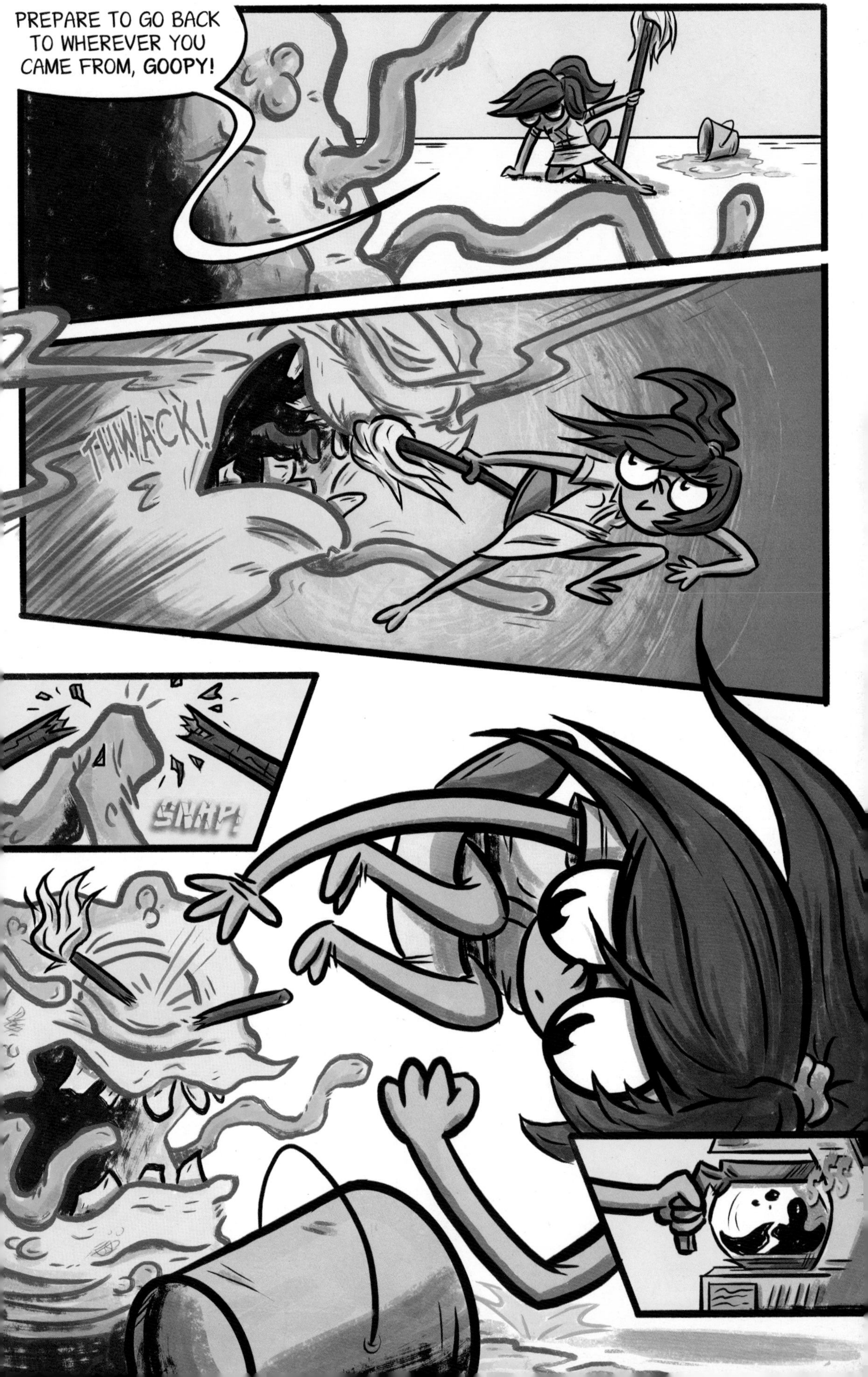
PREPARE TO GO BACK TO WHEREVER YOU CAME FROM, GOOPY!
THWACK!
SNAP!

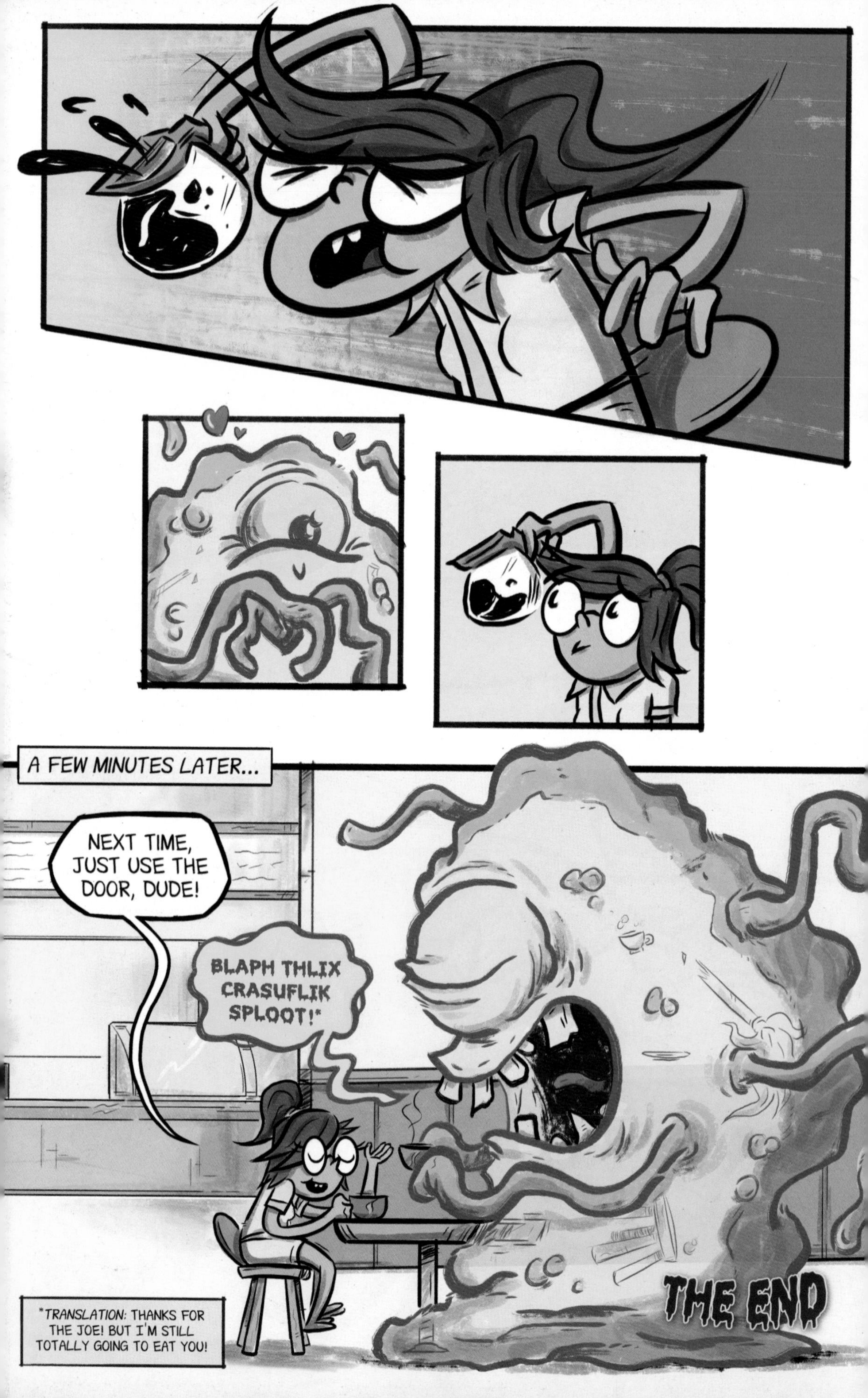
A FEW MINUTES LATER...
NEXT TIME, JUST USE THE DOOR, DUDE!
BLAPH THLIX CRASUFLIK SPLOOT!*
*TRANSLATION: THANKS FOR THE JOE! BUT I'M STILL TOTALLY GOING TO EAT YOU!
THE END

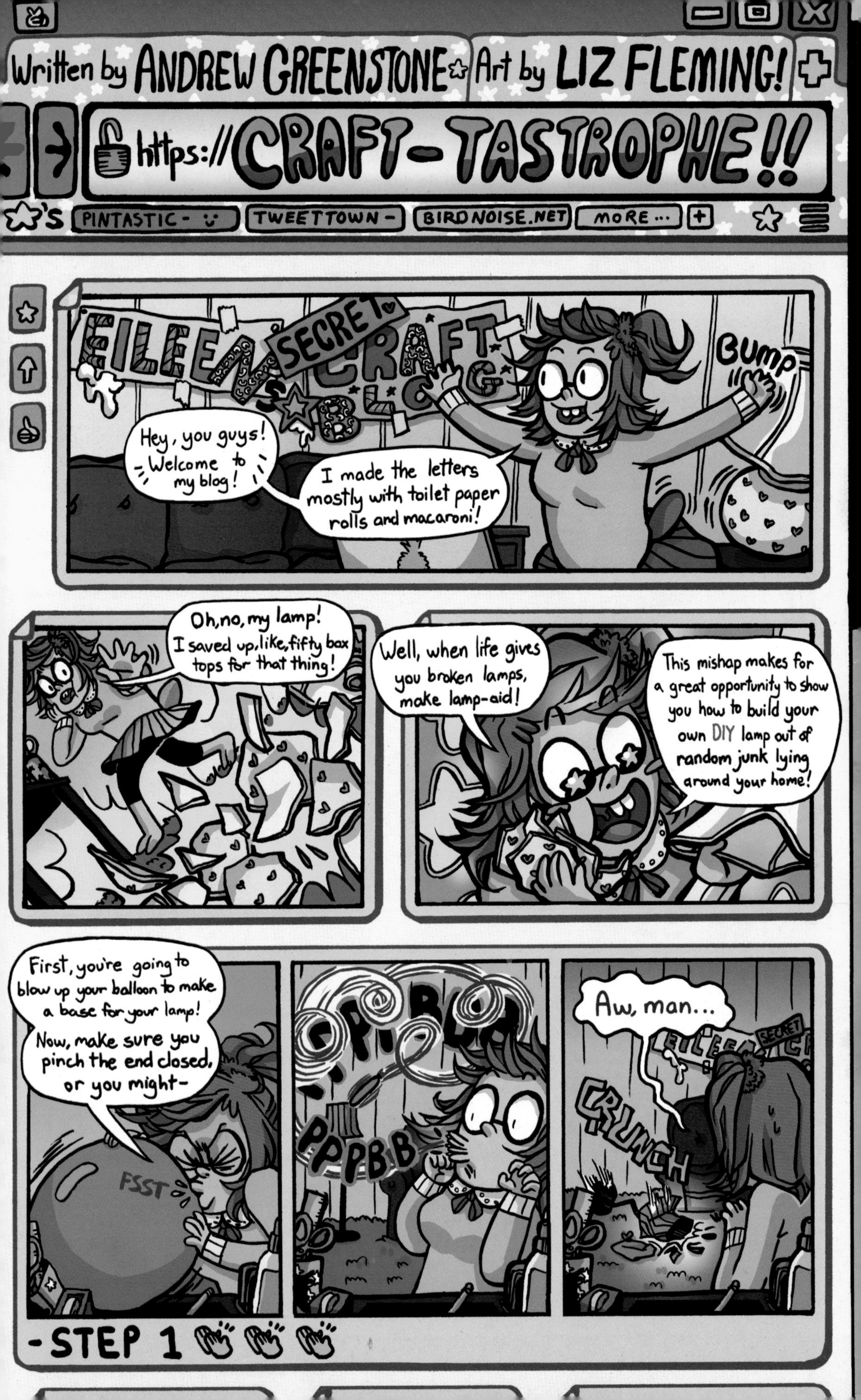
Written by ANDREW GREENSTONE
Art by LIZ FLEMING!
https://CRAFT-TASTROPHE!!
PINTASTIC
TWEETTOWN
BIRDNOISE.NET
MORE...
EILEEN'S SECRET CRAFT BLOG
BUMP
Hey, you guys! Welcome to my blog!
I made the letters mostly with toilet paper rolls and macaroni!
Oh, no, my lamp! I saved up, like, fifty box tops for that thing!
Well, when life gives you broken lamps, make lamp-aid!
This mishap makes for a great opportunity to show you how to build your own DIY lamp out of random junk lying around your home!
First, you're going to blow up your balloon to make a base for your lamp!
Now, make sure you pinch the end closed, or you might-
FSST
PPPBB
Aw, man...
CRUNCH
-STEP 1

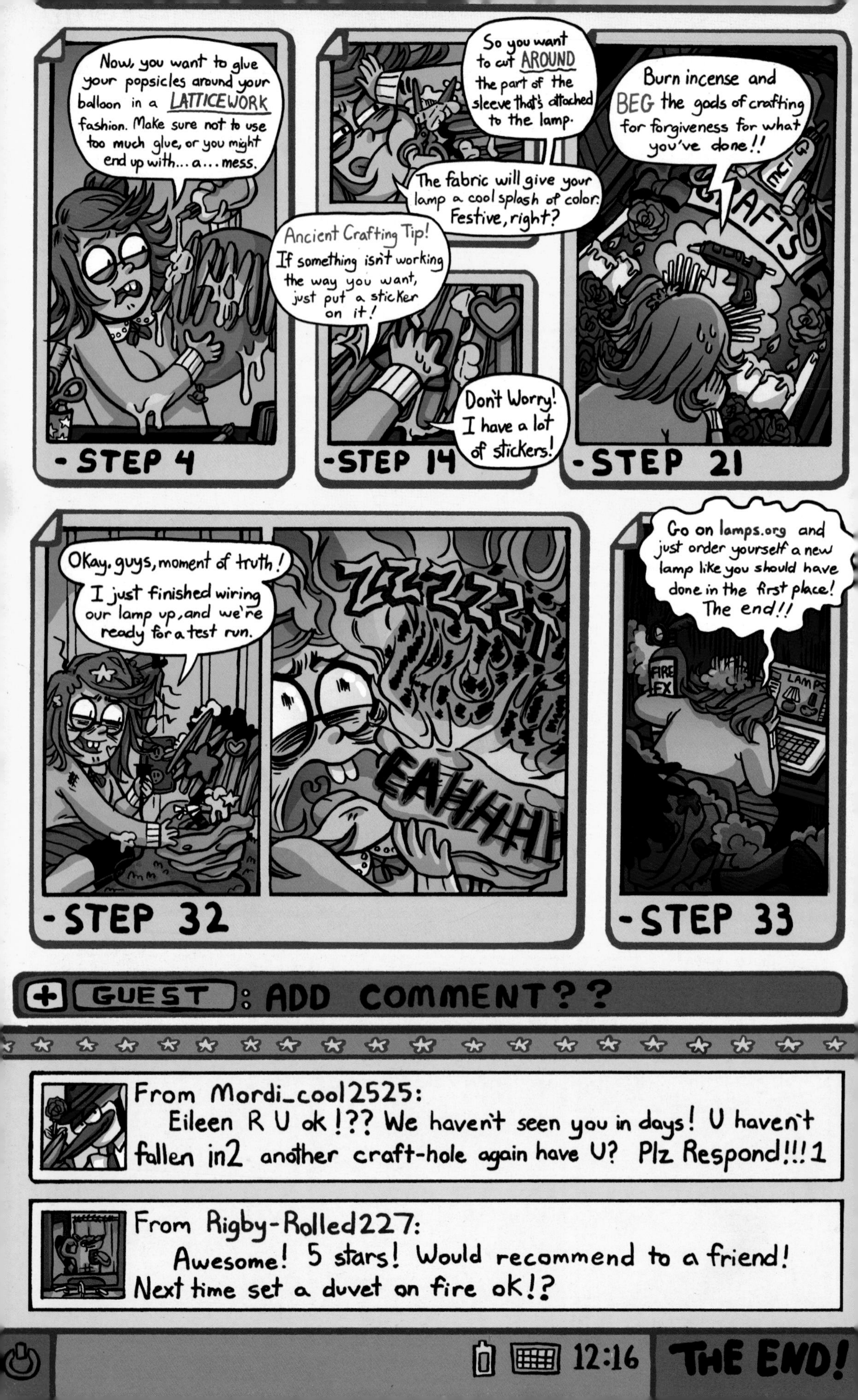
Now, you want to glue your popsicles around your balloon in a LATTICEWORK fashion. Make sure not to use too much glue, or you might end up with... a... mess.
-STEP 4
So you want to cut AROUND the part of the sleeve that's attached to the lamp.
The fabric will give your lamp a cool splash of color. Festive, right?
Ancient Crafting Tip! If something isn't working the way you want, just put a sticker on it!
Don't Worry! I have a lot of stickers!
-STEP 14
Burn incense and BEG the gods of crafting for forgiveness for what you've done!!
CRAFTS
-STEP 21
Okay, guys, moment of truth! I just finished wiring our lamp up, and we're ready for a test run.
ZZZZZT
EAHHHHH
-STEP 32
Go on lamps.org and just order yourself a new lamp like you should have done in the first place! The end!!
FIRE EX
LAMPS
-STEP 33
GUEST : ADD COMMENT??
From Mordi_cool2525:
Eileen R U ok!?? We haven't seen you in days! U haven't fallen in2 another craft-hole again have U? Plz Respond!!!1
From Rigby-Rolled227:
Awesome! 5 stars! Would recommend to a friend! Next time set a duvet on fire ok!?
12:16
THE END!

DANDY DRIVE-IN

SCRIPT BY EDDIE WRIGHT AND ART BY CHRISTOPHER PETERSON

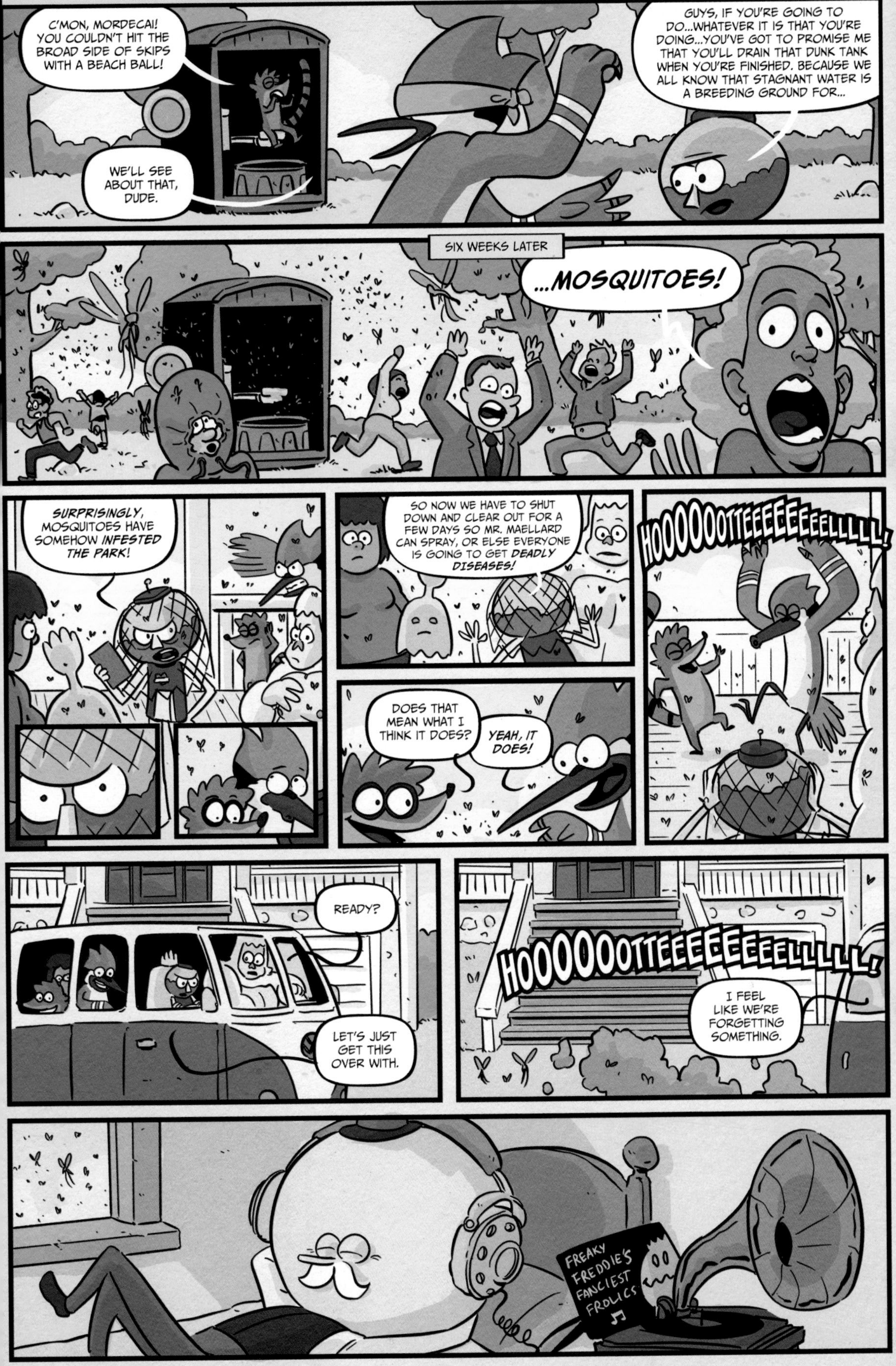
C'MON, MORDECAI! YOU COULDN'T HIT THE BROAD SIDE OF SKIPS WITH A BEACH BALL!
WE'LL SEE ABOUT THAT, DUDE.
GUYS, IF YOU'RE GOING TO DO...WHATEVER IT IS THAT YOU'RE DOING...YOU'VE GOT TO PROMISE ME THAT YOU'LL DRAIN THAT DUNK TANK WHEN YOU'RE FINISHED. BECAUSE WE ALL KNOW THAT STAGNANT WATER IS A BREEDING GROUND FOR...
SIX WEEKS LATER
...MOSQUITOES!
SURPRISINGLY, MOSQUITOES HAVE SOMEHOW INFESTED THE PARK!
SO NOW WE HAVE TO SHUT DOWN AND CLEAR OUT FOR A FEW DAYS SO MR. MAELLARD CAN SPRAY, OR ELSE EVERYONE IS GOING TO GET DEADLY DISEASES!
DOES THAT MEAN WHAT I THINK IT DOES?
YEAH, IT DOES!
HOOOOOOTTEEEEEEEELLLLLL!
READY?
LET'S JUST GET THIS OVER WITH.
HOOOOOOTTEEEEEEEELLLLLL!
I FEEL LIKE WE'RE FORGETTING SOMETHING.
FREAKY FREDDIE'S FANCIEST FROLICS

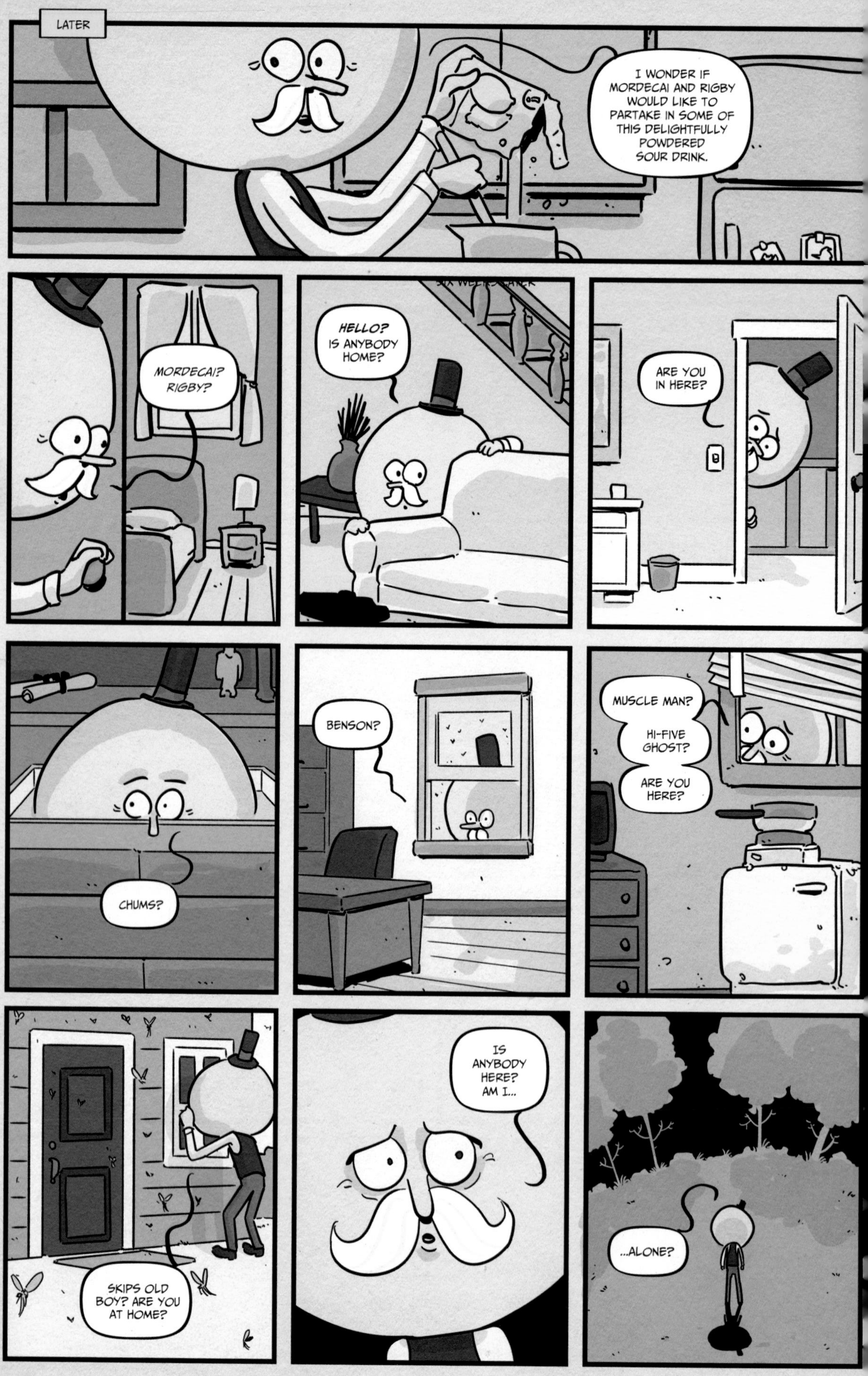
LATER
I WONDER IF MORDECAI AND RIGBY WOULD LIKE TO PARTAKE IN SOME OF THIS DELIGHTFULLY POWDERED SOUR DRINK.
MORDECAI? RIGBY?
HELLO? IS ANYBODY HOME?
ARE YOU IN HERE?
CHUMS?
BENSON?
MUSCLE MAN?
HI-FIVE GHOST?
ARE YOU HERE?
SKIPS OLD BOY? ARE YOU AT HOME?
IS ANYBODY HERE? AM I...
...ALONE?

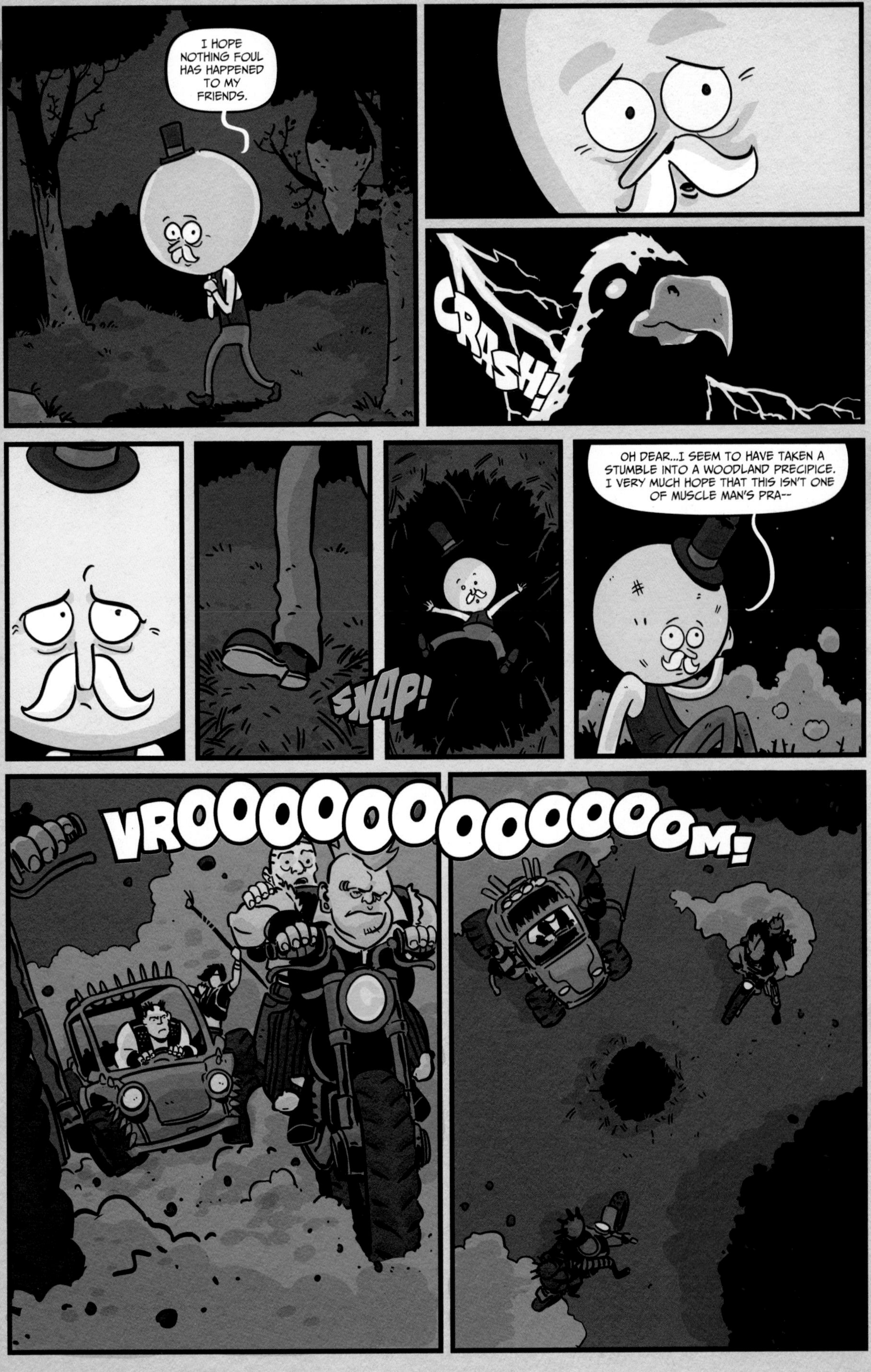
I HOPE NOTHING FOUL HAS HAPPENED TO MY FRIENDS.
CRASH!
SNAP!
OH DEAR...I SEEM TO HAVE TAKEN A STUMBLE INTO A WOODLAND PRECIPICE. I VERY MUCH HOPE THAT THIS ISN'T ONE OF MUSCLE MAN'S PRA--
VROOOOOOOOOOOOOM!

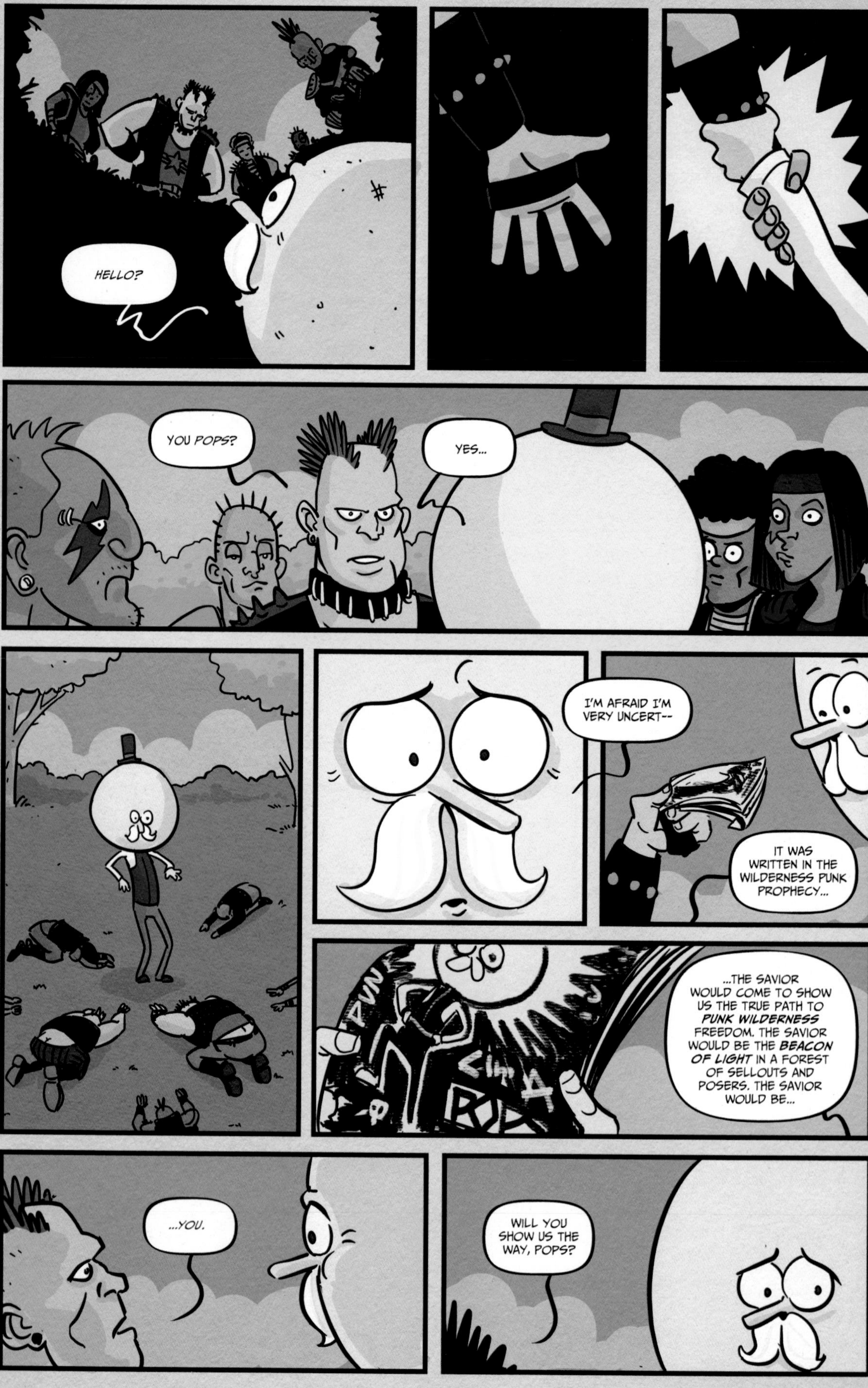
HELLO?
YOU POPS?
YES...
I'M AFRAID I'M VERY UNCERT--
IT WAS WRITTEN IN THE WILDERNESS PUNK PROPHECY...
...THE SAVIOR WOULD COME TO SHOW US THE TRUE PATH TO PUNK WILDERNESS FREEDOM. THE SAVIOR WOULD BE THE BEACON OF LIGHT IN A FOREST OF SELLOUTS AND POSERS. THE SAVIOR WOULD BE...
...YOU.
WILL YOU SHOW US THE WAY, POPS?

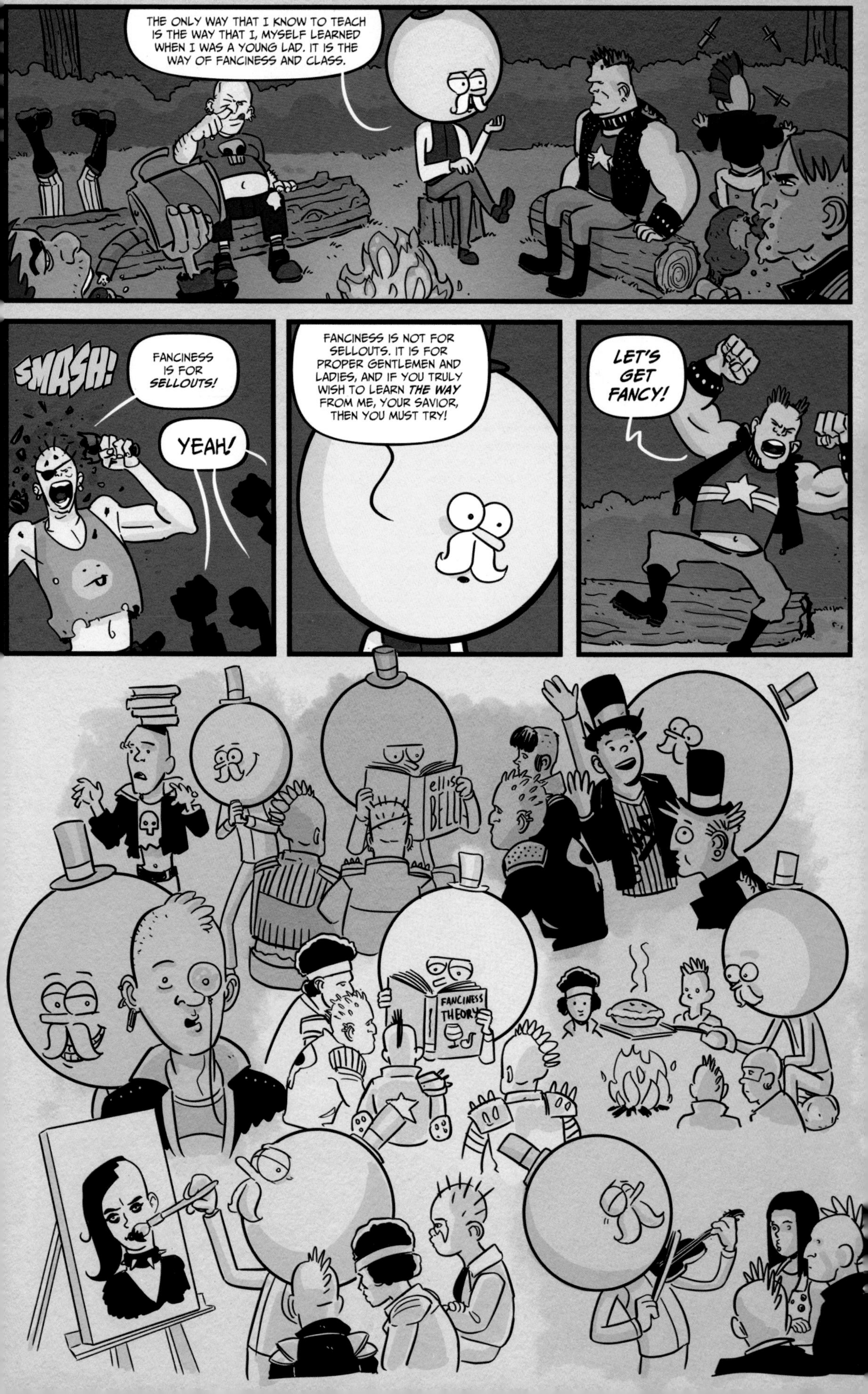
THE ONLY WAY THAT I KNOW TO TEACH IS THE WAY THAT I, MYSELF LEARNED WHEN I WAS A YOUNG LAD. IT IS THE WAY OF FANCINESS AND CLASS.
SMASH!
FANCINESS IS FOR SELLOUTS!
YEAH!
FANCINESS IS NOT FOR SELLOUTS. IT IS FOR PROPER GENTLEMEN AND LADIES, AND IF YOU TRULY WISH TO LEARN THE WAY FROM ME, YOUR SAVIOR, THEN YOU MUST TRY!
LET'S GET FANCY!
FANCINESS THEORY

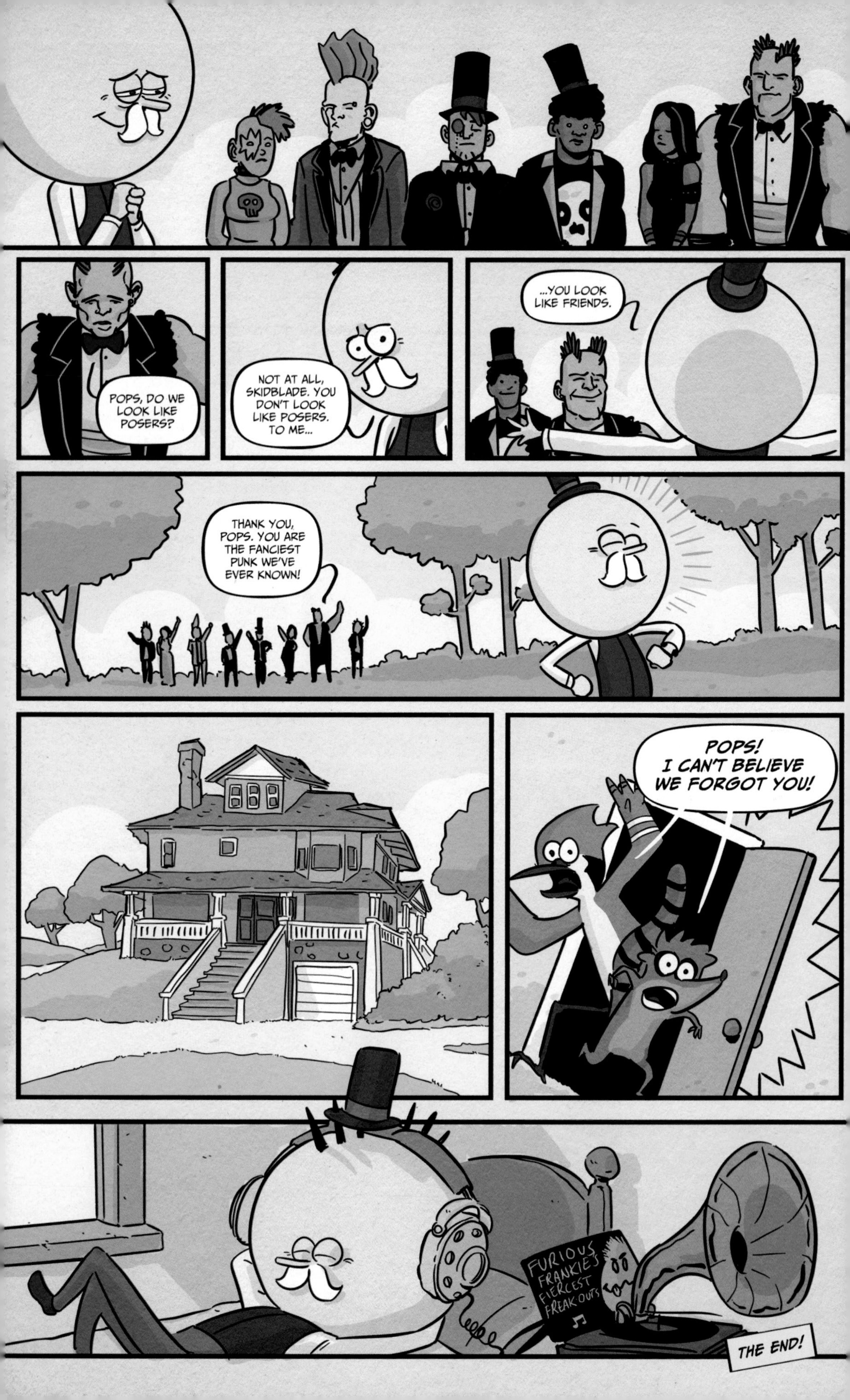
POPS, DO WE LOOK LIKE POSERS?
NOT AT ALL, SKIDBLADE. YOU DON'T LOOK LIKE POSERS. TO ME...
...YOU LOOK LIKE FRIENDS.
THANK YOU, POPS. YOU ARE THE FANCIEST PUNK WE'VE EVER KNOWN!
POPS! I CAN'T BELIEVE WE FORGOT YOU!
FURIOUS FRANKIE'S FIERCEST FREAK-OUTS
THE END!

COVER GALLERY

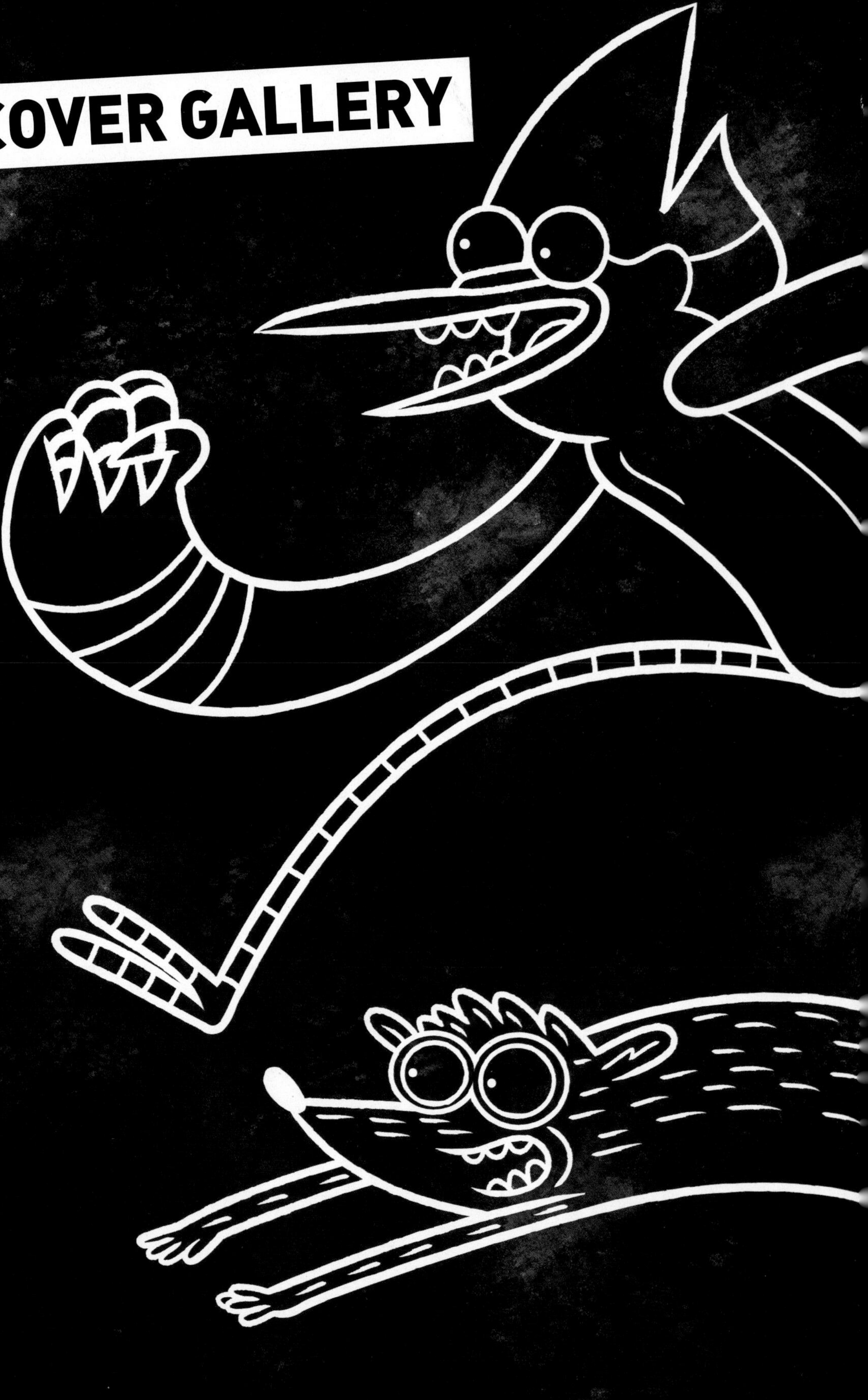

ISSUE TWENTY NINE Main Cover
FELLIPE MARTINS

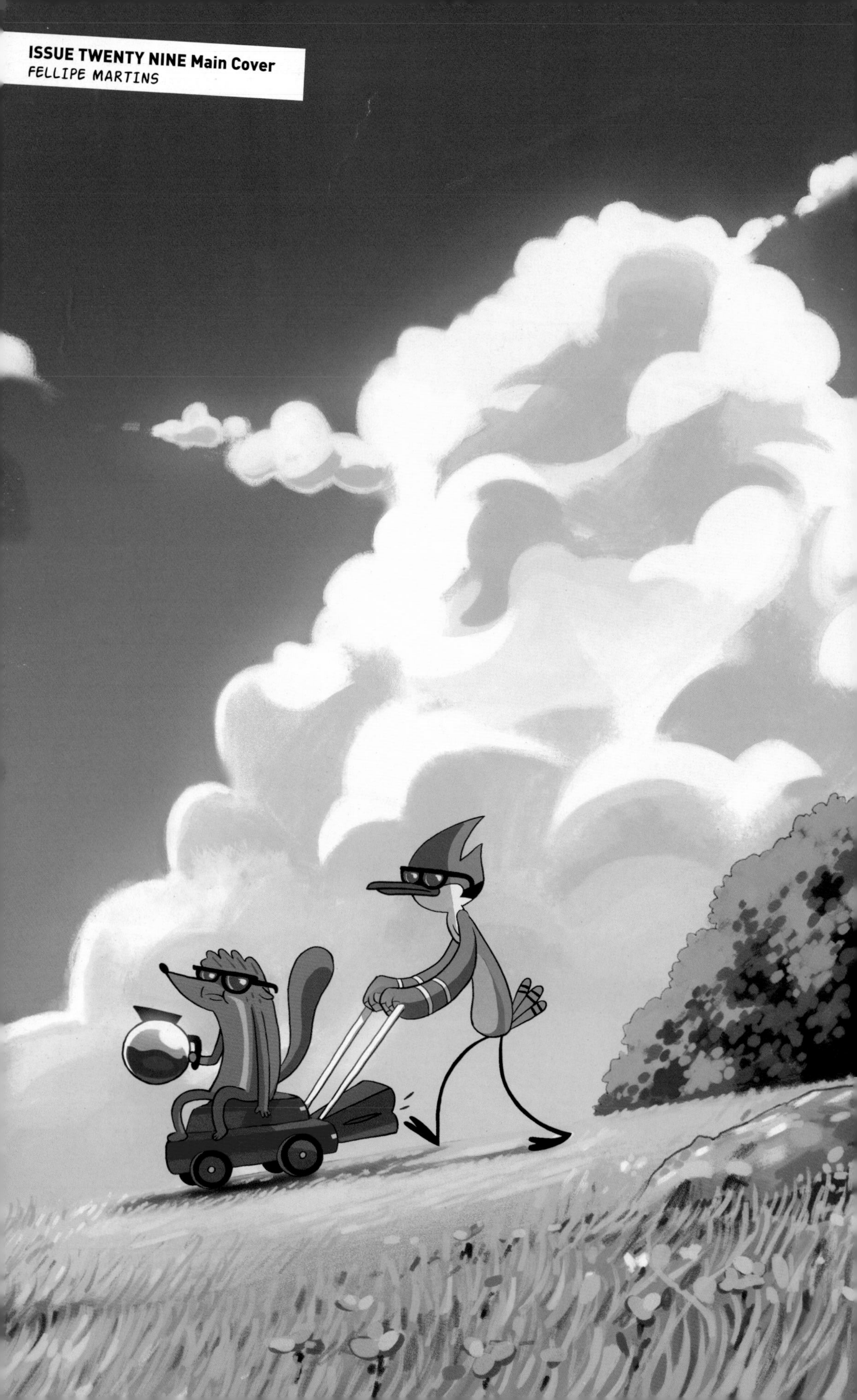

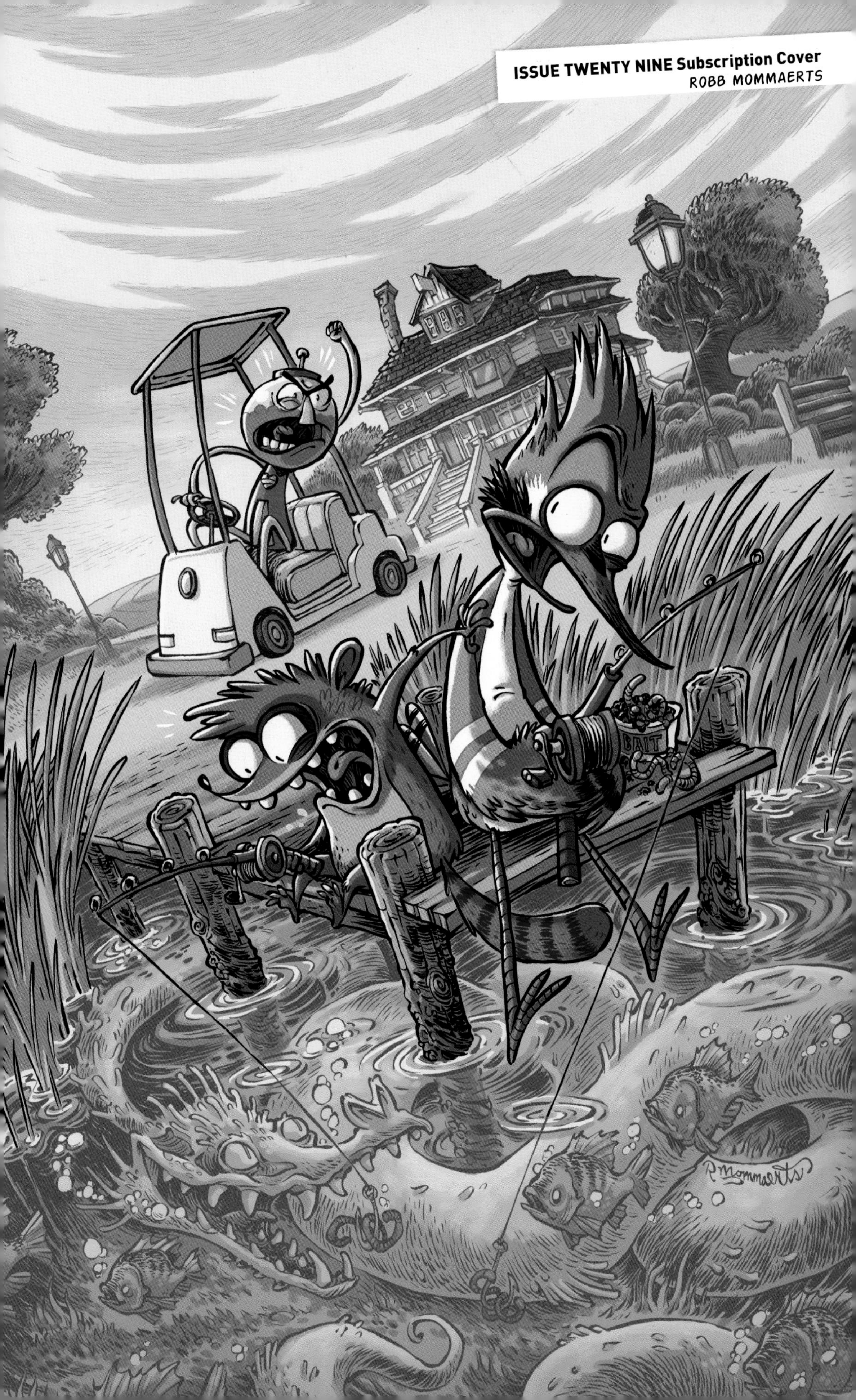
BAIT

ISSUE TWENTY NINE Subscription Cover
ROBB MOMMAERTS

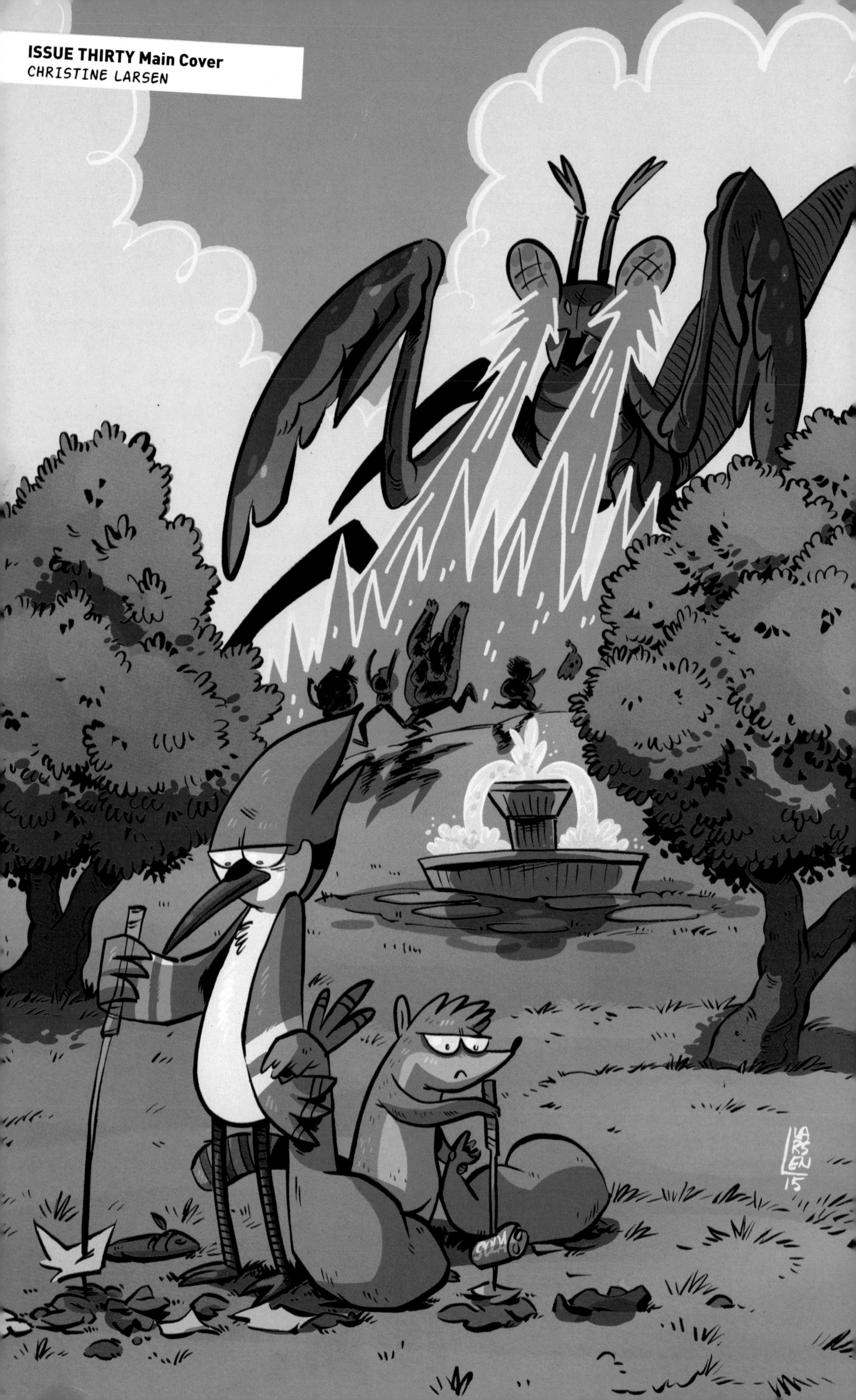
LARSEN 15

ISSUE THIRTY Main Cover
CHRISTINE LARSEN

ISSUE THIRTY Subscription Cover
KYLE SMART

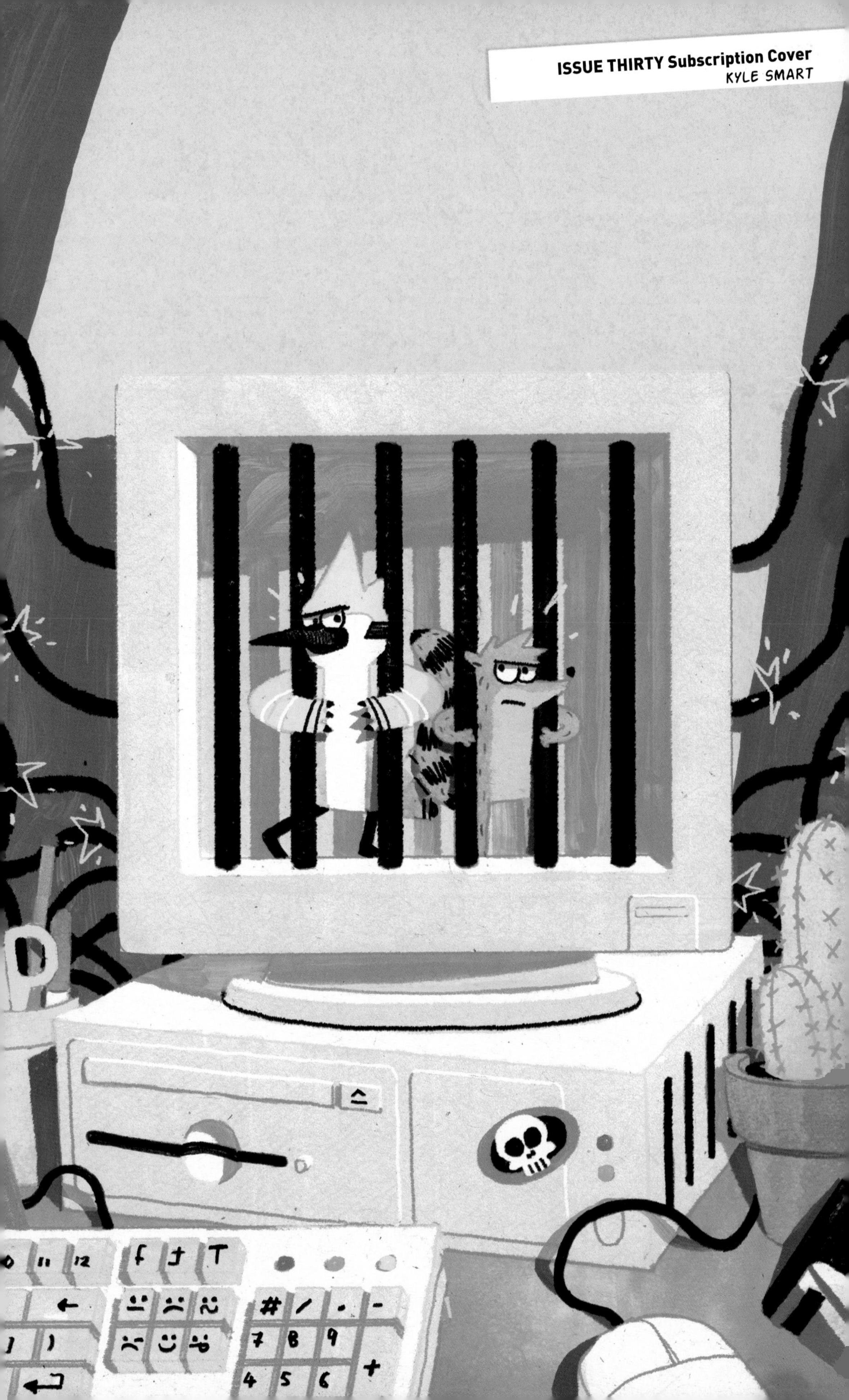
11 12
T
7 8 9
4 5 6

ISSUE THIRTY ONE Main Cover
JEREMY DE LA GARZA

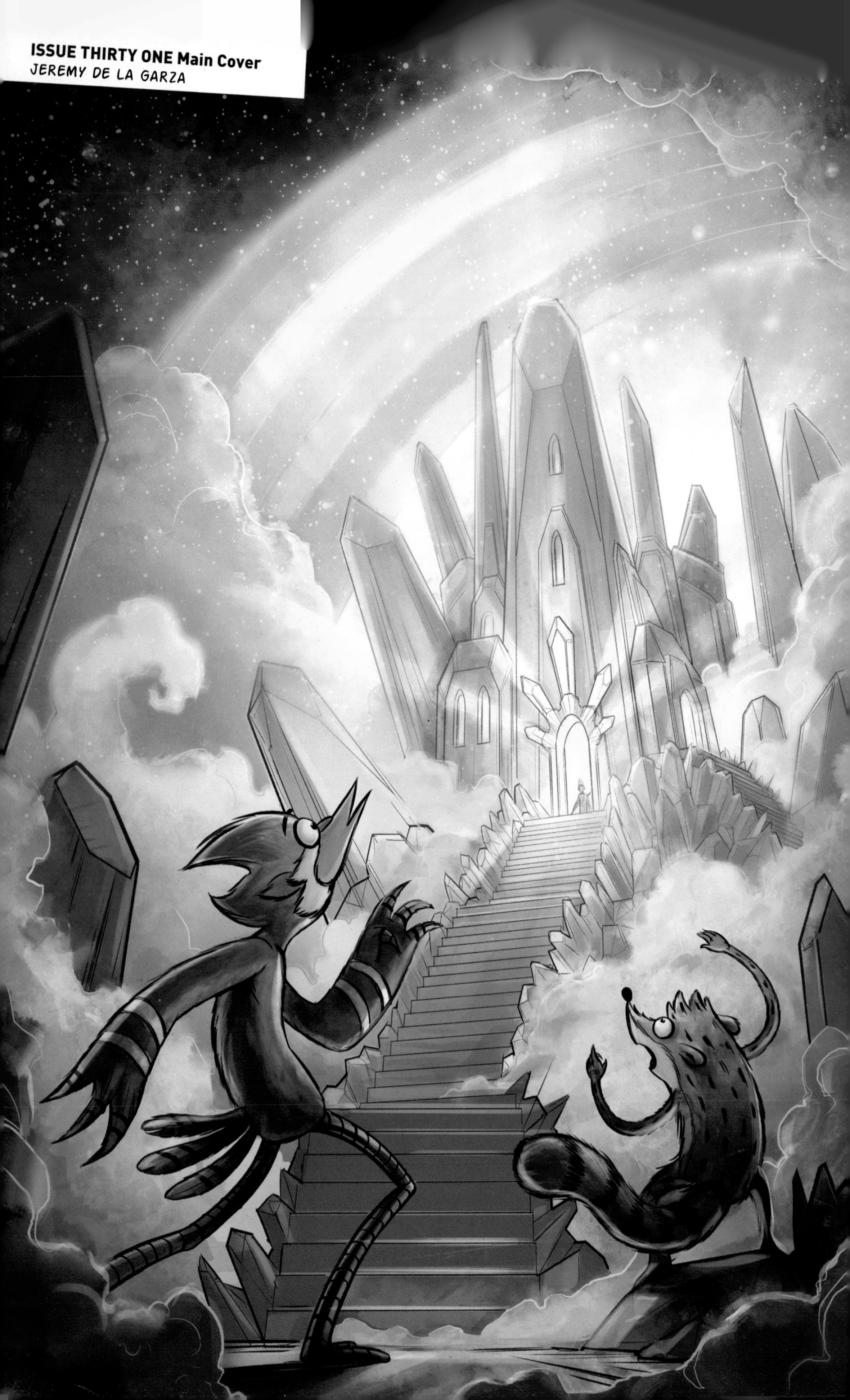

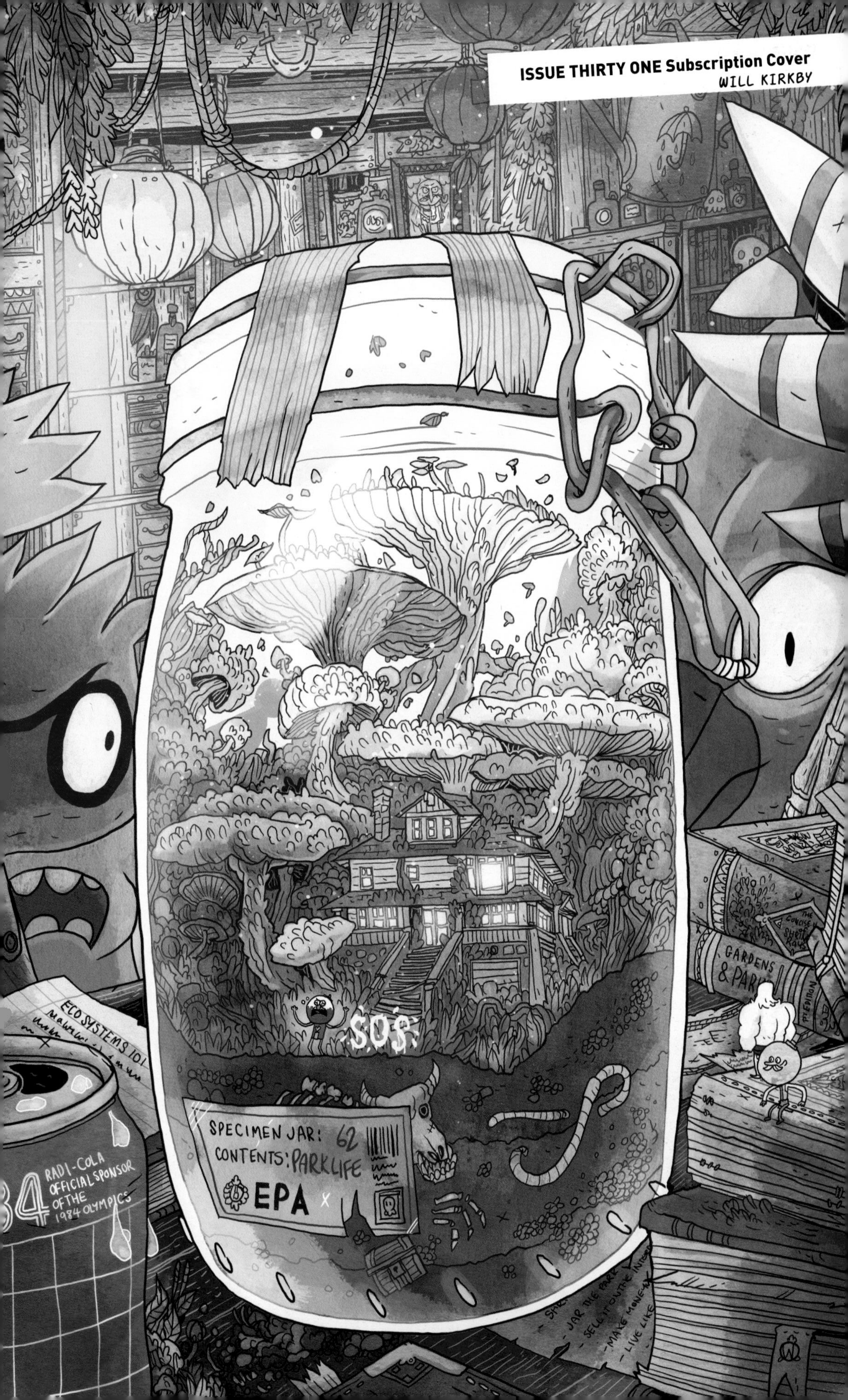
SOS
ECO SYSTEMS 101
RADI-COLA
OFFICIAL SPONSOR
OF THE
1984 OLYMPICS
SPECIMEN JAR: 62
CONTENTS: PARKLIFE
EPA
GARDENS
& PARK
JAR THE PARK
MAKE MONEY

ISSUE THIRTY ONE Subscription Cover
WILL KIRKBY

ISSUE THIRTY TWO Main Cover
IGOR WOLSKI

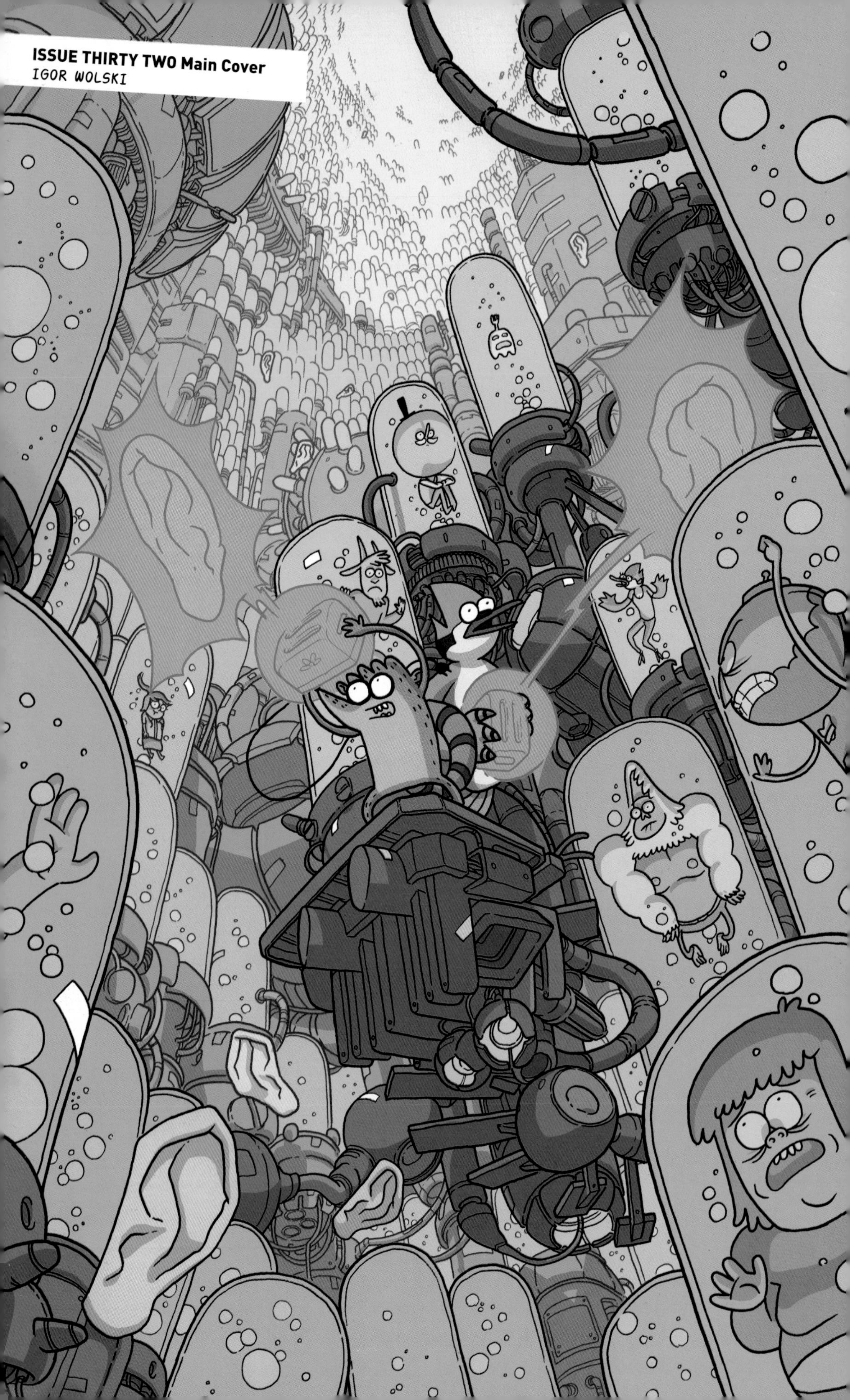

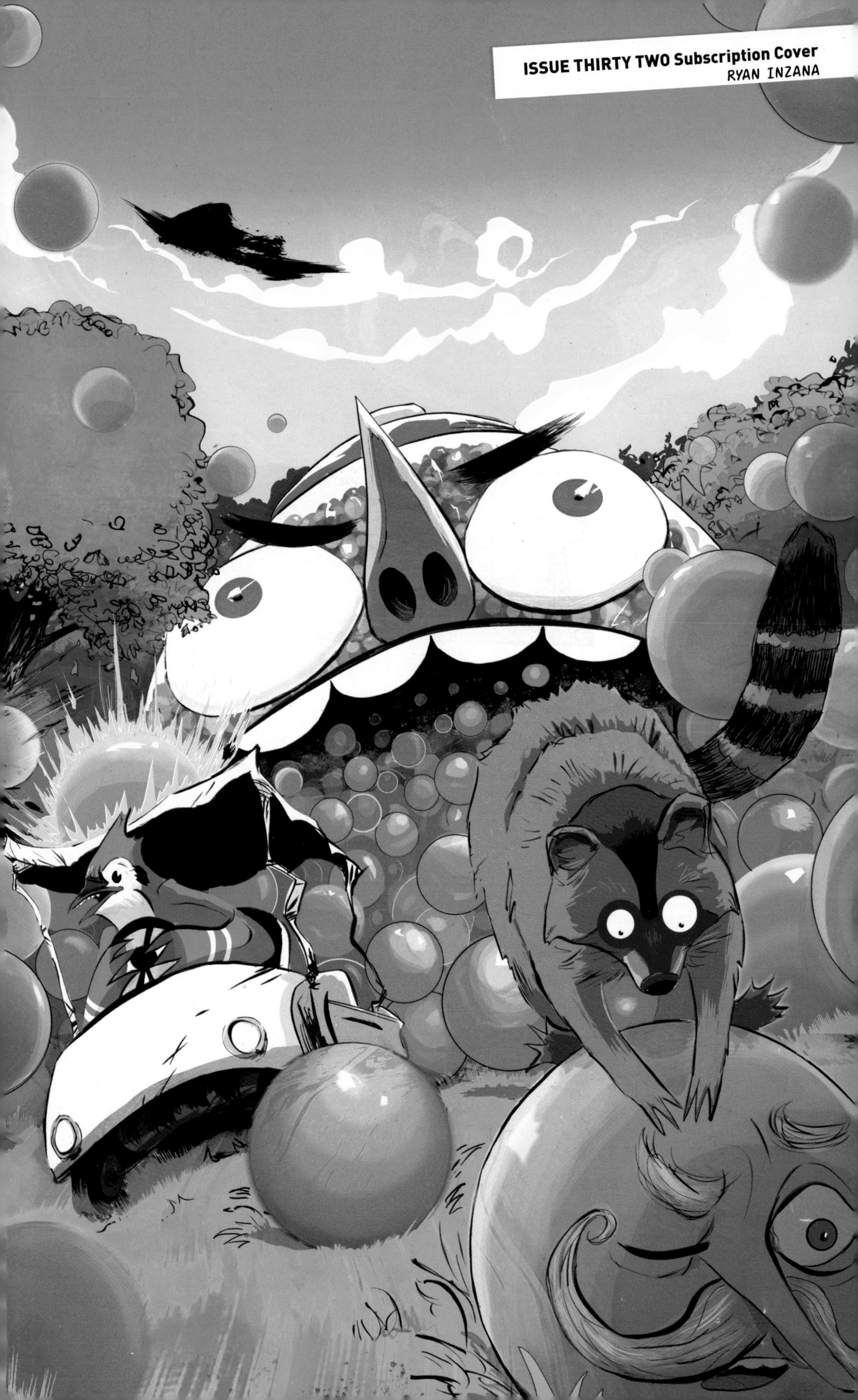

ISSUE THIRTY TWO Subscription Cover
RYAN INZANA

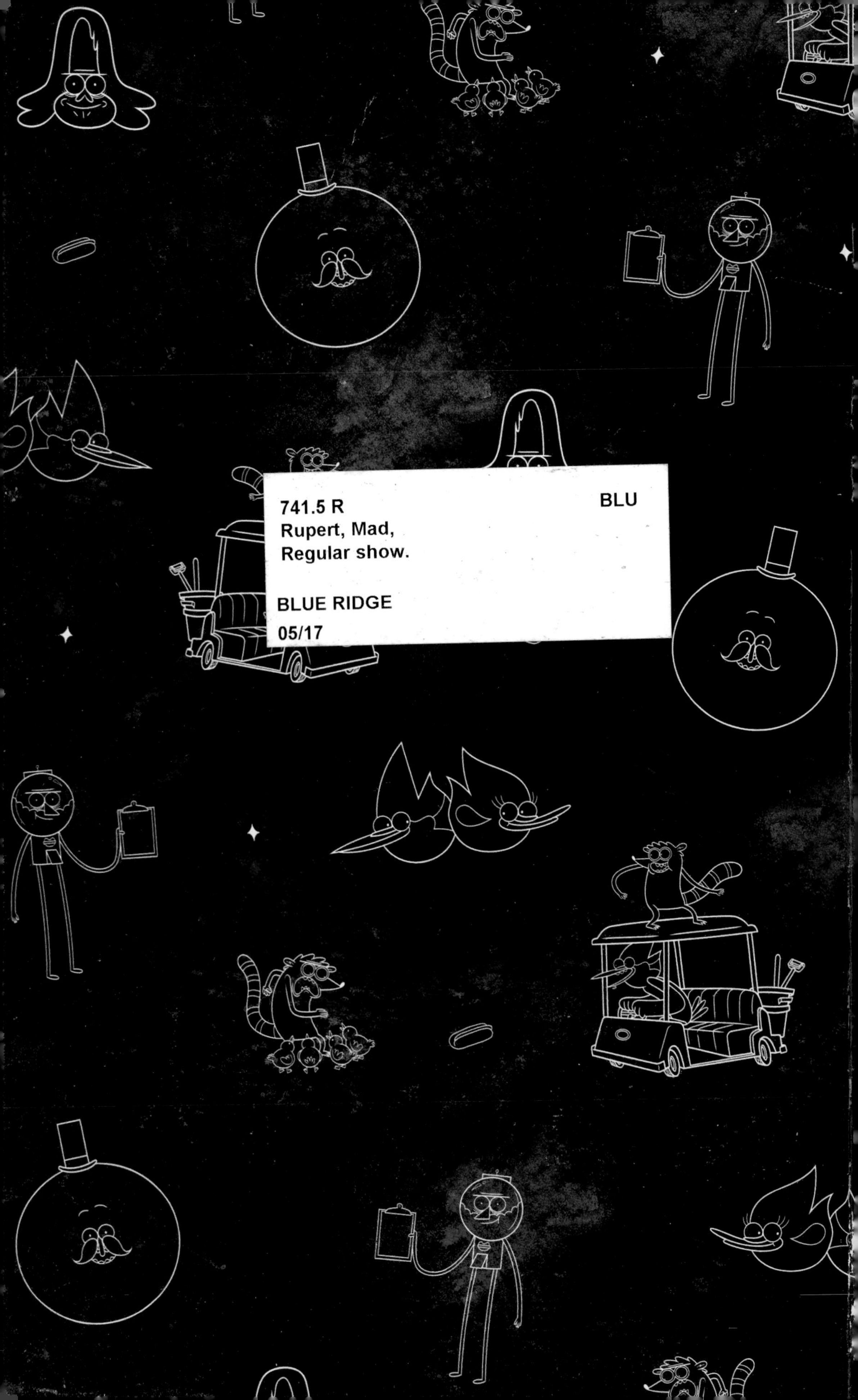